My body is a cage
That keeps me from dancing with the one I love
But my mind holds the key

- My Body is a Cage, Peter Gabriel

To new friends, to true friends,

You might not think anyone appreciates how well you're holding yourself together in the face of a world gone mad, but I do.

I see you.

RABID

Sierra Prynne

Book Five in *The Garden of Beastly Delights* series

CHAPTER 1

My strange half-raven, half-wolfen chimeric body soared through the air above the Aegean Sea as if it had been born to fly. It sped out of range of the silver bullets shot by Rav's men from the cliff face. It veered around the sail of an anchored catamaran and spun to knock away the ravens who pursued us out to sea. And once we were alone out there in the empty, it rose higher to glide to save energy. But really, it did it as a mercy for me and my exhausted mind and body.

The agony in my shoulder had only worsened with every turn and twist as we escaped. Every flap of my wings riled the bullet wound again; I could feel a trickle of blood running down my leg, pattering the water far below.

The suffering in my mind wasn't much better, though. I sat, pale and shaking, in my inner sanctum, trying to decide…anything.

Trying to will myself to see a *reason* to decide anything at all.

Ruined. I was ruined. What else could I be?

This wasn't just escaping a wedding to the most powerful shapeshifter in Europe; this was escaping as a beast of legend, a monster feared more than any other. All I'd ever heard was that beasts were broken, confused perversions doomed to lose their minds and go feral, devouring anything—human or otherwise—in their gravity.

Was that my future?

Could I even trust myself to know?

I'd been having migraines for weeks, dipping in and out of magick as often as a quill into ink, losing pieces of time, losing memories, losing friends.

My friends! My family! Cass!

Oh, that last one.

If I was going insane *surely* I could will the sight of his lifeless body away, banish it from my mind and forget it like I had so many other things.

Horrible. Devastating. Unfathomable.

And *not real*, my mind decided, maybe to protect me.

"*He's not dead, he's not dead, he's not dead,*" I said over and over to myself in the inner sanctum. "*Tell me he's not dead.*"

"*Rest,*" my raven said.

"*Calm,*" my wolf said.

"*What are you talking about?*" I almost screamed. "*How can I ever be calm again? My life is over!*"

"*Trust,*" my raven said again, this time begging. "*Need energy. Rest.*"

Shaking. I was shaking. But not just in heart and spirit. I could feel the exhaustion in my physical body—my wolf's body, my raven's wings. The need to conserve every morsel of strength I had left was undeniable.

And yet a deeper panicked part of me asked, was it even worth it to keep going?

The answer, of course, was yes.

"*For them,*" I reminded myself.

My mom might be with my friends, but she'd be out of her mind with fear. Scarlett was still at Hamingja; if nothing else, I could use the last of my sanity to save her. And the others? Fern? Yasmina? I hadn't done any formal paperwork for my line of succession yet. I'd planned to leave it all to them, and to…Cass, so I would will myself to live long enough to give it to them. To ensure Rav never got his hands on the Eighth Kingdom.

Planning my last wishes was a flimsy sort of distraction, but it held me together as the shaking worsened and my body weakened and my raven used the last of her flagging energy—*my* energy—to raise us higher so we could glide as far as we could before crashing.

Even my crash, they tried to soften. My raven flared her wings to slow us down. My wolf tucked her legs tight to our body to give us those last few feet of airspace. And then they struck together at a soft angle that allowed the water to cushion us without skipping our body across the wavy surface.

There was a splash. A bolt of blinding pain across my wound as the saltwater hit it. Then silence.

The warm water cradled me, lulled me. After a time, my wolf's form retreated and she joined me in the inner sanctum, looping around the room to let me pet her—to examine her gorgeous thick silver coat and bright green eyes—before she walked over to the fur-lined cubby that matched her and curled up inside. My raven soon followed, landing on the perch in front of me.

"*Your turn,*" she said, making me laugh. "*Island.*"

I was so tired the word barely registered. I sat there for ages catching my breath, drifting in and out of consciousness until the word snagged like a bit of loose kelp on the shore of my mind.

"*Island?*" I asked her.

She nodded. "*Your turn.*"

I blinked out of my inner sanctum slowly to find myself staring up at the dusky evening sky. I rolled and coughed at the sea water as it poured into my mouth. Floundered for a moment as I instinctively leapt to cradle my wounded arm.

At first, all I saw was sea…until my patient raven laughed, "*Turn around.*"

There, half a mile away, was an island. And not a small one either.

I could make that. I could reach it. Even kicking and swimming with one arm, I could do it.

I *did* do it. Length by length, scream by scream as the saltwater lapped at my wound.

Until finally, with nothing left in me to give, I let a soft wave carry me onto the white sand beach and crashed where I lay, desperate for rest.

There was no telling how long I laid there, curled in a sandy naked ball, but I knew the warmth of day gave way to the chill of summer night before somebody found me. They cast a blanket over my body. Tucked it around me gently. Lifted me into their sturdy, unharried arms.

"*It's okay, you're safe,*" I heard the Greek man whisper with the voice of a father, of a man who was unsurprised to find a tired, battered body washed up on the shore.

I mumbled, "*Where are you taking me?*"

With warm reassurance he told me, "*To the labyrinth, my lady. To the minotaur,*" and I accepted what that answer really was.

Proof that I was losing my mind.

Proof that there was nothing left to do but drift away into a dreamless sleep.

CHAPTER 2

I learned quickly that pain is insanity proof. Or rather, pain doesn't care whether you're insane or not; it can pierce through sleep, through fear, through the deepest depths of exhaustion to reach you.

I woke up screaming on some sort of stone platform, cold and damp and gratingly sandy against my back. All I could see was rough rock wall. All I could feel was pain…and hands. Hands held me down—on my ankles, legs, hips, my arms, my shoulders.

And a man gently held my head in a fixed position turned toward the wall while he cooed in my ear, "Relax. *Relax,* Natalie!"

I knew that voice, but there was too much pain to think clearly, to do anything other than whimper, "W-What are you doing to me?"

"We're removing the bullet, okay?"

"It h-hurts. *It hurts!*"

"I know. I know. Forgive me. Relax please. Just a few more seconds."

It didn't just hurt. My flesh was flame and acid; my entire left arm was *burning-searing-melting*. And someone I couldn't see was…rooting around in my shoulder.

"*Almost,*" I heard the man say. "*There it is. I've got it. I've got it!*"

He seemed happy about it—*thrilled* even—but the pain was happy-proof too. A flash of scalding fire shot through my arm, causing the rest of my body to clench and scream. Or maybe that was just me. Then a tide of darkness stole me away into dreamless slumber once more.

When I woke next, everything was different. Softer. Warmer. Cleaner. Brighter.

The rounded white plaster ceiling overhead curled around the bed in which I lay like a cocoon. A cocoon punctured by large wooden beams and a small brass fan blowing air across me. Turning my head, I realized I was in some sort of cave—a luxury cave bedroom. I could see the suggestion of a beautiful full bathroom nearby, and an indoor-outdoor seating area beside a small private pool, as well as giant glass doors that served as the room's windows. These opened onto a terrace, which I had to assume overlooked the sea, given that I could hear its gentle lulling roar as it broke across rocks below.

Soft pillows cradled my head. Softer sheets covered my body. Somebody had dressed me in cotton pants and a pale purple tank top and used strips of gauze to form a makeshift sling which "sealed" my bandaged arm to my body so I couldn't accidentally pull away or stretch it and hurt myself.

Someone had taken great care of me. And they must've given me something for the pain too because there was none so long as I didn't move my arm. The absence of discomfort was so lovely, my brain felt as if someone had drawn a warm bath and left it to soak—

Until I realized someone had drawn me an *actual* bath. Through the open doorway, I could just see curls of steam rising from the large tub right before I heard the soft *squeak* of the faucet shutting off.

"Hello?" There was no answer. No footsteps. "Is anybody there?"

I expected the response to come from outside me—from a housekeeper, from the man who had saved me—but it came from within, scaring the ever-loving soul out of me.

"*Safe*," my wolf suddenly said, her voice ringing through my head.

I startled at the sound of her. Her voice was deeper than my raven's. Raspy. Less harried. Distinctly her own.

"*Rest*," she added. "*Safe*."

That seemed like an insane thing to say, given her mere existence. But calm *radiated* off her where she stood in my inner sanctum. Alone, I realized. She was alone in there.

"*Where's my raven*?"

"*Patrolling*," my raven said, drawing my attention to the viewing windows. She was soaring over a rocky, dry coastline above an opalescent sea. Her body shifted slightly as she swooped low across a massive, tiled terrace outside a cave home, turning her head so I could see myself lying in bed in passing.

It was *trippy*.

My raven laughed at the thought and echoed the wolf, "*Safe*."

But I wasn't sure if I should believe her either. I mean, would someone losing their mind even know? When it came to something as complex as insanity, it was anyone's guess. Fast or slow. Complete or incomplete. Would it happen suddenly and all at once or in small slips and bursts? Would my mind crack in half like an ice sheet? Or would I descend slowly and madly into a quicksand that robbed me of myself over time?

Delicately, I pushed up to sit and drew back the bed covers, studying my traitorous body. There was nothing different about me that I could see, save for the bandaged arm. I didn't look insane. I didn't look like I was going to pieces. I looked like myself.

I felt like myself. Clear and calm and in control of my own nature. Like a still lake recovering after a storm.

But the big emotions of recent days were there just under the surface. The escape, the transformation, Rav's sham of a rushed wedding—just the thought of those things broke the surface tension and rippled *remembering* through me. Along with worry. Dread. Sorrow.

So much heartache.

Cass had come for me, like he'd always promised he would. He'd found a way through the guards and Rav had shot him in the head for it. That silver bullet had struck right between Cass's beautiful eyes and stolen my friend from the world in a single violent second.

Sharp pain rippled away from the memory, as if it was cutting me every time I tried to touch it. And with the pain came tears that never fell. Not outside my body anyway. There was some version of me deep inside wailing like the world had ended. She was inconsolable and no one was there to comfort her, except me. But I couldn't do that; another part of me remained willful. In obstinate denial.

I…

I didn't know how to process what had happened to him. It felt wrong, somehow. *Untrue*. My mind *rejected* it again the second I tried to think about him being gone.

And then my raven cut in, her voice sharper than I'd ever heard it, "*Not gone. Here.*"

I didn't know how to process that either. That was also demonstrably *untrue*.

But then she said it again, "*Not gone.*"

And all I could do was snap back, "*Then where is he?*"

I didn't expect an answer, because there couldn't be one—

"*Bathroom.*"

I froze where I was. "*Don't lie.*"

"*Never lie. Bathroom.*"

I…

Despite the aching exhaustion still in my body, I was on my feet half a second later, tripping over a rug in my haste, narrowly avoiding the door jamb with my wounded arm, practically skidding on my heels as I launched myself toward the bathroom.

"Cass?"

But…the bathroom was empty, save for the humidity from the filled tub and my lonesome shadow stretched dark across the floor. Save for the sound of the crashing waves outside. Save for the shattering heart inside me.

"*He's not here.*"

"*Yes, he is,*" she said just as confidently…and I…broke a little realizing the madness must already be setting in.

Tears splashed down my cheeks. Everywhere they struck, they carried fear with them.

I couldn't trust myself anymore. And if I couldn't trust myself, who else was I supposed to trust?

CHAPTER 3

I thought the door leading to the rest of the cavern house would be locked when I tried it, but it wasn't.

It also wasn't a cavern house, it turned out. It was a hotel. A very posh, very *empty* luxury hotel. I met no one as I moved down the hallway toward the lobby. I met no one again at the front desk, or in the spa or restaurant. It was a small place, maybe set up to hold a hundred guests at most, but I didn't see a single soul until I stepped out onto the public terrace…

…and the soul I *did* see terrified me. His curly hair, his young face lined with stress and worry; it looked vastly different than it had when I'd last seen it…at my wedding.

"Asterios?"

The name escaped my lips as a soft breeze, but he heard it above the roar of the sea, and turned where he stood by the terrace edge, offering me a cautious smile. One that didn't match the worry I could see in his bright blue eyes.

"You're looking well, Lady Damarand."

I didn't get closer to him; instead, my gaze snapped back to the hotel lobby behind me, scanning it for any signs that this was a trap, that Rav was nearby. Or Eike. I didn't know which would be worse.

But my raven heard me, and assured, "*Safe*."

Then I felt a rub of soft fur along the side of my leg, and my massive wolf stepped out of me, silver with the faintest sheen of pink, ethereal and translucent—a bubble in wolf form. She took a step forward and then sat between me and him, like a guardian. My guardian.

"Absolutely beautiful," Asterios said after a moment. His smile deepened and reached his eyes as they rose to meet mine. "What does it feel like?"

"Going insane?" I asked.

A wince flitted across his features, but he didn't respond to that. Instead, he turned and stared out to sea again. It was casual. *He* was casual, despite the tension and unease I could sense in him. I'd expected…more of a reaction. He'd been at my wedding. He'd stood there and watched Rav drag me down the aisle with a smile on his face. I hadn't noticed Asterios's reaction to my transformation then, but he didn't seem bothered in the slightest by my beastliness now.

"I'm going to leave."

"I wouldn't. Our dear king is hunting you."

His hand rose and pointed to the water, and I almost didn't look. Once I did, I couldn't look away. I stepped toward the terrace edge and clutched it for reassurance, as my gaze skimmed the surface of the sea…tracking *dozens* of boats as they zipped back and forth. Several helicopters slowly searched overhead too.

I didn't know what to make of it. Not the boats—the search, I understood. I didn't know what to make of him. Asterios wasn't acting like a jailer, like a threat. If anything, he was acting as if he was protecting me. Technically he was. It was his voice I'd heard when I woke up in agonizing pain. He'd held my head gently in his hands to keep me from looking as someone pried the silver bullet out of me. It was likely he'd brought me here too.

He could have called Rav at any time while I was unconscious. If an entire armada of ships was scouring the sea for me, that suggested Asterios hadn't.

"*Are those boats really looking for me?*" I asked my raven.

"*Yes.*"

Then… "Why haven't you told Rav I'm here?"

"I wouldn't do that," Asterios said. "I *won't* do that. I swear it."

"Why not? You were at the wedding supporting him. You didn't try to stop it."

"No, I didn't," he said quietly. "But you wouldn't believe me if I told you why."

My gift of honesty was on. He shouldn't have been able to lie, so I pushed. "Try anyway."

"Because I hoped the bond would save him," he said.

"Save *Rav*? Save him how?"

He hesitated before speaking, and when he spoke, he threw me for a moment with a seemingly random remark.

"Mating for life is quite rare in animals, did you know that?"

I shook my head gently.

"Rare and yet, there is a certain reassurance in it, isn't there. Maybe it's the possibility that someone else can stand you for so long, or that the bonds are so steady. Or the fact that you are willing to *surrender* yourself to something that isn't entirely selfish. Maybe it's just the romance of it. Or that the Goddess favors such bonds.

"Whatever it is, we are blessed to know those bonds are real. Where others wish for soulmates, we *know* they exist. We have all seen the power of these connections. Witnessed it with our very eyes. Lady Sorina and Lord Bogdan, Lord Aldric and Lady Giselle, King Ivar and Queen Tenna—when it was good, it was *spectacular*. And when it was not…"

Asterios blew the world's saddest raspberry with his lips.

"I have known Rav Elivagar his entire life. He's smart, strategic, confident in himself…and inflexible when it comes to getting what he wants. I dreaded the day he found a mate just like him, Lady Damarand. Not just me, others too. You Americans have that saying about people "drinking their own Kool-Aid," yes? We feared him finding his copy, or his cave echo." At that, a real smile danced across Asterios's face. "Instead, he found you. You're smart, strategic, confident in yourself…and humble enough to know you don't know everything. And you're kind as well? Imagine our surprise—our *relief*. We could not wait for you to mate with him. We could not wait to see who he would become with your influence."

I doubted he knew how raven mating worked. I didn't feel the need to hide it, though, considering I wasn't a member of the raven court anymore.

"Yeah, well, Rav told me raven mating was absolute. That the stronger of the pair usually took over the bond."

Asterios's brow furrowed in soft derision. Staring at me, he said, "Did you never consider that might be you?" He grinned and added, "I did. Still do."

Anger crept into my confusion. "So, you stopped my team from rescuing me because you wanted to force me to mate with him just to see if I came out on top? You know that's messed up, right?"

Asterios didn't answer my question. After a moment, he pushed away from the terrace wall and motioned toward the lobby. "Allow me to show you something, Lady Damarand."

He didn't wait to see if I would follow him. Instead, he walked through the lobby, down a hallway to a far door, which he held open for me.

I hesitated, but my wolf didn't. She charged ahead, right past him through the door, and after a few moments, her voice rang in my head, "*Safe*."

My feet were moving before I really thought about it. Or rather, the reluctance came after I was already on my way to follow her, as if my body and some part of my subconscious already trusted her implicitly. Suppose I shouldn't have been surprised; she *had* already saved my life.

"Absolutely incredible," Asterios murmured to me again in passing. "Just keep going until you reach the very bottom of the stairs."

Easy for him to say—there appeared to be *five thousand* of them. The rough-hewn stone steps descended for several hundred feet, and several stories. I passed four doors that led to who knew where before reaching a T-junction. In either direction, electric lights lit the corridor for a few lengths before darting inward out of sight.

"What is this place?" I asked when Asterios reached me.

"It was used as a refuge for civilians—alters and man alike—during the great human wars. Before that, well…"

He beckoned me to follow, so I did, deeper. At first, I thought it was a maze, but it wasn't. Or it wasn't anymore. Where there had once been other hallways, someone had sealed them with brick and mortar, narrowing the paths down to a select few. This one seemed to cut through several cross paths before bringing us to…a natural cavern lit by a narrow gap in the rock overhead. Green trees grew from scraggly stones. A pond full of little stalagmites sat at the center. And an archeological site consisting of the remains of a small stone house clung to the far wall.

"My ancestor, Asterion, shared your unique gift," Asterios said. "He could command individual parts of his animal form. This came in very handy as he was a sad little soul who hated other people. To scare them away, he would sometimes grow the head of an aurochs, sometimes the tail, sometimes the hooves while keeping his human hands. It worked for a time…until word spread of a creature with the body of a man and the head and brawn of a bull."

The Minotaur. The *original* Minotaur.

"But his sorry tale can wait for now. This way, please."

Asterios grabbed two flashlights set nearby and handed one to me before picking his way across the cavern and leading me into another corridor. This one was rough and natural, and carried on for what must have been *miles* until we reached…a stone wall with a small lever to the side. Asterios smiled at me so proudly before he pulled it, opening the wall like a secret door.

"Living your best Indiana Jones fantasies, Asterios?"

He grinned wider. "Oh yes."

The door slid sideways to reveal…an artifact crypt, just like the one at Rav's castle in Denmark and Bear Glen in Scotland. I could feel the energy of it before I spotted the impossibly delicate golden spire and one of the artifacts we had created at Versailles hovering above the point. Unbothered tendrils of magic swirled around it. Just like the original relic at Bear Glen before I removed it, this one was steady. Magick filled the space, but it wasn't pulsing erratically, on the verge of tossing people into walls like it had at Fylgja Castle.

The walls here were beautiful. Painted with frescos, instead of carved. But just like Rav's crypt, it held almost nothing otherwise. It was built around the spire, for the animalmass that spun gently in the air.

"I wanted to thank you," Asterios said after a while of just watching the delicate thing twirl. "If it weren't for you, I never would have known this was here. I would never have known my kingdom contained such a beautiful ancient technology as this."

"Well, at least something good came out of that whole fiasco," I joked.

Asterios frowned gently at that. "It can be difficult to look for good in disaster. That doesn't mean it isn't there."

"Doesn't mean it *is* either," I pointed out.

"Some disasters are just rotten luck," he admitted softly. "But others are warnings. Signs, if you choose to see them that way. In any case, there is always something to learn from them."

I didn't have anything to say to that. Fear and despair weighed down my heart until it was practically in my stomach, souring it awfully. I didn't need him to tell me some platitude like *everything will be okay* or *you'll get through this*. I didn't need baseless fantasies either.

But Asterios didn't offer those.

"When the relic broke and the first waves of spontaneous alterations began in my kingdom, you became desperate to undo your mistake, Natalie. I, on the other hand, was curious to know if it *was* a mistake. I researched these paintings, carbon-dated this chamber, and reached out to our neighbors asking if *they* had any relics like this in their kingdoms."

"Neighbors…in the Middle East?" I asked for clarification.

"And Africa, yes," he said.

"Do they?"

"None that they know of," Asterios said. "But would you like to guess how many asked me for the relic creation ritual instructions once you showed us?"

I hadn't thought to suppose they would, so my guess was that they had *all* asked. His soft smile suggested as much.

"I wasn't my father's first choice for an heir," he pivoted. "I wasn't even his second choice. Or his third."

"Oh?" I asked, as my eyebrow rose.

"If you can believe it, aurochs have very rigid social hierarchies. There is a dominant bull, a dominant cow. Aggression, size, and so on—it all matters. We are a matriarchal species, so technically it should have been a sister that rose to the position. My father only became Alter Supreme because his father failed to sire females. Same thing with my grandfather. A smarter group of men would have wondered if the Goddess was trying to tell us something—especially considering our form is extinct now and we are the last of our kind…*I am*, now. Instead, they decided that they knew better—the male line must continue."

With a twinkle in his eye, Asterios added, "Imagine my father's disappointment that I was all he had to leave as a legacy."

I frowned at that. "You seem like a good leader. More or less."

"I was too curious for my own good," he countered. "Always asking questions. Questions like, why does my family only seem to produce males? Why does the magick skip some people and not others? Why do the sabbat rituals require sacrifices? And if they do, why doesn't the Goddess come to collect them herself? He hated these questions. Refused to answer them when I wouldn't accept performative answers. Demanded I stop asking and forbid me from attending Gathering Table meetings until I learned to control my…outbursts."

I'd asked myself most of those questions too.

"And did you?"

"I taught myself to keep quiet…until he died."

"What happened then?"

"I went in search of answers and found that most were the same."

He shrugged. "Greed is as strong a force as gravity. Stronger. It can disrupt the natural order and warp our perception of what is just. It can make monsters of the most earnest of men, and demons of the worst."

I tried to answer his questions in the context of that response. I had no idea how greed was connected to the magick skipping some people and lavishing itself upon others, but…

"Your family produced males because the males in your family wanted to keep power for themselves." Off his nod, I continued. "And the sacrifices aren't for the Goddess at all, which is why she doesn't come to collect them herself. We sacrifice people…to take their power."

"Why spend time cultivating gifts naturally, through your work and achievements, when you can rob someone else of their power by simply killing them and consuming their flesh? And how convenient it is that we gave ourselves the authority of kings and queens, to execute at will with unquestionable judgement and often vague justification. And how lucky is it that our records of criminal investigations are held privately so only we might review them.

"If you did look through them, you might notice a surprising pattern in our sabbat offerings—so many otherwise lawful subjects are suddenly found guilty of something after the Goddess bestows her gifts upon them. And wouldn't you know it, the better the gift, the faster they are found guilty."

Corruption. Manipulation. I hadn't applied those words to the reservations I'd had about everything I'd done and been expected to do since entering the shifter world, but I think I knew subconsciously. The sacrifices had never made much sense to me. Not in practice. Not in purpose. After all, despite only consuming a single bite of shifter heart at Yule—and throwing it up—the Goddess had given and continued to give me plenty of gifts…

Too many gifts, in fact.

I opened my mouth to say as much when Asterios beat me to it in a way I never expected.

"Makes you wonder why beasts never make it to trial, no?"

I rolled that question around in my mind, along with all the ways he could mean it, but…

"What do you know about beasts, Asterios? Have you ever met one?"

At that, another happy smile broke the intensity of his face. "I have now."

He acted as if that was a good thing…and didn't even bother to answer my first question.

"What aren't you saying?" I asked after a moment.

His smile fell and he motioned me to follow him with a jerk of his head. We didn't take the path back toward the hotel. The crypt had another set of rough-hewn stairs leading steadily upward toward the surface, which eventually arrived at another levered door, horizontal this time. It opened into a…construction site.

A *mansion* under construction, I realized, as we left the tunnel and cut through rooms of dry concrete block and timber to reach a rocky hill overlooking a village and the sea in the distance. Even from here, the search boats were unignorable. As numerous as waterbugs. If anything, it looked as if their numbers had doubled while we were underground.

"Come with me," Asterios said, turning our attention to the half-built house. He doubled back through the construction and pushed open a door to reveal a perfectly beautiful apartment with white stucco walls and blue curtains and a lived-in quality that felt jarring in contrast to the construction zone just outside. Close the door and you'd never know you weren't already in someone's completed home.

"What is this?"

"It is quite common here to build houses in stages. When I found the crypt, I had this built to disguise its entrance. People tend to leave unfinished homes in peace."

My wolf and raven didn't trust that at face value. My wolf circled back to my side and heeled at my feet before my raven soared through one of the open windows, shot past Asterios close enough to take his nose off if she wanted, then out through another, as if in warning.

"You are safe here," Asterios assured. "You will be safe here until I can help you escape."

"Escape how? To where?"

"They will search the ocean until the last streaks of sunlight color the sky just like they did yesterday. But after nightfall, I will ferry you out of Rav's empire."

"I need a phone—"

"There are no phones here, Lady Damarand. No electricity either." After a moment, he added, "And I would not recommend attempting to leave on your own. They are not just searching the sea. With me—with my gifts protecting you—you are safe."

"What gifts?"

"The kind a nosey child who wished to hide from an unloving father would ask for."

He eyed me with a mix of confidence and heartache that was as easy to read as a fortune cookie—he *could* protect me but wouldn't tell me more if I asked again. It wasn't my business, of course, except for the fact that I didn't know how to risk my life on more cryptic half-answers.

"Rest. Let yourself heal a little more. I will make us some dinner in the meantime, and when night falls, I will see you to true freedom. I swear it on my life, Natalie."

Lovely words. A lovely promise. And in the face of the exhaustion I still felt, it was much needed. However far we had walked, the sea was miles away. And my skin was dampened with sweat and cave grit now. More than that, I had…nothing. No money. No phone. Nothing but the ability to fly or fight, if I needed to. And if he meant what he was offering, letting him spirit me beyond Rav's borders might mean the difference between enough time to save my kingdom or a swift and sudden death.

"*Is he telling the truth?*" I asked my creatures, just in case.

"*Trust,*" they both said together…and I reluctantly agreed to try.

CHAPTER 4

Asterios showed me to the bedroom, and I tried to rest. I let my body lay down, at least, while my mind ran circles around itself and I dipped in and out of my inner sanctum to patrol with my raven and wolf. It was strange to watch through the viewing windows while they were both outside my body. I had…more options now. Like a television with a mental remote, I could switch back and forth between their perspectives like I was changing the channel. Except the channels felt unique; they changed the inner sanctum as if they had their own thermostat settings. My raven was lighter, airy, and cool. My wolf was grounded, sturdy, and warm.

Together, there was a weird homeostasis. So strange and lovely.

More than that, it was *easy* to shift between them. Emotionally, physically, psychologically. I was in one, then the other, then both, then neither. There was a gymnastic agility to it. The more I switched, the easier it became, and the less strange it felt.

But…

That ease scared me. It felt slippery. Oily. The sort of sensation you could lose yourself to. Wasn't that what insanity was? No longer being able to distinguish between what was 'real' and 'unreal?' How could I know the difference as a shifter?

Did I need to resist the natural urge I had to talk with both of them, walk with both of them, know both of them? Yes, right? To buy myself time?

I felt a peck from my raven at the thought. "*Not insane.*"

But again, how could I trust myself enough to know?

Blah. Like it mattered at all in that moment.

They were all I had…and I couldn't be alone with myself. The moment I stopped using them as a distraction, the moment I reentered my own body and the bedroom in which I was laying, cold, brutal *loss* swept back into me.

It came in waves, building one on top of the next.

Loss of my mom, my friends, even Rav. I missed the 'before times' when the worst thing I had to deal with was Rav's treachery.

Loss of my future. Loss of all the things I could be. I'd been given a terminal diagnosis with a question mark written in for how long I had left to live. Insane or not, there was now a bounty on my head. Alters were out there right now *in droves* hunting me, fully prepared to end my life on sight. I might have six years or six hours left.

Yet as terrified as I was of the reaper's scythe suspended by a thread above my head, it was nothing compared to the…*other* loss, the one that squeezed my heart—crushed it—in the palm of the reaper's hand.

Cass was gone. My friend. My first love. My…mistaken mate. I'd yelled at him in London. The last words I'd said to him before Rav's wedding were spoken in anger and frustration. And *still* he'd come to help me.

Tears tore from my eyes as stinging rivers.

My chest threatened to collapse.

And when my wolf and raven sang out in my head, "*Not dead*," it only made me cry harder.

I curled into a ball in the sheets and began to weep the *hopelessness* out of me. That and the heartache I was being forced to carry alone; they were bitter oils leeching into my body, souring my flesh, exhausting me. And when unconsciousness finally claimed me, I was grateful because it spared me from the pain of being awake without him.

***

Hours later, I woke…to the terrifying texture of fur against my skin. It tore me from peaceful oblivion in a panic; I was only lucky my body didn't flinch like my mind did, giving me away. No, I kept my eyes closed, pushing awareness through my body.

I wasn't alone.

There was someone else in my bed.

They had their…arm around my waist.

I could feel puffs of air against my hair.

Their legs were curled around mine, as if they too were asleep, resting peacefully.

But the touches were fur-lined, it was the strangest thing. Terrifying.

Until my raven said, "*Safe.*"

"*What is it?*" I whispered in my mind.

"*Mate.*"

I plunged into my inner sanctum at the claim, "*Show me.*"

But they already were. My wolf was in the room with me, laying on the floor beside the bed. Through her vision, I saw—

My eyes jolted open in the real world. I spun so fast in bed, I tangled in the sheet and hit the wall with a dull *thunk!*

I hardly felt it.

He was there.

Right there!

Eyes of moonlight. Hair of flame.

My friend.

My ginger gentleman.

He was…dressed differently than he had been at the wedding—a slate blue shirt and dark jeans hugged his form tightly. His body was still strangely proportioned in that new beefy way that would take getting used to. His silver eyes were open and unblinking, fixated on me in a piercing way…but there was no bullet hole between them. For a moment, my heart tore a frantic rhythm in my chest, both at the thought that he *was* there and that he wasn't, that this was just some horrible waking nightmare.

"Cass?!" I whimpered.

I startled as his hand moved, pushing him to sit up. That curl of longish saffron-orange hair fell across his forehead the way I'd seen it do so many times before and my hand rushed ahead of me, swept it aside, tucked it behind his ear.

His warm ear.

His soft hair.

I couldn't help myself; I threw my good arm around him tightly and clung, savoring the feel of him.

"You're alive!" I breathed. "Cass, w-what on earth happened?! How did you survive? How did you find me here?"

My heart *soared* with joy, relief, hope. Seeing him—*feeling* him under my fingertips—was everything. It stirred an emotion in me I hadn't felt in a *very* long time. Not since Versailles. It was safety, and more. It was longing, and more. It was…something unquantifiable.

Soft—subtle, even—but unignorable. Essential.

More than that, I wasn't alone. I wasn't completely cut off from everyone I knew and cared about. And *Cass was trustworthy*. We could get through this together. He would help me secure the Eighth Kingdom. He would help me protect my family and our friends. And if I was truly lost, he would be able to keep me from hurting anyone else. If I couldn't trust myself, I could trust him.

But…he didn't speak. The corners of his eyes crinkled with joy. His hand reached forward to cup my face—his fur-lined calluses skated across my skin and settled warmly—but words of reassurance didn't come pouring out of his heart-shaped mouth wrapped in his beautiful sophisticated accent.

Then I sniffed…and my heart sank. He didn't smell of campfire. He didn't smell of anything. For a moment, I thought maybe he was wearing the concoction he'd told me about all those weeks ago—the combination of angelica and mugwort the Goddess had told him would obscure his scent.

But…I felt no lick of snowflake attention across my skin even though his eyes never left me. In fact, he wasn't blinking *at all*. His gaze darted across me, reacting to my every movement, but not once did the lids hemmed in long red lashes close across his silver eyes.

"Cass—?"

—The bedroom door wrenched open suddenly, tearing my attention away.

"Natalie, are you all right? I heard something." Asterios was there at the door, staring at me. His eyes swept over the bed, then down to my wolf on the floor before returning to me.

I knew before I looked to confirm that the bed beside me was empty; Cass had disappeared in the blink of an eye.

A rusted blade of loneliness sliced through my gut and twisted the cruelty of it deeper. Even though I had seen and touched him, he wasn't real. He had been nothing more than a symptom of my brain's rapid deterioration.

And I…lied. "I'm fine. Sorry."

I was breaking. Pieces of me were crumbling to dust.

And Asterios could see it. A tiny fleeting glimmer of worry deepened the lines along his forehead before he said, "All right. Dinner's ready when you are."

He went to shut the door—

"Wait! I'm ready. I'll come now."

I hustled after him, knowing if he left me alone, I'd burst into tears. Or worse, I'd see someone who wasn't really there again.

***

Asterios had set the table by the open window so prettily. A white tablecloth. Blue plates. A little vase holding a violet-green plant stalk that flared on all sides with tiny purple and white flowers. Among and between these sat the freshest food I'd seen in ages.

"A village salad with feta from the farm not far from here. Fried zucchini. And spanakopita. I'm sorry I don't have more to offer."

"Is…this all vegetarian?" I asked, taking my seat.

"That's what you are, yes? Just like abstaining from the sacrifices, this is yet another side of myself I have been able to recover…thanks to you."

"You're vegetarian?"

His nod was a sweet, nervous thing. "I am learning to be myself again."

"You *do* look lighter," I admitted.

"You have no idea. A great burden has been lifted."

I smirked, thinking whatever burden he'd freed himself from had probably found its way onto my already overloaded shoulders. I would have to hand some of it back.

"Asterios, I need your help."

"I am helping you—"

"No. I mean, yes you are, but…I need to reach out to my people. There's paperwork I need to make sure is finalized. Before I can't make sure of anything anymore."

"Tomorrow, after we escape—"

"There might not be a tomorrow," I countered. "If there isn't, or if I'm caught, I need you to do this for me. Rav cannot have the Eighth Kingdom. Neither can Archer Mahon. I should've put failsafes in place before things went wrong, but I didn't. I can write everything out; a last will and testament. I just need your word that you'll deliver it to my team. O-Or my lawyer. Please?"

Asterios studied me for a long moment with a strange twinkle in his eye. "What about Cassian Mahon?"

The name summoned crushing sorrow.

"He's…gone," I strained.

The twinkle in Asterios's eye darkened with…play? "But he came for you. Supposedly died for you."

I bit down on my lip and tasted metal on my tongue.

"May I ask you something personal, Lady Damarand?" he asked after a moment.

My gaze snapped back to his, already defensive.

"A little birdie told me you were able to help Yasmina Kramar alter for the first time, even though she had never been able to do so before. Is that true?"

Was that sensitive information to divulge? Would it harm her to reveal it? I…didn't think so.

I nodded softly.

"Then it is safe to assume you did the same for Master Mahon?" he asked.

"Does it matter now?"

Again, he eyed me with a mixed expression on his face that was difficult to read. He looked frustrated by my answer, but also amused by it?

"Do you know what this flower is called, Natalie?" He drew my attention to the stalk of delicate purple and white blossoms. "It is the national flower of Greece—Bear's Breech, we call it. Fitting, no?"

No, but if he was trying to make a punny joke about the Bear Lord's son, Cassian Mahon, breaching the wedding to save me, he wouldn't know why the joke didn't land. No one—outside Fern, Yasmina, Dr. Martin, and I—knew what Cass really was.

"The late Bear Lord, Goddess rest him, had many dreams for his son. But dying to protect the raven alter who usurped his throne wasn't one of them."

"William Mahon named me his heir," I said. "I didn't steal his throne."

"No, but Cassian helped you keep it. In turn you helped him alter—something *no one else* was able to do. Then suddenly he is there, stopping your wedding, sacrificing himself to help you escape."

"…So?"

He chuffed a tiny laugh, like a puff of air. "So, there is a game happening all around me, and I would like to play, if you'll let me."

Discomfort rankled my body. "This isn't a *game*, Asterios! Cass is dead. Rav's an asshole. And sooner or later, I'm going to die—"

"*Pfft*, you're not going to die. You're far too well protected for that."

"If I don't die, I'm going to go insane, and frankly that sounds worse." Off another one of his friggen puzzling grins, I snapped, "Why are you smiling?"

"Is there no way for me to convince you that I am on your side?" he asked finally, confusing me more. "Believe me, Lady Damarand, I could be as tremendous an ally to you as you have been to me. I have much I can share, much that will make this transition of yours easier."

Frustration replaced the discomfort I felt. It was as if we were having separate simultaneous conversations. Worse, I couldn't tell him that I genuinely had no clue what he was talking about because he meant what he was saying. He thought I was up to something, that some grand conspiracy was afoot. And even though he didn't know any details, he was genuinely offering to join me in it.

It was a good reminder of how I needed to be. There was no time for self-pity, or even for mourning. I needed to protect my kingdom with the little life I had left, and I needed to pull from Cass's strengths, now that he wasn't around to use them. If Asterios was willing to help me because he believed I knew more than I did, I would have to lean into that.

I took a deep, steadying inhale before I said, "Help me contact my team, get me out of Rav's empire, and we can talk."

Blue eyes still twinkling, his grin widened. "Then we shall talk tonight, my queen. I am looking forward to it."

I spent the rest of the afternoon at that little table with a pad and pen, writing my last will and testament. The actual laundry list of *things* and *stuff* I owned was the easy part; putting together a set of directives, of steps to take now that Cass was gone and I was dying was harder.

But Asterios helped. He talked me through parts of my kingdom I hadn't thought to safeguard, like earmarking funds to ensure special interest projects kept going—like the wildlife parks I'd started, like the beach cleanups and the elder care facilities for alters and the healthcare recruitment initiatives. He showed me how to prevent a future heir (or Rav) from getting rid of them.

And then, when the pages covered with my shaky handwriting were finished, he summoned a trusted man on his team to leave immediately for London to deliver the will to my lawyer.

My raven and wolf helped too. They kept calling out little warnings to me, regarding the army, which I'd left in Cass's capable hands, and resources I needed to double check, along with steps I needed to take.

"*Production lines. Ammo. Weapons. Silver.*"

"*Call Brodie. Millie. Idalia.*"

"*Call witches. Belina. Jane. Fiadh.*"

"*Warn Fern—Walshingham.*"

"*Walshingham? Who's that?*"

"*Will know.*"

It was that last recommendation that stumped me. The name was entirely foreign, not something dredged from the depths of my mind; I had no idea who 'Walshingham' was and I'd never heard that name before. Yet, my wolf seemed adamant Fern would understand.

In between their recommendations, my raven and wolf called out the arrival of approaching cars carrying Asterios's guards who brought updates about Rav's search. He'd begun a sweep of homes across the nearby islands, and it was only a matter of time before he began one here, on Crete.

"This is a big island," Asterios assured me. "We will be long gone before he gets here."

It still made me anxious. My gaze kept darting to the west as I watched the sun sink lower in the sky, counting the minutes until Asterios finally said…

"Natalie, it's time to go."

A tiny beat-up silver Toyota appeared outside at sundown and my wolf inspected it before I darted into the back and hunkered down out of sight. We drove nearly 45 miles in complete silence as my raven soared ahead of us, on the lookout, and I peeked over the back door as we passed through village after village.

There was an undeniable tension that thickened the hot, dry air. The village streets were empty, save for swarms of black motorcycles, and every time I glanced up, I caught a local person peering out of their shuttered windows as we passed by.

"*This can't be for me,*" I said to my raven.

She didn't answer, but her silence was heavy with reply.

And then, as the island's southern coast came into view, I spotted two black motorcycles parked outside a lonesome rural house at the center of an olive grove. Through the closed car windows and even from a hundred feet away, I could hear shouts of anger and cusses in Greek. We didn't stop, and Asterios offered no explanation, but right before the house disappeared from view, I spotted two tall blond men stomping out, pursued by a local-looking man and woman—the owners who had very obviously not consented to having their house ransacked.

"Asterios, how is Rav justifying this? I mean, I know why he's hunting me, but most of these people are probably human, right?"

"I will explain once we're safe."

That seemed like an arbitrary point in time, but when my raven suddenly cried, "*Hurry!*" and I parroted it to Asterios's driver, he picked up speed immediately. We were down an old narrow road to a main road, to a gate, and past it to a boat marina in moments.

I expected to find a speedboat waiting for us.

Heck, I expected a *dinghy* that I'd have to row across the sea myself.

Instead, a mega yacht sat anchored at the very end of an otherwise empty pier, as flashy as a neon bar sign in the growing darkness. What could Asterios have possibly been thinking when he chose this as our escape vessel?

There was no time to ask.

Just as the Aurochs Lord opened my car door, my raven cried, "*Danger!*"

"Asterios, someone is here."

His eyes snapped to the boat and for a long moment, he froze there, blocking my way out of the car, before he and my raven said, "*Eike,*" and my system flooded with dread.

CHAPTER 5

"Natalie, I need you to hold my hand and not let go, do you understand me?"

"W-What?"

"Hand! Now!"

My uninjured hand shot for his the moment he offered it. I felt the tiniest zip of magick, barely a bee sting on my palm, as his soft, dry fingers folded around mine.

"Get out quietly. Remain silent. Do not let go of me for *any* reason. Not if I'm injured. Not if I am knocked unconscious. And if I am killed, you must tear open my chest and eat my heart. *You have my permission to do so*."

"*What?*"

"Hush!"

I slipped out of the car and tucked myself behind him.

"Can't we leave before—"

"No," Asterios whispered. "She already knows I'm here."

"Lord Talon." It was a voice that had narrated almost all of my nightmares since entering the shifter world. Raspy and growling and eerily calm.

I peeked under Asterios's arm. Eike stood on the small piece of wood between the yacht and pier, as if she'd been waiting on board for him to arrive. She walked off the gangway and paused, wearing that piercing stare that always gave me shivers.

Every *clack* of her shoes across the wood spiked terror through my body. She was only twenty or so feet away; I kept waiting for the moment she noticed Asterios's awkward gait. Or my shoe slipping out from behind him, or his hand tucked strangely to his side.

Instead, she asked, "Have you had word from your men?"

Asterios's body language shifted before my eyes. His shoulders squared, his slightly hunched back straightened. Even his voice deepened a little. "Yes, they've scoured the western half of the island. There's been no sign of her."

"And the water?"

"They haven't found her there either," Asterios said. "But they've searched every boat they've encountered."

"You understand how dire this situation is. You understand how important it is to His Majesty that his mate is saved before anything happens to her."

Saved?

"Of course, Eike," Asterios scolded. "I've known Rav far longer than you have. I know how much he cares for her. My men will continue to search throughout the night and the days ahead. We will bring her home if we can."

It was such a strange moment. Such a torturous limbo to find myself in, both convinced that she would see me and reassured by every continued second of un-discovery that she couldn't. More than that, what he was saying—what they were *both* saying—set me more on edge in confusion. My body fritzed at the mixed messaging and the reassuring feeling from my wolf and raven to trust that he was lying to her. I was too out of the loop to feel safe. I felt like a cat around tinfoil, ready to leap at a moment's notice.

But their conversation continued as if I wasn't even there.

"We?" she teased, glancing at the yacht. "Are you joining the search, lord?"

"For a time… Is there something I can help your men find?"

"No," Eike replied. "They are just being thorough."

Peeking under his arm again, distant bodies came into focus. Men were searching his yacht; there was one on the bridge with the captain, two more on the next promenade down, and three on the main deck. They pushed past the yacht's crew with raider bravado, tugging open hatches and yanking cushions up to peer underneath.

A strange tetchy silence stretched between them as Asterios waited for Eike's men to finish their search. Eike never took her eyes off him, and Asterios never blinked. He simply waited, hiding the raging thrum of his heart, until the six men walked off the yacht to join Eike on the pier.

Then, he offered, "Can I give you and your men a ride back to the mainland?"

"The sea between here and there has already been heavily searched," Eike purred in frustration.

"Then I'll head around the island to join the armada. We can expand our search to the southeast."

Eike continued to study him for a long moment. So long, he eventually added, "You may join me for that if you like—"

"No," she said. "We have our own orders. But Rav has asked that you call with an update tomorrow morning."

"Very well."

Again, no one moved. Not until Asterios gave my hand the tiniest squeeze and tug, warning me that we were about to walk. It was a useless warning; terror spiked through me again with his first step, then the next which I took with him. It was like walking on broken glass, more and more uncomfortable the closer we drew to his ship. I kept my eyes on the ground, watching his feet, mirroring his steps. It was all I could do. That, and trust the magick.

"*They can't see me, they can't see me*," repeated in my mind like a prayer.

But…there was only so much distance between us and Eike. With each step closer I knew there would come a point where they couldn't help but see me…

My heart seized as I caught sight of the first body in my periphery—one of Eike's men. Then another, then another.

No one moved.

Asterios never flinched.

And Eike didn't react.

I did, at the sight of her. I couldn't help it; my body knew where the real threat was. It was like seeing a shark in the water. The men around her were the fin above the surface warning that the shark was near; but she was the teeth and the wide-open mouth ready to tear me in two.

Asterios tightened his grip on my hand at the first moment of fear and kept me moving, despite my body's knee-jerk need to run away.

It was impossible, their nonreaction.

Wrong.

I peeked up to look at her in passing and found…her gaze wasn't on me. It was on Asterios, welded there like she expected to find me hiding in his eyes. The men, too; their gaze swept across my general location as if I was…

"*Invisible*," I whispered in my mind. My wolf rubbed against me in confirmation. "*I'm invisible, aren't I?*"

"*Trust,*" my raven replied.

And I did…all the way onto Asterios's yacht, clinging to his hand as his crew rushed around readying the boat to leave. I remained barnacled to his back until the engines kicked on and a breeze began to blow, and a crewman tossed a rope onto the deck and climbed back aboard. Then we were turning, speeding away from Eike, who stood on the dock staring after us until we disappeared to the east out of sight.

Only then did Asterios release my hand. And when he did, he ignored the whispered curses of several crewmen at my sudden appearance.

"*This is my burden,*" Asterios toned. "*You are blind sailors tonight.*"

He shot me a small, reassuring smile before barking orders to the nearest man and rushing up to the bridge, sealing himself away with the captain. Through the tinted windows, I watched them talk, then bark, then argue. About me. The captain glanced my way half a dozen times, all but confirming it.

My spine itched with a wish to know what they were saying, and in answer…

"*Confused,*" my raven said.

"*The captain?*"

"*Willing to help,*" my raven said.

"*Scared,*" my wolf added.

"*Where are you?*" I asked my raven. In answer, a tiny flicker of orange-pink drew my eye to a spot near the bridge—a wingtip as she flicked it at me. My little spy.

I found a quiet spot inside the main cabin to sit by the window and wait for…whatever came next. We sailed for nearly two hours until we reached the far eastern edge of the island, and Asterios came to collect me.

"Is everything okay?" I asked.

"As good as can be expected, given the circumstances," he said, gesturing me up from the seat. "While the water is calm, we will leave my crew here and continue on the next leg of our journey alone."

"O…kay."

I had trusted him this far, and heard no warning from the duet of voices in my head, so I followed him. A crewman was already waiting for us down a side hall beside a shallow shelf on the wall; he pressed some small button to the side and the shelf slid sideways, revealing another staircase. This wasn't a hidey-hole or some weird jerry-rigged addition to the boat; this had clearly been put there by design, built in as a secret lower level, half above and below the waterline. Trying to visualize how the ship had looked as we approached, I couldn't imagine this being here, until the crewman opened another door at the bottom.

"Oh wow."

There was…an entire mobile seaplane base down there. The deck stood at water level wrapped in a U around a slip, where a boat—or in this case, a seaplane—could dock. At the moment, the small blue plane with white stripes was drydocked above the water, dangling in a sling. And the back of the boat wasn't solid like it had seemed from the outside; it was a door.

As I watched, Asterios and the crewman slowly lowered the plane onto the water's surface. Then the man detached a gas line from the plane's body as casually as you might a car at a gas station. This clearly wasn't the first time they'd put a plane here, or taken one out.

And I knew before Asterios said that this was the real ferry out of Rav's kingdom.

"Don't be scared, Natalie," Asterios said, motioning me toward the plane.

"I'm not scared."

"Really? Most people are terrified when they see Helios," he joked, patting the plane with love before tearing open the door for me.

"I have wings," I reminded him with a smile.

"Does that mean you would abandon me if we went down out there?"

I didn't mean to hesitate, but I did…and Asterios laughed.

"Good, I want you to," he said. "If you are ever in danger, leave me behind without a second thought. Hop in."

My raven crashed back into my body just as I crawled into the passenger seat, and we watched Asterios finish preparations before he joined me. When he did, the crewman opened the ship's stern and the last tether connecting the seaplane to the yacht was removed. The yacht slowly sailed forward as we remained in place, until we were clear of the door and suddenly adrift on a miraculously calm sea.

I didn't bother to ask where we were going; I didn't think he would tell me. Instead, I tightened my safety belt and set the headphones he handed me on my head and left Asterios to do his thing. He flicked on the ignition and busied his hand twisting various knobs and pulling levers until he suddenly pulled back on the vibrating yoke and we sped across the glassy sea and up into the deep violet sky.

CHAPTER 6

"We're flying south."

"Yes."

It shouldn't have been that surprising. With Rav's kingdom to the north, south was the obvious direction to head to get me out and away from everything associated with the Raven King. Every mile we flew was a gift I could never pay back.

Still, surprise rippled through me, then wonder when a great city winked into my awareness on the far horizon a couple hours later. The metropolis stretched wild and golden and massive along the coastline in the dark. Before going to London, the largest city I'd ever seen was New York City, and this was larger than that by a wide margin.

"Holy moly," I whispered.

"Welcome to Alexandria, Egypt, my queen," Asterios said. "Welcome to the Crocodile Court."

I shivered in my seat, gawking. It was beautiful. Magnificent. And terrifying, given his identifier. Of course, alters existed everywhere, on every continent on Earth and in every sea—Eike and my own research had taught me that—but it was something else entirely to be told I was entering the territory of a new kind of shifter. Many shifters. Not just crocodiles, but wading birds, cobras, beetles, and camels.

From the little I'd been able to read about the Crocodile Court on my own, I knew it was ruled by a Dual King, or "king of two lands," which was the most fitting title I'd heard for an alter yet, especially one that ruled both the land and sea. They weren't kings by royal blood. They earned the title and position through battle and brawn, and they all took the name Dual King Sobek upon coronation. Sobek, I'd learned, was the name of the ancient Egyptian god of crocodiles, and no matter who they had been before, they were all Sobek after. They were all "His Excellency."

It was one of the world's oldest alter houses, after the Outer Sea Court of the Atlantic—the shark court.

Intimidating, to say the least. I felt smaller and smaller the closer we drew to the city, but also excited and relieved. This place felt distinct. Separate from all I was leaving behind, and therefore reassuring. Scary because of that too, but there was more anticipation. Just a couple of days ago, reaching this place had seemed impossible to me; now, with Asterios's insane and perplexing generosity, anything seemed possible. My reactive doom and despair had given way to…a tiny flicker of hope.

We flew over a narrow strip of land into a harbor before Asterios told me to prepare for landing and glided us down onto the calm surface of the water…right between a naval yard and a white, domed palace standing on the lip of the sea. In the darkness, it glowed like a long pearl.

As Asterios guided the plane up to the palace's seaplane dock, I could sense dark uncertainty. A small contingent of soldiers wearing tan uniforms, blue berets, and assault rifles over their shoulders were waiting to greet us, led by…a young woman just a few years older than me. She had sharp dark eyes and shoulder-length black hair and wore a sort of lethally relaxed smile as if she knew she was never in any real danger.

A crocodile's smile, I realized, as a soldier opened my door for me, and I caught a strong whiff of warm figs and…stagnant water. Like pond water on a hot day. It wafted off all of them, especially her. They were all alters.

"*As-salamu alaykum*, Lady Damarand, Lord Talon," she said, her voice low and sweet. "Welcome to Ras el-Tin Palace."

"*Wa alaykum as-salam*, Sayyida Mesi," Asterios replied. "Natalie, this is Mesi Ahmose Raed, daughter of Dual King Sobek."

"Nice to meet you," I managed in the face of her unwavering stare. She stared for so long and so contentedly I felt on trial somehow, even though I sensed no animosity from her and no warning from my creatures.

Then I realized…she was reading me. Whatever her gifts, they were activated and aimed straight at me. Who could blame her? I certainly couldn't, until I knew what Asterios—or even Rav—had told her family about me.

"My father is away on business," she said, motioning for us to follow as she turned and strode for the palace. Her guard fell into position around us as we walked. "He will come to speak with you when he can. In the meantime, we have set out a dinner and arranged rooms. Our physician can redress your wound as well. Anything you need, just ask."

"Thank you, Sayyida Mesi," Asterios said. "We'll need a secure, untraceable phoneline as soon as possible."

Mesi considered this for a long beat before nodding. "You shall have it tomorrow."

My heart sang at the easy promise, at how true I hoped it was, considering I couldn't turn on my aura of honesty just yet. Not while Asterios might need to lie to help me.

My creatures, too, were off limits.

As we walked, both warned me that while it felt safe to be there, they weren't taking any chances. Neither would reveal themselves unless my life was in danger, but they were on full alert inside the inner sanctum. I could sense them peering out of me, like twin eyes in the dark, gawking with me as Mesi led us up the palace's enormous ceremonial staircase, past the throne room and private offices, and away to a pair of suites she said were ours to use as we needed.

The building was beautiful, bedighted with gold accents and grand scalloped archways and lofty ceilings that echoed our voices for ages down the halls, although I was surprised by how many similarities it shared with Versailles in terms of décor. Apparently, it had undergone renovations in the Italian and French styles over the years, and had become an architectural staple of the skyline of Alexandria as seen from the sea.

"This palace is a summer home for the human president," Mesi told us, when we eventually reached the palace's inner courtyard. "It *publicly* belongs to him and his administration—but it is most assuredly my father's. It has belonged to the Dual Kings since it was built in the nineteenth century. It is also closed to the public, the military, and the police without explicit permission from my father. The president himself would be turned away if he showed up unannounced. You will be safe here while you decide your next steps."

It was another easy declaration that made me anxious to speak with Asterios in private. To have that big conversation he promised we would have once we were finally out of Greece.

So it was with no small amount of relief when we finally arrived to a long table crowded with dishes of food, and Mesi bid us goodnight, summoning her guards to follow her.

In her absence, silence descended. I dropped into the seat closest to me and took the first deep breath I'd taken since Rav had trapped me at Hamingja all those days ago. Or…or had it been weeks?

"Asterios? What day is it?"

"July nineteenth," he said quietly, taking the seat beside me. "It's been seven days since the wedding."

I fell silent, mulling that over. It was earlier than I'd expected. I thought I'd spent a long time clawing myself free of the endless magick at Hamingja, but it really hadn't been long at all. Less than a month ago, I'd been in Ireland with my friends planning our annual holiday, Lunasa. I'd visited Scotland to interrogate our prisoners, learned of the coordinated attacks all over Europe and helped to prevent five of them.

Or…at least four of them.

"Were you able to stop the attack in your kingdom?" I asked him.

"Yes, thanks to you."

"What about the others?"

"I don't know. Oriol said nothing to me at the wedding. Sorina was preoccupied by other things. I don't trust Oskar enough to ask him. Giselle is missing. And something happened with Idalia. She's sealed herself away at Arachne's Revenge."

Again, I didn't know if I should reveal anything about what had happened in the days since Rav turned on me.

So instead, I asked, "Arachne's Revenge?"

"It's the ancestral home of Idalia's family. Now it acts as the Spider Court's official seat."

"Where is it?"

"Nobody knows. Italy, of course, but other than that…"

I laughed at that. "You're joking."

Asterios shook his head.

"You mean, Rav's never visited? You've never visited?"

"No one has," he said. "Spiders are naturally quite secretive, and, well—to be delicate about it—ravens are one of their natural predators. Her kind have a long history of clinging to the shadows to avoid them."

"Have you spoken with her?"

"No."

"So then…how do you know she's sealed herself away? Let alone in a place you've never been?"

The moment the question left my mouth, I felt a shift in him. A soft smile rose to his face as if he'd been baiting me to ask exactly that.

"That is a complicated question. But…I owe you answers, Lady Damarand. I *promised* you answers."

"Yes, you did."

"Before I tell you anything more, I must warn you, you cannot ask what my gifts are. You can *guess* what you *think* they are, and I can say no if you've guessed wrong and nothing if you guess correctly, but on my life I cannot name them for you, understand?"

I didn't, really. And I had the sudden urge to flick on my aura of honesty gift now that we were alone, so the truth might slip out anyway. But the moment I reached for the switch in my mind, my raven gave me a vicious mental peck.

"*Hey! Watch it!*" I yelped.

"*Trust,*" she scolded me.

I blew out a breath instead and said, "Okay. Fine. I won't ask."

"In exchange, I won't ask what happened between you and Rav to drive him to the extremes I've seen in the last few days."

My shoulders sagged with guilt…and gratitude trickled in. For a moment, I'd forgotten just how much I owed Asterios, beyond bringing me to Egypt. "Thank you."

"Believe me, I would tell you many things if I could, but as I said before, I was not my father's first choice and the lock around my tongue is one reason why. Not that it matters now, of course. As for Idalia, well. I only know where she is because of the wedding."

"The wedding? I didn't see her there."

"She wasn't, but after you leapt away from that altar, all hell broke loose. The guards that were still standing chased you. The ones taken away by whatever darkness Cassian brought with him caught up with the hunt too. In their absence, the other Supremes went after Rav, for harboring a beast, for killing the son of William Mahon…"

Asterios eyed me then soberly and added, "And for telling you to run."

Rav had done exactly that; despite everything that had happened between us, Rav had sort of saved me again. I was so frozen in the wake of Cass's death and my sudden transformation that I knew it was only my wolf's quick footwork and that strange command from Rav that had saved my life.

"I don't know why he did that," I admitted quietly.

Asterios's eyebrow rose. "Yes, you do." But he pushed on before I could disagree. "For anyone else, the decision to help someone like you would have been a death sentence. Rav, however, is singularly well equipped to deal with the fallout of such a dangerous choice. Do you know why?"

I wasn't sure which answer he wanted.

Because he's the king, seemed too simple.

But so did the other option, "Because he's invincible?"

"He has certainly done everything in his power to appear so. But no. Like me, Rav was born into this world. From the moment he could toddle, he was groomed for the very position he now holds. Granted access to wisdom far beyond his years and experience, both magickal and political. His father Ivar wasn't just a king; he was a seeker. He dedicated his free time to absorbing all the knowledge he could and then used it to find…shortcuts."

Shortcuts. Tenna's journal had mentioned those. That Ivar had tested them on her and Rav.

"Ways to accrue power, influence, advantages beyond the ones he earned personally. He naturally passed many of these onto his son, and Rav has continued that tradition. Why wouldn't he? It is no different than a family with a restaurant teaching their very young children how to cook. What the grandmother learns at fifty, she teaches her granddaughter when she's five. That is how wisdom is supposed to work.

"In this way, Rav succeeded and outperformed his father when he was still a child. Until Ivar grew jealous and stopped sharing so freely with him. By then, of course, it was too late. Rav already knew how to ask the Goddess for gifts, and how to hide them. He already knew how to solve his own problems. And he had to. Ivar could be a formidable adversary."

This seemed like important albeit random information; I couldn't help wondering what that had to do with everything that had happened. Until I realized… "You've known Rav his entire life. You were—*are*—friends. You know things the others don't."

His eyes sparkled at that. "I also had a father who grew to despise me. I asked for gifts I needed to survive mine…and so did Rav. He wanted his father to listen, just to listen, and from that need grew a dangerous and very useful ability. The ability to influence others."

"I know he can make people feel things," I said. "I know he can erase people."

"He can also inspire them," Asterios added, pinning me with a cautious stare.

"Inspire them how?"

"To think differently. To act differently." I didn't know what look on my face had him sitting forward in his seat, but he did and added, "It is especially potent with humans. A touch and a careful word. Advice spoken with sincerity. Not much at all, really. Just a seed planted that takes root in the person's mind and grows until they believe they spawned it themselves."

With that Asterios smiled darkly, "It's amazing how the softest suggestion can change everything you think you know about yourself."

I blinked, soaking his words in. "That's…so dangerous. Anyone could be influenced to believe anything."

"Well, this is just a heightened version of what already exists in the world. We are social creatures. We are influenced by what we are told, what we are shown, and what we want to believe. Especially those of us who never bother to ask questions. How many people have you met who believe literally anything they're told if they trust the person saying it? Even the most suspicious among us *want to believe* that there is someone who can be trusted, and usually this is true. In Rav's case, his gift simply convinces them he's worthy of being believed."

A small moment flashed inside my mind—a memory from Hamingja. Rav had insisted on coming with me to speak with Violette about becoming an alter. He'd sat with her, holding her hand. She'd acted mesmerized by him. I hadn't recognized the influence as anything magickal in the moment, but looking back? Sheer *terror* had flitted across her features when he'd suggested becoming a wolf, and yet a few soft words from him and she agreed to it.

I thought back farther again, to her home in the woods near Barcelonnette, France. The barbed wire she'd said her late husband had put up to keep creatures like us at bay. In the Wolf Court, the most likely creature to keep at bay was a wolf. Would she have chosen to become a wolf if Rav hadn't been there? I didn't think so. Hell, she'd even asked him to choose *for* her.

Who else might he have influenced the same way?

"You said it works better on humans?" I asked. "But it *does* work on alters too."

He nodded. "After you escaped the wedding, Rav seemed torn between chasing after you with the guards and remaining with the Supremes. In the end, he chose us. He stayed and touched every one of us on the shoulder and whispered a new truth into our ears. He said there was no beast. Instead, we had all watched wolves from the cult raid the wedding, kill Cassian Mahon, steal you away. He pointed at the guards Cassian had wounded as proof of this. He told us we must all search for you, save you from harm…because once you were safe, we were going to go to war. We were going to destroy the thieves who had taken you, and get revenge for the cult's crimes against all of us."

"You're saying the Supremes believed that?"

"As truly as they believe their own name."

"But…you weren't affected?"

Asterios smiled again. "Like you said, I've known Rav his entire life. I'll never forget the first time I saw him wield that power against somebody. And once I saw its devastating effect, I knew what gift to ask for next."

The gift he couldn't name. Some sort of resistance or shielding, maybe.

"I pretended I was bewitched like the others. Once he'd finished with us and the guards returned, he did the same to every single one of them. So simple, his words were—*You don't remember today, but you failed to protect the queen. You must make it up to me.* Over and over, into each man and woman's ear."

I shivered with unease…but also disbelief. For months, I'd watched Rav struggle with the Supremes. It was like herding cats sometimes, how unwilling one or another would be to follow his commands. The last time we'd visited Crete, in fact, I'd watched him try to persuade Sorina to let him have control of her military with zero success. Aldric and Giselle had been unwieldy too.

And Idalia? I doubted she'd ever done anything she didn't wholeheartedly want to do.

"But if he has that ability, why is anything ever difficult for him?" I asked Asterios. "Why isn't he already the tyrant he wants to be?"

"Well, some are less susceptible to influence than others. Some are bull-headed, as you might say." He winked at that. "And even the sweetest liar risks discovery if the truth is obvious enough. But emotions are much easier to manipulate than facts. Say you tell a man he is a failure. That man might believe you or he might not. But go to his wife and whisper that her husband is a failure. Go to his son, go to his boss. Their behaviors change and he notices. By the time they're no longer under Rav's influence, that man doesn't know what to think of himself, because he is surrounded by suggestions that Rav's original insult is true."

My mind spiraled thinking of all the ways in which that had played out throughout history, in much bigger conflicts with much higher stakes. Influence and propaganda played just as big a role in war as brute force did. And it sometimes made war unnecessary at all. The witch hunts, for example, had rarely erupted into battles—at least, none that made the history books. It didn't have to, when whispered character assassination was enough to condemn women to death at the hands of their churches and communities.

Asterios could sense my mind starting to wander, it seemed. He pulled me back with, "But Rav was *determined* to hide you. Protect you. He *exhausted* himself convincing us that what we had seen with our own eyes was not true. And I think he would have sacrificed much more, if necessary."

I looked away at that.

"You don't believe me?" he asked.

"I don't have to," I said. "I asked Rav if he loved me and he said he didn't."

"Did he say the words 'I don't love you'?"

"No, but—"

"Rav shares a misconception common among men. That to actually care about something or someone makes them weak and vulnerable rather than stronger. They destroy so many good things clinging to this harmful belief. But Rav was in transition. He was changing. I've never seen him do the things he has done for you for anyone else, Natalie."

"Because he wants a mate."

"Two things can be true at once." I opened my mouth to reply but he beat me to it. "I do not claim to know what your relationship was like—*that*, he did not share with me—but I do know he has been fascinated by you since the very beginning. Since that first Gathering Table meeting at Hrafnagud, when you stood up to him and took your rightful place beside him at the table. We could all see how he looked at you."

I didn't respond. I…didn't know if I believed what he was implying. But then again, I didn't know why Rav would go to such great lengths to protect me either. He'd hidden so much, though, I could only assume it was because he had plans for me, even now. Even…ruined.

"Anyway," Asterios finally plunged ahead. "Once Rav reset the wedding party, he commanded the others to search the sea for you. Me, he commanded to search the islands. He had planned to come with me—which is why I suspect he sent Eike to Crete in his absence—but on our way to the airport, he received a call from his men in Italy. For one reason or another, they were following Idalia. One said he believed he found the entrance to Arachne's Revenge, and that was all Rav needed to hear. He didn't even wait for me to board my plane; he ran off to ready his own plane to fly."

"To Italy," I said, just to confirm.

He nodded. "When I arrived in Crete, I had a strange message waiting for me from a local fisherman. He claimed '*Talos*' had led him to an injured alter girl washed up on the shore. He and his family helped me take the bullet from your shoulder and carry you to the hotel."

"Talos?" I asked.

"It's from an old Cretan legend," he said, waving that away. "To the point, I know something happened between Rav and Idalia. I just don't know what. He wouldn't say why she wasn't at the wedding. And when he bid us to search for you, he commanded Oriol to scour the Ionian Sea, between here and Italy, and then turn his eye on Italy itself."

"He thinks I'd go to Italy?"

"Perhaps. But he's planning something for Idalia as well. Right before he left, Rav warned me to prepare for an incursion into her kingdom. When I asked why he simply said she could no longer be trusted and that all would reveal itself in time."

I winced at that. "I'm guessing you would rather have me reveal it?"

Asterios grinned. "If you would be so kind."

I didn't tell Asterios everything. Or rather, I hadn't had enough time yet to organize my thoughts in any coherent way. In terms of the war and the choices everyone was making, it was still like catching pieces of confetti as they flew through the air. I could only hope to make sense of them eventually once I laid them all out.

As for Asterios, I told him what was mine to tell.

I told him what I had learned of the Knights of the Rising Sun.

I parroted what I'd learned from Rolfe and the other prisoners at Kinloch Castle, without saying it came from them.

I revealed that I'd warned Rav about the impending attack, and he claimed he was going to warn the Gathering Table, but I didn't trust it and called them myself. Then I let Asterios confirm what I suspected—that Rav never did.

I laid out what had happened in Eike's hometown, with Antonio and his spontaneously combustible friends…as well as the Noctaran Order, the emergence of a Ninth Kingdom.

And I explained that Rav and I had arrived back to Hrafnagud to find Idalia freeing Giselle and fleeing before Rav could do anything about it.

After I finished, a few moments of silence passed before Asterios murmured, "Fascinating."

"Any part in particular?"

"We have the Knights claiming there is a just and noble goal behind the mayhem they have caused, which includes creating these new shifters—these *tall wolves*. We have an Emperor making moves on his own, to who knows what end, but to the detriment of his own closest allies. We have a Gathering Table splintering as we speak. And we have…you."

"Me. The ruined abomination."

"Natalie," he barked almost *at* me, as if scolding me, before he settled himself. "Do you *feel* ruined?"

"N-No…?" I whimpered it, but the moment the answer left my mouth, I realized I meant it.

"After everything you've accomplished, everything you've learned since entering our world…do you feel like you know enough to condemn yourself that way?"

"I've read the legends—"

"Those were stories."

"I've learned some of the history—"

"Who benefited from writing it that way?"

Frustration riled in me, even though I knew what he was implying. "Asterios. *Something has to be true*. If you go down that road of questioning *everything*, then what's left?"

"Exactly."

"Huh?"

Asterios sat forward again, almost into my space. "*Questioning everything* isn't the answer. It's the method for finding the answer. It will always be better to question what you think you know than to defend it blindly. But that isn't enough. You must then go one step further—dig, tear, burn through what you have been told and what you fear, and stand in what is left. That is where the truth begins."

CHAPTER 7

A few minutes later, after Asterios took his leave and said we'd talk more after he'd had time to think, his words churned and churned in my mind, caught in the eddy of my thoughts.

He was right, of course, about getting to the bottom of the war, the conflict, Rav's strange behavior, and so on.

But, more personally, he was right about me. I'd spent so much time that summer learning to trust myself, my instincts, my desire to help people. Why would I throw all that away because something had changed? Granted, it was an enormous life-altering change, but still…

My beastliness was a reality I just had to deal with. If it killed me in the end, so be it, but until then I refused to die. I was a seeker. I had things to do. Truths to ferret out myself, to help my kingdom and whoever my allies turned out to be in the war ahead.

But it wasn't just Asterios urging me to expand my mind and remember I didn't know everything. The universe itself seemed determined to prove Asterios's wisdom right.

When I entered my suite in the palace, I found a gift waiting for me. A strange pile of tiny electronic pieces gathered and smashed at the center of the marble floor.

"*What are those?*"

"*Ears*," my raven replied.

"*Listening devices?*"

My raven ran her feathers down my spine in confirmation.

"*Who found them?*"

"*Mate*," she and my wolf said together, and I shivered.

"Cass?" The name echoed against the vaulted ceilings of the room. I waited in the silence for ages afterward, on bated breath, both hoping he would appear and terrified that he might.

***

When I woke in the morning, I threw open the suite door to find Asterios there holding…a black box.

"I hope I didn't wake you, Natalie, but Mesi delivered our phone just a few minutes ago."

"Come in." He hesitated, so I moved aside and drew his attention to the small pile of electronic bugs I'd left in the middle of the floor. "Come in, come in."

As soon as the door was shut, I took the box from him and carried it to the closet, which was the only room in this suite with low ceilings and no echo.

"Do you think those are just your standard-issue palace listening devices or did they put them in *our* rooms specifically?" I asked as I sealed us in and set the phone on a shelf.

"No way to tell," Asterios murmured.

"What did you tell Mesi and her father about me?"

"It's complicated." I raised an eyebrow at him until he added, "They don't know anything about you other than that you're Rav's betrothed. No one who was outside that wedding even knows it happened yet, I don't think."

"So they don't think I'm missing or kidnapped or trying to run?"

"I don't believe so. They don't even know about the Knights, or the brewing war. Rav's gone to great lengths to hide that from the rest of the world."

I knew that was only mostly true. While still at Hamingja, Rav had sent missives to a handful of Great Courts across the world warning them of brewing tension in Europe, requesting alliances in the event that the secret war became less so and he needed resources or support. He'd warned a handful of "lesser" families in Europe too.

There was no telling if he'd told one too many people. Secrets were like contagious viruses. Even if you trusted the people you told, the more people came in contact with the secret, the more risk there was of that contagion spreading.

"They probably know something's coming," I told Asterios. "There's no reason to assume the Knights are only operating in Europe. Hell, as secretive as everyone is, there could be a branch of the Knights working to undermine every empire in the world. They could be everywhere, waiting until the person at the top tells them their time has come."

In that spirit, I opened the box containing the so-called untraceable phone. I didn't know if it was courting disaster to speak with my team this way, but I had to risk it. Just in case I didn't get another chance.

"Show me how to work this, so I can call my team."

It took no time at all, and before I could really ready myself to hear their voices, I heard a click. Then Yasmina said, "Yes?"

"Yas, don't hang up. It's me."

Her volume rose instantly. So did Fern's, as they yelled at once.

"My lady, thank Goddess!"

"Are you okay? Are you free?"

"I'm fine for now. Is Mom okay? Did you get to her in time?"

"Yes, she's here."

"Honey?" My mother's voice filled the room with panic. "Are-Are you okay? Where are you? What's going on?"

"I can't tell you where I am, but I'm safe."

"Are you sure? You can't disappear on me like that!"

"I didn't want to leave—"

"Of course you didn't. What the hell was that woman thinking? What was Rav thinking?"

I wasn't lying when I told her, "I don't know. He was scared. He was stupid. Rav tried to keep me against my will—"

"We know!" Yasmina suddenly bleated.

"You do?"

"Yes," Fern said. "Your mom called us immediately to tell us what had happened and Scarlett called us from Hamingja when he was holding you there."

"Scarlett?" Gah, that name shot *blinding fear* through me. "H-Have you spoken with her?"

"Not since she warned us," Fern said. "We flew to Norway, but we were turned away. By the time we returned with soldiers, you were already gone. Cassian sent us back to England while he went after you."

"Is Cass there with you?" Yas asked and I flinched as if I'd been struck.

"He's gone." My voice broke like glass. "Rav killed him."

Asterios's eyes snapped to me at that, with a strange look on his face as if he'd forgotten Rav killed Cass in front of him too. I turned my gaze away. And when my raven pecked me again, I ignored her. They deserved to know.

"What?" Fern sounded sick.

"That can't be true," Yas yelped.

"He did it right in front of me," I said gently. "I'm so sorry."

"Why are you sorry?"

Tears welled in my eyes and my throat stung as I forced all the pent-up sorrow in my stomach out through my mouth. "Because I should've done more. I should have stopped him. I didn't believe Rav would really hurt him. But he did. He did! Right in front of me. He commanded a guard to shoot him in the head. My Cass, like he was nothing. I should have leapt in front of him. I should have fought against Rav harder. I failed him—"

My voice cut like a rusty chainsaw. But Asterios was there a second later, pulling me into a tight hug, whispering, "Hush, it's all right," against my hair. It made me want to cry harder. It was a comfort I didn't deserve. Not when I'd made so many mistakes.

Vaguely, I heard Fern ask who was there with me, and Asterios introduced himself to them, giving them a little play by play as I went to pieces in front of him. But after a time, a voice cut through the storm in my mind. "Little bird? Don't cry, okay?"

"I'm fine, Mom," I sniffled.

"He loved you so much."

My diaphragm hitched with anger and laughter at the same time; leave it to my well-meaning mom to make me feel worse while trying to make me feel better.

"You hardly knew him," I murmured.

"The couple times I met him were enough, kiddo," she countered. "He would've gone after you no matter what."

Yas leapt forward to add, "Once he knew where you were, none of us could have stopped him."

Their words didn't *exactly* make me feel better, but some residual warmth hugged me as I stepped out of Asterios's embrace.

"I hate to push on so quick," I said after a moment. "But if you don't have Scarlett, we need to find her. We need to get her away from Rav before he can use her to force me back. One of you, please call Brodie o-or Millie and ask them to put everything else aside to do this for me as soon as possible. Warn them Rav is dangerous. Please."

"We will, my lady," Yasmina swore. "I'll call as soon as this call ends."

"Thank you. As for the rest of you…I need your help."

"Of course," Fern said.

"Anything," Yas echoed.

I opened my mouth to speak…and hesitated. It was the most natural instinct I had, to tell my team the truth of my transformation, that I…wasn't just a raven anymore. But beyond the sudden (and I thought most likely nonsensical) fear that my team would abandon me, my mother was there. In the face of so many things going wrong, I couldn't stomach the possibility that she'd pay for my beastliness. Whether she would want to be part of this world if I told her or not—if that was an option anymore anyway—this wasn't the time to make her responsible for a secret like that. It was too big, too dangerous given what I was. If we saw each other again, I could tell her the truth in person.

So I spent another ten minutes coaxing my mom to leave the room so Yas, Fern, and I could speak freely. Then, I used euphemisms anyway.

"Things have changed in ways you can't imagine. The war is here a-and I'm not on Rav's side anymore, which means we need to act quickly and safeguard the kingdom as much as we can before he can do something rash."

"I'm here with paper," Yasmina said. "I'm ready when you are."

We plunged into war talks faster than it took the last tear on my cheek to dry. I made Brodie the head of my army in Cass's absence, and a thousand little responsibilities landed on his broad shoulders like flakes of snow. I also told Yasmina he needed to call me from an untraceable number as soon as he was alone.

Then they ran me through a CliffsNotes version of everything Cass had done for me in that position. Turned out, we had exhausted an entire silver mine to make ammunition. Our soldiers were already on alert because Cass had warned them before he came for me. And when I mentioned *Walshingham* to Fern, she said she'd be right back and disappeared off the phone line before I could ask what it meant…which genuinely surprised me. *Walshingham* was clearly a code word to her; it wasn't something my confused, crazy mind had come up with on its own.

And yes, Brodie's teams had prevented the attacks from happening in Dromineer, Ireland, and Conques, France. It was a miracle. *Two* miracles, because he'd managed to capture two more Knights of the Rising Sun in the process, both of which had already been spirited to our makeshift prison in Kinloch Castle.

We stood in that closet for *hours* talking about priorities. Audience hours would have to be pushed back. Yasmina promised to call Jane Lakeland to act as an intermediary between us and the witches, and to track down Belina to see if she would help us too. And I would need money, so I could survive on my own without relying on unmet foreign dignitaries for shelter. Here, they surprised me again; Cass had already covered that in his bugout plans.

"He deposited money into every major bank in Europe, my lady," Fern revealed. "One account available to all of us, including your mother, and one for you. There's a five-thousand-dollar daily limit; you just have to go in and provide your information."

"Boy, he really thought of everything, didn't he?" I half-joked.

Fern only said, "He had a feeling we would need it."

We also discussed what to do *when* Rav came to speak with them…because it was inevitable. After all, Lunasa was a little less than two weeks away and all the guests had already been invited. My disappearance wouldn't stop the holiday from happening. I supposed Idalia and Giselle wouldn't make it, but everyone else would and in my absence, Fern and Yasmina would have to run it. Rav would probably orchestrate the Wedding of the Dawn, but other than that they'd have to pull the whole event off on their own.

"We won't tell him anything," Yasmina swore.

"Don't let him touch you either," I added. "He can make you do things, forget things."

"You see?" Fern said, aside to Yasmina. "I told you I was right."

"You definitely were," I admitted. "I'm sorry I didn't believe you."

All those weeks ago when we'd first arrived at Hamingja, she'd warned me. Tried to get me to leave for my safety.

Fern didn't accept my apology. "Stop that. You didn't know. None of us did."

That brought up a good point; I didn't know all of Rav's powers, or those of the rest of the Gathering Table. And assuming they were the only ones with abilities was a type of hubris we couldn't afford to entertain.

"Hey, I think we need to add an azurite stone to every soldier's gear, and our own."

"The transforming stone?" Yasmina quirked. "Why?"

"If we're ever in a bind, being able to shift at a moment's notice might come in handy. For escape. For a fight. To heal ourselves if we desperately need to. Who knows what we might be up against."

"We'll distribute them immediately," Fern swore.

Eventually the meeting began to wind down and the conversation shifted to me.

"Why can't you come back, my lady?" Yas asked eventually. "We could *surround* you with soldiers. Rav wouldn't come for you like that. He wouldn't risk a scene. And at least you'd be back on Eighth Kingdom soil where you're safest."

Even without my potential death sentence, I didn't know if the Eighth Kingdom *was* the safest place for me. Not yet. Not while Rav was hunting in his secret way, using his powers to hide my true nature from the world. Not until I knew why he was hiding me.

Sure, maybe he genuinely cared about me and maybe I didn't know him well enough to know his motivations for everything...but I knew Rav wasn't a sentimental guy. Logic. Power. Strategy. Those things drove every decision he made.

Which meant that he was hiding my beastliness *for a reason.*

I just had to figure out what it was.

By the time I said a heartfelt goodbye to my mom, and cut off her repeated attempts to tell me where Fern and Yas were hiding her, the great weight that had been crushing my shoulders from above finally lifted.

The will was on its way to the lawyer.

My team had been warned about Rav.

A rescue mission had been planned for Scarlett.

At least I'd had the chance to do that.

And when the call finally ended, Asterios clamped a reassuring hand on my shoulder and said, "*That* was beautifully done, my queen. *That* is one of many reasons why I choose you."

But there must be some great cosmic two-plate scale that swings wildly in search of balance every second of every day. No sooner had our productive, uplifting meeting come to an end than I heard a noise, a crunching *skitter*, and opened the closet door to find a wide-eyed maid sweeping the little pile of electronic bugs off the floor. Her nervous gaze met ours and she *bolted* as if our discovery of the 'electronic ears' was dire, dangerous, or the real reason she'd come in to clean the room in the first place.

CHAPTER 8

I'd thought, given the terrified look on the maid's face, that it was only a matter of time before Mesi or her father or their royal guard came to confront us about the listening devices I'd found in my room, but they didn't. No one came to speak with us for over a week.

We were fed. Our rooms were cleaned.

But no one came. It was the strangest thing.

Especially since I could *feel* the tension rise after our discovery. In subtle and unsubtle ways, the palace tightened around us. Additional guards arrived each day, just a handful at first, then more, until they lined the halls like meaty statues wrapped in modern armor.

I tried only once to communicate with them when I caught two guards whispering at the end of a hall one day.

"*Sayyida Mesi says we shouldn't worry about it, so why should we?*" one said.

"*She asks us to guard when there is already a guard. It seems like a waste of our time.*"

"*It could be worse. Good food, at least.*"

"*Excuse me,*" I said. "*Could you tell me where to find Sayyida Mesi?*"

The two men leapt almost three feet in the air, gawking at me like a nightmare.

"*She speaks Arabic!*" one yelped. "*Go warn the others. Warn the others!*"

And that was the last any of them spoke at all. No one talked to me, but everyone was aware of me. I was being watched every time I left my suite. No matter which room I entered, guards with blue berets and assault rifles were there waiting. It felt like being back in Hrafnagud all over again.

I, of course, didn't trust it. Why would I? With each passing day, as my bullet wound healed and the heartache of Greece softened, I was waking up to the uncertainty of staying here. Especially on days when I woke up to find neat little piles of smashed listening devices on my floor. As if some cat was leaving a dead bird on my doorstep. I tried to hide them in a vase this time, but eventually the vase filled and the maid freaked out again and two silent men arrived to haul the thing out while I tried to tell them I wasn't the one doing it.

"They know you're not," Asterios tried to reassure me when I told him. "It's happening all over the palace."

"Do you mean you're not doing this either?" I asked, already sensing the shake of his head before it happened.

"*Are* you *doing this?*" I asked my creatures too.

"*No*," my wolf swore.

"*Still safe*," my raven added.

"*Do you know who's doing this*?"

This time, they didn't answer…which was a very obvious yes.

I wanted to leave *immediately*, genuinely worried that I'd wake up one morning to the sound of the door banging open and a gun cocking in my direction.

But I didn't know where I was supposed to go yet.

I finally managed to stop the maid from fleeing long enough to ask her to ask Mesi for a computer, but when it finally arrived, it was…glitchy. I would turn it on, the screen would light up, then darken suddenly before the whole thing shut off again. The next day, I woke to more electronic bugs on my floor, and the computer worked just fine, as if there had never been an issue in the first place. But when I went to scour the web for ideas of where to go, how to move forward without just disappearing to another part of the world until the war was over or Rav forgot me, the internet kept diverting me to…Italy.

Genuinely the country of Italy.

I'd open a webpage for the news or a history text pdf only to have the browser reroute to a Genoa tourism page or a flight leaving Alexandria for Rome…not that I could take it, since I didn't have a passport and I wouldn't risk revealing my location to my team in case someone was listening to their calls.

The Italian glitch only happened when I left the room, I noticed. I'd go to the bathroom, and return to a map of Tuscany. I'd be called to lunch and when I returned, news of a "spider infestation in a small

Italian alpine town" would be waiting for me.

Again, I asked my creatures, *"Are you doing this?"*

But their answer was the same, "*No.*"

And this time, I heard suspicion in their voices.

"*I can't go back to Europe,*" I pointed out anyway. "*That would be dangerous. Insanely dangerous.*"

They didn't disagree. They didn't tell me to trust it either.

But the fourth time this happened, my raven asked quietly, "*What if...Italy?*"

I countered with, "*Why Italy*?"

She shrugged, unsure.

Eventually, I found myself with Asterios at dinner again in the courtyard alone and brought it up.

"Why on earth would you go there?" he almost yelped. "Rav is targeting it. I told you he's looking for Idalia. He has his sights set on her."

"I don't know." I shrugged. "Maybe that's why. Idalia and Giselle...aren't my enemies. If anything, they're the ones I'm closest to on the Gathering Table. They're helping each other, I've helped both of them, and I feel like I should keep doing that. If he's going after them, I need to warn them. There's strength in numbers, right? On top of that, Italy's where another ally of mine is. Or used to be."

Belina Saldo had crept into my thoughts just the other night, when I'd retreated into my inner sanctum. I'd sat for a while considering my wolf and raven, along with the two additional cubbies that were different from the others—the one lined in cinnamon-colored fur and the one slicked with black that caught the light in passing and shined like a rainbow.

I...assumed those were dormant forms waiting to claim me.

That's...what they must be, right?

I didn't know which animals they belonged to, but they stood right beside my wolf's cubby, where she rested when not outside my body.

The implications of that, of those cubbies, of all the cubbies, threatened to send me into a panic, though, so I set any thought of them aside in favor of something more important.

I sat in my inner sanctum until the confetti of information that had been swirling around me for weeks finally began to settle. In it, I could see a pattern emerging. Or rather, a gap in my knowledge I wanted to fix. *Needed* to fix.

Weeks ago, when I'd dome-walked into the Goddess's domain, she had warned me we were heading toward a cataclysmic shift in the world. Not just me, but everyone. Without more to go on, I might have let my worst fears—that I would somehow be responsible for that—consume me, but she'd told me I *had* to survive or many other people would die.

She'd also told me to "gather, meet, seek, and protect" with intention.

I'd done exactly that. I'd protected and healed Giselle. I'd met with the Witches Council and the prisoner Knights at Kinloch, and spoken with Rolfe, and listened to Antonio as he said these hybrid wolf-vampires weren't beasts at all…

I'd managed to seek a little information in Hamingja's library too, but not before obstacles had thrown themselves in front of me one after the other, cutting me off from that vault of knowledge.

I desperately needed to find another ancient source of knowledge as soon as possible, but even when I did, I needed help to go through it all. Which is where I thought Belina Saldo could be helpful.

She was a seeker like me, and by her magick or her curiosity, I thought she could help me fit all the puzzle pieces of Rav, my nature, and the Knights together. She didn't shy away from difficult questions or dangerous possibilities; if anything, she doubled down on them.

She was also generous and open to working with alters. When she slapped me in the face before fleeing Fylgja Castle all those months ago, she'd still left the door open for me to reach out to her again. She, like my friends, had tried to warn me about Rav too.

Considering all of that, she felt like a valuable person to count as an ally.

So did Idalia. So did Giselle.

But I didn't know where any of them were. The number I had for Belina was disconnected, and my fellow Alter Supremes had gone to ground. All I knew is that they were all likely somewhere in Italy.

"Asterios, I don't think there's a place on this planet I'd be safe for long with Rav hunting me," I told him finally. "Do you?"

He shook his head, but added, "Let's just wait until Dual King Sobek comes to speak with us. A-And we have Lunasa coming up. We won't make any rash decisions before then."

I smothered the grimace that threatened to emerge on my face. "I don't know how much time I can waste here, doing nothing, Asterios. Not when this court is clearly suspicious of us. Soon, there'll be so many guards here, I'll have to assume it's a prison."

"You're not wasting time, my queen," he countered. "You're recovering."

"I can recover while I work," I said.

"What kind of work?"

"If I'm really not ruined—"

"—You're not—"

"—then I'd like to know for sure. I need…all the information I can find, you know? An archive. An ancient library. *Any bit of proof* that I'm not…doomed."

I caught the desperation in my own voice and glanced away, embarrassed.

But Asterios surprised me. "I may know someone who can help you with that."

I smirked, not really believing him…but I really had to stop doing that. That evening as the sun sank over the sea, there was an insistent knock at my suite door. When I tossed it open, I found the Crocodile Princess herself there waiting for me, along with Asterios and four of her largest guards yet.

"Could I interest you in an adventure, Sayyida Natalie?" Mesi asked, her dark eyes glowing with humor.

My gaze bandied between them. "What sort of adventure?"

"I mentioned you have an interest in ancient libraries," Asterios said, his voice high with excitement.

Mesi shrugged. "We happen to have the most famous."

My heart jolted inside me at the implication. "You don't mean…"

"Oh yes. The Library of Alexandria is right there," Mesi said, holding out a modest full-body bathing suit to me. "Would you care to see it?"

CHAPTER 9

I shoved the wrist-to-ankle blue bathing suit onto my body with a shaking hand. Took the sling off my injured arm and fed it carefully into the fabric. Rubbed my tight chest to relieve some of the pressure as I shoved shoes on my feet. Then I forced a fake smile on my face as Mesi's guards led us out of the palace to a waiting dark-tinted SUV.

Should I have been leaving with this woman I didn't know and her silent guards as big as hippos?

Should I have gone *night swimming* with a *crocodile* and the men sworn to protect her with their lives?

Probably not.

But Asterios was going too.

And the first thing I'd asked my raven as Mesi handed me the bathing suit was, "*What do I do?*"

And the first thing she'd said was, "*Trust.*"

"*You keep saying that!*" I sniped.

In reply, I felt a phantom smile and she teased, "*Always right.*"

"*But can you read her?*" I pressed anyway.

"*Some.*"

"*Is that supposed to be reassuring?*"

"*Here with you. Safe.*"

From everything I'd ever gained from entering the alter world, that was the most important. I was only alone if I sent my creatures away or they left to their other tasks. Otherwise, I always had company. I always had somebody on my side.

Multiple somebodies now. I felt my wolf "curl around" me, her fur like a strange invisible coat across my skin. Then reassurance flowed through me like a warm spring and confidence came with it.

"You don't *really* mean *the* ancient Library of Alexandria?" I asked as the SUV tore out of the palace grounds and dove into the city proper.

"The one and only," Mesi said. "Its ruins lie approximately five to eight meters down on the harbor floor now, but many of its pieces are quite preserved."

I almost thought to ask why she was taking me to see a submerged library ruin twenty feet below the ocean's surface, but…I knew she must have her reasons, and I was too curious to jeopardize the trip. Too excited. Despite my nerves, my mistrust, there was more…adrenaline. I'd never been diving before. I'd never seen ancient sea ruins before either. I was sure there were plenty of people who would've said no to this sort of adventure if offered. But I no longer counted myself amongst them.

And I desperately needed the emotional distraction.

It took only a few minutes, maybe fifteen, to navigate the heavy city foot and car traffic and arrive at the Eastern Harbor's edge. The massive semi-enclosed sink of water was turquoise and wavy in the retreating sunset light; the warm breeze blew a sunny kiss across my skin. Dozens of sailboats crowded the harbor's western edge, near the Citadel of Qaitbay, a massive stone fortress Mesi told us was situated where the ancient Lighthouse of Alexandria once stood. That's right, I was standing maybe a quarter mile away from the site of *one of the Seven Ancient Wonders of the World*! And I was about to dive to see another.

My hands shook monstrously as Mesi led us down a pier to a speedboat loaded with state-of-the-art diving suits.

I could barely sit still as she dropped into the captain's chair, cranked the ignition, and sped us away, deeper into the harbor.

And when she finally maneuvered us into position and her men dropped the anchor, I could barely breathe, my heart was beating so fast.

She could sense it. Pausing by me, she motioned to the water with her head. "What do you see?"

At first, I saw nothing. Just gorgeous opalescent water begging to be cannonballed into.

Then…

"Oh no way," escaped me in pure joy.

There, not five meters down, was a statue. A *beautifully preserved* life-sized lion statue. From above, it took a moment to orient my eyes to how it was laid out, but…the shape of its body gave it away. The slender hips, the bushy mane, the tail. It stood regal and watchful, its massive paw resting on a ball.

"A fixture in Cleopatra's Palace sixteen hundred years ago," Mesi told me, as casually as if she was describing the weather.

"*The* Cleopatra?"

"The one most people are familiar with, yes. The great ruler who took her own life with her lover Mark Antony. Her palace sank after an earthquake and tsunami rocked the city. Over time, many other things were lost here as well. Let us visit a few."

It took a few minutes to figure out the high-tech diving suit, basically watching how Mesi and Asterios put on their own and copying. Then Mesi pointed out the submersible pressure gauge on our arms and said we'd return to the surface when it was nearing 50 psi.

"What happens if it drops below?" I asked.

"You run out of air." Off my obvious fear, she added, "Don't worry. We will surface long before that."

The last piece to go on was the helmet, which swallowed my head and sort of suctioned to my neck. It had a full-face viewing window, and a radio built in.

"Ready?" Mesi's voice boomed in my ears. I shot her a thumbs up. "Just remember, whatever you see down there…none of them will harm you. I swear it on my life."

My mind *tripped* over her phrasing. "What was that now? Who is '*them*?'"

But she didn't answer. Neither did Asterios. They simply tossed themselves backward over the edge of the boat, leaving the guards to gawk at me until I decided whether I was following.

I was awkward. Very awkward. But I took a deep breath, sat back on the boat's rim…and pushed. The air tank and my back hit the water first. Then I sank down below the surface watching the guards slowly retreat from view. The water in the harbor was *hot* after baking all day in the desert sun. Practically bath water. And it was dark at the point where my field of vision ran out; even though the water around me was crystal clear, there was a distance at which definition was swallowed by dark blue. That made a logical sort of sense, I guess, but I'd never experienced it before and I was *not* prepared for it. I'd been in endless expanses before, like the technicolor infinite of the Goddess's magick, but that had been soothing, almost womblike. Not once had I thought about the creatures that might lurk in it. The sea's endlessness, by contrast, wasn't comforting at all. It was staring into a void and hoping not to see monsters staring back.

Not to mention the water was growing darker by the second as day gave way to night.

A sound escaped me halfway between a whine and a yelp.

But…

Then I let myself drift. I let myself *be* adrift in the expanse and remembered that I was also technically a monster in the void now. And once that thought entered my mind, I surrendered to the water like a bit of flotsam and the creeping dread from moments ago gave way to…peace.

To say the splendor of the sea was a balm to my soul would be doing it a disservice. Neither blue nor green but its own color that enveloped me, warmed me, soothed me. Quiet and awesome. Magnificent and entirely humbling. I was…afloat. Empty of churning thoughts for the first time in weeks. And that was *before* I saw the bevy of architectural wonders awaiting us.

"Are you all right, Natalie?" Asterios asked, swimming over.

Off my nod, Mesi added, "Come, let me give you the grand tour."

Mesi's tour was a crash course in ancient history. Cleopatra's palace with its still intact marble floors. Foundation blocks of Mark Antony's unfinished palace. Broken statues of priests from the Temple of Isis. Dozens of columns running the length of ancient city streets made from Aswan pink granite. Huge slabs carved with hieroglyphics and papyrus motifs. Giant heads knocked off giant statues. And a gorgeous black granite sphinx.

Mesi drew my special attention to this last one, brightening the black sea around us with a massive aquatic flashlight she'd brought with her. As all three of us floated there, holding onto the sphinx's head to avoid drifting with the tide, she turned to me.

"I feel we must be honest with you, Sayyida Natalie, before the main event begins," she said, plunging along before I could ask any questions. "The ancient library isn't down here. Bits and pieces once fell into the sea, but the area where it once stood before the great fires destroyed it did not sink into the waters like the rest of these things."

"Then why did you two bring me here?"

She didn't answer that question right away. Instead, she asked, "Do you know what a sphinx is?"

"Um…a mythological creature?" I tried.

"Creature is correct…What *is* it? Physically, I mean."

"Lion body? Human head? Wings? Tells riddles, right?"

I didn't have to see their faces to know they were smiling as they glanced at each other.

"You are thinking of the Greek sphinx," Asterios said.

"Or perhaps the Thai variation," Mesi added. "Can you tell me what the *Egyptian* sphinx doesn't have?"

I glanced at the statue and realized, "Wings. It's missing wings."

"It doesn't tell riddles either."

"Pity," I joked. "I'm pretty good at those."

"They are also benevolent guardians," she said. "But those who live in Europe wouldn't think so, I suspect. No, you call creatures of many parts something else..."

My spine tightened as I realized what she meant. "A beast."

Panic bolted through my mind as lightning. I glanced at Asterios, trying to see his face through the mask, trying to decide if he had trusted this alter with *my* terrifying secret. I couldn't tell. I had the sudden desperate urge to swim away, swim to shore, find a taxi, drive out into the desert and let my wings carry me as far as they could. To another kingdom. To another world. I didn't care!

But...she'd called them *benevolent guardians*. After the panic receded like a tsunami, those words remained stranded on the beach of my mind.

And on the off chance he hadn't told her, I stayed where I was.

"The sphinx is not the only ancient creature of varied form. Most of the ancient Egyptian gods were depicted with animal parts or had the ability to shift into animals. Our own Sobek—god of crocodiles—is depicted with a human body and a crocodile's head."

"I can picture it..." I said, trying to keep my voice steady.

"Because you yourself have wings, yes?"

"...Yes."

"There are so many creatures and deities in our stories that share this gift," she said. "I wonder how they would feel to hear you call them '*doomed*,' as you call yourself."

I glowered at Asterios, even though he probably couldn't see it. Whether he'd told her I was a beast, he'd certainly told her about our conversation.

I opened my mouth to snark or grumble a reply, but something happened, knocking the words back down my throat. A low, breathy sound drifted in with the tide. It was musical, soft, intentional...and absolutely *not* the sort of sound we should have been able to hear through our masks.

Through our *chests*; the dulcet note vibrated my heart like a purr.

It was magickal. There was nothing else it could be.

"Natalie, remember what I told you," Mesi suddenly said. "They will not harm you."

"Who won't—"

Bu-BUH. Bu-BUH. Bu-BUH.

Three more notes boomed through the water, each different. Each as bright and clear as a herald's trumpet.

I turned and twisted, glancing around, on the lookout for 'them' and whatever might make them seem dangerous enough to fear—

—My gaze snapped to the dark void of the deep water. The mouth of the harbor leading out to the sea. It was just vague shapes at first, growing sharper, more impossible by the second, until 'they' became undeniable.

'They' had long hair that flowed behind them like a ribbon as they swam.

'They' had eyes like golden spotlights.

'They' had tails where there should have been legs.

And 'they' were headed straight for us. So fast, I thought for a moment they were going to swim over us, toward the shore, in a school of human torsos and fish tails.

But they didn't.

Oh no.

My breath caught inside me as the golden eyes of one with a pale turquoise tail turned to me, and her body followed with it, serpentining through the water, snagging my uninjured arm, flipping us back toward the sea, and then we were moving so fast I might have screamed, if there had been enough travel time to do so.

One moment I was in Alexandria's Eastern Harbor. The next, we arrived at a tiny, rocky islet with Alexandria as a distant backdrop. The mermaid—*it was a mermaid*—held onto my arm and swam us forward through the tide to the shallow waters on the islet's far side. Then she let me go as two others dropped off Asterios and Mesi beside me.

Not that I could see them very well. It was almost pitch black out there; a new moon was faintly visible overhead, like a coin submerged in inky water. The cove beach was little more than a vague gray strip below a low rocky wall.

But there were…beings…moving in the low light. Dozens of them.

Giggling.

Whispering.

Singing.

Splashing.

Combing each other's hair.

As a wave carried me into the very shallowest water, I forced the dive mask off my face just to marvel at them without something in the way.

Mermaids!

"You are very quiet, Natalie," Mesi said a second later, taking off her own helmet. "I expected more from you."

"This might be the best day of my life," I admitted, my voice high and yipping.

"The best?" she teased quietly. "So you are not afraid? You aren't going to swim screaming for your life? They are not monsters?"

My gaze snapped to her. "I never thought they were monsters."

"Good. Because they seem decidedly *un*monstrous to me." She motioned to one that seemed to be sieving shells out of the sand a few feet away. "Perhaps easily distractable, but who isn't in the presence of a coven of mermaids?"

"They're just…letting us be here?" I asked.

Mesi motioned again to the shell searcher. "We are guests of Sayyida Rawan, Tidebringer of the Widows' Wail Coven. I told her you were in need of wisdom."

I…don't think I'd ever heard two more beautiful sentences in my life.

"Tidebringer…" I whispered. "Their version of an Alter Supreme?"

Mesi nodded.

"Why are they called Widows' Wail?" I asked.

Her voice grew soft and lonesome. "That is not for me to say."

"But… Why are they here? *How* are they here?" I asked, motioning to the dark sky.

"These ladies take advantage of the darkness of the new moon," Mesi explained. "They learn to turn at will, or they use *lazaward*."

"*Lazaward*?"

"Another name for azurite," Asterios explained.

They were *magnificent*, no matter how they altered. But… "Why are they only half fish, if they're using azurite?"

"What else would they be?" Mesi asked. "This is their form."

I balked at that. "Their altered form is half woman, half fish?"

"Yes." Mesi shrugged as if this was obvious. "This is the way with hybrids—some of one form, some of the other."

"*Hybrids*?" I almost yelled. Asterios hushed me, but I couldn't be quiet if that's why they'd brought me. "You don't mean like our tall wolves?"

"Hybrids like the sphinx. And the chimera. And the griffin," Mesi said.

"We have daughters of the sea in Greece too…and the minotaur…and the Pegasus," Asterios added. "Almost every culture on Earth has legends of humans that alter into animals. So the same, almost every culture has legends of creatures that are half-human, half something else or many creatures put together."

They were *common*. That's what he was insinuating. Not exceptions. Not perversions. Not abominations. Whatever the extraordinary version of ordinary was. Mundane.

I felt I had to ask. "Are hybrids beasts? Are beasts hybrids?" I pointed toward the shell-seeking mermaid. "Either way, are they…allowed?"

Asterios seemed to understand what I was really asking. "King Ivar hated how dangerous they were."

I recoiled in confusion. "Dangerous? But Mesi just said they're not monsters."

"They kill men occasionally." Mesi shrugged, as if that was hardly something to get worked up about.

I glanced at the only man among us; Asterios didn't seem nervous in the slightest.

"Most creatures when driven to desperation are dangerous," Asterios clarified. "As are most people in power who feel entirely too comfortable calling one danger unacceptable and their own inevitable. But that is not why King Ivar feared creatures he could not easily define. He hated how…disruptive…they were to the established order. They "encouraged open-mindedness." An unforgiveable crime to those who rule over closed minds."

I fell quiet watching Rawan continue to search for shells, drawing closer and closer to me down the water's edge. I felt like I should have dozens of questions for her, but they never made it to my mouth. It didn't feel like the time for them. So instead, when her search brought her closer, I reached into the sand and offered her the curled pointed shell I found there.

She studied it, then me, a sharp curiosity in her golden eyes. "*What would you ask of me for this*?"

"*Nothing*," I said. "*Thank you for having us.*"

"*You would hang this debt over me*," she said.

"*No!*" I swore. "*It's just a gift.*"

But she pursed her lips at that, almost playfully, and snatched the shell away with webbed fingers, shoving it into a net bag she wore around her waist. A tinkling *jangle* filled the air as she dug through the shinies she already had in there before she pulled back with a curled pointed shell much larger than the one I had given—almost the size of a coconut. Even in the low light, I could see it was bright coppery brown on the outside with stripes of black and white along the mouth. Triton's Trumpet, I would later learn it was called.

"*If you have need of me, I shall answer*," she said with a put-out tone, as if I had greatly imposed on her.

She plonked the shell into my hand and then with a wave of hers, we were moving, being pulled into the water *by the water itself*, which tentacled around our ankles and dragged us under. I only had time to shove the diving mask back over my head before I was fully submerged. Then the mermaid from before grabbed my arm again and in a literal flash of movement, we were back in the Eastern Harbor, just under the boat.

I watched the mermaids swim away into the deep, admired the little shockwave that rippled away from their tails a second before they disappeared, and shivered. *Amazing*. Perhaps the most amazing thing I'd seen yet.

And yet, the universe still tried to ruin it.

Mesi and Asterios were already swimming toward the boat, so I turned to do the same.

But…

Overhead, through the wavy veil of water, I could see…a flash of saffron orange. A pale face around silver eyes staring down at me. Cass was in the boat. He was standing right there, across from Mesi's guards.

I tore toward the surface like a bullet. Broke it with all the grace of a drownie.

And my heart sank.

The boat only held Mesi's guards, waiting to help us back aboard.

Cass wasn't there again.

And all I could think was that Asterios and Mesi may have shown me their version of "proof" that there wasn't anything wrong with hybrids…but they hadn't shown me proof that I wasn't doomed to go insane.

CHAPTER 10

The morning after our visit with the aquatic coven, I woke to…a mostly empty palace.

No Asterios or Mesi.

A normal number of guards who ignored me.

And a note on my door that read *Natalie, I have been called back by Rav. Taking the long route to hide your location. Please don't run. I asked Mesi to clear the palace for your comfort. I swear on my life you are safe there and there are grave things we must discuss when I return.*

It was a lot to pack into a note.

And I'd be lying if I didn't have the *immediate* urge to, like, buy a car and just…drive off toward Libya or Sudan, then beyond, as a nameless unknown. Not because I wanted to run from my responsibilities, but because that felt like the safer thing to do, even when you planned to fight for your kingdom. Perhaps, *especially* so. Out there, I would be known to no one. I wouldn't be easily surroundable by guards, or waiting on the best friend of my enemy to return from *meeting* with said enemy.

As much as Asterios had done for me, this seemed like the sort of scenario that gave him way too much pivoting power. He could pretend to be my friend ninety-eight percent of the time and decide at the last second that it benefited him to hand me over to Rav, and I'd be doomed anyway.

That train of thought led me to chastise my raven for not leaving with him, so I could have a head start if he betrayed me to Rav.

She only laughed and said, "*Not leaving. Might need wings*."

"*Should I leave now anyway?*"

"*Unsure,*" was all she gave me.

In the end, though, I chose to stay. Just a little while. Just while I researched, and prepared.

I still had the computer, so I stood at that thing all hours of the day until I went to sleep, stopping only for bathroom breaks…and the strange *ingredient trays* that would appear outside my door three times a day.

That's not a joke. Little golden trays of…"almost snacks" would appear like model kits for me. A loaf of bread with a bottle of olive oil and a jar of dip. A loose pear rolling around beside a wedge of cheese and a knife. Random dates and spiced nuts placed on a plate.

Either there was a *super* passive aggressive chef who resented being left behind at the palace to feed me…or…?

Whoever was doing it, I never found them. I found the kitchen. I *heard* someone messing around in there. But it was empty when I entered, and the shadows freaked me out too much to go back.

The snack trays fed me, though, and I was grateful for that.

And in those couple of days, I realized where I *really* needed to go. The fake-out about the Library of Alexandria had me *jonesing* for a real alter library…and the closest one I could access was also exactly where I wanted to go.

Italy. Rome, I remembered Yasmina telling me. I texted her for the address from the list she'd curated for me and had it in seconds, along with a cryptic series of instructions for how to find the library once I got there.

But that was enough to set my wolf's tail wagging. Idalia's great library was there, ripe for exploring. *She* was in Italy too. Maybe not in Rome, but that'd be as good a place to start my search as any. I needed to find her because she was in danger. Until we knew how far Rav was willing to go to find Arachne's Revenge, we all were.

In the spirit of trying to get inside Rav's head, I also realized that I wanted to be "present" for Lunasa in any way I could.

"*Not going*," my raven said almost immediately, as if she thought I'd tell her to make the long trek across the continent alone. Or that *I* would be dumb enough to go in person. Both made me laugh.

"*I don't need to be there to hear what's going on*," I told her. "*I just need a little help from my friends*."

***

"Testing, one-two-three. Natalie, can you hear me?"

"You're coming in loud and clear, Fern."

"Yasmina?"

"I can hear you both."

It'd taken a couple of days and a few errands, but I was standing in my closet in Alexandria, in front of the black-box phone listening to my team in Ireland test the audio wires they'd hidden under their clothes in preparation for the Lunasa celebration that night.

They'd gone all out for the festivities, hiring security, selecting pre-paired guests for the lover's chase, bedighting half the trees in the forest near Glengarriff with twinkly lights and decorations so the whole thing looked like a fairy kingdom. And I knew it did because they'd been taking pictures for me and storing them in a private account, which I could access through a VPN. It was my favorite way to wake up, opening the account to see what new details they'd added. Giant resin sunflowers acting as umbrellas. A large inflatable globe to contain the band and dance floor in case of rain.

As a surprise for me, they'd even hired a group of local artisans months ago to create a "path of petals," hexagonal tiles made of clear resin inlaid with violently orange and red and yellow and pink blossoms. They'd laid these along the central walk through the forest to the location we'd chosen for the Wedding of the Dawn. And they'd made sure to make enough tiles so each guest could take one home as a gift.

"Technically, we did this so we didn't have to figure out what to do with them after the holiday," Yasmina admitted.

"Two birds, one stone," I praised her. "It's a lovely keepsake."

"It was Cass's idea," she added, and I wasn't surprised.

"Save one for me, okay?" I said, ignoring the squeak in my own voice. "Has Asterios arrived yet?"

"No," Fern said, her tone cautious. "Are you *sure* you should trust him with this?"

When I'd come up with the idea of having my team wear wires so I could listen in on the festivities, I'd realized I needed more than that. I needed to hear what Rav told the other Supremes during the sacrificial ritual, so Fern had had the area around the ancient plinth and stone circles wired too. Then, I'd asked her to pull Asterios aside when he arrived and put one on him as well.

He hadn't returned to Alexandria since he left to go talk with Rav, and there'd been no communication otherwise. *But*…no one had come to kidnap me either, which made me think he'd kept his word. He hadn't told Rav where I was.

Or Asterios was already dead, a quieter part of me worried…

"I want to know what Rav's planning," I told Fern. "If Asterios comes tonight, ask him to be my ears around the king."

"Fine," Fern said. "But if he endangers you, I won't hesitate to defend you."

"Fern, I'm a million miles away. I'm safe for now."

"To be honest, my lady," she countered, "I was tempted to poison all of them tonight. You can't be a fugitive if all the people hunting you are dead."

A shiver ran through me at the suggestion. I supposed that *would* be the easiest way to ensure I remained unfound, but the thought made my soul squirm. I had no idea what the political or moral argument might be for doing something like that, but I was pretty sure a good leader would never even consider it. I mean, half the Gathering Table thought they were searching for me to save me. Killing my rescuers seemed like a great way to get myself karmically cursed.

Not that any of that mattered, ultimately. Fern didn't know I was already on borrowed time. Gathering Table or not, my time as Alter Supreme of the Eighth Kingdom was nearly over anyway.

"Thanks, Fern, but no thanks," I said limply. "Let's just get through tonight, and then we can move on."

"Move on to what?"

"I'll tell you after Rav's gone," I told her. "After *all* the Supremes are gone. Remember Sorina has a lie-detector gift."

I'd forgotten about it, in the midst of everything else, but I'd seen it in action at the last Lunasa celebration and knew we couldn't risk it. I still didn't know what Oriol's gifts were, or Oskar's, either. It was too dangerous to reveal my plans; they were safest when only I knew them.

"But you do *have* a plan, yes?" Yasmina cut in.

An insane one, but, "I do."

"Good because Brodie and his team just landed in Bergen."

My heart almost leapt inside me at the news. While Fern and Yasmina had been busy prepping for Lunasa, Brodie had made plans to go after Scarlett. He'd chosen tonight because he knew Rav and Eike would be away from Hamingja for the holy day.

"Did you arrange the uniforms?" I asked.

"Yes, my lady."

"And the tinctures? The charms?"

"Yes. They're ready," Yasmina assured. "He's updating me as he goes."

His plan had been deceptively simple when he described it to me—he was going to sneak into Hamingja with a small contingent of soldiers—to avoid a head-on assault and any guards who might be "suped up" on Hamingja's aquifer of *raw magick.* They would dress as staff, which is where the uniforms came in. I'd told Brodie and Brodie alone about the tincture the Goddess had given Cass to obscure his scent—angelica and mugwort distilled into an oil worn on the skin—and he'd arranged for Millie to fly to Kinloch Castle to collect and make it for the team. Then, we'd found a pine marten alter living in Wales and asked for locks of his hair in exchange for investing in his business. It was the most expensive hairball in the history of the world, but Brodie's team had woven the fur into little charms they could wear around their neck while in Hamingja.

"They're nearly to the fjord, my lady," Yasmina added.

I couldn't wait. If he could get Scarlett out of there, Rav would have nothing on me. I'd be free of the guilt and fear that had weighed heavy on my heart since I was forced to leave her. With her and my mom out of harm's way, I could make bolder choices, reach for loftier goals, and die free of the fear that I had failed my family.

It was enough. It had to be enough.

Fern yanked me from my musings a few minutes later. "He's here! I see Lord Talon now. I'm going to grab him."

I took a deep shuddering breath. "Let the holy day begin."

CHAPTER 11

"Hey. Where are you taking me?"

"Just this way, Lord Talon. Lady Damarand is expecting you."

"Don't be ridiculous—hey!"

I could hear hastened movement through leaf litter. A foot splashing through a puddle. Some sort of bird SCREAMING overhead so loud it sounded as if it was attacking them.

"Go away!" Yasmina whispered loudly before I heard a close, frantic flap of feathers and the bird fell silent.

It was like listening to a radio drama. Heavy breathing. Grunts. Weird silences. Until finally, the "wide" sound of their voices in the open quieted around them, as if they had entered an enclosed room.

"What's going on?"

"Here, take this."

"What's this?"

"Natalie's on the line for you."

I heard interference, the rub of fingers over a microphone, a muffled *bonk* against something, and then, "Natalie?"

"Hi Asterios."

"I told you I was coming back."

"I believe you. I just realized I needed to be there with you."

He quieted for a moment. "Oh-kay?"

"Would you wear a wire tonight so I can hear what Rav says?"

"Uh…sure."

His answer came so quickly—so *easily*—it genuinely surprised me. "Really?"

"Yes. I told you you can trust me." It was seeming more and more true that I could. Then he added, "The king is arriving soon, so we should hurry."

"Fern?"

"I'm unspooling it."

After a moment, new interference noises filtered in. Fabric rubbing against itself, tape being cut. Yasmina began a step-by-step commentary, letting me know they were attaching the wire to his body.

I heard him bark, "Careful of my chest hair, please!" and then Yasmina told me it was done.

"Testing, testing."

"I can hear you," I said. "Thanks everyone."

"No thanks yet," Yasmina suddenly yelped. "It looks like Lord Oriol has arrived…and Brodie is calling; I have to go."

"I'll see to the Lords," Fern said.

"And I'll be…around," Asterios added, in a way that told me they'd left him alone already.

It had only been a few seconds, and a rough welcome for my savior, so after a moment I said, "Asterios? Sorry for ambushing you. I would've been able to tell you if you'd come back."

"I wanted to. But Rav didn't call me to Greece. He called me to Zurich."

"Zurich?"

"He was meeting with Oskar and Oriol—and me—to discuss next steps into Italy."

Friggen Italy. The center of the world, it suddenly seemed.

"So, he's serious about going after Idalia," I said.

"Seems so."

"But they haven't found Arachne's Revenge yet, have they?"

"No," he chirped, almost proud.

"Have *you* had any luck contacting Idalia?"

"Unfortunately not," he replied, suddenly sheepish. "Rav says it doesn't matter. With everyone scouring the country, it's only a matter of time before we find someone willing to reveal her location."

I almost snickered at that. "But…doesn't he already have people there looking for her?"

"Yes, he does."

"Then…?"

"He's not being his usual strategic self right now," Asterios said. "Or if he is, he's keeping it all inside."

That sounded more likely. Rav could, and had, kept plenty of strategy to himself while I was living with him at Hamingja.

However…if he was still planning to invade—really, *smother* Italy in soldiers—it meant none of his people had found any leads.

"What *did* he tell you?" I asked.

"Very little. He yelled at me for disappearing during the search for you, and for not finding you…until I reminded him you have wings. I've never seen him so sulky in my life."

Competing emotions burbled inside me. Knowing that he no longer had access to my wings made me feel like laughing, like cheering…or like doing some mix of the two. Cackling with triumph, maybe? Being separated from the powers he cared about more than me was a punishment he deserved for how he had treated me. But of course, there was another part of me that felt sorry for him. To think if he'd just…let me in…a few weeks ago, I might have been able to give him everything he'd ever wanted. Friendship. Love. A family. Neither one of us would have ever been alone again. It was sad, to see someone almost get everything they'd ever wanted…and fumble it.

"He's hiding something," Asterios said, pulling me from my thoughts.

"Well…yeah?"

"No, I mean, from *me*. He said the Gathering Table would soon look very different. 'More friendly,' he said."

My stomach dropped at that. "More friendly *to whom*?" Then a horrible thought hit me. "You don't think he's going to *kill* Idalia, do you?"

Asterios didn't say anything, and sour rot filled my stomach.

Idalia wasn't alone in Italy. Giselle was with her. One loss would be devastating, but both? Both would be the end of everything I had planned. No alliance. No friendship. I would truly be forsaken then.

"I-I'm sure he would be more clever than that," Asterios stammered, reassuring me in no way whatsoever. "He *is* more clever than that, my queen."

I didn't have the chance to reply. Half a second later, Fern's voice erupted around me in the small room. "The king is here…and so is…"

Her voice cut off with high surprise, and my anxiety spiked.

"Who's there with him?" There was no answer. "Fern? Who's there with him? Yasmina? Asterios?"

"I must stay where I am," Yasmina yelped. "Brodie has just landed at Hamingja."

And just like that, my anxiety split like a fault line. I didn't know which took precedent, or which to worry about more. I was suddenly *made* of worry. Of panic.

"I'm nearly there." Asterios's voice cut in, breathy and nervous, and around him I could hear crowds. Laughter. Music.

"Almost…Almost."

I waited on bated breath. I waited on tiptoe. I waited for *anyone* to tell me *anything*.

"Who's there, Asterios?"

"It's…Oh…Oh, *gamó*!"

My built-in translator wouldn't have been necessary to know he was cussing…and shocked and angry and maybe a little bit scared.

"Who. Is. It?!" I begged.

"It's…Archer Mahon, my lady," Fern said after a moment. "Archer Mahon and—"

"Ulric Garand," Asterios added darkly. "The wolf princeling is here."

CHAPTER 12

What was Rav playing at? What was he trying to do? Inviting both Archer Mahon and Ulric Garand to *my* holy day was no accident. It was a statement. An open-handed threat to me.

"Fern, be careful not to let him touch you," I said. "Asterios, get him away from her as quickly as you can. Figure out what he's doing, okay?"

Their voices jumbled as they said, "Yes, my lady," and "On it, my queen."

"Yas? What's happening with Brodie?" I added.

"He's inside Hamingja. His team has split up."

I hated that I hadn't been able to narrow down where in Hamingja Scarlett might have been for Brodie, but…I had no clue. When Rav had caged me in the Goddess's infinite magick, I'd only managed to find Scar once when I woke up, and it was entirely by accident. Then, Rav had put her in our bedroom with me and when I'd woken up, I hadn't bothered to ask her where her room was. I'd only had a few minutes to tell her she was in danger and that I needed help before Rav forced me under again.

Which meant she could be anywhere in Hamingja. Brodie and however many people he'd taken with him were basically hunting for her in a building the size of a small city. A new sort of guilt settled in the pit of my stomach as I found myself wishing I hadn't bothered to send Brodie's team at all. But it was only a half-wish, and a passive one. Only the worst version of me could have left Scarlett there.

And then…

"Asterios, there you are."

Rav's voice cut through the mire of my thoughts like lightning. I literally flinched where I stood, he sounded so close in the small closet.

"My king! Happy Lunasa," Asterios said. "And you bring unexpected guests. Master Garand…Master Mahon."

"Not for much longer," Ulric growled proudly. I could almost hear the words curling around his canine smile.

"What do you mean?"

"You'll excuse Ulric. He's forgotten his manners," Rav said. "Let's wait for the others to arrive and then we'll have formal introductions. First, I need Natalie's team. Where are they?"

"Your highness, welcome," Fern said a second later, her voice steady as a river. "Happy Lunasa."

"To you as well, Lady Saeli," Rav said. "This is quite the celebration you've put together, considering your lady is missing."

His tone was just south of accusatory, still light but only barely. As if he wanted to blame her for not joining the hunt for me all the way across the continent, or to trick her into revealing something.

Fern took it in stride, "My lady designed everything you see tonight. She was excited to surprise you with it. While she's away, the least I could do was hold the holy day in her honor."

It was a simple lie—I'd been responsible for maybe twenty percent of the choices this year—but she said it with just enough emotion to make it seem genuine. And to my surprise, when Rav spoke again, his voice sounded tight and…grateful.

"Good," he coughed. "It feels like her."

"Would you like me to show you the—"

"No," he cut her off. "How long have the guests been celebrating?"

"Since sundown, my king."

"We'll begin the chase early tonight. The moment the last of us arrives, ready the guests to run."

"Lord Savall and Lord Lange are here," Fern told him. "We are still waiting on Lady Ilias, Lady Garand, and Lady da Carra."

"My mother would pay dearly if she dared show her face tonight," Ulric laughed darkly.

"Lady da Carra won't be coming either," Rav added. "Lady Ilias is the last. Take us to the gathering place now and send her to us once she arrives. In the meantime, I would have words with you—"

"Don't trouble the woman," Asterios suddenly laughed. "She is a mistress of chaos tonight without her lady here to guide her. I know where the ritual site is. Come on, I'll show you."

My mind bumped on his phrasing, his tone. Quietly I asked, "Fern, does he actually know where it is?"

"No," she said, and I could hear she was moving. "Rav reached for my arm. Asterios pulled him away."

"Guide him!" I urged.

"Left, Asterios," she said. "Take the path lit by lanterns to the trail blocked by warning signs. Follow that and you will find the altar in a hollow. The others are already there."

"I'm over here already," Yasmina added. "I can guide you once you're on the closed path."

It sounded like the blind leading the blind, but it worked. I listened as Asterios exchanged small talk with Rav while Fern and Yasmina secretly guided him, until other voices filtered in and Asterios said, "Should we leave Masters Garand and Mahon here so they can celebrate the evening?"

"No, they belong with us tonight," Rav said. "After you."

They belong with us tonight. My spine tightened with dread and discomfort at his words.

"Asterios, does he mean what I think he means?" I couldn't help but ask.

Asterios tried to pry. "A-Are you saying they're—"

But Rav wouldn't let him. "Patience, Asterios. All will reveal itself in time."

My mind barely had time to overthink. A second later, Yasmina's voice yelped at a slight distance away from her microphone. "Brodie? Brodie, what happened? Can you hear me?"

"What's happening?" I squeaked. "What's wrong?"

Yasmina didn't answer me; she was still talking to somebody else. "Millie?" … "He said he was entering the third floor when I heard shouting." … "No, he hasn't responded." … "Hurry, please."

I waited until she stopped speaking. "Yas?"

"I-It's fine, I think, my lady," she said. "Brodie encountered someone. Millie said she's going after him."

Damn. Who had he encountered? Was it Eike? Had Eike stayed behind?

"Fern? Asterios? Is Eike at Lunasa?"

"I haven't seen her," Fern said after a moment.

"My king, I haven't seen your Second tonight," Asterios tried.

Rav seemed distracted. "I can't tell if you're disappointed or relieved, my friend."

"As scary as she is in person, she is more terrifying when

unaccounted for," Asterios joked.

Rav grunted. "She isn't needed here tonight."

"What do you mean?"

"My mate is missing," Rav almost growled. "Until she is found, nothing else matters. I almost canceled the entire holy day to continue the search, but…after Greece, I need the rejuvenation."

I felt my heart tighten with confusion and something warmer. Rav was saying that using his gift of inspiration to convince everyone I wasn't a beast had taken a lot out of him, I just knew he was. And the emotion I felt was complicated and insane.

On the one hand, I knew Rav was in for a rude awakening. There were no sacrifices at Lunasa this year. I'd planned to host it, after all, and I had had zero intention of sacrificing anybody.

On the other hand, I felt…sorry for him. Just a little. That desire to take care of him was still there in me, which made sense. Despite everything he'd done, I *had* been ready to spend the rest of my life with him only a few short weeks ago.

"…Is he okay, Asterios?" I asked quietly.

"You do look a little tired, my king," Asterios said in response.

"I'm fine," Rav barked. "Look, there are the others. Let's make this quick and go home."

They'd reached the ritual place. Faintly, I could hear Oskar and Oriol jabbering on about something.

"I can barely hear them, Fern," I said.

"The microphones at the altar are on a different frequency," she said. "I'll switch us over now."

Not a second later, the sound coming through the black-box phone boomed *wider*. Suddenly I could hear birds and crickets and the Alter Supremes turning to welcome the new arrivals.

"Well, well," Oriol hummed. "If it isn't Giselle's puppy, out in the open at last."

"Not her puppy anymore, Oriol," Ulric chuckled. "And not your—"

"Patience, Ulric," Rav said, his voice dark and irritated.

Patience? If anything, there was too much patience. No one spoke after Rav cut Ulric off, and all I was left to wonder was *why wasn't anyone else bringing up the fact that a man who had killed his father—killed an* Alter Supreme*—was being welcomed into that sacred place like he belonged there?* Did they really not care?

Thankfully, I didn't have to be patient for long.

"She's here. Lady Ilias is here," Fern whispered a second later.

I heard a whip of wind, a soft *boom* of arrival and Sorina said, "No need to announce me, darling. I can smell them from here."

There was another whip of wind and Fern said, "I have to start the chase. I'll be listening."

Then I heard Sorina say, "I'm here. I'm here. I was hungrier today than usual. Needed to stop for a quick bite."

"Good," Rav said. "Everyone, to your stone."

"My king," Oriol laughed. "So early in the party?"

"There is no party tonight, only a feeding," he said. "Unless recent gossip proves correct and she's returned to me soon, we're all to continue our hunts for the queen, understood?"

The others grunted.

Everyone save Sorina. "The wolf pup and bear cub are joining us, my king?"

"Yes," he said. "We deserve a full meal and a full Gathering Table."

"What are you saying?" Asterios asked.

"Lord Mahon and Lord Garand are to be welcomed as one of our own tonight."

I…

I cannot tell you how those words broke my heart. Not just my heart. My spirit.

He was…

"Rav's taking my kingdom away," I whispered. "He's giving it back to the bears. Can he do that? He can't do that. *Why* would he do that? He can't think I'll come back to him if he does this."

I felt sick. *I felt sick!*

"But…he is a bear," Asterios said for me.

"I hope you haven't forgotten *my father* was the Bear Lord," Archer snapped.

Asterios ignored him, "And *that one* butchered his—"

"I saved my kingdom from two selfish pack leaders," Ulric suddenly growled. "A weak man, a feeble woman. You should be thanking me, but in time you will come to love me."

"My king," Asterios almost barked. "You must believe Lady Damarand is alive somewhere!"

"She *is* alive!" Rav roared. "She will be mine again shortly."

Asterios plunged ahead. "How will she react when she returns to see you have given her kingdom away?"

"She will understand," Rav said.

"She will *never* forgive you, my king," Asterios warned.

"She will," Rav challenged, but in his voice, I could hear doubt, misguided hope.

"No, she won't." It wasn't Asterios saying those words. It was Ulric.

"Mind your business, Wolf Lord," Rav growled.

"I know it for a fact," Ulric chuckled.

"You couldn't."

"Ah, but I do," Ulric said, smiling. "Lady Damarand just said as much."

"*What* did you just say?"

I heard a scuffle. A yelp. A growl and a low laugh.

"You bring the wolf pup back just to kill him?" Oriol snickered. "I am not complaining. I *love* a good show."

Rav ignored him. "Speak, dog."

"Woof," Ulric said…right before I heard his voice tighten and strangle. "Take care, king. You have a traitor in your midst."

My spine tightened at that, in warning. "Asterios, I think he knows."

"You have three seconds to speak, Ulric, or I *will* rip your head off," Rav swore.

"I am trying," Ulric coughed.

"What do you know about my queen! Speak!"

"Lady Damarand may not be here in body, my king," Ulric said. "But she is here in spirit. Right there, in fact, listening through the microphone under Asterios's shirt."

There was a loud moment of silence.

And then quiet as a dying breath, Asterios said, "*Run*."

CHAPTER 13

I'd forgotten about the wolves' hyper-hearing. Or rather, I'd never had "Ulric showing up to Lunasa" on my bingo card in the first place. Either way, he'd probably heard us talking the whole time. That's all I could think as all hell broke loose on the other end of the phone. It was a cacophony of noises—grunts, growls, things being ripped from the earth and thrown.

But…*run*, Asterios had said. His last word before I heard microphone feedback and…he stopped speaking.

Was he telling *me* to run? Maybe. Definitely.

But I wasn't in immediate danger.

"Run, Fern. Yasmina, run!" I almost screamed the words at them, hoping they could hear. Hoping they were far enough away from the ritual site to flee.

But what about the guests? There were *hundreds* of them. And they were all running through the forest, completely clueless about the true predators in their presence, hunting for real.

"*Friends first*," my raven consoled me.

Gah, she was right. I hated that she was right!

"Yas!" I barked again, "Fern? Someone say something!"

"I'm hidden," Yas said. "But it's too dangerous to speak."

She was gone with a *click* and I was left talking to myself.

My mind wasn't just reeling; it was running away with me, with my creatures. I could *feel* their panic, their strategizing. It was like a buzz under my skin. And I only contributed to that panic trying to think of ways I could help my team from afar.

Until everything got worse.

"*Danger*," my raven suddenly warned. "*Window.*"

I crept to the closet window and peered out, but all I could see from here was one of the guards standing at attention at an interior gate that led to the back courtyard.

"*What is it? What's happening?*" I asked.

My raven didn't need to answer. As I peered out, the guard suddenly stepped out of position…and four armed men I didn't recognize walked right through.

"*Hunters,*" my wolf said, and my diaphragm tightened with dread.

I was certain of only two things.

I couldn't help my friends.

I had to help myself. I had to run.

The pain. The *loss*. They had to wait. I had to go.

My sneakers were in the closet. I shoved them on my feet. I'd prepared a small pack for myself too, containing a plastic bag full of papers covered in important phone numbers and other things like my passport number and UK ID number. The shell Tidebringer Rawan had given me was loose at my feet, so I shoved that in too. I had little else but my laptop. Should I take it? I didn't know. If I didn't take it, I had to smash it.

"*Destroy,*" my raven said. "*Quiet.*"

I crept to the closet door and softly opened it, peeking out. My suite was empty. I ran for the desk, grabbed the laptop, raised it over my head to slam it on the ground…and then I hesitated. Too much noise. I ran to the bathroom instead and tossed it in the tub, turned on the shower.

"*What now? I need to leave.*"

"*Wait.*"

I froze. "*Wait for what? For how long?*"

I knew I had to get out of the palace, and I had options depending on who was here and if I was already surrounded. I could fly, but the only direction to do that was directly north, across the sea, which wasn't a problem except there was a thousand-foot-long stretch of land between here and the Mediterranean. Enough distance that I knew the second I soared into open air, I'd most likely be met with gunfire. The harbor on the other side of the palace was much closer but I dismissed it out of hand. Or I could run. The exit to the city streets was barely half a mile away. I could disappear into the crowds.

I reached for the window latch to let myself out—

"*Wait!*" my wolf growled.

"This is the back of the palace. The path to the delivery drive is *right there*!" I didn't even say it in my head, I was so impatient.

"*Three.*"

Three?

"*Two.*"

I didn't know what we were counting down to, but I reached for the window latch anyway, and unlocked it, ready to leap through the moment she said…

"*One—*"

I lunged…and stopped. A hand was on my bicep, yanking me back. Another went to my mouth, covering it.

My hand fisted instinctively. I turned, ready to attack. Ready to *blind.* Ready to beat the ever-loving daylight out of *anyone* who dared to touch me.

But my fist froze midair…and I left it there, completely forgotten when I saw who had ahold of me.

"Cass!"

His finger rose to his lips, begging me to be silent. I nodded. He tapped the same finger to his ear…and I quieted my own breath enough to listen.

"*Search everywhere.*" That was Eike.

Holy hell, the sheer sound of her voice iced my veins in fear. How had she gotten here so quickly? Had she been listening in on my conversation with Asterios too? Had she traced the call or had her search already led her here? Had Mesi betrayed me? Or was it sheer bad luck? I didn't have time to think about it.

"*Every room. Every closet,*" she snarled. "*The rest of you, line the walls. Leave her no path of escape. If you see the bird, fire*!"

As quietly as I could, I asked Cass, "What do we do?"

"*Distraction,*" my raven suddenly said, erupting from my chest in a splash of orange-pink. She shot away through the wall and disappeared.

A second later, my wolf slunk out of me from behind and I watched her bolt away through the opposite wall

Then Cass slid his hand into mine and gestured at me for trust, little more than a nod and an earnest look.

But this being that smelled like nothing and never blinked *wasn't him.* Was it? I didn't know. I didn't know! I was about to lay my life in the hands of a…a…hallucination? A split personality? A ghost? Heck, a *ghost* I would have trusted! Maybe that wasn't smart either, but at least I would know it was him.

He gently tugged on me to follow, but I hesitated and begged, "Are you *real*? Are you *him*?" He nodded, and I clarified one last time, "Are you *my* Cass?"

His eyes tightened with some emotion I couldn't understand. But then…like some sort of tiny miracle…he raised his hand to his chest, the way Cass had done so many times before to reassure me *every beat of his heart belonged to me*.

It brought tears to my eyes. Tears that dried a second later, when he tightened his grip on my hand and yanked me out of the bathroom.

At the suite door, he paused us and listened. I heard a faint shout…heard running feet…and then—

POW-POWPOW-POW!

Gunfire. So close I could feel each *boom* in my spine. It was instinct—pure instinct—to raise my hands to cover my ears. I felt a slice of pain along my wounded arm as that knee-jerk reaction took over and my arm began to rise, jerking against the constraints of the gauze sling that held my arm to my body—

Cass stopped me. He grabbed the forearm on my wounded limb, shook his head, and held my arms down at my sides as more gunfire erupted and my body began to shudder and shake with the *desperate need to cover my ears*. Shame filled me at my reaction, but I had no control over it. Ever since France, ever since Ulric had shot Rav in the chest while aiming at me, gunfire had had this effect on me.

"I'm sorry," I mouthed as we waited.

But Cass only nodded, his brow high with pity and compassion.

And then, the gunfire ceased. Cass held firmly to my hand and pulled me out into the hall behind him.

We ran to the corner. Waited. We ran down a short hall. Waited. More gunfire erupted at a distance, just far enough away not to trigger my freeze response, and I was grateful. Two halls farther along, we found the closest exit…but…

Three intruders with guns were standing just inside the open doorway. Three more were visible just outside. Beyond them, I could see choppy dark water, not fifty feet away beyond the lawn. It wasn't the side of the palace I would have chosen—this side was a harbor, not open sea, and shared water with a naval yard and commercial traffic. There was a rainbow-sheen of gasoline on the surface. But maybe there was a boat we could steal? Maybe we could swim across to the other side?

Not that I could do any of that unless we could *get outside* and run the fifty *completely uncovered* feet to the water.

In answer, my wolf suddenly appeared beside us.

She stepped into view of the men down the hall.

"*Hey. Hey! What is that*?" One of the intruders stammered, practically slapping the arm of the man beside him. "*Isn't that a…*"

"*Wolf!*" The second intruder screamed the word as if she was already attacking him.

My wolf didn't move, not an inch. She waited as they raised their guns. Waited until they were aiming properly. Until their fingers were on the triggers.

"*Fire!*"

POWPOWPOWPOW!

Cass pulled me back, covered me, covered my ears, while the vaulted halls around us amplified the roar of gunfire until it was cataclysmic and had all but obliterated the golden mirrored wall to our left.

Silence finally descended upon us minutes later, but it wasn't because the men had triumphed against the ghostly wolf facing off with them. When Cass took away his hands, I could *hear* the continued *click-click-click* of their empty guns as they caught their breath.

"*Where did it go*?" one asked.

"*I-I-I don't know!*"

I peeked my head around the edge just to see what was happening…and saw more than I hoped for. All six of the intruders with their empty guns in hand were standing by the exit door peering down the hall in our direction…and all six were *torn off their feet* a moment later as my wolf barreled into them from the side, knocking them into walls like bowling pins.

Cass yanked me forward down the hall before I could blink.

We reached the open doorway in seconds…and I heard a horrible click.

"*Don't move!*" It was a feeble voice, belonging to the only man still conscious a few feet away. He had a handgun aimed straight at me. "*Stay right where you—*"

His voice died with a yelp as my wolf's ghostly head suddenly emerged from the wall right over him. She gave him a second to decide. She gave him a chance to lie down.

He didn't. He twisted his gun as if to shoot her and he was gone, his head clutched in her mouth as she dragged him the length of the hall and smashed his head into the wall as she ran through. I could literally feel the graze of something being jerked from my mouth as her hold on him slipped; it was the strangest sensation.

There was no time for guilt, though. Only running. Cass pushed me ahead of him across the open stretch of lawn, toward the water, and we made it nearly halfway across before we heard someone shout, "*There! She's there!*"

I turned for only a split second, and saw a wall of men and women bearing down on my location, guns in hand. I had seconds—*seconds!*—to reach the water.

I didn't walk off the sea wall so much as launch myself off and I splashed down into the harbor like a stone. I spun, just in time to see Cass wasn't with me. He had turned to face the coming tide. And beyond them, my raven was swooping down on Eike's soldiers from behind, as my wolf tore through the palace's façade on lightning-fast approach.

"You! Down on the ground!" someone yelled at Cass.

"Down now or we'll fire!"

But my raven and wolf were there before they could. Claws went to eyes. Teeth tore legs out from under bodies. And Cass…disappeared in the blink of an eye before reappearing behind an intruder aiming his rifle at my raven ten feet away. Cass jerked the gun skyward as the intruder fired before disarming him and smashing the gun across the man's head. Cass did the same to the next man over.

They were winning, in the moment, and my soul sang in triumph. But more were coming. I could hear them. Then I could see them, just turning the far corner of the palace. My creatures were running out of time.

I couldn't leave them. *I couldn't leave them*! Who could I possibly be without them?

There was only one thing I could think to do…and the thought pulled at me like the tide. I didn't know if Tidebringer Rawan was even in her altered form tonight—for all I knew she was a million miles away camping in the Sahara—but she might answer if I called for help.

I reached for my bag. I reached for the shell she had given me. Turned it in my hand, trying to figure out how to use it. There, along the curved tip was a tiny hole.

I'd only ever seen someone blow into a shell in the movies. So I followed their lead. I pressed it to my lips and blew.

Bu-BUH!

It rattled my throat. It rattled my soul. Where the notes I'd heard before sang like trumpet song, my notes erupted like a siren.

Bu-BUH!

There'd never been a more beautiful sound in the world…until I heard a splash behind me. Just the tiniest ripple of water.

Rawan was there. *Right there*, her golden eyes almost neon in the darkness. She studied me, then the scene on the shore behind me…and then she closed the short distance between us. Her hand went to my wrist.

"*Dangerous men,*" she hissed. "*You wish to escape*?"

"*Please*," I begged.

"*Where shall I take you?*"

I heard a scream. My gaze snapped back to my creatures as my raven picked up an intruder by the scruff of his neck and hurled him into an approaching battalion. But no sooner had those men fallen, then I saw Eike behind them. Her predator eyes locked on me at a distance, and icy *terror* poured into my body when she began to sprint.

I had seconds. *Seconds*!

"Come now!" was all I had time to scream at my creatures before I turned to Rawan and yelped, "Rome! Take me to Rome. Please!"

And the daughter of the sea dragged me under.

CHAPTER 14

I had no air this time, no tanks of oxygen, but I didn't need them. The second I was fully submerged, Rawan's tail flicked underneath me and a bubble as big as I was enveloped me. The wrist she held was the only part of my body outside this magickal sphere of air.

I sensed splashes, felt the sensation of my raven and wolf slamming haphazardly into my back, right before people plunged into the water behind me.

Right before a hand fisted in my hair.

I turned to see Eike there in the water with me, clawing for purchase on my body as Rawan clung tightly to me in a mad tug of war that made my wounded arm scream with pain.

I kicked. I kicked Eike as hard as I could, ignoring her nails as they shredded my shoulders and Rawan's as they scratched my wrist. Ignoring the little nicks salted by the water lancing sharp pain through me.

Until Cass appeared behind Eike. And with long vicious wolfen claws, he pierced her eyes and wrenched her away from me like a barnacle from the bottom of a ship.

Then, Rawan and I were moving. Careening. Slicing through the water like torpedoes.

It felt like being pulled down a drain. Ahead of us, the water churned in a growing vortex that encased us, blotting the sea from sight in a whirl of fast-moving water.

My stomach lurched.

Pressure squeezed my brain.

Pain popped in my ears.

And just when I felt unconsciousness threatening to steal me away, it all stopped—the discomfort, the movement, the air bubble, all of it—plunging us into an alien world so beautiful I could hardly stand it. We had arrived beside a massive coral reef system; to one side of me, a wall of coral extended in either direction into the dark and above me, nearly to the water's surface. Great fuchsia-colored fan corals wafted in the waves. Fish and eels peeked out at us from the reef.

It was beautiful. And startling. And I wished I had more time to explore it.

But water rushed into my mouth the moment I opened it in wonder, and I sputtered, clawed for the surface, and drank in the salt and rosemary-scented air until I thought my lungs would burst.

And then Rawan took hold of me again and *dragged* me along in her wake at a speed just shy of jet ski toward the far shore I could see in the distance. It made me want to scream, but if I screamed, I knew I would vomit.

Eventually, though, she slowed as we reached a beach devoid of anything remotely human. Houselights glowed in the far distance, but otherwise I could just make out an empty beach and scrubland. An empty beach…and beautiful bioluminescent algae that frilled the soft waves in neon blue.

"Italy?"

"Italy," Rawan confirmed. "*The ancient reefs of Tor Paterno. Unless I risked the filth of the Tiber—which I am not willing to do—it is as close as I can take you to the city without feet.*"

I wanted to smile, but I was too tired. Still, I said, "*Fair. Thank you.*"

To say I staggered into the shallowest shallows and flopped down like a soggy dog would be an understatement. It was gross. I was tired of being wet and sandy. More than that *I was exhausted*, so limp and breathless and disoriented from traveling hundreds of miles in mere moments that I had an urge just to lay down on the sand and fall asleep in it for decades. But the pain and fear for my friends, my kingdom, wouldn't let me. I felt like weeping. I felt like screaming. I was a jumbled mess on the shore.

"*Rest!*" Rawan urged, reaching for my uninjured shoulder to hold me down. "*The motion sickness will pass in a few moments.*"

I couldn't even fight her on it. My head was spinning.

"*While we wait, I would take the shell back.*"

With leaden limb, I held it out to her. "*Is that why you gave it to me in the first place? I don't think you really thought you owed me for the shell I gave you.*"

"*Of course I did,*" she chuffed, playfully. "*But...*"

"*But you knew I might be in danger soon?*"

Lit only by the low glow of the blue algae, it was difficult to see the full expression on her face, but her golden eyes crinkled with what I thought was sorrow. "*Water is an emotional conductor. All who enter unknowingly feed their feelings into it.*" She paused for a moment and nudged herself closer to me in the shallows. "*Your pain was felt by many.*"

"*When?*"

"*When you crashed into the sea many days ago,*" she said. "*I was not in Greece then, but I heard of you from others who were. They thought I would want to know.*"

"*Why?*"

She made a little amused noise and rolled over to prop her upper half up on her elbows as the neon waves washed over her tail. "*It's complicated.*"

"*I have time,*" I grumbled, still recovering.

"*Well, let's just say I did not become what I am to...rule. To lead others. I became a daughter of the sea because I thought I was utterly alone in my grief. Forsaken and doomed to be forgotten.*"

My heart tightened at that. "*I'm sorry for your loss.*"

"*My loss?*"

"*You lost your spouse?*" I offered. "*I thought maybe that's why you call yourselves the Widows' Wail Coven?*"

At that, she threw her head back laughing so hard she sounded like she was barking.

"*Goodness, the moonmother has a wonderful sense of humor! No-No-No. I* wish *I'd lost my spouse. If he had gotten lost, he'd still be alive!*" she laughed. Then she grew pensive and added, "*But if he had I would not be here.*"

"*I'm sorry, I don't understand.*"

"*My marriage was an offense to the Goddess, an awful mistake I spent ages being punished for. After the wedding, he became someone I didn't recognize. A cruel and bitter man who needed me to feel small so that he could feel large. He would take any opportunity to ruin my joy, any opportunity to shame me for finding peace within myself, or for asking for rest. And for the longest time I had convinced myself that if I only tried harder, if I only gave more of myself, if I only made myself smaller, he would eventually recognize my dedication and sacrifices...and show me the same in return. He did not.*

"But when I tried to leave? When I tried to give him the freedom he claimed to want so badly? Dear Goddess, you would have thought he truly loved me for how devastated he pretended to be. He would make empty promises and weep and threaten himself, and I would feel too guilty to leave, and by and by I would find myself in the same miserable place all over again when nothing ever changed."

"So...what did you do?"

"I wasted away until I hardly recognized myself. And then...one day...a little voice in my head told me to follow him. Not fifteen minutes from the house we shared, I saw him there with a woman. He'd brought her flowers. FLOWERS! Ha!"

She laughed, but in the sound, I could hear devastation; even after however long it had been, the memory still bit at her.

"I went home that instant, packed a bag, and left. I crossed my entire country before he even noticed I was gone. I thought that was the end of it. He was free to be with her, and I was free to be myself for the first time in my life."

Again, through the triumph in her voice, I could hear looming sorrow. It was coming. The twist in her story was coming.

Her voice began to quiver and quake. *"Until he found me. Until he broke into my home and attacked me, raging about how I had humiliated him for leaving. ME, humiliate HIM! I wasn't prepared. I wasn't as strong as I am now. I listened to him make more empty promises, this time while he broke my bones. I listened to him threaten himself while all but destroying me. I kept thinking that if I didn't fight back, he would take pity on me eventually...*

"And then, he drove my battered body to the sea. Dragged me out of the car, unable to walk. Grabbed me by my hair—the thing he'd once told me was my most beautiful feature—and threw me from the cliff. I can still...I can still feel *my body break as it hit the rocks again and again before the water caught me."*

"What happened then?"

"I wept to drown faster." She shrugged. *"And the pain leeched away into the water until a daughter of the sea found me. Lifted my body to the surface so I could breathe. Asked me if I wished to live, and bit me when I said yes. She told me the full moon would heal me, and I floated, broken and forsaken, in that cove for nearly thirty hours before that healing silver light spilled out of the sky."*

I didn't know what to say, so I sat there with her in silence for a long moment, letting her recover instead. And when she did, she surprised me again.

"*Before I killed him, the coward called me cold-hearted. But he never took responsibility for stealing its warmth in the first place. Does that seem right to you?*"

"*So...Widows' Wail is a battle cry*," I said in answer.

Even in the low light, her smile was as bright as the full moon. "*At first, I was the only guest at my own party, but in time I found others. Women thrown into the sea. Women who cast* themselves *into the sea. Their pain would leech into the water like oil. I could sense it from fathoms away. I took them in, became a collector of lost souls, trying to help them in the ways I was never helped. In my human form, I have since become a divorce lawyer, if you can believe it.*"

I chuckled at that.

"*And in this form, I am a widowmaker. I became one leading many. I am who they call whenever a new daughter cries tears into the sea.*"

Me. She was talking about me. I couldn't remember if I'd cried when I crashed into the waters off Crete after my wedding, but my emotions had certainly been high. I wondered if I had laid there a bit longer whether someone with golden eyes and a beautiful tail would have come to save me.

"*Do you accept men into your coven?*" I asked.

"*Of course.*" A cheeky smile twisted her lips, as she added, "*But Widows' Wail has a nice ring to it.*"

"*I can't be a widow*," I pointed out.

"*No, but your pain was excruciating*," she said. "*When the others told me of you, when they told me you landed on Crete, I put my ear to the sea until rumor reached me of a stolen Alter Supreme. But if an Alter Supreme had truly been stolen, surely every kingdom and queendom on this planet would have been informed, no?*"

"*You didn't believe the story.*"

"*I allowed myself the space to disbelieve it, waiting to be proven wrong if your king summoned the might of us all to find you...but then Sayyida Mesi and Lord Asterios asked me for a favor, and I saw for myself that you were not stolen.*"

My throat tightened without my permission, as heartache swept into me. "*I wasn't, but my queendom was.*"

"*Then take it back.*"

"*Sounds so simple when you say it.*"

"*Because it is.*"

I disagreed. "*I'm...different.*"

"*Good. So am I. It can be quite lonely to be a stranger among others who are also strange.*"

I shook my head. "*There's...something wrong with me. I'm not...fit to be a Supreme anymore.*"

"*Do you think I declared myself an Alter Supreme? No,*" she tutted. "*The power to lead is granted by those who follow, not by others who lead. If your people remain with you, if you have earned their loyalty and remain worthy of it, then you are still their queen. And they are still counting on you.*"

Damn, more responsibility. And another reminder of what the Goddess had told me—that I still had a part to play in whatever lay ahead of us.

"*There's a war coming,*" I warned her, although I couldn't say for certain who was an enemy and who wasn't. "*Would you...*"

"*Would I what?*"

"*Could I count you among my allies, if I needed you?*" I asked, hating how small and quivering my voice sounded.

"*You would have my kind as allies?*" she asked. "*Even though the truth of creatures like us scares people?*"

"*Yes,*" I swore.

"*And would you come to my aid, if I needed it?*"

"*Yes,*" I swore again.

Rawan cooed happily beside me. I turned and caught the Triton's trumpet shell as she foisted it back into my hands.

"*I had decided that if you had the courage to ask, my answer would be yes,*" she said. Then she motioned toward the scrubland across the road. "*That land belongs to the Italian human president. If you manage to cross it to the northeast without being caught, you will soon find yourself in Rome. Call if you have need of me, and I will come.*"

As she pulled back into deeper water, I held up the shell and jokingly asked one final question, "*What's the range on this thing?*"

"*Much farther than you think!*"

With a flick of her tail, she was gone, and I was alone again.

No, not alone.

"*Will search ahead,*" my raven said, soaring out of me across the scrubland. "*Must hide before rest.*"

A second later, I shoved myself to my weary feet, staggered across the sands and road, and plunged into the brush after her.

CHAPTER 15

"Thank you, sneakers. Thank you, backpack."

The scrubland was…scrubby. Dry and tangled and hard under my feet. I was still sandy, chafing. I was growing heavier with each second of wakefulness I forced out of myself, but I was fading fast. The only thing I could do to stay standing was talk to myself, to…show gratitude for the little things that were making this trek through the pale brown duney thicket bearable.

Like my wolf who returned from her own trek with…a pomegranate clutched in her mouth.

"Thank you, friend," I murmured, taking the fruit and tucking it in my backpack for later.

Then my raven soared into view and spun overhead. "*Follow. Rest.*"

I'd never wanted anything more. I stumbled after her through a thick, gnarled bramble of dry bushes that tore and scratched my already tenderized skin before arriving at an…ancient Roman ruin. At least, I had to assume that's what it was. Still-mortared half walls with a doorway ringed an old mosaic-tile floor. The ceiling had long collapsed, but columns still stood, and from those columns, vining plants had created a wild pergola. Some, like morning glory, I recognized. Other vines, like the ones covered in bursts of star-shaped white flowers that smelled of vanilla I didn't. But it was a protected place and there was room to lie down.

I made it all of three feet through the doorway before I stumbled to my knees and just curled up where I fell.

"*Thank you,*" I said to my creatures.

"*Rest, will keep watch.*"

Unfortunately, despite the aching fatigue in my body, sleep was slow to come…and not just because the hard floor was brutal. I just kept *listing* things in my mind. I needed a phone…but to get that I needed to find one of the banks Cass had stashed money in. Then I needed to call Fern, Yas. I needed to call Brodie and make sure he and his team escaped Hamingja alive…and to find out if he'd saved Scarlett. I needed to know if Asterios was dead, if any of my guests at Lunasa were dead. I needed to know if my lawyer had received my instructions for my queendom, and whether she would still carry them out now that Archer was in charge.

I needed to find the alter library in Rome.

I needed to find Idalia and warn her.

It was so much. *So many little steps* that were actually enormous, considering I'd never been to Rome in my life and I had to do it all alone.

Not alone, I had to remember.

As I went to tuck my uninjured arm under my head to use as a makeshift pillow, I found there was already an arm there. One that looked human and normal but felt like it was covered with invisible fur when you touched it. It made me leap up like a startled cat again. I turned to find Cass there, lying beside me on the floor with his arm extended, staring at me.

Gah, it was *so uncanny*. It was him, but it wasn't. I couldn't feel any magnetic force when I touched him, there was no dappled snowflake attention when he looked at me, but he'd fought Eike, and I could physically feel him when we touched. *What was he*?

Maybe he was a gift from the Goddess? Some silent consolation prize for knowing how this would all end for me?

He stared at me, almost frozen, waiting. There was a mixed expression on his face as if he was both defensive, assuming I wouldn't accept the arm pillow he was offering, but determined to offer it regardless. To be a gentleman anyway, even if I didn't deserve it.

But as I stared back, all I felt was…guilt.

I scooched closer to him, wincing as his body stiffened, and dropped my head on his muscled arm; if he was offering, I wasn't going to turn it down.

"I'm sorry," I said quietly. Tears prickled my eyes. "Cass, I'm so sorry I lost the Eighth Kingdom."

He just stared, those silver eyes unblinking.

And I began to cry harder, letting it out. "I'm sorry I yelled at you over the phone, in London. You didn't deserve that. You annoyed me sometimes because I thought you cared more about sacrificing for some imaginary idea of me than actually being with me, but I was mad and mean, and if I'd known it was the last time I'd get to talk to you—the *real* you—I would've told you so many things."

At that, his fur-lined fingers curled under my chin, turning my head so I had to look him in the eye. He wore an expression of…confusion? Curiosity, maybe?

"You deserved so much better," I told him. "I wanted you to be so happy, as an alter. I am *not* sorry I found a way to force your alteration. I'm just sorry you didn't get to enjoy it."

It was so unfair. He'd gotten the life he wanted and barely lived it. And I'd gotten a taste of ruling the way I'd only dreamed of, before Rav—and my beastliness—had taken it from me. I now understood why Cass had wanted this life so badly, to the extreme of letting vile beasts like the Russian monster bear Dobrynya attack him to get it.

"If you had survived, I would have left the kingdom to you and Fern and Yas," I told him eventually. "And I would have asked you to be the one to end my life."

His brow furrowed at that, but I knew no response was coming, so I continued. "Whatever you are, are you going to stay with me until the end? Are you going to be there when I go mad?"

His brow furrowed deeper, his grip on my chin tightened a little…but he nodded.

"Will you kill me when the time comes? If I lose my mind and start h-hurting people, will you promise to stop me?"

His eyebrow rose at that in a…scolding way. But my chest tightened to pain; this was so important.

"Please promise me," I whispered, shoving tears away so I could see him. "I don't want to become a…a…m-m-monster."

The moment the word left my mouth, a flash flood of tears and fear tore out of me impossible to stop. No matter what happened, no matter where I was, it felt important to have *someone* willing to do the terrible thing for me, just in case.

But the tears blurred my vision too much to see whether he'd given me a nod or a shake; all I felt was his head and free arm curl around me, clutch me, as my body finally crashed into darkness.

***

I woke to shaking. A hand on my good shoulder, shaking me awake.

I looked up and found Cass there motioning me up off the floor. He was silhouetted by the sun, his eyes like spotlights above me, his finger back on his lips telling me to be quiet again.

And all I could think was *what now*?

"*Danger*," my wolf said in answer.

I was half-way to more panic when my raven clarified, "*Annoying*."

I almost laughed. It was *not* what I expected her to say; her tone, too, was irritated and snippy.

Then I heard it—*snarfling*. Snorting, squealing, hooves upon the dry earth. Hogs. *Boars*. Dozens of them just outside the ruin, rooting and running and shoving at each other with razor-sharp tusks, some short while others jutted out from their jaws nearly a foot long.

Vaguely, I remembered learning from some video long ago that boar were dangerous—and I knew from experience that Millie could be deadly both in and out of boar form—but…in the moment? The stampede was mesmerizing. Earthquaking. So normal in comparison to all I'd seen and done in the last few hours-days-weeks, it was a breath of fresh air.

Until one massive hog snarfled his way into the ruin's open doorway. As he let out a raging squeal, I found myself swept off my feet…but not by the thousand-pound animal sizing me up.

Cass had me in his arms like I weighed nothing, cradled six feet off the ground as the creature charged and sprinted straight under me *through Cass's legs*. As if they were made of air. As if he truly was the ghost I'd originally thought he was.

But…how could a ghost carry me?

I glanced down and watched the boar run through Cass again, a look of confused frustration on its face, before it finally darted out of the ruin.

"Unreal," I murmured.

But to that my raven and wolf replied, "*Real*."

***

"So…like…*what are you*?"

A couple hours later as we walked through a bright, airy forest of stunted oak trees, I couldn't help but ask Cass that all-important question, if for no other reason than to distract from how far we still had to go to reach the city. We'd been bouncing between short, fast walks along the property's narrow, paved lanes while dipping into the brushy forest to avoid the presidential guard patrols that drove down them at random intervals.

"Are you a ghost?" It felt like the sort of thing to ask outright.

Cass waggled his head, giving me no clarity either way.

"Are you a hallucination?"

He shook his head firmly at that, but…c'mon, like my brain would actually tell me if he was.

"I wouldn't be surprised if you were," I told him, ducking under a branch as he held it out of the way for me. "I'd be grateful, honestly, that my brain let me keep you for a little longer. No one wants to die alone. I bet most dying people would take a hallucination of a friend if they could have it."

As we reached a ruin wall too high for me to jump, he leapt down and held his arms out to me, and as I leaned into them—felt the pressure of his hands against my sides, how he took my full weight and lowered me so gently to the ground—I couldn't help but wonder…

"Maybe it's a mate thing."

But as I said it, his hands tightened their grip on me. I glanced up into his piercing gaze, surprised to see concern and a question in it.

"I just mean…Maybe this is my mind's way of…handling…the loss of you, you know? When Giselle lost Aldric, she wept and screamed and went almost catatonic. If I hadn't been there to guilt her into moving, the Knights would've probably captured her by that riverbank. Killed her, maybe. My mind probably knew losing my mate would paralyze me too, so it figured out a way to protect me from the truth. Maybe you're the beautiful lie keeping me alive."

He continued to cling to me with that confused look on his handsome face. And I…let myself enjoy it. The illusion of him. I slid my hands up his strange invisible-fur-lined arms, pressing gently, wishing I could feel that magnetic tug under the skin one more time, or smell his bonfire scent.

"Or maybe I just want to believe that," I laughed at myself. "After all, *you* didn't accidentally mate with me. *You* didn't make one more silly disastrous mistake in a string of them."

I could have left it there. I probably should have. But when was I going to get another chance to tell him how I felt? Eventually he'd be gone, or I would be.

"To be fair," I admitted, "I don't think accidentally mating with you was a mistake. Or, if it was, I'm not ashamed of it. I'd like to think you wouldn't hate me for it—don't tell me if you would, please. I don't want to know."

Cass finally released me and, even though this ghostly touch was incomparable to his touch when he was alive and with me, I missed the connection as soon as it was gone.

But again, he was so…odd. He seemed like an impossible thing, both solid and ethereal depending on what the moment called for. Like some sort of useful tool in a pretty package. A Scottish army knife.

And then, it hit me. "Are you…one of my new powers?"

From the light switches in my inner sanctum, I knew at least two more abilities were due to kick in at some point. One of the switches featured me with a larger version of me overlayed. The other featured me surrounded by copies of myself. I didn't know how either would explain him, but…

His reaction was immediate. Cass nodded soberly, lifting and dropping his chin just once while staring me straight in the eye.

"You're a power," I repeated.

He nodded again!

"Oh!" I said, both excited and disappointed by the possibility. "Okay. W-What sort of power would you be?"

In response, he held his hand out palm down and slid it slowly away from him.

"…You're a…skateboard?"

The very edges of his lips curled up momentarily as he shook his head and did the gesture again.

"You're…something to pet? Like a therapy dog?"

He shook his head adamantly against that, his lips still trying not to grin.

"…You'll…tell me later?"

He nodded, and a smile that did brutal things to my belly, and lower, bloomed across his beautiful face. Then, he held out his hand to me, and when I took it, he pulled me along, hustling me faster through the forest.

Hours later, when night finally fell and we'd navigated an entire central area on the property around a massive presidential palace, and long after we left the scrubland and forest and passed into green pastures and more signs of civilization, Cass guided me to an old, disused fire pit hidden at the base of a tree and sat me down. He motioned for me to wait and disappeared into the brush without disturbing a single leaf.

I must've waited there for an hour, long enough that both my raven and wolf had come and gone on surveys of the local area. They informed me that the edge of one of Rome's outermost neighborhoods was mere blocks away, and I would be in the city tomorrow morning. Then my raven returned with a crisp 20 euro note clutched in her beak, which she dropped into my lap before soaring away again.

"*What's this for*?" I asked. "*And where did you get it*?"

"*Travel*," she replied, ignoring my second question.

I added the tiny blip of guilt I felt to the mountain already inside me. Then I smirked, wondering how many alters with my ability to farsee had ever used their creatures to steal. Probably more than I'd care to know.

Then Cass returned with a collection of more stolen things and I added those bits of guilt to the mountain too.

"Where did all of this come from?" I asked, not expecting an actual answer.

There was a large metal pot, a small bowl, a lighter, a bottle of water, and a random loaf of bread in a bag, as well as a weird gnarly root that looked like spindly fingers and a huge bunch of reddish-brown flowering stalks. These he laid in a heap to the side as he passed me the loaf of bread and gestured for me to eat it. Then he set about building a small fire. He placed the large pot over the flame and then laid a flat stone at the bottom of the pot. He placed the smaller bowl on the stone. Then around it, he poured the water. Just enough. Barely an inch or two. He broke the root into pieces and dropped a few into the water. Then he crushed some of the flowering stalks and added those to the water too. And at the very end, he took the pot's lid and flipped it upside down before covering the pot with it.

It was a fascinating little ceremony, even if I had no idea what he was doing.

At least, not until steam stopped escaping from the pot, and he removed the scalding lid to reveal…a thin layer of oil and water that smelled of herby aged wood and celery in the smaller bowl. He'd…he'd steamed the oil out of the plants. A miniscule amount, but…still impressive.

"Is that angelica and mugwort?" I finally asked.

Cass nodded and my heart leapt again with gratitude. In all the chaos, I hadn't thought about hiding myself that way, even though I was about to wander into one of the biggest cities on Earth, at the epicenter of a foreign Alter Supreme's court.

"Thank you, Cass."

He simply nodded and grabbed my backpack, tucking the rest of the unused root and flowers inside. I supposed we'd need to make more whenever we got where we were going.

"Are you going to tell me about this power now?" I asked.

Again, he made the gesture for "in time" and I supposed that one-sided game of charades would happen when we got where we were going too. Then he laid down in the dirt and held out his arm as a pillow for me again.

This time, he didn't wince when I drew closer and tucked myself in the space he'd left me, and a funny-sad thought struck me.

"You know, this is probably what it would have been like for us if we'd run away together last year," I said. "Us sleeping in the dirt, trying to find a place to hide in plain sight."

To my surprise, Cass shook his head at that, a look of disdain on his face…and I didn't know what to think about my own power being repulsed by the thought of running away with me.

I knew how it made me *feel*, though. Inappropriate anger spiked inside me as sour as candy.

"Don't shake your head at me," I scolded. "You *would* have run away with me if I'd been brave enough. And I would have run away with you if I knew everything I know now."

Cass's disdain deepened. He rolled his eyes and shook his head harder, as if he didn't believe me.

Even though it didn't matter—or perhaps because it didn't—I said the scary part out loud before turning away, "Well, maybe *you* didn't really mean it when you offered, but I did."

CHAPTER 16

Dawn colored the world around us a few hours later, as if someone had steeped a teabag of it in the sky. Tepid purples gave way to dusky reds, then daisy yellows, before the blue seeped in and the rising sun set the world on fire.

Cass had remained beside me all night and I found his eyes open and unblinking, studying me, when I opened mine. At the sight of him, my stupid sleepy heart leapt with hope and relief and peace, which my brain crushed a moment later. For one glorious second, I'd forgotten it wasn't really him.

"Good morning," I said anyway, although I couldn't keep the disappointment out of my voice, as I replaced the waking fantasy with every-day reality. "Bus. Bank. Phone. Then we'll know how screwed I really am."

It felt like there was a leak inside me as I rose from the ground. Sour rot slowly filled my stomach from below as I dabbed the little oil from Cass's distillation experiment on my arms, legs, and neck, poured the tiny trickle left into the water bottle for later, and gathered the few things we had into my bag before I walked four blocks to the nearest bus stop. I paid for a ticket and glowered at Cass where he sat beside me, completely clean despite sleeping on the same dirty ground as I did for multiple days. I looked like a crunchy, crusty dust bunny by comparison and more than a few people kept their distance as I boarded the bus and picked a seat at the back.

Arriving in Rome felt like stepping into a time traveler's theme park. Everywhere you looked, there were people on cell phones, on Vespas. Everywhere you looked, there were ruins and museums and signs telling tourists how to reach one ancient wonder or another. The young and the very old were smashed up against each other in every nook and cranny of the city.

We passed the Colosseum.

We passed the Roman Forum.

Then a Basilica the size of a small town beside a gyro shop.

And once we finally got off the bus and started walking, we passed the Spanish Steps, then the Trevi Fountain. That one was wedged between gelato shops that were so crowded you couldn't even read all the flavors until you reached the counter.

Lemon, coconut, espresso, wine—I had a scent headache long before I smelled my first alter, and when I did? Holy moly, I added a pharmacy to our list of errands to run. I'd need painkillers *asap*, unless I was willing to risk walking up to random alters on the street to ask them their form.

I had anticipated the electric honeysuckle scent of magick, though, and I wasn't disappointed. Magick was *everywhere*, so thick in certain spots, I could tell where ancient ruins were hidden under the streets simply by identifying which gutters were flooded with orange-pink energy. No joke, the entire city seemed ankle-deep in magick; it kicked up into the air in little spritzes with every step I took.

But…and it was a *huge* but…

I'd picked this city to do two things—to gain access to the alter library and to find a spider. Not just any spider, the Spider Lady of Silks and Secrets.

Sounded simple enough.

There was just one problem. Of all the alter forms I'd encountered since joining the shifter world, there was only one animal I knew of that *didn't* have their own unique scent. Or rather, that smelled like *nothing*…and happened to have eight legs.

No, the identifier for spider alters wasn't their scent, but their eyes. That momentary flicker of silver that happened every time they shifted their gaze quickly from side to side.

Which wouldn't have been a problem if *every third person* in Rome wasn't wearing sunglasses.

I couldn't tell who the spiders were.

But I *could* tell who the ravens were, the wolves, the bears, the dragons, and the deer. On a certain store-lined avenue, we even passed by a lion in the presence of a couple of vipers and I whipped my head so fast in that direction to check if it was Oriol that it hurt my already-sore neck.

None of them looked at me strangely, or did a double-take. None of them lingered as I passed by. It was only once I realized nobody recognized me that the discomfort in my stomach finally settled, and I let myself assume that Cass's little tincture had worked. Or, maybe, that my filth disguised me.

I would have kept the camouflage, honestly, if I could have, but…the moment I saw the bank where Cass had stashed money for me, I knew I couldn't. It wasn't just a local branch of a bank chain; it was *the* national bank, located in an actual Renaissance revival palace. There was zero chance I was walking in looking like a tangle of sea garbage washed up on the shore.

Luckily for me, there was a fast-food chain literally across the street. With the change I had from my bus ticket, I bought a meal and used their bathroom to take a sink-shower—the best I could do until I had cash in hand. Honestly, I didn't do a bad job. I looked presentable, at least. And thankfully the dirt on my clothes was entirely dry so most of it brushed right off.

After applying more of Cass's scent eraser, I sat and ate my meal slowly, until my hair dried. Then I walked into that bank like I owned it.

It was amazing what you could get away with when you feigned confidence…and knew how to magickally speak the language. They had me with a bank manager less than ten minutes after entering. And with a soft lie that I had been mugged and therefore had no ID or debit cards to show, they simply presented me with a list of security questions to answer while the man chided with the tone of a father that, "*you should let me call the police for you. Your safety is a national point of pride, signorina. This is a terrible thing that your valuables were taken from you.*"

"*Thank you, signore, but I just want to get home.*"

"*Perhaps that is best, so you can dump this young man who does nothing for you.*"

I blinked at that, following the manager's fatherly scolding eye to Cass, who was waiting and watching from a few feet away.

"*If he will not protect you from thieves, throw the whole man away,*" the manager said, so seriously. "*A civilized young lady like you deserves a prince.*"

I smiled at what the manager didn't know; that Cass *had* been a prince once upon a time, technically, and that he'd done far more for me than I could ever repay.

Like the bank's security questions. Cass had made them all

personal. The answers, easy to guess.

A word for emotional trust—grace.

Our shadow man's haunt—Galdere.

My nickname for you—heart.

Not a bear but a…—wolf.

Twenty minutes later, I had a debit card, a line of credit, and a bank statement for the *hundred thousand pounds* Cass had stashed in Italy for me through a business account under both of our names. I couldn't help wondering how much he'd stashed elsewhere…and in how many places.

But as I went next to get a phone and a SIM card, I guessed the most likely answer to that question—everywhere. Cass had likely stashed money in every country on this continent. He'd had no way of knowing I would end up in Italy, so he'd planned for every outcome just in case.

It…It was how I had to be. Thorough. Careful. So, the first thing I did was log into the bank account, change the passwords, and add a security question of my own: *What five-word phrase means 'I love you?'*

All the questions Cass had chosen were vague enough, I doubted anyone else could guess the answers, but that fifth one? Only Cass and I knew the answer to that, so…now only I knew.

***

"*Is it month to month?*"

"*Yes, signorina, but we would need to see proof of savings.*"

"*I'll take it.*"

Becoming a fugitive had already changed me in ways that made sense after the fact, but which surprised me in the moment. Before, I'd been nervous to make doctor's appointments. I'd dreaded phone calls and called my mom to fill out official paperwork even though it was easier to google most of the time. I'd made royal decrees and declarations while squeezing the arm of my chair out of sight of the people I was talking to. Now? I didn't have time for fear. Or rather, some Bigger Dread had *pushed* the fear into a very specific box in my mind related to running out of time. There was a structurally unsound dam looming over Italy. Who knew how long it would be before the dam broke and Rav and his allies poured into the Spider Court and drowned everyone inside?

I couldn't leave until I either found Idalia and Giselle, or the invading horde drove me out, so I chose to settle in instead. Before attempting to call my friends, I hired an *agente immobiliare* to find me a stronghold to survive the coming flood. And she'd found one, right in the center of the city.

It wasn't fancy by any stretch of the imagination—I wasn't trying to speed-spend the savings Cass had laid aside for me—but it was a beautiful two-bedroom apartment with enough space to hold my friends if they'd survived. In that way, I guessed, it was aspirational. Wooden beams stretched the length of the ceiling, art was everywhere, and it had a private patio. Someone had *started* to tear through one of the interior walls, then stopped for some reason, so there was a large "artistic" hole looking in on one of the bedrooms. And the building also had round-the-clock security and a rooftop access that overlooked a large park, which would make for a semi-dependable escape option with my wings if someone tried to surround me.

One thorough inspection by Cass and my creatures, one massive deposit, and some paperwork later, and I was entrenched in Rome like a slow tourist. And the first thing I did the moment the door closed behind me was tear open my backpack, rip open that plastic bag full of phone numbers and dial every. single. one. after turning on my phone's VPN.

There was no answer from Fern. Or Yas. There was no answer from Mom or Scarlett, and I tried to hold back a swell of vomit. I even tried Corby's number. Nothing.

But then, I tried Brodie's. It rang for almost a minute, ratcheting my anxiety higher and higher with each buzz until—

Click. "Hello?"

It wasn't Brodie. It was… "Millie?"

"M-My lady?"

"Oh my Goddess, Millie, yes, it's me! A-Are you okay? Is Brodie okay? Is Scar—"

"She wasn't there, my lady," Millie said, yanking on my heart when she clarified, "Scarlett wasn't in the part of Hamingja we were able to search."

I swallowed my heartache. "O-Okay. But are you all right? Are you safe?"

"Yes, but…hold a moment, Brodie's here. He wants to speak with you—"

"My lady?" His rich Scottish brogue burst through the phone, tight and stuttering.

"Brodie, a-are you hurt? What happened?"

"Big fella got me right in the arse with his *cabar-fèidh*." He griped, and I couldn't help laughing—he'd been stabbed in the butt by an antler. "Then a bunch of the wee ones—the little furry beasties—bit me all to shite, but…I'm all right, dinnae worry about me. Give me a few days an' the moon'll fix me right up." Then his voice dropped as he added, "Couldn'y find your friend, I'm sorry."

"Everyone survived?"

"My team did, but…"

"But?"

"Master Mahon's brother has summoned me to Denmark."

"*Denmark*?"

"Aye. He said he and the Raven King wanted to speak with me. Said that Cassian was no longer in charge, which I already ken on account of him being dead.

"Master Mahon—the one wedged inside the king's arsehole—told me I'm to take orders from him now, and…well…I dinnae take orders from anybody but you, my lady, so we haven't returned yet."

"Where are you?"

"Iceland."

"I-Is that safe? That's the Raven King's territory."

"I have a way out," he replied. "Tell me where you are, and we'll be there tonight."

At that, Cass stared at me and nodded, urging me to say yes. But I didn't know which would be more useful—Brodie here, protecting me, or him there helping Fern and Yas. And technically Archer was right; I wasn't his lady liege anymore.

I swallowed nervously and turned away from Cass. "Brodie, Archer's not wrong. The king gave my queendom to him. As for Fern and Yasmina, I-I can't get ahold of them. I don't know if any of the guests from my holy day are dead. I was about to call Asterius, but Ulric Garand drew a target on his back at Lunasa and I don't know if he's even still alive. I-I'm safe for the moment, but… You don't have to help me anymore—"

Cass's hand landed on my good arm and spun me to face him. There was confusion and frustration on his face.

"And it's probably safer not to," I added.

Cass's brow bunched at that, imploring. He glanced at the phone as if he wished he could speak for himself, which…surprised me.

I continued anyway. "No matter what, Brodie, I-I don't think you should go to Denmark. You know about Rav's power. If he touches you…"

Brodie chuffed. "My lady, I cannae decide if Archer Mahon is just a bawbag or if he's a full-on rocket, but whatever he is, he's not my lord. And that king took you captive. If I caught him with wings, I'd rip 'em straight off."

"But—"

"No buts. Give me a few hours and the might of your army will go to ground until you need them. Mahon can recruit his own hot air for all I care. In the meantime, what do ye say we split the difference. I'll send Millie and Jonesy to ye while I go to Glengarriff and see what's what."

His words were the warm hug I'd needed for days now.

"Thank you, Brodie. I'm in—"

"Nah-Nah! Wait a tick, don't tell me, tell her."

A second later, Millie was back on and we made a quick plan for her to meet me in the Piazza Navona in two days. Then I said goodbye to them and ended the call, dialing the next number on my list and putting it on speaker before I'd even taken a breath.

Asterios was probably dead. And I *hated* how high that probability was. It was like standing at the epicenter of an earthquake; Asterios had been right beside Rav when Ulric called him a traitor. I couldn't imagine a scenario where he survived that…unless Rav took him as a prisoner.

And I was accidentally calling the very person trying to hunt me down.

No sooner had that possibility come to mind, but I heard a *click* on the other end of the line.

A click…and silence.

No one spoke, not on his end and not on mine. I suddenly couldn't. Cass stared at me in confusion, but I didn't know who was on the other end of the line…

"Say something, *min skat*."

I almost swallowed my own tongue as Rav's voice filled the air around me. And his pet name for me hit like a sucker punch. So did the loneliness I could hear in him. I knew Rav was by himself from that tone alone; he would *never* let anyone else hear him like that.

Cass prickled at the sound of Rav's voice too; he stepped away as if he couldn't be near me with the reminder of Rav's existence there.

"Talk to me," Rav whispered when I remained silent.

I didn't know what to say, but the words found their way out anyway. "How could you do that? How could you take my queendom away?"

"*Min skat*—"

"What were you thinking? Do you hate me that much?" My throat tightened.

"Hate you?" His voice rasped. "*Hate you*? The woman I nearly butchered half the Gathering Table to save. The woman who clawed the eyes out of my Second rather than return to me. The woman I haven't been able to stop thinking about even though you broke my heart and threatened to leave me forever because I pointed out you don't have enough experience yet to rule equally with me. Oh yes, I must hate you."

Competing emotions tore at each other inside me. He was saying true things; I didn't need my aura of honesty to know that. But those truths were twisted, and they didn't erase other, more hurtful ones.

"You called me weak. You took me hostage. Trapped me in magick. Tried to force me to marry you! You *murdered* my friend—"

"I made mistakes!" he roared.

I froze. That…that surprised me. So did the hiss in his voice, the desperation.

"*The moment* I trapped you in magick I knew I'd made a mistake. The moment I suggested you weren't incredible I knew I should have shut my mouth because I was speaking nonsense. But my greatest sin was trying to minimize my feelings for you because I was afraid of losing control. The moment you pulled away from me, I lost something far more important. Tell me how to apologize for it and I will. Tell me how to *show you* how much I can't live without you, and I'll do it."

I didn't know how. Mostly because half of me didn't believe him. This…had to be a trap, didn't it? He thought some pretty words would trick me into giving myself up.

Stupid. Me for thinking any of this was real and him for thinking I'd fall for it!

I steeled myself and let the moment settle. "What happened at Lunasa?"

"To your precious accomplices?" he growled.

"To the guests, to *your friend*, to mine," I clarified.

"Are you just gloating now?"

His question surprised me again. Gloating? Why would asking about the status of our friends seem like gloating to him? Unless…unless they'd all gotten away. Fern, Yas, Asterios. He would have brought them up as potential leverage to force me back.

I realized: "You don't know where any of them are, do you."

Which meant…!

"You don't have Scarlett either."

He would've brought her up *immediately* if he still knew where she was. My spirits soared as I realized he didn't have anything. Not Scar. Not Fern or Yas or Asterios. Not my mom. His next words all but confirmed it.

"Take care, *min skat. You* may have immunity from what's happened between us but they do not. Every one has a bounty on their head, one which will only lift once you're with me again."

My relief fizzled at that. It didn't really matter if they were free; they were still in grave danger…and Rav didn't care if they died.

But maybe…

"Rav…" —I swallowed a throat tightening ball of fear— "If I promised to end my own life so I wouldn't be a danger to anyone, would you promise not to hurt them?"

The moment the words left my mouth, two things happened simultaneously. The first was that Cass recoiled, his face awash in incredulous anger. At me. He looked betrayed. The second happened a moment later as I heard a horrible low purr of rage erupt from the phone.

"*Min skat*," Rav hissed. "If you harm yourself in any way…If you attempt to end your life—or Goddess help you, *actually succeed*—I will punish every single person you love, do you understand me? I'll hunt them to the ends of the earth and everyone who dies trying to keep them from me will be *your fault*."

…huh?

"I don't *want* to die, Rav. But…it's inevitable. It's going to happen sooner or later and I don't want to hurt anyone before I go. I don't want to be responsible for the Great Secret being revealed either. This is the best option for all of us. You don't have to hunt me down; I won't hurt anybody. It's a win-win—"

His voice snapped as he cut me off. "You will live or there will be terrible consequences, do you understand me?"

I *didn't* understand. I couldn't imagine any consequence could be worse than losing my mind and becoming a plague of terror upon the earth, a creature feared more than any other.

I was just trying to do what was best for everybody. I mean, I *fully* intended to protect my allies first, but afterward, I was prepared to make that sacrifice if I had to. Heck, if at that point I still had the mental clarity to ask the Goddess whether I'd fulfilled my purpose and she said yes? It seemed like the best way to ensure I died peacefully. Painlessly.

Unless…unless he *really* wanted to kill me himself.

"Rav, do you…*want* to hurt me? Do you hate me—"

"Again with that word!" he barked, almost laughing. "Come to me and let me show you just how much I hate you when I tie you to your throne beside me. See how much I hate you when I slide our wedding band onto your finger for the Goddess and all of creation to see."

The record scratched in my head again. He still wanted to marry me?

A deep molasses chuckle escaped him as he added, "Hate you… Come here and say that to my face while it's nestled between your silky thighs."

At that, Cass turned and walked right through the wall, out of the room.

And I…just sort of froze, my mind reeling from everything Rav had just said.

"I'm coming for you, *min skat*. Hide, if finding you is my penance for all I've done wrong. Run from me, if chasing you is how you wish me to show you my love. Anticipate me. Delight in your impending capture. *That* is inevitable. And once we are together again, you'll finally understand you call it hate only because I love in ways the world has taught you to fear."

Then I heard a click, and the Raven King was gone.

CHAPTER 17

Scarlett is safe. Mom is safe. Fern is safe. Yasmina is safe. Corby is…safe.

I kept those words on a running loop in my mind, believing in some small way that thinking them might make them true, as I walked the early morning streets of Rome. It was drizzling. The air smelled of wet soil, rich coffee, and buttery *cornetti*, a perfect perfume for my solo trek across the city in search of Idalia's library.

I was alone, but I wasn't. My creatures were with me, sure, but "the power that was Cass" was too, even if he wouldn't show himself.

After Rav's mention of faces framed by silky thighs the night before, Cass had left the room and refused to return, even when I talked at the apartment walls for an hour, swearing I hadn't wanted to hear any of that. But later, in the middle of the night, I'd felt him slide onto the bed behind me. His arm materialized back in its familiar place beneath my head in lieu of the bed's terrible pillow I would need to replace.

Cass was gone—or rather, he *disappeared*—when I woke up. He didn't reappear when I dressed or stepped out of the apartment, but I caught a flash of him standing guard outside the *pasticceria* where I bought breakfast. He blinked away again the second I opened the door to leave.

He was mad at me…which…I guess made sense? After all, my raven had been ticked at me plenty of times since entering my life. This new power might share the same attitude.

But…something about his behavior rubbed me the wrong way. It seemed so…human, at times. Maybe it was a mirror of me? Maybe my addled mind had manifested Cass instead of showing me myself?

Goddess, I *hoped* I didn't have to deal with another one of me. I had a very healthy respect for everyone in my life who tolerated my presence, but there were plenty of times I didn't count myself amongst them.

If this Cass-power *was* supposed to be me…what sort of power would that be anyway? I wasn't some vanity project walking around with a hand mirror in my pocket just in case I needed to practice kissy faces or something. I didn't have some deep psychological flaw that I knew of which required me to face off with myself, but maybe some part of me needed to face off with Cass about something. Or maybe my subconscious was just…supplying me with a friend. Ugh, why did that both fill me with relief *and* make me feel a little pathetic?

Ultimately, though, I was just grateful to have someone with me while I tried to figure out the directions to Idalia's archives.

You see, in between my original trip to Ireland to help with Lunasa prep and that day Rav and I had returned to Hamingja to find Idalia breaking Giselle out, Yasmina hadn't had time to get permission for me to visit the library. And after, Idalia had been unreachable. So all I had was the instructions for how to find the library without a guarantee that I could or that I would be welcome when I got there.

Which meant I was walking a mile and a bit across the city in the rain on a wish and a prayer that the librarian at Idalia's archives was feeling generous. Or, a large part of me hoped, they had some sort of direct line of communication with Idalia and I could solve two problems with one hail Mary solution.

But…

Any dreams of "easy" died the closer I came to the address Yasmina had given me for the library, as my GPS brought me to the foot of the ancient Roman Colosseum, then veered to the Northeast only a few hundred feet to the base of a soft hill and a gate, then beyond to an unassuming side driveway.

There wasn't a giant building full of books waiting for me, not that I'd ever actually expected one. There wasn't a group of weirdos with silver-flashing eyes and too-long straight white teeth loitering nearby either. No, there was nothing at all to suggest one of the world's most extensive and secret libraries was nearby.

There was, however, a ticket kiosk and a perfectly friendly human woman selling admission to a guided tour of the Domus Aurea, the ruins of the Roman Emperor Nero's once great and enormous palace. And this fit the instructions Yasmina received when she had called the library initially for information. They read:

Buy a ticket.

Graze the golden spider in the room where its legs can touch every wall.

Follow its silk to the west along the forbidden path beyond the two guardians.

There you will find our lady's web of silk and secrets.

Follow the path to its end.

Bring light. Bring water. Do not get caught. Enter at your own risk.

Did *graze the golden spider* sound naughtier than it probably was? You betcha. And were those the most promising set of directions to a library I'd ever received? I mean, obviously. I was almost vibrating with excitement.

"*Good morning, two tickets?*" the woman asked as soon as I stepped forward.

I had to turn around to confirm what she already had; Cass was standing right behind me, not quite looking at me, looking totally out of place in his completely dry clothing despite the rain.

"*Yes, please,*" I said, making a mental note to buy myself a wallet as I pulled out the small wad of cash in my pocket and counted out the nearly fifty euros I was about to fork over before her sweet voice interrupted me—

"*No, no! Sweetheart, only two dollars for locals.*" Her tone was so lovely, panicked with insult.

"*Oh, I'm not a local,*" I told her gently, forcing myself to pay attention as I manually made my mouth form English words. "I would like an English tour please."

At this, she tutted, refusing to take all the money I offered her. "Well students are two euros too. *Give the rest as a gift to whoever is teaching you Italian. Your accent is perfection.*"

I didn't fight her on it, but I did pop the rest of the cash into a nearby donation case as we passed.

I'd lucked into coming at the right time. Tours were different depending on the day, less in-depth on the weekdays, and more complete on the weekends. It was a Saturday, so we were getting the full show. I'd also lucked into a tour group that was entirely human.

What I *hadn't* lucked into was getting through Cass's icy façade. We stood by the entrance, staring out at the rain together while more arrived for our guided tour and I kept sneaking glances at him waiting for him to thaw. He didn't. I knew he could sense me looking, but he kept his eyes squarely on the park outside, refusing to meet my gaze. I wanted to scold him. I wanted to argue with him. I wanted him to act more like my friend again, if that was ever possible. But this wasn't the place to bring up why he was angry. We had more important things to do.

When the tour guide finally assembled us all together and motioned us down the long, winding ramp that led underground, I fell to the back of the group and handed Cass my phone to read Yasmina's instructions.

"Will you help me find the entrance?" I asked him when he handed it back.

He scowled at me and nodded as if it was obvious.

"Will you go with me to the library?"

His scowl deepened with annoyance as he nodded again, and I grinned.

"Will you dig me out if this whole place suddenly collapses on my head?"

I was only teasing—of course, I was only teasing—but his scowl gave way to a scared frown the likes of which I hadn't seen before. He finally met my eye, hurt and concerned. This time when he nodded, it was a soft gesture, such a small sincere nod it almost broke my heart.

I left it at that. I hated seeing that devastated look on his face. I'd hated it the night before and I hated it now.

We passed under a low arch, which Cass had to pretend to duck under to maintain his human persona, and found ourselves in a ruin I couldn't have anticipated without seeing it in person. It was…enormous. *Labyrinthine*. Where Asterios's tunnels in Crete had been short, narrow, and sealed off in some places, these were gargantuan and open like a rat's maze. The hallways were wide and nearly forty feet tall in some places, while the checkerboard configuration of adjoining chambers and closets and alcoves were smaller or larger as necessary for their function. And it was all built with 2000-year-old brick and stucco that had survived the passage of time despite other buildings being built right on top of it.

It was so easy to picture the palace as it had once been, regal and opulent and painted with frescoes, especially since so many of the frescoes were still intact featuring not just Roman gods, I was surprised to see, but Egyptian iconography too. Sphinxes and lotus flowers and human figures arranged like those in Egyptian hieroglyphics were everywhere you looked. Literally, I'd seen similar artwork just a few days ago, at the bottom of Alexandria's East Harbor floor.

And there was a reason, I soon learned.

"Egyptian artwork, styles, and even religions were very popular during the time of Emperor Nero because Rome ruled over Egypt from 30 BCE to 641 CE," the tour guide said. "Roman emperors depicted themselves as ancient Egyptian pharaohs not only because they technically *were* pharaohs, but also because Nero existed three thousand years after the period we refer to as "belonging to ancient Egypt." Dressing like the ancient Egyptians was like wearing a costume."

It was fascinating, but…that wasn't the piece of information that made me stop in my tracks and squeeze Cass's arm like I was about to scream.

A few minutes after entering the ruin, our guide led us into one of the palace's most recognizable features, the Octagonal Room with a large oculus in the ceiling that had once been open to the sky but was now covered in some sort of hard plastic. This room with its five adjoining chambers had been turned into a museum exhibit, containing statues of Nero depicted in his Egyptian pharaoh getup and artifacts from the Cult of Isis, and it was here that the tour guide shocked me.

"Nero had several notable teachers, including Seneca the Younger and Chaeremon, who served as the head of the Museion and Library of Alexandria."

I couldn't believe it. I'd ended up in Alexandria, Egypt, just a few blocks from history's most famous library by chance…only to arrive at the house of one of history's most infamous rulers, who had received some of his early teachings from the head curator of that very library.

It felt cosmically intentional, that journey somehow. Like a wink from the Goddess that I was on the right path…even if I didn't know where I was going or why yet.

That feeling of being on the right path struck again a second later when I realized…I was standing in a room with eight walls.

"Graze the golden spider in the room where its legs can touch every wall." I turned to Cass. "This is it, Cass. This is the first clue."

I turned so abruptly from the group, it probably looked ridiculous to anybody paying attention to me. That, or suspicious. I couldn't help myself, though. I wanted to find that golden spider so badly, I would've let it bite me just to know it was real.

"*Do you see anything?*" I asked my creatures, after the first chamber revealed nothing.

"*No*," they said.

Cass, too, shook his head as he emerged from the adjoining chamber across from the one I'd picked.

I was already stepping into the next chamber along the edge of the room before he turned toward his own on the other side. Nothing in that one either.

And then…

I have no idea how I spotted it…

The third chamber contained an ancient flue, a gravity fountain where water had once poured into the chamber as an aesthetic addition. It was dry now, but there, just inside the lip, in the dark, I saw…magick.

An unmistakable, undeniable spark of golden magick in the shape of a spider.

"Cass," I whisper-yelled. "Cass!"

He appeared out of nowhere behind me a moment later, and I pointed it out to him.

Even though I knew he was me, and I was basically asking for confirmation of my own opinion, I still asked, "Isn't that beautiful?"

His nod and soft awed smile made my heart sing. So did the encouraging motion of his head for me to reach for it. He didn't need to tell me twice. My fingers were already reaching, already grazing the glowing spot on the wall before I could stop myself—

"Excuse me. We do *not* touch the exhibit, please!" the tour guide shouted.

I jerked back, ashamed of myself. "*Sorry! I didn't mean to!*"

My accent and language, I could see, caught her off guard…and I felt a tiny twinge of guilt for using my gift that way, but it seemed like the only reason why she stopped glaring at me from where she stood twenty feet away.

Once she did, I turned back and found Cass smiling. *Beaming*. Staring at the wall.

For a moment, I couldn't tell why. There was nothing particularly standout about the basic brown brick wall—

Until a tiny glint of gold caught my eye as I moved my head. There was a spider-silk-thin line of gold running from the water channel, along the wall, and out into the center chamber. It was so fine, I could've held up a single hair on my head and completely hidden it from view.

At least, until I entered the central chamber again, chasing that thin thread of gold, and discovered my touch had summoned much more.

Magickal graffiti.

A web of gold had materialized across the ceiling of the domed room. No one but Cass and I could see it, but it was there, above everyone's heads like a net over the world. And there, on the far wall above the doorway through which we had entered, was a massive golden spider with legs as sharp as needles and as long as oars. It wasn't like my raven or wolf; it didn't have *weight*. It was two-dimensional.

Even so, it suddenly, and unceremoniously "rose" from where it laid along the wall and skittered right out of the room.

I darted to the doorway to follow it, but—

"We will continue our tour in just a few moments, please be patient," the tour guide said, stopping me cold.

I watched the golden spider scurry down the hall before it turned right and disappeared.

Impatience was a polite word for what I was feeling. A little despair was mixed in too.

But then Cass was there. His hand landed on my shoulder so reassuringly, his unblinking eye snapped in the direction the spider had fled, and he was gone. *Literally* gone, dematerializing like sea foam in a hard breeze.

Gah, I wanted to follow him so badly!

"*Trust*," my raven chided.

"*I do trust him. I'm just excited*," I told her, trying my best to pay attention to the woman sharing so much incredible information with us that I just couldn't focus on.

Not even when she finally told us all we were leaving the chamber and her suspicious eye turned on me like a teacher's against a wayward student. "*Where is your friend?*"

"*I...*"

"*We told you at the start of the tour, we must stay together. If he's gone off on his own, we will have to escort you both from the site.*"

Cass had incredible timing. He walked right through the far wall behind the entire tour group at that very second.

"*No, signora, he's there!*" I said, pointing. "*He's been here the whole time.*"

My gaslighting didn't dampen her suspicion; her gaze whipped in his direction in disgust, as if she could see through the "proof" of him still being in the room and refused to believe he was there. Still, she didn't kick us out, so that was a win. But I could feel her mistrust against the back of my head like a sixth sense as our tour continued.

I waited until she was talking again before I whispered to Cass, "Did you see where it went?"

And he nodded with a smile on his face that ratcheted my impatience even higher.

The golden magickal graffiti didn't stop in the Octagonal Room. Oh, no, it was *everywhere*. Outlining mosaic tile floors and frescoes. Webbing almost every domed ceiling. Crawling across the floor as tiny herds of golden spiders. The entire place felt alive suddenly, as if it had always been in use and the "ruin-ness" of it was just set design. A cool vibe they were going with this month.

And then, we entered the criptoportico, a *long* hallway chamber decorated in beautiful frescoes of Isis and palm trees…and griffins and black sphinxes and hippocampi and satyrs.

Hybrid creatures.

Creatures of multiple forms.

All in honored places along the walls. All connected by those thin threads of magickal golden spider silk.

It was there that Cass reached for my hand and drew my attention to the far end of the hall, and I almost screamed again in excitement.

"Follow its silk to the west along the forbidden path beyond the two guardians. Cass, that's amazing!"

Two white sphinxes—two *guardians*—blocked the hallway and any further tour in that direction. But beyond them, the giant golden spider loomed like a neon sign upon the wall, swaddled in more of that ephemeral magickal silk, urging us on.

I…got an idea then. As unsuspiciously as I could, I edged closer and closer to the sphinxes until the guide took a concerned step toward me, at which point I backed up until I was nearly pressed against the wall, and I waited for one of the other tourists to draw her attention away.

"*Can you see that?*" I asked my raven.

"*Yes.*"

"*Fly through the wall. Check out the way ahead. Where does it lead? What can you see*?"

I felt her leave my body a second later. Then I closed my eyes to watch her journey through the viewing windows in my inner sanctum.

There was brick-darkness-more brick-darkness, on and on like a sideways layer cake for eons. Until she reached a descending staircase and flew deeper-deeper-deeper right before she came to a sudden, view-shaking halt.

"*Dropoff*," my raven said suddenly, turning again.

She found another tunnel shortly after, but she declared that one a dead-end too. Three more of these and I called her back as the guide said that our time in this part of the site was coming to an end.

But as my raven returned to me, she warned, "*Darkness. No magick.*"

That didn't seem possible. The golden spider was *right there* on the wall, as if it was waiting for us to chase it. Maybe that's what the problem was. It wouldn't move on again until it knew we were following.

Unfortunately, there *was* no following. We couldn't. Not when we had the guide's nearly undivided attention. Not when she finally, bluntly stepped between us and the sphinxes, coaxing us back in the opposite direction.

Still, it was there. The entrance was there. We just needed a way to slip through.

CHAPTER 18

"Millie!"

"My lady! Thank goodness!"

I was standing in the Piazza Navona hiding under my hoodie using the thousands of flowers being sold by vendors at the center of the plaza to stave off a migraine, when Millie Davies spotted me waving through the crowd and ran for me. Enveloped me in her muscled arms.

"It's so good to see you, Mills," I said, so choked for words I had no idea what else to say. What *could* you say to someone who'd put themselves in harm's way so many times for you?

"You as well! We arrived just this morning. Couldn't wait to find you."

At that, she turned and revealed Jonesy to me; I'd met him before, at the camp just outside Giselle's chateau in France, a young kid barely older than I was with dark skin, dark eyes, and a scent of musky coriander—he was a water buffalo alter. He'd also been the one who asked me to teach their entire squad how to farsee with their animals.

"Jonesy?" I said, offering him my hand.

"Hello, my lady." He shook it, then gave me a quick, nervous bow anyway. "Glad to see you're still with us."

"But why are you alone like this, out in the open?" Millie scolded. "This place is chock-a-block full of our kind. I'm surprised no one's spotted you yet."

Then she sniffed and bristled with concern. "Why do you smell…human?"

"I'm wearing something to mask my scent," I explained. "Something Cass came up with."

Their eyes tightened with sympathy for me, at the loss of him, I knew. But they also looked…concerned.

"Your scent and hair might be disguised, but your face isn't," Millie said. "You should really be wearing more. An actual mask. Glasses. Dye in your hair. You have one of the most famous faces on the planet."

I snorted at that. That seemed a little hyperbolic.

"I don't think so, Mills."

Millie and Jonesy eyed each other then, before she pulled out her cell phone and offered it to me.

"Yes. You do," she said, motioning to…a picture of me on her phone.

Ten minutes later, as we stepped into the apartment and locked the door behind us, Millie had to guide me by my shoulders to keep me from walking into things as I continued to swipe through the images on her camera roll. There were *hundreds* of me. Or rather, there were hundreds of images featuring *the same* picture of me. That photo Cass had once taken of me at Hrafnagud in the beautiful green dress. The one he'd sent to all the other Alter Supremes. My official portrait, more or less.

All the pictures on Millie's phone were candid; none were of the picture itself. No, she'd *found* my portrait in a hundred different places while traveling across the continent with Brodie and Cass and our army, hunting cult members, hunting Rolfe. The picture appeared on the bodies of tall wolves and vampires, as well as in abandoned encampments, ruins, even those workshops where the air was so choked with silver particles that members of Rav's militia had died breathing them in.

This all meant that the picture of me Cass had found on the tall wolf Idalia had killed wasn't a fluke.

When I called Brodie shortly after, he confirmed he'd also seen the pictures of me distributed all over the place.

"I don't understand," I told him. "Why would my picture be everywhere? I mean, *after* Rav made me a fugitive, I could almost understand sharing it, but these pictures are from months ago."

"We don't know either, my lady," Brodie said. "There's the obvious possibility—the cult is hunting you."

I grunted my agreement. It *was* obvious.

"But wouldn't they be hunting *all* of the Supremes then?" I asked.

Millie shrugged. "We found photos of Cassian scattered in places as well, along with half a dozen other people, but none of them are public figures."

Curious.

"And Cassian had a real bug up his bum about it," Jonesy revealed. "He commanded us to burn any pictures we found of you on sight."

At that, I pushed. "Cass would definitely have had a theory about it."

Brodie sighed over the phone. "He…suspected the cult put a bounty on your head, lass. What better way to destroy the king before a war than to kill his queen? Cass reasoned that if you mated with the king and that bond was severed, the Raven King would be…handicapped in the fight ahead, so-to-speak."

That made a sour sort of sense. And…it made me wonder something about Violette and Ulric that I hadn't previously. Before trapping me in the magick of Hamingja, Rav had said sending Violette to mate with Ulric would "neuter him" somehow.

Had…had that been Rav's plan? To mate Violette to Ulric and then kill her?

I shivered at the thought. And added Violette to the list of people in my mind who might need saving, before the end of this.

But then, Brodie told me something that broke my heart.

"Your place in all this was always on Cassian's mind, my lady," he said. "Before the cult attacked you in France, he believed they just wanted to kill you. But when I went to relieve him at Lady Garand's chateau, during the cult's attacks, his opinion had changed. He said he heard them talking about capturing you. He said it was one of their priorities. I dinnae ken how he knew that, but he was convinced of it, which is why he wanted all images of you destroyed."

That *also* made sense. Too many little things had happened to suggest they saw me only as a bit of target practice. When we had escaped Violette's home in France, Lilla had called out to me, teasing that she wanted to talk. The wolf prisoner at Kinloch Castle had implied he'd heard enough about me to think I was important to somebody on their side. And Antonio, the Knight we'd met in Eike's village, had spoken to me not as the mate of the king but as if he respected my independent influence in this conflict.

"Maybe they *do* want me for something," I murmured after a moment. "The Knights I've met—at Kinloch and with the king—kept calling me 'poisoned princess.' I never found out why."

"Wager I could," Brodie replied. "Glengarriff's deserted, my lady. There's no sign of the king or Fern and Yasmina or anything at all to suggest anybody died. The whole town's full of humans and all they said was that they'd never host that sort of party again, on account of how much garbage was left in the forest."

Around a bitter taste of guilt, I told him, "If it's safe, let's hire a cleanup crew in the area, get it cleaned as soon as we can, okay? I'll pay out of the funds I have access to."

"Yes, ma'am," Brodie said. "But why not let me go to Kinloch, eh? Let me interrogate the old and new prisoners until I have somethin' juicy for ye?"

"No torture," I said, hoping it was obvious.

"Not even tickling?" he whined, genuinely put out. "Not even Peppa Pig all hours of the day?"

Millie and Jonesy smiled. I did too. "Uh…"

"I swear I dinnae need to harm a hair on their heads, my lady, but…let me have *a little* fun. I'll have information for you quicker than ye can say haggis."

Millie nudged. "Who knows how much time we have?"

"Only if you have to," I said begrudgingly.

A deep, mischievous cackle escaped him in triumph. "That's class. Gimme a few days."

Then he was gone, and I was left with the image of that giant Scottish man with a giant feather tickling vampires and wolves with a bearded grin on his face.

But…Millie's phone was still in my hand, and the moment the call ended, one of the stored pictures of me on a barn floor somewhere popped up again.

"Why didn't any of you *tell me* about this ages ago?" I chided.

"You were still in the king's shadow," Millie said politely. "And Cassian…just wanted to handle it for you."

My shoulders sagged, wondering if Cass hadn't told me because he'd been keeping things from me like Rav, or simply because he'd never gotten over his anger toward me before he died. I hated that I couldn't ask him. Even the phony bologna unblinking version of him that followed me around couldn't tell me. *Why the hell couldn't he talk?* My raven and wolf could!

"Speaking of Cass," I said. "I need to warn you two; you might…see him around here."

"Is he alive?!" Jonesy leapt forward to ask. "I knew he was too smart to die."

"My Goddess, that would be amazing!" Millie echoed.

"No. No." I grimaced. "The Goddess gave me a…gift…and for

whatever reason, it looks like him. It has his face but it doesn't blink. It doesn't smell like him or speak. And I don't have any control over how it looks."

Confusion muddied their expressions, and I got the urge to just prove it to them, so I added, "Cass? Can you come out please?"

They waited patiently for a few seconds before *the nothing* that was happening began to stretch.

"Cass," I tried again.

This time when nothing appeared, some look passed between Millie and Jonesy that spiked my embarrassment sky high.

"Cass, come on!"

Why…why wasn't he coming?

"It's all right, my lady," Millie offered. "We'll see him when we see him."

Her tone was high and gentle, so delicate, and it riled my embarrassment more. Dread, too, poured into me in a torrent. What could this possibly look like to them, but that I was going insane?

"Sorry, forget it," I said, moving us along. "Right now, a few pictures of me don't matter. What matters is pushing forward. Our forces are scattered and nobody on our side is talking to each other. While Brodie's doing his thing, we *have to* reconnect with our allies. We *have to* prepare. Rav's coming for Idalia and Giselle…and me. If we don't find them fast, more than one queendom will be lost."

***

"It's too hot for this."

"It's that or we're dying your hair bright blonde, my lady."

After the embarrassing Cass moment the night before, I'd told Millie and Jonesy the entire reason I'd come to Rome in the first place—to find my way into Idalia's library. That and to find Idalia, of course, but I figured one would lead to the other.

I'd told them about my tour of Domus Aurea, about the magickal spider and the over-vigilant tour guide, and they had both agreed to help me look for a way in. Then, they'd argued with me for nearly an hour about the dangers of walking around this city with nothing but a hoodie to hide my identity before Millie left the apartment "on an errand" and returned with all manner of disguise. From wigs to baseball caps to niqabs to ridiculously giant sunglasses, which we ultimately decided against since the search was underground and I needed to actually be able to see where I was going. She brought back so much stuff I had to demand she return most of it once we settled on my costume.

Hoodies that were big enough that I could wear a baseball cap under them.

A baseball cap that made me look like a noob tourist.

A wig that made me look like a twelve-year-old boy.

And a camera worn around my neck on a strap so I could bring it to my face to cover up whenever I needed.

The disguise was *hot.* And Rome was hot. So, I, in turn, was *melting* by the time we reached the Domus Aurea for our "weekday" tour that turned out to be much less extensive, and ultimately only useful to show them the spider and the start of the magickal graffiti.

The next day, we returned and toured the forum, down the hill, to get a sense of whether the tunnels might run under it.

The day after that, we toured the Colosseum and learned that the hypogeum—the underground tunnel system where the gladiators and animals were kept—was only available for tours on certain days…if you booked in advance…and if the tickets weren't already sold out.

They were.

And the earliest we could buy them was over a month away.

It was day after day of this (and trying to spot-identify spider alters when we went out to dinner) until Millie just said "screw it" and started having us walk side by side across the park above the ruins, looking for a hole, a crack, or any way into the tunnels below without alerting the guards.

"The ceiling collapsed in 2010, so…it's possible," she told me while a *literal river* of sweat ran down my back in the sweltering heat.

Oh, and we discovered the entire park was under video surveillance, so…somebody had hours of footage of three weirdos combing the hillside day after day.

By contrast, the evenings, at least, were…well, they were stressful. Filled with updates and strategy sessions and meetings with Brodie and the heads of different departments of the war effort.

One, a woman named Heledd, the brigadier who commanded our Welsh forces, let us know that Archer Mahon had contacted her after Brodie went AWOL. She didn't know how he'd found out her name or rank, but she told us he'd offered to promote her to the general of "his army" if she agreed to go to Denmark and swear her fealty.

Off that piece of intel, Brodie discovered Archer had made the same offer to our other regional commanders, and one had accepted—the brigadier in charge of our forces in England, a man named Geoffrey who stopped replying to Brodie's messages a few days before. With Heledd's help, we were able to replace Geoffrey before he returned from Denmark.

Brodie also arrested him and took him to Kinloch Castle. Then he used his "playful" interrogation techniques to squeeze as much information out of the turncoat as he could…which turned out to be very little. Rav was *definitely* brainwashing anyone he or Archer lured to Denmark.

We *did* learn, though, that Rav had swept through the UK, Greece, *and* Egypt after Lunasa, searching for me. And from the new cult prisoners Brodie had captured during the full moon attack, we discovered that the Knights of the Rising Sun had been suspiciously quiet in the aftermath of their failed attacks against each kingdom…because they were gearing up for something catastrophic. What it was, Brodie wasn't able to glean no matter how much Peppa Pig he made them listen to at full volume.

There was good news, though.

A few days into this routine, two familiar faces staggered up Kinloch Castle's front walk, robbing me of a *huge* portion of my anxiety.

"My lady! My lady! It's Fern and Yasmina!"

I nearly leapt out of my oversized hoodie when Jonesy came sprinting across the park with the phone in his hand and thrust it at me.

"Hello?"

"Natalie, it's me. We're here, we're safe," Yasmina almost shouted through the phone. "Your mother, too, is safe."

Mom.

"I-Is she there? Can I talk to her?"

"No, my lady, we thought she'd be safest where we hid her, away from all of this," Yasmina yelped. "Is that all right, or—"

"No, that's probably the right call."

Probably. Because she was *probably* also losing her mind with worry.

"Is there a way to contact her?"

"Yes! Do you have a pen?"

I'd never expected that keeping in contact with people—stealthily communicating—would be our biggest issue, but I supposed it made sense. The world was a big place, even with our technology. It was incredible how quickly we'd been totally scattered because one or some of us lost our phones, or couldn't trust who might be tapping the line in search of our location. Or because we were forced to alter at inopportune times.

That was how Fern and Yasmina had escaped Lunasa. They'd shifted using the blue azurite I'd told them to always carry with them. Yasmina's polecat had hidden in the forest and Fern's elephant had stomped her would-be attackers until the party grounds were deserted and they could retrieve the stones and shift back again.

Now. Had I listened to my own advice? Had *I* started carrying a piece of azurite around with me just in case? No. But that was because I was terrified to tempt fate that way. Who knew what I might transform into, if I ever did again. Still, better safe than sorry. I remedied my hypocrisy immediately by buying a long, loose necklace with an azurite pendant that buzzed gently where it touched my stomach. Something which might not be lost if I was forced to transform.

After altering, Fern and Yasmina had been forced to take shelter while Rav's people hunted them. Without being able to call me or Brodie for aid, Yasmina called the only number she could easily look up.

"Fiadh helped you?" Fiadh Clarke, the Irish High Priestess from the Witches Council.

"Yes, my lady. I-I remembered she worked at Trinity College, so I called her office. Her people came for us before the sun had even set. Fiadh snuck us out of Glengarriff. Hid us in her home."

"We'll need to thank her," I said at the exact same moment Yas did. "Jinx."

"She still wishes to speak with you," Yas added.

That remained to be seen; she might not, now that my official title had been stripped from me…and I was preparing to go insane. Although, to be fair, even with my beastliness, she still had a better chance of brokering peace between the witches and shifters working with me rather than Archer.

"Jane Lakeland does too, my lady," Yas said after a moment.

"Did you ask her about Belina?"

"Yes. Jane gave me her number. I called her."

A tug of panic tightened my stomach. "What did she say?"

"She had a message for you, but I don't understand it."

"What was it?"

"Belina said, '*the cult now knows what William Mahon always knew.*'"

I…didn't know what that meant, but the moment I heard the words, my raven ran her feathers down my spine and my wolf "licked" me, sort of the way a friendly dog would. To reassure. To remind me I wasn't alone.

"*Does that mean anything to you?*" I asked my creatures.

"*Ask him,*" my raven said.

I recoiled almost laughing—surely she couldn't mean I should ask *William Mahon*. The guy who'd died a year and a half ago.

"*Yes. Him.*"

"*Are you nuts? How would I even…*"

I didn't finish the thought…because I already knew. Idalia. Her holy day, Ognianima. The one Rav had refused to let me participate in. Idalia had helped the other Alter Supremes commune with the dead, with their loved ones. She'd even complained about how mad Sorina was after the fact. She'd gotten to speak all night with Lord Bogdan only to lose him again at the break of day.

I…I could talk to the dead. I could ask for Idalia's help speaking with William Mahon.

And Cass, a quieter part of me said.

At that, my raven ran her feathers down my spine again.

Goddess, I really needed to find Idalia.

"Thanks, Yas. I-I want to talk to Belina. Can you send me her number?"

"It's useless now, my lady," she said. "Belina told me she was disappearing after the call. She warned that things were about to get very bad for us and she had to get some place safe before it was too late. But she told me to tell you that *she* would find *you* 'after dawn.'"

Despite the oppressive summer heat, I suddenly felt frozen, full of icy dread. Weeks ago, Rolfe had warned us that the Knights of the Rising Sun were making plans for some future event, alluding to it in their messaging, talking about all the things they'd finally get to do 'after dawn.'

"After dawn. She said that?" I asked for confirmation.

Yasmina's voice trembled when she answered. "Yes, my lady. I-I think we're running out of time. I think dawn is nearly here."

It was for me, at least.

Less than twenty-four hours later, Millie, Jonesy, and I arrived back at the Domus Aurea so we could take a weekend tour and I could finally show them how the great golden spider teased of further directions to the library past the white sphinxes.

We never made it through the door.

A few steps from the queue for the ticket booth, the choking scent of bonfire struck my nose and I froze, grabbing Millie and Jonesy's hands so fast they almost tripped as they slowed to a halt beside me.

"What is it? What's the matter?" Millie asked.

There was a wolf in the gathering crowd, and I didn't know which one of them it was. I only knew that if I said the word *wolf* out loud, they would hear me. *He* would hear me.

It was already too late.

Not a second later, a man at the front of the queue stepped away, turning in my direction. His gaze flitted across me indifferently before he, too, froze and his eyes landed on me again.

I watched him recognize me—*identify* me—in real-time. We'd never met, but he *knew* my face.

He took a step towards me and—

"*Go!*" my raven suddenly squawked, and I was moving. Turning. Rushing back down the path toward the anonymity of the city. Millie and Jonesy caught up seconds later, glancing at him again and again as they whispered about what we should do. I resisted the urge to look until we were nearly to the end of the path leading to the Colosseum.

Only then did I turn back, and when I did? I found him staring straight at me, with a phone pressed to his ear.

CHAPTER 19

"My tour is about to start."

"Mine too."

"Can you hear us, my lady?"

"Loud and clear."

Our run-in with the wolf had inspired the exact reaction in my friends that I *didn't* want. Millie and Jonesy told me under pain of being locked in the bathroom that I would have to stay behind until they knew whether or not the Domus Aurea had been compromised for me.

Millie was there, preparing to take the extended weekend tour.

Jonesy was at the Colosseum; he'd managed to buy a ticket off a tourist for the hypogeum tour, to check whether there might be a way into the tunnels under Nero's palace through there.

And I was stuck in the flat listening to their adventure over the phone like the world's saddest podcast listener. I mean, they were in *one of the seven wonders of the world*! And here I was straining my ear to hear drips of water in the background, scraps of lecture from the tour guide, echoes of voices bouncing off the high brick walls.

I hated being left behind. I hated being...precious. Yes, yes, I knew it was the smart move; that didn't mean it was the fun one. No, I was stuck in the kitchen, cooking more of Cass's angelica and mugwort tincture over the stove like some sixteenth century apothecary.

And of course, the moment Millie and Jonesy left, Cass had reappeared in the apartment with me as if he'd always been there. Jerk.

"Any wolves?" I asked, grumbling.

"No, but blood is in the air," Millie said.

I froze at that. "Do you mean...dragons? There are vampires there?"

"Ah-huh." The confirmation escaped her like a noise caught in her throat. As if a vampire was too close to risk answering clearly.

"Here as well," Jonesy echoed a moment later.

"Vampires at the Colosseum," I said just to clarify.

"At least a dozen," he replied.

"Is it safe? Should you two leave?"

"No, Mom, look we're heading down now. I might lose you, if I do I'll call you back as soon as it's over. Love you!" Millie replied, her tone artificially happy and bright…right before her voice garbled and her line dropped.

"Jonesy?"

"We're heading underground as well. Can you still hear me?"

"Yes."

"Okay, I'll talk when I can."

At least I still had one of them. Through his side, I listened intently in silence. I couldn't hear what the guide was saying, but I could hear their voice drifting in and out as Jonesy moved around searching.

For nearly an hour, I did nothing but watch a pot with an upside-down lid bustle with steam and listen to Jonesy's stream-of-consciousness commentary.

"Nothing over here…wait, that might be a…no, definitely not…not unless you want to get shit on your wings…you could *definitely* fly down here though. *Plenty* of birds roosting in here already."

Until finally, Jonesy said, "Oh, hang on," in a quietly excited voice that made me stand up straighter with anticipation.

"Jonesy?"

"Give us a second. I…I'm going to send Jel through to check if this leads anywhere."

Jel was Jonesy's water buffalo. In between other tasks, he'd revealed he'd been practicing the farseeing technique I'd taught him. He'd even managed to coax the buffalo out of his body several times, which he did again in the living room for me after a bit of huffing and humming, straining his brow in a way that made me giggle. Jel was…beautiful. Nearly as tall as the ceiling and a rich green color that surprised me.

But… "Jonesy, he's *huge*. Are you sure nobody will see you?"

"I-I don't think so. He's…he's through. He's through the wall."

Again, I waited, this time with Cass right beside me, his impatient gaze fixed on the phone.

"Can you see anything in your mind?"

"Just dirt…smaller tunnels…wait. What is that?"

I opened my mouth to ask "What is what?" but the words were cut off by a sudden serrated scream on the other end of the phone before the line dropped.

"Jonesy? Jonesy!"

I had my hoodie and keys in hand before I stopped screaming his name. I flicked off the stove, shoved the terrible wig over my hair, and tucked my phone in my pocket, ready to sprint the twisty-turny mile to the Colosseum if I had to.

Cass was already waiting by the door to open it for me. He followed me out and down to the street, reaching for my hoodie to shove it up over my head.

I dialed Millie as I ran, dodging pedestrians like I expected them to tackle me at any moment. She didn't answer. I tried Jonesy again. Nothing.

"*Could you fly below the city surface?*" I asked my raven. "*Could you just cut through without being seen? Make sure they're okay.*"

"*Left,*" she shouted in my head.

The second I turned, I found myself on an empty side street and my raven flew out of my body, skimmed the cobble as if soaring across the surface of a still lake, before she plunged right through the rock and disappeared.

I wasn't built for running; I wasn't wearing the right bra either. My whole chest mutinied halfway there, but my raven could go the distance easily. And she did.

After a few moments she said, "*Here. Looking,*" and I had to force myself not to hold my breath as I ran on despite the pain.

"*Do you see him?*"

"*No…no…there!*"

"*I-Is he okay? Is he hurt?*"

"*No,*" she replied, and I almost stuttered in confusion. Which was it? I didn't get to ask before I felt a slight shift in her direction and she added, "*Millie now.*"

He must've been okay if she left him, right? But…if he was okay, why wasn't he answering the phone?

"Cass? Can you get to him faster?"

His lips tipped down as he turned his gaze from me, offering no answer either way. He didn't need to; his expression was plain to read. He absolutely could, but he wouldn't.

Frustration burbled in me. "Why not? If Jonesy is in danger, you need to help him."

"*Must protect you*," my wolf answered for him.

I opened my mouth to argue, but Cass held my gaze and pointed at his eye; he was telling me to look. Telling me to be careful.

When we reached the edge of the Piazza del Colosseo, I understood why. A smell I knew and loved more than any other saturated the Roman air, along with a scent that turned my stomach to rot. Smokey bonfire and the metallic tang of blood. The scent was so heavy, I half expected to see a massacre, but there wasn't one.

No, there was an infestation.

Vampires and wolves—maybe even tall wolves, although I couldn't differentiate—swarmed the area as far as the eye could see. There were dozens of them scattered amidst the unsuspecting human crowd, blending in. They were seated at café tables. Waiting for crosswalks. Playing on their phones. Behaving in perfectly appropriate ways for the warm Roman summer.

And yet, everyone else of magickal persuasion was fleeing. It wasn't a mass exodus, but it was noticeable. Several alter families hustled past me away from the piazza, and arriving alters turned back immediately as they tried to enter the square. Even in traffic, I saw several Vespas calmly enter the intersection before the drivers' heads whipped in every direction, and they sped off as quickly as possible.

Cass tapped my hand and drew my attention to a nearby rooftop where a human-shaped grump of a man was surveying the street from above, then a tree-shaded hilltop where a woman was doing the same.

"What do you think they're doing?" I asked, wishing he could *just answer me*. Heck, just *humor* me.

Cass eyed me again, and again his look said everything he couldn't. Either they were here for me…or they weren't. And from the look of things, neither was going to end well.

I couldn't walk across that piazza to reach Jonesy or Millie. They might as well have been on the moon, and they would have probably been safer on the moon to be honest.

All I could do was ask my raven again, "*Have you found Millie yet*?"

"*Yes, safe. Leaving now*."

"*Then it's just Jonesy unaccounted for*," I said right before a sudden eruption of screams tore my gaze to the Colosseum.

From our location, to the west, we couldn't see what was happening, but we had a clear view of dozens of wolves snapping their attention toward the noise, and at least half a dozen vampires disappearing in the blink of an eye, clearly racing over to investigate.

But…the screams weren't frantic and terrified. They were high yips of disgust.

As I watched, a gaggle of teenage girls burst for the nearest intersection at a *sprint*, oblivious to the cars screeching to rubber-burning halts to stop from hitting them. The girls didn't even seem to notice the traffic. They were…

They were hitting themselves. Tearing at their clothes, clawing at their hair.

Others, too, were running out of the mouth of the Colosseum in strange zigzag patterns, frantically pawing at their clothing. A baby was screaming. One man was flapping his arms like a chicken, as if attempting to fly.

I speed-dialed Jonesy out of sheer curiosity as much as concern. Still, there was no answer, so I called Millie instead.

"My lady, sorry, I lost signal in the tunnels, but I saw the magick. Let me call you back, something's happening—"

"I know, I can see it."

"*My lady!*" she hissed with disapproval. "Go back! Get away from here. The piazza's dangerous."

"Something's happening at the Colosseum, Mills," I said. "Let's get Jonesy and go."

I told her where we were standing, and within a couple of minutes, her and Jonesy's forms materialized out of the growing crowd, antsy to be anywhere else. Millie had Jonesy by the arm, pulling him behind her like a kid. And he was frantically scratching at himself, wiping the crown of his hair as if he thought something was sitting on top of his head.

Cass, of course, had disappeared in the meantime.

"What happened?" I asked when they finally reached me.

Millie didn't say anything, she just pressed her hand to the flat of my back and rushed me away from the piazza.

Jonesy, on the other hand, had a lot to say. "S-S-Spiders! They were everywhere! Came pouring out of the walls like ants out of an anthill."

"Spiders? Like, *normal* spiders?"

"There's nothing normal about spiders, my lady," he said, slapping his back. "Bloody creeps, the lot of them. Crawling *all over* me. Probably still are. Probably going to lay eggs in my brain! Ugh, Goddess, can you see any? Please tell me if you see any."

When we made it safely back to the apartment, he told us what happened while frantically stripping down to his underwear. Turned out, his buffalo had run through a wall and landed in a massive nest of spiders at the bottom of a long slanted tunnel. There were so many, he said, the frescoes on the walls and floor of the chamber looked like they were moving.

It was a nightmare to Jel, who'd run back toward Jonesy seeking safety, seeking retreat into his alter's mind, riling the entire nest of spiders to stampede ahead of him into the Colosseum.

"Well…that has to be it, doesn't it?" I offered, trying to see the bright side. "That's probably a way into the library."

"Maybe," Millie shrugged. "Or maybe it's a death trap. I didn't see any other way down, except through that tunnel past the sphinxes, my lady. But there were vampires on my tour with me. When I got outside, there were wolves too. It's not a coincidence that one spots you and suddenly they're everywhere."

"Let's give it a day," I suggested. "Maybe they'll be gone by tomorrow."

CHAPTER 20

The wolves and vampires around the Colosseum were not, in fact, gone the next day. Or the next. Or the next.

Every day at dawn and dusk, Jonesy or Millie would schlep across the city to check, and every day they returned with the same news—that the infestation was spreading. More and more vampires and wolves were arriving daily, crowding streets farther and farther away from the Piazza.

And once the pattern was obvious, we called Brodie to discuss.

"They're still concentrated around the Colosseum and the Domus Aurea," Jonesy told him. "But there were a lot of alters gathering by Trajan's Forum too."

"They're spreading in our direction," Millie said.

"I could fly in a battalion with eight hours' notice, but the cult'll ken something is happening the moment I do. How long before they reach your location, do you think?" Brodie asked.

Millie shrugged. "Depends. If they have those sorts of numbers, maybe two days? Three?"

I knew what she wanted me to say to that. I knew she wanted me to admit I was better off giving up on this whole endeavor while there was still time.

I couldn't do it.

"That gives us three days to get into that tunnel," I said.

"That gives us three days to flee the city, my lady," Millie tutted.

"I don't want to leave without doing this."

"Why not? It's just a library. You can come back later."

I couldn't tell them the truth, about my beastliness and the looming fear that at any moment I might shed my humanity and rampage through the streets as a monster. Or the fact that I thought the library might hold the key to my salvation.

I also felt like words couldn't quite do justice to the *desperate craving* I had to gain access to more knowledge, given everything Rav had done to me and the Knights had done to us. It wasn't an exaggeration to say that I believed the information we needed to save us in the war was locked away in those archives.

Not to mention the *next* closest alter library was in the friggen Netherlands, which was technically part of the Wolf Court and belonged to Ulric, now. And *way* too close to Denmark for my tastes.

But I went with the simplest reason: "I told you. Italy's about to implode; from the looks of it, *two* invasions are happening now. We're running out of time to find Idalia. I *have* to find her."

Millie's brow rose at that. "My lady, you don't need a *library* to find her."

"Well, no, but…two birds with one stone. Find one and we'd probably find the other."

A twinkle rose in her eye. "Exactly. We find one, we find the other."

Of course, it made sense that locating Idalia first would mean gaining easy access to the library…if we could. But I'd honestly thought tracking Idalia down would be impossible. From the glint in Millie's eye, though, she didn't seem to think so.

So, I asked the obvious. "…What did you have in mind?"

***

I didn't know why I hadn't thought of it when I'd first arrived in Rome. Genuinely, I was *mortified* when Millie told me her idea for locating Idalia.

We needed to find an alter bar…and cause a scene until the spiders revealed themselves and we found someone willing to help us. Or, if need be, we could do something to get us brought before the Spider Lady for sentencing. That was it—find a bar, talk to people.

It was so simple, so obvious, I wanted to try it *immediately*.

"Fine," Millie said. "We'll go tonight. But, if it doesn't work, you agree to leave the city tomorrow."

"But—"

"No buts," Brodie leapt in. "I've given the order to pack. Our soldiers will reach the city tomorrow. By then, you need to be *gone*, my lady. These nutters aren't gathering for a tea party; they're up to something—something *you* probably want *no* part of."

I couldn't argue with that.

Nor could I argue a few hours later after Yasmina researched the nearest alter bar and Millie informed me that I would *obviously* not be going on the mission myself.

"With all due respect, are you *out of your mind?!*" she scolded when I tried to argue anyway.

"They might call her," I pointed out. "Or if we make a good enough case, the spiders might take us right to her."

Millie recoiled as if I was insane. "Exactly! No secondary locations for you! *If* one of them offers to take us, *we* assume that danger, not you. They might be lying. They might kill us on the way. It's far too dangerous."

"But they won't be able to lie to me," I reminded her. "You need my gift of honesty."

Millie's eyes softened as she realized I was right, but… "It's too risky; someone from the king's men might recognize you. Stay here. Pack your bag. Let us do our jobs, all right?"

It wasn't all right. Damn it, *I wished* I could be in multiple places at once! But without that friggen option, I didn't want to be a burden either.

So it was that I found myself with my bugout bag packed again, listening to their mission *again* from the comfort of the flat, feeling like some sort of useless diamond in a display case, overprotected and pointless.

And, of course, the second they left, Cass reappeared in the room with me.

This time, I muted my end of the phone and approached him where he stood peeking past the closed curtain out the window.

"Go with them," I begged.

He shook his head only once, not even looking at me.

My hackles rose in frustration. "Why don't you want them to see you? I've told them about this gift, they know they might see you, so *why are you hiding*?"

He, of course, didn't respond, but…I saw the faintest flicker of discomfort in his eye, that very human tell that seemed wrong for a power I should be able to control.

To that thought, my wolf said, "*Must protect you.*"

"I'm safe. *I'm safe here,*" I pointed out. "They might need your help. Go!"

Cass ignored me, rooted to the spot.

"I said GO! You're my power. I'm telling you to go!" I sounded silly; I know I did, but…I commanded it anyway. "Get out of here! Catch up to them!"

Again, Cass shook his head, refusing to look at me and I…I hated the absence of his attention. He'd done this before he died too; in those weeks after Versailles, he'd only looked at me when he couldn't stop himself. Even at the very end, at my wedding, he'd refused to meet my eye.

I couldn't take it anymore. Before I could stop myself, I grabbed his face, cupped his stubbled cheeks in my hands and physically turned him until he couldn't help but look at me. But…the moment his gaze connected with mine, I saw so much *hurt* there. So much pain and anger and longing. It struck my chest like a sword to the heart. His hands rose to mine, limply tugging at my grip as if he wanted me to let him go, but also *didn't* want that. Not at all. The push and pull left him clinging to me, holding onto my hands, my wrists, for dear life.

"Cass." My voice broke. "You're here to protect me, right?"

He nodded.

"If something happens to them, I'll be alone. That's more dangerous, isn't it?"

My raven answered, "*Not alone.*"

"I'll be okay here by myself, I promise—"

But at that, Cass's face quirked with a sneer that meant only one thing.

"You…don't believe me?"

Cass's eyebrow rose defiantly. He shook his head.

"No one knows I'm here," I said, but he rolled his eyes in frustration as if that wasn't the problem at all…and I froze as a realization struck me. It was the phone call with Rav—that had to be it. He was angry about what I had said.

"Do you think I'll hurt myself if you leave?"

He shrugged. *He shrugged* as if to ask, *would you*?

"Cass, I…"

As I watched, more hurt flooded his gaze along with fear, and his grip on my hands tightened. He pulled me slightly toward him, and he lowered, pressing his forehead to mine. The moment we connected, his eyes finally closed.

It broke my heart, even as it confused me. He understood why I'd made that offer, didn't he? To protect our friends, our family, our kingdom? To give myself an out in case I felt my sanity slipping. To prevent Rav—or anybody—from…keeping me as some sort of caged thing he could harvest blood from to make cures with.

There were so many awful possibilities that made the solution I'd offered seem reasonable.

Surely, *as a part of me*, he must know those things, right?

Unless…he *wasn't* a part of me.

It happened so quickly, I didn't know what to think. His head was pressed to mine, his hands were clutching my wrists, when he moved the tiniest bit…and his nose trailed away across my cheek. Eyes still closed, his lips grazed my skin next. Feather-light, they landed on my cheekbone before gliding across to my temple then up to my forehead. These little pattered kisses scattered sparks all the way to my tailbone.

A whimper of surprise escaped me, but I couldn't pull away. I physically couldn't. Even without that magnetic tug under his skin, everywhere he touched came alive as he activated it.

His hands slid down my wrists to my forearms, squeezing rhythmically, as his lips continued their soft skimming tour of my face, landing again and again at random intervals. Faint as breath.

Goddess, it was…

I shivered suddenly and accidentally turned just enough to feel the brush of his lips against the very edge of mine. The zing of that graze sent the shiver bounding off every surface of my body. And I savored the deeper squeeze on my arms he gave me in reply. Savored the sudden pounding of my heart inside me.

With it, though, came heartache. More confusion. Tears rushed for my eyes.

"I miss you," I whispered.

His next kiss landed harder against my jaw, then my neck-my neck-*my neck*. Nuzzling until my knees weakened against my will. Until tender sensation spiraled away through my body and my hands reached for him, clinging, as my heart pushed more tears into my eyes. Cool liquid trickled across my skin.

"I miss you s-so much, Cass."

That was why he was there, I knew. He was what my brain had created to protect me, some likeness of my friend. He had to be.

But how did that make sense? Was he imagination? Fantasy? Was he the dream I thought I could spend the rest of my life exploring…because he wasn't real?

I got *some* piece of an answer to my questions a moment later.

Cass's hands rose to cup my face. So tenderly, he studied me, his unblinking eyes like full moons shining up above. His thumbs slid across my skin, soft as breath. And his lips were there hovering inches above mine. It would've taken nothing—*nothing* but a push—to narrow the space between. And I wanted that too much to care whether he was real or I was pathetically about to kiss myself.

Until he suddenly licked me.

Licked me.

It took me totally by surprise. I did nothing but blink as his tongue gently, savoringly landed against my cheek and lapped the tears away. First one side, then the other, then again when another errant tear streaked to my jawline. I even felt the tip of his tongue brush the edges of my eyelashes in passing. Watched his eyes dilate with…some quiet excitement…as he tasted each tear. It was electrifying and bizarre and…

A reminder. It was a reminder.

"What *are* you?" I asked again quietly.

But in response, he pulled back and stepped out of my grasp. Defiance colored his face, and he brought his hand flat against his chest. He pressed at his heart, then reached for me and pressed the same hand to my chest, before he jabbed his finger at the floor, as if to say *I'm yours, I'm staying here, and that's the end of it.*

Then he turned back to stand guard at the window and ignored my existence entirely.

***

"What does it look like?"

"Just like any old manky pub."

"…Can you describe it?"

"Like every other pub you've ever seen, I don't know," Millie griped. "Stools with green cushions. At least, I think that's green; it's bloody dark in here."

"*Night* dark," Jonesy murmured in the background. "I can't see two feet in front of me."

"Stained glass and tiles," Millie continued until I heard a gasp.

Faintly, Jonesy said, "Whoa. You don't see that every day."

"What is it?"

"Fairy lights," Jonesy said, leaning into the phone. "The whole place is pitch black except for red fairy lights overhead. There's a whole web of 'em."

"Don't think we'll have much luck finding a spider," Millie concluded. "I mean, *I* can see just fine, but Jonesy—"

I heard a soft crash, drinks spilling, an apology, and Millie groaning.

"Fine. I'm fine!" Jonesy swore. "Sorry. Thanks."

"Look for the eyes, Mills," I said when they'd recovered. "Silver flashing eyes."

"Hold. Let us get settled and we'll tell you what we find."

I waited patiently as I heard them order sodas, then move to a table and sit, chairs screeching across the wood floor as they pulled them out. Other sounds reached me too—music, human talking, but also strange chittering noises and odd *fwoomp-fwoomp* noises that sounded distorted but so familiar.

It wasn't long before Jonesy grunted, this time in fear and disgust.

"What's happening? What's wrong?"

"Some of them share your gift," Millie said. "It's fine. We're fine."

But Jonesy didn't seem to think so. "Wings, my lady. Ugly ones."

My brow furrowed. "Ugly wings? What do ugly wings look like?"

"They don't have feathers," he said. "Sort of pointy. And see through a little bit? Every time they flap them, I can see the fairy lights behind. It's horrible in the darkness. I hate this."

Well…those were either butterflies or… "Bats? Are they bats?"

"Yes," Millie said. "Seems to be a lot of those tonight."

"Any vampires?" Vampires, I knew, shared a unique, very ancient relationship with bats. They often worked together, disguised one another, and where you found one you were likely to find the other.

"No, not that I can tell," she said. "Look, I don't have a good feeling about this. I don't want to be here long. I'm going to try to get things going, all right. Hold tight."

"How?"

I heard her messing with something on the other end as she strained, "I brought one of Jonesy's spiders."

Jonesy's spiders. After the Colosseum, he'd stripped off his clothes to rid himself of any lingering creepy crawlies, discovered one clinging to his sock, and hurled the whole thing out the window with a high scream. That was the only one I'd seen.

"What spider?"

"Found it sitting on the heap of clothes by his bed this morning. Put it in a little stopper bottle just in case."

My stomach sank. "Millie, don't crush it or anything. Until you touch it with azurite, you can't be sure whether it's an alter or not!"

"Relax, my lady, I wasn't going to crush it, I was going to…ah, hell!"

Whatever she planned to say died as a horrible sound unlike any I'd ever heard before erupted from the phone. Halfway between a shriek and a roar from some beast that had crawled clear out of the depths of hell to make it. So loud through the phone, I had to cover my ears.

So loud, my raven and wolf began to wail inside me in pain.

So loud, the lightbulbs around us in the apartment burst in great sparking fireworks, scattering glass everywhere.

Cass was already beside me, shielding me from the flying debris.

Then he hit the END CALL button, plunging us into blessed silence.

Dark silence. I finally took my shaking hands away from my ears and sat up trembling to find it wasn't just *our* apartment that had been robbed of its light. The lit edge around the curtains was black. I crawled to the window; the damage radius had darkened half the block in either direction, as well as the building across from ours. And a crowded restaurant at the far corner had emptied into the street, with diners surveying the destruction.

I didn't think I could stay there even if I wanted to.

The alter bar wasn't far. I rose to my feet, prepared to run—

Cass caught me by the arm. My spine stiffened, expecting some reaction from him to suggest he wouldn't let me go…but when I looked at him, that wasn't the expression I saw on his face.

He was peering out the window, looking gobsmacked. Awed and cautious at the same time.

Then I heard a *fwoomp*. And another. Then the roar of a distant crowd, which grew louder and split as something drew nearer, until it sounded like a thousand tiny things screeching into the night.

Shadows flitted across Cass's features, and I lunged for the curtain, drawing it back just enough to peer out again. The sky was…*clouded* with bodies. *Bats*. Thousands. *Hundreds of thousands s*treaming by in the darkness like a plague.

But there weren't *just* bats up there. Among and between the bodies, I spotted several enormous bat alters with their taut gray slick wings spread above them, flap-flap-flapping to keep them in the air. They were attempting to use the bats as camouflage, but…it failed spectacularly. The bats made the winged humans among them look like harbingers of some sort of hellish apocalypse.

"My Goddess, what are they thinking?"

This was...*stupid.* It was *dumb* to reveal yourself like this. I couldn't *imagine* an excuse that could explain it away. There would be no mistaking them for angels, the way Violette had mistaken mine and Rav's wings as belonging to such; if anything, these creatures looked like *demons*.

Especially when one of them suddenly drew to a flapping hover above the street outside. She—a bat alter with beautiful red hair flowing nearly to her hips—turned her gaze to the radius of destruction around us. And I knew, I *just knew*, from the look on her face that they'd set a trap for me. A sound trap. They knew I was listening. They knew their screams would blow the power where I was, so they could identify my hiding spot from above.

It was brilliant.

And horrifying.

And step two of their trap was about to begin. As I watched, the bat alter opened her mouth and unleashed another one of those *horrifying, ear-splitting screeches*.

Awful. *Painful*!

My hands slammed down over my ears without any input from me whatsoever.

When it stopped, I was ready. "Cass we have to go."

But his hand was still on my arm, fusing me to the spot. His gaze was on the door.

I whipped my head in that direction just in time to see it *slam* inward, breaking the lock clean off. A wall of air—a soft shockwave—blew our hair back a second before a vampire appeared in the doorway, holding Jonesy by the throat. He was tall with light brown skin and dark long hair, and a rocker look that made him seem larger than life.

"Well-Well-Well," he crooned, his voice dripping with an accent I couldn't quite place. "At last, poisoned princess. It is an *honor* to finally meet you. We have been looking for you everywhere. I am Oded—even though I am very much alive, as you can see." He winked at me, so pleased with himself. "Very soon, I will be your humble and trusted servant...after I have delivered you to the *Voyante*."

Cass took a step forward, putting himself between us. The vampire's unbothered gaze snapped to him with a smile.

"And Cassian Mahon. I have heard a *great* many things about you."

A deep melodic chuckle escaped him as he added, "This double blessing was unexpected, but with the Announcement of the Dawn coming, I suppose it is fate you are both found at last."

His hand rose to cover his mouth playfully, as if he hadn't meant to say any of that.

"Is this your truthsayer gift, my sovereign?" he asked me. "I can feel it in the muscle, right at the back of my throat. And in the squigglies of my brain! Amazing! Ask me for my bank pin number, next. Please…All right, I'll just tell you—it is 0430. My birthday. I think we have this in common, yes?"

I…didn't know what to make of him. Nor did I have time to dissect his dazzling, *genuine* smile as if he thought we were already best friends.

"Put him down!" I demanded, motioning to Jonesy.

"Of course, my sovereign," Oded said…right before he tossed Jonesy into the wall. I felt the shatter, felt the drywall and wood break, as if *my* body had been thrown. Watched Jonesy crumble to the floor unconscious like a ragdoll. Watched the vampire turn back to me and offer me a charming smile instead of attacking…

And I realized Oded was wasting our time.

"Cass, more are coming. We have to go—"

"*Go?* Go where?" Oded asked. "You are exactly where you're meant to be."

Cass disappeared before I could blink. Reappeared across the room behind the vampire like a nightmare. And they were suddenly at each other's throats. A blur of red and brown cycloning around the room, twisting around itself, smashing into things.

I ran for my backpack and shoved it on before I darted for Jonesy. Slapping his face, I managed, "C-Come on, Jonesy. Wake up. Wake up!"

Right before the vampire's claw snapped around my throat from behind. Oded jerked me to my feet, then lifted me right off them before I could breathe.

But Cass was there, like some dark sentinel, wearing a look unlike any I'd ever seen on his face before. He didn't flinch. He obviously didn't blink. Barely strained…as his fingers curled around the vampire's and *wrenched,* breaking four of Oded's fingers with all the effort of crushing a tin can.

Oded howled in pain and surprise. Cass grabbed his collar and, as I had seen him do before, *hurled* the offending vampire away from us, across the room, clean through the window.

I heard the shattered glass scatter across the street below. I anticipated the heavy thud to follow…but there wasn't one.

"That was very good, sir."

I nearly gave myself whiplash turning around to see the vampire once again darkening our doorstep.

"But I have another hand," Oded teased, tucking his injured appendage behind his back. "And if I went back to my friends with one unbroken, they would think less of me. You understand."

Cass let Oded make the first move. The vampire darted toward me at lightning speed…and Cass caught him by the throat in the middle. Then they were suddenly *speeding* in the opposite direction. He tore the vampire out of the apartment and down the far stairs in a tunnel of air that made my ears pop.

"My lady?"

"Jonesy, thank Goddess, come on!" I helped him up and shoved him out the door without hesitating. "We need to find Millie."

"No. *I* have to get *you* out of here," he countered. "The bar was a trap. It's like they knew we would go there."

"They did," I said. "The *Voyante* told them we would."

CHAPTER 21

Voyante. Seer.

The Knights of the Rising Sun had a seer—a real one, if Oded was to be believed. Offhandedly, I wondered how a fortuneteller fit into the Goddess's "no information about the future" thing. But then my feet hit the asphalt outside the apartment building and sprinted after Jonesy down the street and all thoughts of seers went out the window. I supposed I'd find out whether they were real if anyone caught me.

For the moment, at least, my sole goal was to *escape the neighborhood*, which was currently in chaos. I had to dip, dive, and dodge around half of the humans who were staring slack-jawed at the sky, transfixed by the apocalyptic cloud of bats and winged people overhead. And then I had to dodge, duck, and dip around the other half, who were screaming and running for their lives. It was an obstacle course. A living obstacle course I had no idea how to complete, not with winged alters calling out my location to their buddies as we ran.

Every street we turned down…

Every building we pressed ourselves against…

They were watching. Flying overhead, screaming and destroying the lights, casting a dark trail behind us so we were easier to chase.

The streets were too dangerous. They were just too dangerous. But where were we supposed to go? I'd anticipated potentially having to flee the city before we found Idalia, but…*if* we left it might be weeks, months, or *never* before we knew if she and Giselle survived the invading hordes.

Without them, my army and I would truly be on our own, to face down Rav, to face down the cult, to face down…me, if I finally went feral. Those were, again, all bad options. Two of the three wanted me for their own purposes, and the last would consume me too, in a different way.

This was the epicenter.

I'd chosen Rome for a reason.

And it was time to trust my original instincts.

It was time to break into the Domus Aurea and follow that golden spider to my ally.

"This way, Jonesy!"

"What? What's that way?"

I veered right and bolted for a crowd I could see in the distance. My nose told me they were human. They were…leaving an evening mass, maybe? Or a nightclub? It was anybody's guess. But they were *disoriented*, packed tightly in a plaza, trying to decide what was happening in the sky and on the streets around them.

I hated having to use them to lose our aerial tail, but it worked like a charm. I darted into the crowd and stayed low as I moved. Then I ducked with Jonesy and took off my hoodie while he took off what he could of his own clothes. We found a guy with a shirt draped over his shoulder and stole it. Found a tourist with a wide straw hat and swiped it clean off her head.

"Hey!"

I apologized as I did it.

I made promises to myself to ask the Goddess to bless them in exchange.

But it worked. Changing our clothes while hiding deep in the rabble *worked.* As Jonesy and I emerged at the other end of the crowd, I risked a glance back and saw the bat alters flapping about frantically, scanning faces as they glared unabashedly into the flashes from camera phones.

They'd lost us!

At least, long enough for us to turn a corner and disappear out of sight.

We were only a few streets away from the Colosseum. It was *just there.* And beyond it, the Domus Aurea was waiting up a shy hill past a locked gate.

"Oh, my lady, we shouldn't be here," Jonesy protested when he saw where we were going.

"Underground is the safest place to be," I countered.

"Maybe. But how do we get past *that*?"

The Piazza del Colosseo—what we could see of it from this western vantage point anyway—was crowded. Buzzing with activity. But! Nobody was panicking. They were all cool, calm, and collected, moving around to their various tasks as if the sky to the east *didn't* look straight out of a Bosch nightmare of Dante's eighth circle of hell. Their bonfire and blood scents suggested they were cult members, and they seemed to be building a…dais, the sort a politician would use for a speech, right near the mouth of the Colosseum.

Bizarre.

Disconcerting.

Not my problem at the moment, except in so much as we risked being spotted as I pulled Jonesy across the deserted Via dei Fori Imperiali and ducked behind a line of cars. The corner of the park that contained the Domus Aurea began only a few dozen feet away beyond a narrow green street median, but it might as well have been miles of vampire- and wolf-infested forest for how far away it was.

But after so many trips to this area, I knew there was another way.

"Jonesy, the stairs," I whispered as quietly as I could, pointing to a rough, concrete set of stairs leading away from the Colosseum. "There's another park entrance at the top—"

"*Quiet!*" my raven shouted in my head, silencing me instantly.

Jonesy turned to speak. His mouth opened—

I threw a finger over my lips, begging quiet.

There…not twenty feet away up ahead was a wolf alter. From his cold swiveling gaze, I could tell he was on patrol. He was a guard for whatever was going on in the Piazza. A threat standing between us and where we needed to go.

"*More!*" my wolf echoed a second later, as two vampires arrived in a blur and stopped with a soft *booming* shockwave.

Of the three, I realized, the vampires were the more dangerous while we stood still. For one, they could reach us faster. For another…

One took a big whiff of the air and his nose twitched. Then the other inhaled and his brow furrowed. My eyes snapped to Jonesy, who was sweating his water buffalo odor into the air in massive, heated waves.

The vampires could smell him from a distance.

I shoved off my backpack in seconds, plunged my hand inside, searching-searching for…*the water bottle of Cass's tincture*. The fresh batch I'd made only a couple of days ago!

My hand landed on Jonesy's shoulder. I twirled him around and splashed the whole friggen bottle across his forehead like some sort of hasty baptism.

"Hey! What the—"

I clamped my hand down on his mouth, begging silence.

And we waited. We waited for what felt like *hours* watching those vampires and that wolf. Until their noses stopped twitching and their heads quit swiveling and eventually, the vampires disappeared in a blur. The wolf, too, turned and headed away from where we were hidden.

I didn't waste time. I yanked Jonesy to his feet, *and we ran.*

Across another narrow street to the mouth of those stairs, which were *way* too close to the Colosseum for comfort.

At least the staircase was cloaked in greenery. Farther up, it was swaddled in stone as well. I urged Jonesy on silently.

But I risked one glance. Just a momentary look back at the dais they were building. They were unfurling...*actual banners* with *actual logos* for The Knights of the Rising Sun.

Professional.

Official.

Lunacy.

This was it, though. This was...the moment they were going to reveal the Great Secret, wasn't it?

Damn it all, I felt *sick.* Why had they picked this city in a kingdom on the verge of being invaded to reveal it? Were they announcing it now *because* they'd outed themselves looking for me? Was this my fault in some small way?

As I bolted up the stairs, I did the only thing I could think to do. I pulled out my phone and texted Brodie. I warned him we were in danger, that I had no idea if Millie had escaped the alter bar, that the cult was gathering around the Colosseum. That they were planning to make some sort of 'Announcement of the Dawn' as Oded had said.

But as I reached the top of the stairs and motioned to Jonesy to follow me to the park gate we could see just up ahead, I...decided I had to tell Rav too.

No matter what was happening between us, I *had* to tell him, didn't I? I *had* to warn him.

So I did. I sent the text.

This was *far* more important than some obsession with me, or some vendetta against Idalia. This was the end of the world as we knew it, and the beginning of a new one.

Feet from the locked wrought iron park gate, I felt a slice along my shoulder blades as my blackberry wings erupted and tore through my shirt. My hands, too, transformed before my very eyes into claws. And then I was airborne. My raven was carrying me over the fence, but not before giving me the chance to swoop by Jonesy, clamp my claws under his arms and *lift* him right over the gate.

It hurt. I won't pretend it didn't hurt. He was a *heavy* dude.

But it got us past the gate. And I landed, running. My wings tucked and we bolted across the green hill…to *another* fence. The last between us and Nero's Palace.

"One more time Jonesy," I warned, already exhausted.

Again, my wings tore me off the ground, and I clamped my claws around him. This gate was higher, set on an incline. But Jonesy tucked his legs right before we flew over the wrought iron points and I made it to the other side before my grip began to fail and he tumbled the last foot or so to the ground.

"I'm sorry!" I yelped.

"I'm all right. Go!"

It was *there*. The building leading down into the tunnel was right there, but I knew the door to that one was locked too.

"Jonesy, what do we do?" I asked.

"I have an idea, but it'll be loud and caught on camera," he warned. "We'll have to *run*."

Ugh, more toying with the future of the world. And more running. This time, straight into danger.

Already regretting it, I barked, "Do it."

Jonesy's face scrunched, his brow bent. Nothing happened.

"Jonesy? It's right there!"

We were maybe fifty feet away from the entrance, running at full speed toward an iron door.

"Give us a sec."

He scrunched his face again, straining.

And I knew what he was trying to do.

"Jel!" I growled. "Now!"

I didn't know if my voice helped, but…maybe it did. All I knew was that Jel, that magnificent water buffalo, charged out of Jonesy's body at a full trot and *RAMMED* that door with seconds to spare. The metal sparked as the door flew back into the wall, shattering something, and we didn't slow *at all* as we reached the doorway.

We hit that incline down into the ruin at a full sprint, just as I heard someone shout behind me, "*She's here! She's here!*"

The grating *hunger* I could hear in that voice filled my stomach with rot. They were coming for me. They would take me. Kill Jonesy.

Ugh, I couldn't think about it.

I landed in the underground of Domus Aurea still running.

"*Left!*" my raven shouted, and I turned left. "*Right!*" she added and I skidded into the wall painfully turning to do as she said. Until suddenly, like two ghosts in the near pitch darkness, I saw the white sphinxes up ahead and knew we were in the criptoportico.

A terrifying thought hit me too late—what if I needed to *reactivate* that golden spider in the Octagonal Room before it would show us the way?

But as I leapt between the white sphinxes, and Jonesy followed, she appeared on the wall ahead of us like a miracle. She darted left, and we chased her as I heard pounding footsteps behind us.

Down-down-down a hallway filled with archeological tools, the spider led us.

To a half-collapsed painted chamber full of frescoes.

To a hallway.

To a set of steep stairs plunging deep into the earth.

"Which way did she go!" the hungry voice roared behind us.

"This way!" another replied.

They were gaining. They were coming.

"Hurry, Jonesy! Hur—ahhhh!"

There was no more hurrying. In the inky blackness with no other light source, all we had been able to do was follow that damned spider, trust her blindly…until she ran us right off a cliff. One moment, she was there ahead of us, and the next I felt *nothing* under my feet, and she was above us, growing smaller and smaller as we plummeted into the dark.

CHAPTER 22

"Wings!" I screamed the word as we fell forever and ever and ever. So far for so long my brain tossed up a joke that we would fall straight through the Earth and drift away into outer space on the other side.

But to that, my raven said, *"Trust!"*

And I knew my wings weren't coming.

"Trust what?!" I growled half a second before we struck something and slowed to a springy, vibrating halt.

Past my own panicked breathing, I heard Jonesy's. He was alive, catching his breath between desperate thank-yous to the Goddess.

Then he murmured, "What the *hell* is this? And why is it sticky?!"

It wasn't as dark in this space as in the tunnels above. No, there was…a soft blue and green glow around the edges of this tall cylindrical shaft. As I turned my head and spotted Jonesy struggling on his back a few feet away, I caught faint glimpses of glowing fungi underneath a…

Fear turned my stomach as I realized where we were and what had caught us.

A web.

A *spider's* web dripping with some sort of sticky resin which clung to my skin and clothes as I tried to sit up and realized I couldn't. The more I squirmed, the more glue clung to me, securing me more to the silk.

"Jonesy, stop struggling!" I called out. "It's a web. Stay still!"

"My nightmare," he grumbled loudly in reply, settling where he lay. "My *actual* nightmare. Just kill me now, my lady. I'm done. I'm done!" Then, his voice lilted as he added, "What sort of spider makes webs this big?"

A second later, we heard a high falling scream, and above us, many,

many, *many* feet overhead, we saw a flash of light, then a second. And falling bodies. *Two* of them.

Our pursuers had made the same mistake we did and walked right off the cliff in the dark.

Along with their flashlights, which missed us by *inches* as they fell, slipped between holes in the web, and *shattered* on the stone floor a few feet below.

The men, though, struck the web like we did, catching and sticking before either had stopped screaming.

"Tibor? Jakub?" someone called from above. "*Are you alive?*"

"*Yes!*" the one closest to me called out. "*Help us! We're stuck. We cannot move!*"

"*Can you see the girl?*"

The closest one swiveled his head to look at me. "*Oh yes, she's here. Stuck like we are.*"

"*Excellent! We'll return with rope!*"

I hated the triumphant sound of their voices. And the saccharine smile the closest one gave me a moment after the voices up above faded away.

"*Why are you hunting me*?" I couldn't help but ask.

Even in the soft dark, I could see his face twitch with surprise—I was using his language, whatever it was.

"*That is not for me to say,*" he replied. "*Rest assured, no harm will come to you.*"

But I didn't believe him…and not just because predators didn't deserve to be believed.

Oh no, I didn't believe him because I couldn't. Something was…*moving* in the darkness. A flicker of shadow blotted out a blue mushroom off to my left, and then the webbing itself began to tremble.

"Oh, Goddess *what now*?" Jonesy moaned faintly as the web began to bend.

Then a voice with raspy vibrato rose out of the dark. "*Lucky day! Is this a little web of nosey flies just for me*?"

I didn't want to look. I genuinely didn't want to know what was moving toward us in the dark, but…it was *too big* to ignore. It had…too many legs. A giant round shiny body. And teeth too long, straight, and white to be anything harmless.

Icy dread curled around every inch of me.

It…*she*…would have been a spectacular creature to behold at a distance. A myth come to life. Or rather, the inspiration for myths in the first place. Something that would have made me believe in the old stories, the gods, even if I'd never heard of them before.

Half woman.

Half spider.

Larger than both with a human upper half and a dark purple spider body and silver flashing eyes that *shined* in the glow from the bioluminescent fungi.

"*Shouldn't ignore warning signs, birichinos. You never know what might be lurking in the dark.*"

Our second pursuer mewled, "W-W-What is that?"

The spiderlady reared back in surprise. "A dragon? Silly creature knows it is not welcome here. Not without an invitation!"

She let out a purr; the dragon began to scream. And before I could even blink, she lunged, peeling him off the sticky web and wrapping him in silk until not an inch of him remained uncovered. His mummified, wriggling body landed back on the web mere *seconds* before the great spiderlady purred again and sank her fangs into his neck, silencing him completely.

Then, wiping daintily at her lips, she turned…to me.

Her eyes widened and her smile grew as she drew nearer. And I shrank back instinctively as more and more of her details bled into my awareness. She was *beautiful* and terrifying with many eyes across her forehead, like a blinking circlet. She had two arms and six legs, each pointed like the toe of a ballerina balancing effortlessly on the webbing beneath.

"*A human,*" she purred in delight. "*So long since one of you has fallen in our trap.*"

I-I didn't know whether the same fate awaited me as the other guy, but I didn't take any chances.

"Wait. Please. I-I'm here to see Idalia da Carra, the Spider Lady of Silk and Secrets."

She reared back in surprise again, but there was more curiosity than there had been with her first victim. "Lady da Carra does not entertain humans. Then again, I have never met a human who knew her name either."

"I-I'm not a human," I said.

"You smell like one."

"I know. Idalia knows me. My name is Lady Natalie Damarand, Alter Supreme of the Eighth Kingdom. Ask Idalia. Tell her I'm here, please. She's waiting for me."

"Perhaps," the spiderlady said, her voice beginning to tremble with that threatening purr.

"I swear! L-Look! Watch!"

My raven already knew what I wanted. My wings sprang again from my back; one caught painfully on the sticky web, but the other slid through the gaps and waved frantically beneath me to show her.

"She's telling the truth!" Jonesy echoed.

And then, to my great surprise, the other pursuer began to defend me as well. "Yes, she is an Alter Supreme! Very important to many people."

"Another human and a wolf vouch for you. Very odd," she said, glancing between them.

"The human is my Second," I lied.

"A winged human with a human Second? Stranger still!"

"Please, you must let her go unharmed," our pursuer chimed in. "You must not touch her. The loss of her would be disastrous!"

Why…why was he saying that? Stranger still, why did he look *worried* as he pled for my life. I never turned my aura of honesty off anymore, so…this behavior was genuine. He was genuinely begging for my life.

They were both begging for my life as if it was the most important thing either would ever do. The noise echoed off the stone walls. It vibrated the webbing. It disoriented our captor.

"This is beyond my responsibilities," the spiderlady finally said, recoiling from their grating voices. "I am just an escort to the archives."

"Take us there! Tell Idalia we're here," I tried again. "*She'll know my name.* I'm here to help her!"

"Just let her go!" Jonesy yelled.

"Let her go and fight someone your own size!" the wolf added. "Release me and meet my claws honorably!"

At that, she sprang forward and landed over our pursuer's body, leaning into his personal space like a nightmare.

"Enough! Wolves also know better than to come here uninvited," she snarled, that dangerous purr grumbling at the back of her throat.

The wolf sneered, raising his head as much as the sticky web allowed while clinging to his hair. He pushed himself up into her space. In disdain. In defiance.

"How the *fuck* did something like you survive this long?" It wasn't a real question, although it begged other genuine ones. "Neither human nor spider but some perversion of both. Disgusting monster."

"Shut up, man!" Jonesy begged.

But I…I honestly wanted him to keep talking. He was…a jumble of confusing behaviors and words to me. A contradiction. After all, he was part of the Knights of the Rising Sun—a cult *filled* with "disgusting" hybrids. Why would a half-spider woman bother him at all? Hell, he should have been trying to *recruit* her.

I would've paid anything to see his face once he learned what *I* was. It'd probably make him spontaneously combust.

The spider, though, wasn't bothered by his insults in the slightest. Her purr grew to a soft roar as she narrowed the distance between them to inches, pressing him back into the web.

"You should have spent your last breath defending yourself."

His yell reverberated for ages, but she wrapped him and bit him with a horrible crunch, silencing any last words he might have had to say. Then, she turned back to me.

"I will take you to my lady, and if you are who you say you are, you will not be harmed more than is necessary," she said, tiptoeing closer to me so fast she was suddenly on top of me, looming over me inches from my face.

"*You could just…not harm me at all*," I offered.

Her great white grin widened at that, and I almost fainted at the sight. "*Humans are not allowed in my lady's presence. Not even ones with wings. Rest easy, birichina. If you are who you claim to be, you will wake up again.*"

There wasn't even time to scream as she struck, sinking her inch-long fangs into my neck. And then darkness bloomed in my vision like paint in water, and I saw no more.

CHAPTER 23

I woke in a strange way I never had before. I didn't immediately arrive in the waking world, on a bed or in a cell.

My inner sanctum faded into my awareness and I found myself on the floor by my raven's perch, with my wolf's coarse tongue licking me awake. I sat up, groggy and exhausted. My mental limbs felt leaden and stretched to tearing. But I was awake, I was almost certain I was.

"*Paralyzed*," my raven explained. "*Spider venom.*"

"*Safe*," my wolf promised, and that seemed impossible to prove.

As I rose from the ground, my eye caught on the viewing windows. They were…covered. *Draped* in something white and billowy. Spider silk, I realized after a moment. I was encased in spider silk.

I was honestly sort of awed by it. Humored by it; and I needed all the laughs I could get. How had I ended up here, enveloped in prey wrapping, the prisoner of a magnificent creature who inspired me with wonder and paralyzed me with fear?

Where was I?

Where was Cass?

Where was Jonesy? And Millie? And Brodie?

What was I going to do?

What would happen if Idalia didn't believe the spiderlady and she turned me into a tasty little bedtime burrito snack?

At least I knew I could get out of the silk easily enough once the paralytic wore off. *If* it wore off. I had my raven's wings to slice through it, my wolf's claws and teeth to rip it off, and the piece of azurite I could always feel buzzing softly against my stomach.

I could…

I could…

My busy thoughts fell silent as I turned away from the viewing windows and stopped dead where I stood. The inner sanctum had changed again. The cubbies had changed again. The three larger ones that had been there before were still there, but three more had expanded and altered.

The front of one along the floor had been encased in mud and branches, leaving only a narrow opening at the center for something to crawl through.

The next above it was…full of water. There was no glass—it wasn't an aquarium tank—but bubbly water filled the cubby to its limits magickally and didn't spill.

The last contained…a mossy log wedged into the cubby diagonally so there were spaces below and above it.

I didn't want to know. I just didn't. But I asked anyway, "*Other forms?*"

"*Yes,*" my raven answered.

"*Will you tell me what they are if I ask*?"

She called my bluff immediately. "*Are you asking?*"

I shivered and remained quiet and turned away without another word.

But my wolf stepped in front of me then and said, "*Ask 'why wolf.'*"

I knew what she meant—*Why was 'wolf' the first animal form to emerge from my beastliness? Of all the animals in the world, why had I turned into a wolf first?* They were questions that had nibbled incessantly at the back of my mind since the wedding, but which I'd avoided on the chance they opened a can of worms I wasn't ready for.

"*Will I like the answer?*" I asked instead.

"*Should,*" she replied, but I didn't ask.

As far as anything having to do with me was concerned, there was only one question that mattered right now. One question and one answer.

I needed *proof* that I wasn't going insane. That's all. Ha, "that's all." No seriously, I *needed* it. Everyone I'd met who knew about me seemed to have an opinion about my beastliness but not a single one had offered proof that I wasn't going to lose my mind.

Until I knew I wasn't, anything anyone told me about myself was just as likely to be nonsense as truth.

I needed proof.

I needed Idalia.

And then…like a wish granted…

"For the love of my Holy Goddesses, where is she?"

Idalia's voice trilled like something out of a dream. My heart *soared* at the sound of it.

And then I felt fingers against my face. Long slender fingers with elegant red nails plunged carefully through the silk across my viewing windows and yanked it away.

I was lying in a stone room lit by sconces shaped like spiders. The chandelier, too, was a giant mother spider looming over her glowing egg sacs.

And then *the Spider Lady herself* popped into view above me.

I was *thrilled!* Idalia…was not.

"Natalie, you *cabbage head*! *Has your brain been on vacation?!* I have been waiting *ages* for you to come to me. What a disaster you are!" She sighed dramatically and snapped at someone out of view. "Pick her up. Carry her upstairs. *Gently!* I'll eat you if you drop her!"

Arms slid under me and foisted me up and over a meaty, tall shoulder, shifting my view to one of a man's *enormous* ass and the stone floor far below…then winding circular stairs…and a window out of the corner of my eye…then beautiful mosaic floral tile the color of summer heat and spice. Terracotta, mixed with sage, as we stepped into a room *bursting* with greenery.

"There on the *divano*," Idalia barked, and I was moving—flying—backward as he unloaded me.

I landed with a *fwoomp* on a couch.

Idalia appeared beside the enormous, modelesque African man who had carried me. She smacked him across his brawny arm.

"What did I say?! *Be careful!*"

But then she reached for him more tenderly. Cupped his cheeks and pulled him down toward her for a passionate kiss, which he accepted with a throaty chuckle.

"*Wait in my bed for me, I'll be there after this is settled.*"

"*You better. The longer you make me wait the greater your punishment will be,*" he growled, giving her a swift smack on the butt before he turned and walked away without a glance back.

But as he did, I caught a whiff of something I'd never expected. He smelled of fruit. Papayas. He was an alter—and *not* one of the spider persuasion.

"You sneaky girl," I would've said…if I'd possessed the ability to speak.

Instead, she tutted at me. "Natalie, I know you can hear me. I am going to have my physician administer something to wake you up, all right? If we wait any longer your eyes will dry out like raisins. *Not ideal*."

I felt the prick of a needle lower down, on my thigh. Then Idalia was there tearing the rest of the silk from my body as my fingers began to fizz with sensation, waking up.

Words crawled up my numb throat as croaks: "Is…Jonesy…still… alive?"

Idalia tutted loudly again. "*Of course* he's still alive! *They're all* still alive. You think I am in a position to throw away perfectly useful wolves and dragons with what is going on in my court?"

Even yelled at me like an accusation, the news that Jonesy was alive was a welcome one and made the de-petrification process easier.

After a time, my body became mine again, and I sat up shaking my head to clear the last mental cobwebs away. I was grateful, too, that Idalia had waited until I was in control of myself again to start her tirade.

With the most serious—and therefore most unintentionally hilarious and dramatic—expression on her face, she said, "I will ask you again, *corvetta*. Where have you been? Giselle and I have been in a panic since that day at Hamingja. We heard everybody but us was invited to your wedding and then *nothing*! No announcements. No bragging from the king. Do you know how many obituaries and wedding announcements I had my men comb through for word of you?!"

I tried my best not to smile at her. I really did. But she punctuated her rant by throwing her slender arms around me and tugging me into a tight hug and I couldn't help smiling. I'd done it. I'd found her with a tiny bit of time to spare.

"I'll tell you everything, I promise," I swore, "But take me to Giselle first."

"I'll do you one better, you sweet idiot."

***

"Oh my god, *Natalie!*"

"Scar?"

I thought she was a mirage, a hallucination. Maybe another avatar of my new power, like Cass. But she wasn't. Scarlett was sitting on a far couch when Idalia guided me into a large sitting room. At the sight of me, my best friend in the world leapt to her feet, blonde hair flying behind her, and ran for me. Slammed into my embrace like a freight train.

"Holy hell, Scar, thank Goddess, are you okay?"

"We're fine! We're all fine, I promise!"

We?

She pulled back a little letting me take in the rest of the room. Stupid Josh was there, looking like his stupid sexy annoying self, but…so was Giselle.

She was…*glowing*. Her skin was flushed with rosy pink, her eyes were bright and healthy. And her hair. Her fingers toyed self-consciously with the end of her strawberry blonde new growth, which had grown into a thick *curly* pixie cut since I'd last seen her.

"Hello, *choupette*," she said quietly, rising to her feet.

I stumbled toward her, feeling a swell of *joy* in my heart that made me want to cry. "Are you okay? You look so healthy!"

I wound my arms around her delicately, rejoicing when I felt her hands meet around my back, patting with actual strength and vigor. "Yes, yes, I am well, thanks to you."

But it was barely me. "Thank you for saving her, Idalia. Thank you for saving both of them. I don't think I can ever repay you."

Idalia grinned. "Oh yes you can, but you can thank your little friend for the rescue." She gestured to Scarlett. "She's the one who summoned my helicopter to Hamingja."

Scarlett offered me a wide awkward smile, but it faded quickly as worry rushed in.

"Scar, what's wrong?" I asked.

Tears rose, lining her bright blue eyes in silver. "I'm sorry I couldn't get you out of there. I-I knew Rav was hurting you. I didn't know how but I tried to get you away, I swear. I got you out of the building once. We almost made it to the dock—just ask Josh."

Behind me, I heard Josh say, "True as, she's a bloody legend."

"Rav caught me, and then I wasn't allowed anywhere near you again," she continued. "When he flew away with you, I got my hands on a phone and snuck it to Giselle. The next thing I knew, they were telling me and Josh to run to the helicopter on the roof. It was chaos. The fighting was insane, but Josh helped me get through the guards, and I…left. I left you. I'm so sorry, Nat."

I tugged her into a hug we both needed. "It's okay. It's okay! That was smart, you did so well!"

And a bit of my ire cooled for Josh. The tiniest bit, but it was better than nothing. He'd helped Scarlett escape. There was *literally* no way for me to make it up to him, so…it needed to be enough to pardon his selfish choice to change her into a jay alter without her knowing enough to make the choice for herself.

"Thank you, Josh," I said.

"No worries."

"No seriously, thank you for getting her out. I owe you one."

"Of course, don't worry about it," he said, a little more sincerely.

And again, it was almost enough to warm me up to him.

Except…

The smile on his face didn't quite rise to his eyes. It was a small detail I almost overlooked, thinking I was probably hyper-stimulated and still on alert for danger, real or imagined. But I wasn't the only one who noticed. As a butler stepped into the room to summon us to dinner, Josh gave me a nothing-grin and tugged Scarlett ahead into the hall and Idalia and Giselle stepped up beside me.

"This is of no consequence, I fear," Idalia said with a nothing-grin of her own, "but I do not like that snackrifice. He has been…very dumb since he arrived."

"He *is* very dumb," Giselle echoed, adding, "But it is every young woman's burden to meet a 'Josh' once in their life…so they can learn to avoid them in the future."

"Has he *done* anything bad while he's been here?" I asked, trying to cling to the little goodwill he'd earned for himself.

"Aside from moaning that he is bored every hour of every day like a toddler?" Idalia asked. "No. I just thank the Goddess my tastes have changed since I was her age."

Then she sighed and pulled my shattered phone from her pocket, offering it to me like the electronic brick it now was.

"Suppose it was too much to hope that it survived that plunge I took, eh," I said.

Idalia shook her head at that. "Oh no, I smashed it when you got here, pet. Arachne's Revenge is completely cut off from the outside world. It's why nobody's ever found it. But! I managed to transfer your contacts before I took my stiletto to it, so you can still call your team after dinner."

"I don't think we can wait until then," I warned.

Idalia sighed. "No. We can't."

CHAPTER 24

Everything that had happened, short of my beastliness, came pouring out of me over our several-hours-long strategy meeting, which Idalia *insisted* had to happen over a multi-course dinner to "give me strength to tell my tale."

"We are civilized creatures," she said when I admitted I felt too queasy to eat. "Not eating because our loved ones are in danger only causes two problems. And you are more likely to make impulsive decisions on an empty stomach."

I recounted everything that had happened when I was last at Hamingja over appetizers of mini artichoke hearts and radicchio tartlets with cheese. I told them about Greece and the wedding over *ravioli di zucca*, pumpkin-filled pasta with browned butter and crushed amaretti. I regaled them with my escape to and from Alexandria, along with all that I had done to find them since landing in Italy, as I scarfed down porcini mushroom polenta.

And over a dessert of poached pears in red wine, Jonesy and I warned them about what we had outrun in Rome. The bat alters exposing themselves. The vampire calling himself my servant. The dais by the Colosseum. All of it.

It was the most elegant and nerve-wracking debriefing I'd experienced to date. And by the end of it, Idalia had sent three of her men off on various missions. One to find Brodie when he touched down in Italy; Jonesy left with this one to locate Millie. One to reach out to their spies in Rome for updates. And one to interrogate the wolf and vampire alter that had fallen into the spider pit with us.

"We have been very *antsy* waiting for the king's retaliation," Idalia explained. "We knew it was only a matter of time. Along my border to the north, we have warning systems in place to alert us to mass arrivals, both in the sky and on foot, but…Italy is a peninsula. We can only monitor so much of the sea."

"I…might be able to help with that," I offered. "If you get me to the coast, I can call out to Tidebringer Rawan. Bargain with her for that sort of patrol."

A pleased smile swept across Idalia's face. "In the morning, *corvetta.* Once we know whether this cult of sunrises truly means to destroy the Great Secret at dawn." She turned to Giselle and added, "What do you think the cult is thinking? Do you *really believe* they'll do it?"

Giselle's eyes met mine. "I do."

"Well, if they do, they chose tomorrow for a reason, yes?" Idalia said.

"What reason?" Scar asked.

"It is the day before the full moon," Giselle said. "If they break the great covenant, the humans will have no time to react to the changes that night will bring, and of course many alters who have felt repressed forever will celebrate their freedom loudly. It is *inevitable* that some humans will go looking and be altered. I think they are counting on that."

"Some will also go hunting," Idalia murmured.

"Yes, I believe they are hoping for that as well," Giselle said. "The question is…how will this change the war that is coming? *Is it* still coming? The cascading effects of this decision will echo into eternity."

"What do you mean?" Scar asked.

"King Elivagar is the ruler of the European Continent. By his own laws, he *must* seek out and punish all who reveal the Great Secret, so, in theory, war *would* break out. However, if the secret is revealed, those laws must be rewritten anyway—not just by him but by *all* the world's Sovereign Supremes. They must *all* react to set new standards and legalities. The question is whether they'll unite or divide under the strain. And whether they'll turn away from Rav for his supposed failure to protect the secret. And then there are the human politicians to contend with…We've lived in the shadows for centuries. Exposed to the light, we become a political nightmare."

"Or a political opportunity," Idalia said. "Rav may struggle with some aspects of his station, but he is exceptionally opportunistic. Even more so than his father, the opportunities he exploits tend to work in his favor."

Her eyes slid gently to me then, as she added, "*Most* of the time."

I ignored that. "So let's *go now*. Let's send our forces to the Colosseum. Arrest them before they can make that announcement. I-I don't know how we deal with the fallout from so many videos of flying alters that have probably already been posted online—maybe we claim a company was filming a movie? I could have my lawyer create a production company overnight, if we need that. Throw together a film crew that could be there a couple days from now, after we stop the cult from outing us. The Eighth Kingdom has a couple BAFTA-winning directors and *a ton* of content creators; they could have promos and special effects clips up showing "how the flying was done" in no time. O-Or declare it a hoax if all else fails."

"Those aren't bad ideas," Idalia praised before she grimaced and added, "But…"

"But?"

"At this moment, my soldiers are crawling out of the tunnels under Rome. Oppian Hill will be overrun. Any announcements are unlikely to happen there. We'll arrest cult members. We'll yank bat alters out of the sky like bullfrogs eating flies."

I sat forward at that. That all sounded *great*! "Brodie's probably almost there. He'll help!"

"Our soldiers know their duties, so we will leave that to them while we assume the worst, *corvetta*," she said, shaking her head. "This was not a last-minute plan on the cult's part, as you well know. Assuming the dawn is coming, what do we do once it rises?"

***

It was amazing how…simple the meeting became. Complex—more complex than anything I'd ever had to deal with in my *life!*—but simple all the same. Scarlett took Josh from the room and then it was just us three Alter Supremes planning for an as-of-yet unimaginable future long into the night.

It boiled down to an alliance first and foremost. A military, economic, and spiritually coherent alliance between our three queendoms. One that would be open to Asterios, too, if we found him, as well as Tidebringer Rawan…and the witches, once we had a chance to speak with them and hold a smaller, but long overdue, discussion with the Witches Council.

We made plans to hold a summit among the world's Alter Supremes as well, and to extend our alliance to anyone we vetted and decided sincerely wanted to join us.

I worried the goals were lofty and idealistic, but Giselle countered, "This is our chance to position our kind not just as equals to humanity but *worthy of existing in our own right*. You must remember, the most vulnerable time for our kind will be those precious first months and years when we establish our culture, claim our history, and defend ourselves against those who fear us and would paint us as monsters. And many *will* fear us. It is human nature."

My stomach soured at the thought. So many awful possibilities jostled for space in my brain, tugging at insecurities and fears. I'd never felt younger in my life, imagining how many things could go wrong. Especially representing *so many different creatures*. Sure, we were alters and witches…but in that was a spectrum. Variety the likes of which the world had never seen. Each came with their own complications. Their own expectations. Their own identities and prejudices and dangers.

Not to mention the wild magick, which I hadn't had the chance to tell them still existed yet. Wild magick was alive just like we were; it would need representation too.

It was too big to address in a single conversation but by the time the sun rose the next day, Giselle, Idalia, and I had drafted a long list of potential bylaws, policies, and strategies that could apply to the whole world, if we survived the transition from the shadows to the sunlight.

To my surprise, Idalia made a point of dismissing the very first rule in Rav's bylaws—the one about mixing.

"Mixing *happens*," she whined. "We have never had anything come of it, and soon we won't be able to police it anyway."

I didn't hate the sound of that, even if it was a wish coming too late to matter.

I risked giving a little of myself too. "I don't think beasts are made that way. They're…more the result of magickal mistakes, not biological ones."

Finally, as a *digestif* for the whole evening, Idalia ordered an entire contingent of her men to collect the rest of our scattered people and bring them to Arachne's Revenge—Fern, Yasmina, Rolfe, as well as Fiadh Clarke, Belina Saldo, Asterios, and Corby, whenever they were located, as well as their own trusted people *they* believed would help broker peace or go to war with us depending on how the sun rose that day.

As for Tidebringer Rawan, well, summoning her would be left to me.

As dawn finally broke across Idalia's home, splashing sunshine up the walls, wide sea vistas came into view through the windows. This home—this *estate house*, this *luxurious fortress*—was perched on the sea, at the top of a two-hundred-foot sheer cliff wall. To the left, there was a cozy port village with houses of every rainbow hue, to the right more cliffs and giant cruise ships at anchor in the bay. And across the bay?

"That is Mount Vesuvius," Idalia supplied when I couldn't take my eyes off the enormous singular mountain that dominated the far skyline.

Gorgeous. Intimidating. And…the wrong direction from where I thought we were.

"Isn't Mount Vesuvius to the *south* of Rome?" I asked. "Like, the *far* south?"

"Not that far. A couple hundred kilometers away." She shrugged.

"Are your…archives near here?"

"No, pet," she said. "When our escort in the tunnels—Sofia—warned me of your intrusion, she told me you wished to see both of us, me as well as the library. Unfortunately, we are in opposite directions, and I was greedy and wanted you to myself first. Do you have need of the archives?"

I nodded. "Not today, but I need to go there as soon as possible. And…I also need you to teach me how to contact the dead."

Idalia's already decadent grin widened further as she threw her arm around my shoulders and pressed me into a sideways hug. "I *love* being a bad influence."

To that, I laughed. "I don't think bad influences spend all night discussing how to safeguard the future of entire *masses* of people."

"Everything in balance, *corvetta,*" she said. "Come. We have made plans for the apocalypse. Let us go see if it actually happens."

CHAPTER 25

Was the unraveling of the Great Secret an apocalypse in the making? As we all gathered in the den in front of Idalia's satellite television to wait for…any signs either way, I found myself hoping that Brodie had made it in time. That Idalia's people had flooded the Piazza del Colosseo and destroyed the dais while taking every Knight captive. That *Rav* had gotten my warning and had somehow been able to stop those videos of flying bat angels from spreading.

That everything would be "fixed" again, even if it was only temporarily.

We already had enough on our plates, didn't we?

I certainly did. Between Rav's weird declarations of still wanting to mate with me and him giving my queendom away at the drop of a hat, *and* my beastliness, I wasn't begging to take on more.

Don't get me wrong, I'd never felt more capable in my life, which was a strange realization I'd had during our strategy session and I couldn't tell if it was from exhaustion, delusion, or genuine blossoming pride. I hadn't just held my own with Giselle and Idalia while we talked about some of the greatest dangers we faced integrating into humanity; I'd actually come up with a few policy suggestions that seemed to impress them.

Anti-discrimination laws were a given, but I suggested we hire a slew of lawyers at the very beginning to introduce those laws *everywhere* to avoid pockets of the world finding loopholes that turned our people into second-class citizens.

International recognition of our kind as a legal minority, a distinct class under international law with protections from discrimination in housing, employment, education, and public life. As well as codified language that would make genocide and hate crimes far less appealing to human purists, and to punish them for those crimes if they attempted them.

A right to shift during an emergency, for self-defense…along with a companion agreement to regulate shifting as much as was possible to reassure the humans and avoid introducing chaos into the world at large.

And a few weeks ago, back in Hamingja, I'd read about the atrocious treatment of Aboriginal children in Australia, where European colonizers forcibly removed them from their families to erase their culture, language, and connection to their people through assimilation into western society.

That had led me down a rabbit hole about the same things being done to Native Americans in the United States and Canada, something which had only ever been glossed over when I went to school in the states.

So I recommended special protections for shifter children, legal language that could protect them from being institutionalized or experimented on without consent and oversight. As well as language that codified that shifter children were entitled to their mixed cultural identities, of both their human and animal forms. They were as much one as the other.

Tied to that, we'd need language and regulations for how people and children were marked in the future, so no children were changed against their will, and no parent with good intent was arrested for child endangerment or harm for sharing that heritage with their child.

And yet, despite how well I'd held my own while brainstorming, I could see my life stretched out before me, my future as a public servant unfurling like a neverending brick road of work ahead of me. I hoped one or all of us had thwarted this "Announcement of the Dawn," this latest attempt by the cult to take the bag containing all our secrets and slit it open so our most closely guarded truths could never be shoved back in.

I wasn't that lucky. In fact, I was downright cursed.

At 9:10 in the morning, a guard rushed in and whispered in Idalia's ear, and she changed the channel on the television.

There, in unignorable high definition, stood…a man with blond hair and blue eyes. A perfectly ordinary-looking guy. Maybe an office worker, or a teacher. He wasn't in Rome; he was standing in London—my London—in front of the Parliament building surrounded by signs for the Knights of the Rising Sun.

Idalia didn't wait for him to speak. She switched the channel again, to another station covering an olive-skinned man with chocolate hair and dark hazel eyes standing in front of La Sagrada Familia Cathedral in Barcelona.

She switched again, to a channel covering a similar setup in Vienna.

And Athens.

And Berlin.

And Amsterdam.

A peculiar feeling welled in me as the channels switched by, like alternate versions of the same television show—I was *relieved* to know nothing I had done had contributed to this. There would have been no way to stop this coordinated display. Without more information, more time, more everything, we couldn't have been prepared to stop them everywhere at once.

But of course, with that relief came bitter dread. There was no stopping this. And there was no doubt what they were about to do.

Idalia switched the channel again and I saw someone I recognized out of the corner of my eye.

"Wait, go back!"

It was Lilla. *William Mahon's Lilla* was standing at the back of a dais in the Champ-de-Mars in Paris, with the Eiffel Tower framed in the background. In front of her, a beautiful, serious woman in her late 30s, with coffee-dark hair and matching eyes and pale skin stood at a podium, waiting to speak.

There was something about her…some indefinable quality that had all of us leaning in, on bated breath. When she looked at the camera, it was as if she was peering through it. As if she could see us there watching. For a long moment, I had no doubt she could.

And when she finally spoke, her French accent hugged her English with dedication, as if she had practiced many times for this exact moment.

"People of France. My name is Robine Danton."

"Robine," I murmured, telling the others, "She's one of their leaders."

"I am a member of the Knights of the Rising Sun and the Noctaran Order. I am a representative of a people you did not know existed, but who have lived among you since the dawn of humanity. I am a two-form, an alter, a shapeshifter."

They'd done it. They'd said the secret out loud.

You could have heard a pin drop, both in the sitting room and in

France. No one spoke. Not a single camera flashed despite there being hundreds of people in front of Robine as the camera slowly pulled back to reveal them there watching.

"The time for hiding our nature is over," she continued. "We are not myths. We are not monsters. We are your neighbors, your physicians, your teachers, your friends. Twenty-six days of every lunar cycle, we *are* you. No matter where we were born or how we were marked for change, we hold the same values as every human being watching this broadcast.

"We hid our nature, not to deceive, but to survive many centuries of persecution. There is nothing to fear from us. Our differences do not make us dangerous. We are here to live peacefully and honorably beside you, just as we have done since the beginning of time. We ask not for privilege, but for protection. Not for control, but for coexistence. Not for fear, but for understanding.

"We are real. We are here. And we will work with you, speak with you, stand by you, and welcome you as we work toward peaceful coexistence together."

Again, she paused, and silence filled the space around her as she watched heads in the crowd turn in disbelief. Maybe even humor, as if this was some elaborate prank. In the face of that, she smiled.

"And just so there's no misunderstanding, in cities across this great continent, my brothers and sisters are standing by to show you exactly who we are."

The men and women to either side of her on the dais stepped forward. Then they raised their right hands into the air holding…

"Azurite!" I pulled out the long necklace I had under my clothing, showed everyone my own pendant of the stuff. "Those are azurite stones. They're not going to alter, are they?"

Oh, but they did.

It happened in a flash of blue light and crimson flesh unraveling. One moment four people stood to either side of Robine, the next, there were wolves, dragons, tall wolves, and…a raven.

"Who is *that one*?" Idalia asked under her breath. I knew she meant the raven.

She didn't wait for an actual answer. She flipped the channel instead. Again and again and again, there were altered animals everywhere. In Budapest. In Warsaw. In Oslo. Larger than their wild counterparts. More magnificent *and* intimidating. Magickal. Undeniable.

Especially when the cameras started flashing.

And the questions came pouring in.

Idalia found her way back to Robine's channel, where her cohorts had already transformed back into their human forms and were standing in dark robes with the Knights' logo on them like they'd stolen them from a posh spa or something.

Proud, regal, unintimidated, Robine stood at that podium, taking the brunt of the noise and light like a queen. Like *she knew* those images and moments were being recorded for the history books.

And then, the crowd simmered, and she pointed to a man holding up his hand, "Yes, you have a question?"

She answered dozens of questions, from journalists and civilians alike, until the audience was smiling with curiosity and wonder, and one of her men had distributed new laminated pamphlets of some kind to the people in the crowd.

Each question was another piece of secrecy given away freely.

Each answer was designed to entice all who were seeing this to dream of a world of night they'd never thought possible before.

It was educational, more than anything. Not dramatic. Not set up for ridicule. They were simply laying us bare in the light of day.

And for a moment I could almost imagine the world embracing these revelations rather than being torn apart by them…

Until, like some terrible cosmic joke, a journalist raised his hand and asked a question that changed my life forever: "Madame Danton, are you the queen or president of these people? What should we call you?"

Robine smiled coyly. "No, I am just a humble representative of the Noctaran Order—the Ninth Kingdom of Alters in Europe. Our queen—Arch-Sovereign Natalie Damarand—is not with us today, but rest assured, she will make her debut to the world very soon."

CHAPTER 26

"Arch-Sovereign Natalie Damarand."

"Arch-Sovereign Natalie Damarand."

"Arch-Sovereign Natalie Damarand."

"It has to be a joke, right?"

"Arch-Sovereign Natalie Damarand."

"Arch-Sovereign Natalie Damarand."

It was everywhere. On every channel, almost perfectly timed as we switched through. The representatives of the knights were being asked who their leader was, and each replied the same.

"Arch-Sovereign Natalie Damarand."

I felt sick.

I felt like laughing.

Maybe the insanity was spreading.

I glanced at Idalia and Giselle, hoping that maybe it was all in my head and this was just a symptom of my *own* mind starting to slip, but no. They glanced at each other, then at me, then Idalia leaned into the ear of the nearest man in the room, and he darted away.

"Why would they do this?" I asked, because no one else did. "Are they trying to get me killed? Are they putting a political target on my back? So I take the blame if things go wrong?"

If so, the joke was on them; I was going to die pretty soon anyway so they wouldn't be able to use me as a scapegoat for very long.

"That might be part of it," Giselle said, her face set in a way I knew she was calculating something in her head, considering this new development carefully.

"What else could it be?" I asked.

Giselle eyed me gently. "Do you remember that woman's house in France? The one we took shelter in?"

"Violette's? Of course."

"Do you remember what that vampire said to you as we escaped? She said your meeting was inevitable and that she had much to say to you."

"Right."

Giselle grew quiet again, still calculating.

But Idalia soon snapped. "Don't suddenly learn how to hold your tongue now, Giselle."

"Before Aldric died, when the cult had us, I heard something I didn't give much weight to then, but now seems to weigh quite a lot." She sat forward delicately. "I heard one of the female vampires *command* my son to be patient. It was like a spell or something. Ulric went limp, his eyes fogged, and after, when she snapped her fingers at him, all the impatience of moments before was gone."

"The vampire Lilla can hypnotize," I offered.

Giselle nodded, absorbing that information too. "She also told him that nothing could be done before the dawn, and only their Arch-Sovereign could cause the sun to rise."

I blinked before saying the obvious, "Well, I can't control the sun. I know they mean a figurative sun, but I didn't tell them to do this. I've never spoken to any of them unless forced…or I was interrogating them."

Giselle shook her head. "But…*dawn has risen*. Which means that if you are their Arch-Sovereign, some change in you or the world took place between that day and this one. What do you think it is?"

I certainly knew what it *could* be.

Before I could even open my mouth, my raven shouted, "*Lie!*"

The word was so loud and sharp in my head, I felt actual pain near my ear.

I snapped back at her, "*I wasn't going to tell them I'm a beast.*"

"*Good,*" my raven said. "*Lie.*"

But…*was* my beastliness the reason the cult had chosen to claim me as their leader? Was there any way for me to know for sure?

Yes, I realized, there was. And it made me sick to think of it.

Yasmina had called the witch Belina Saldo. Belina had told her, "*The cult now knows what William Mahon always knew.*" And then she had sworn she would find me "*after dawn.*" That chosen phrase wasn't a coincidence. It couldn't be. And William Mahon *had been* a knight at one point.

It suddenly felt like there was no air to breathe.

Worrisome thoughts bullied their way into my brain.

Once, I had thought I knew William Mahon relatively well, but…that was as a kid understands people. Since entering the alter world, I'd learned many things about him which colored his motives, his politics, his decisions differently.

Had…

Had William Mahon always known I was a beast?

How could he have?

And if he had, *Goddess why* wouldn't he have warned me? Why had he only left me a riddle to figure it out?

Why was I surprised that was all he had done? He'd ended his riddle with the words: *Natalie, I'm sorry.*

He'd known.

The swell of sickness that had been in my stomach since the start of the broadcast rose into my throat.

He'd known. Somehow.

I needed to talk to Will as soon as possible. But I couldn't mention that in relation to this, and there was another way to confirm my suspicions anyway—one I thought my allies would approve of.

So, I tuned back into the room. In my silence, the other women had been batting possibilities around; I had no idea what they were, but I heard Scarlett suggest, "Natalie left Rav. Could that be it? Maybe they chose her because she didn't marry the king?"

"That would make sense politically," Idalia said, seemingly unconvinced.

"Maybe it's something else," I offered. "Idalia, I think the answer might be in your archives. This cult has been around a while. I'd like to go there and find answers for myself. I'd like my team to be there with me—Fern, Yasmina. Corby, if we can find him. Not to mention, Rav is still coming for us. Whatever the fallout of all this, we need all our people together in one place, we need information, and…I think we need to call Robine."

CHAPTER 27

It was amazing how quickly Idalia shifted gears.

With a dramatic, "*Che coincidenza!*" she leapt from her chair and told us to take an hour to gather ourselves while she made plans to leave. As if she had struck a group of billiard balls, the entire room erupted into action and the men who had been standing around the fringes of the room scattered.

"We'll relocate to Arachne's Revenge as soon as the helicopters have arrived."

"Arachne's Revenge?" I asked. "Isn't *this place* Arachne's Revenge?"

She smiled that long white smile at me again. "I am Arachne, *corvetta.* It is wherever I am."

Then she clarified that she had another fortress to the far north right near the archives where we could stay while I did what I needed to do.

"There is also a very special thing I would like to show you there, so this is a perfect recalibration. By the time we arrive, your team will be there waiting for us, along with any stray allies we can find in the meantime."

Her men packed her necessities while *her man*, Jasiri, reached out to his own contacts in the African Elephant, Lion, and Bonobo courts, to see how news of the Announcement of the Dawn was being received. After all, Robine and her knights hadn't just outed European alters this morning; they'd outed the entire world.

Giselle went to call her contacts as well, which gave Scar and I (and an entire *battalion* of spider snackrifices) time to go down to the dock below Idalia's home and summon Rawan for a quick meeting. I'm glad we did.

Tidebringer Rawan *burst* out of the water before I'd even finished blowing the conch shell.

"What on Earth just happened?!"

"I'm so sorry; it wasn't me. I swear, Rawan, I am not *their leader. I think they're trying to get me killed. Please tell everyone you know."*

She eyed me gently, then cautioned, *"Don't tell anybody that yet. Being their "leader" may give you leverage you won't want to throw away. But also...don't do anything that would make you a target. I'm telling everyone in my coven to prepare for the coming storm. For now, the bigger question is why was it allowed to happen?"*

Guilt trickled back in, but she wouldn't let me dwell on it. She didn't believe for a second that the king didn't already know this was coming in one way or another, and I couldn't confirm or deny that. Instead, I told her everything that had happened in Rome. Then after, I asked her that all-important question—whether she still wanted to be my ally.

"Yes, I do. So long as you uphold your end of this, I would like to be kept informed and help any way I can. Especially in what comes next."

"...What's coming next?"

"There's already talk under the sea of a gathering. The Sovereign Supremes are furious. Whatever happens, I have five thousand souls under my care and I would like to keep them safe. You understand?"

I nodded because I did. Of course I did.

"What if I make you a deal? What if I offer you a seat in my cabinet so you can help mold policy for your kind in the years ahead?"

Her golden eyes widened with intrigue. *"What would you ask of me for this?"*

"We need someone to patrol the shores of Italy. We need someone to warn us if large numbers of alters land anywhere."

"I could do this," she said. *"How should we report to you?"*

I couldn't guess where we were going, but that information could reach me through Brodie while he was stationed in Rome.

"I know you were reluctant to swim the Tiber River," I said. *"Maybe for this you'd be willing?"*

Rawan scowled at me, but her eyes were smiling. *"For this. For you."*

And we shook on it.

***

Four hours later, our entire menagerie set down in a clearing outside a little Italian alpine town called Cison di Valmarino and rode up a tiny funicular to an *enormous* Roman fortress on the hillside. The castle loomed over the village like something out of a medieval romance, with great foundation stones and portal entrances that led up to what was essentially a village, complete with its own theater, spa, and temple to the Goddess.

Every staffperson's eyes flashed silver as we passed.

Every room we entered was grander than the one before.

And it was easy to see why Idalia considered this a place of retreat in times of uncertainty. Idalia explained as we walked up the path to the main building that, with the exception of aerial attacks, they could cut the castle off from the outside world entirely and for long stretches of time.

"As for flying pests, we have other precautions in place." Idalia didn't specify and I thought it better not to ask.

There were so many guards lined up along the battlements outside and the halls inside, it felt like the Ras el-Tin Palace in Alexandria all over again. Except this time, I had my own people with me.

"Finally!"

The moment I stepped into the central salon, there were two sets of arms around me, squeezing me between them like they were trying to turn me into a diamond. Fern and Yasmina even pulled Scarlett into the cuddle puddle, rejoicing that we'd finally found our way back to each other.

Rolfe had arrived too, and it almost made me cry watching Giselle run to him and hug him, and him admire her health as tears welled in his eyes.

A couple hours later, though, Millie arrived with Jonesy in tow. I was so relieved to see them, but dread seeped in when I caught a look of…trauma…on Millie's face; one she was trying so desperately to hide. She looked healthy physically, which was a perk of being able to alter at will, but when pressed she admitted her injuries had been extensive in the attack in Rome.

"The spider I took with me to the bar was…dead…when I pulled it out of my pocket," she said, shooting Idalia an apologetic frown. "One of the alters there saw it and…all hell broke loose. It was insane. Like some sort of frenzy. Not even really directed at me. I can't explain it; the others in the bar began to hiss, then I was suddenly thrown backward through a wall and I couldn't see Jonesy. Three bat alters came after me. I used the weapons I had on me to hold them back at first. But when they realized they couldn't get through the hole, they started using their wings to reach through for me, stabbing and jabbing and hitting. They broke my arm, sliced into my neck.

"I was in so much pain…Eventually, I had to use my azurite stone. Transformed for a moment just to heal myself, then transformed back, but they were reaching for me again and the knife I'd brought couldn't hold them off forever. I was there for an hour fighting in a puddle of my own flesh, hacking at their wings, transforming when I needed to buy myself more time, but it was exhausting. I was s-so tired, I didn't know how much longer I could take until…"

"Until what?" I asked.

Millie's gaze connected with mine, then, in a strange way I hadn't expected, given her story. It was pointed, secretive, and I instinctively switched off my aura of honesty.

"Until Brodie's team hit the city, I suspect," she lied. "Suddenly, the bats fled and I looked out to see the bar was completely empty."

"I found her in the apartment when I went back," Jonesy added.

"I'm sorry I couldn't get to you," I said, even though it didn't alleviate my guilt in the slightest.

"My lady, it's the way of things," she said, shrugging. "It was our job to keep you safe."

"You did," I swore.

Turned out, Idalia hadn't been joking when she said her men were going to tear the bat alters from the sky like bullfrogs eating flies. The spider alters who could shoot webs did exactly that, lassoing them with adhesive before yanking thirteen bat alters to the ground where they were captured and gagged to keep their screams of the damned from destroying anyone's eardrums.

"Brodie thought we'd have to call you to interrogate them, given your gift," Millie said. "But they told us straight away that they were on the Knights side in all of this."

"Why?" Giselle asked.

"Survival. Bats are the most numerous alters in a world that sees them as pests. Millions of the animal are killed every year, and the alters die for the same reasons. They said it was either they come out of hiding and be given the chance to save and protect themselves nonviolently, or they'd have to choose a different path."

It was a curious thing, hearing that explanation. How could I fault them for wanting to represent their own interests in the world? For wanting to claim their place and build a better future for their people? I didn't know enough about the bats yet to know whether their goals were unreasonable, but they didn't *sound* unreasonable. I supposed the devil was in the details. Only time would tell if that was truly why they wanted this.

But… "They must've been in on this for a while," I said. "This isn't the sort of thing you decide overnight."

"No, my lady," Millie said. "They've known for years."

"I figured as much," I said. "Earlier this summer, there was a massacre in Sweden, of a bat family. Afterward, bats all across Europe told Rav they wouldn't fight for him against the cult because they were afraid of retaliation. I think that massacre was an excuse they created. A justification they could use to stay out of Rav's army without arousing suspicion."

I took a deep breath and added, "Suppose this is all just guesswork until I speak with Robine, isn't it."

At that, Millie pulled a laminated fold of paper from her pocket and handed it to me. "I took one just in case."

It was one of the brochures we'd seen the cult distributing in major cities all over the place this morning. It was similar to the cult brochure I'd seen before, but there were no illustrations of how tall wolves were made. Instead, there was a web address and numbers on the back page.

If you would like to learn general information, visit our website KnightsoftheRisingSun.org.

If you're interested in becoming an alter, dial this number and listen for instructions.

If you are already an alter and wish to join the growing collective of nightshifters seeking change, dial this number.

If you would like to speak with a representative of the Knights, dial this number.

It was so mundane. So casual. So…unsecretive. It was just…*here's the information.* There was no sense that the cult was trying to take over the world, or start a war. The brochure read like it belonged to a non-profit.

Idalia, Giselle, and I left the others and gathered in the only room in this castle where cell reception was possible, let alone permitted. There, one of Idalia's men foisted one of those heavy satellite box phones onto the table between us. With zero ceremony whatsoever, as if we were ordering take out, we dialed the number on the back of the brochure.

The ring of the phone echoed into the room's gables overhead. Once…twice…

"Thank you for calling the Knights of the Rising Sun. Please listen for your language. For English, press one—"

I felt silly pressing the button. I couldn't unfurl my amused brow as I did so. Then Debussy's "Clair de Lune" began to play, done on a xylophone, and a shiver ran up my spine. Such a small touch, but it was intentional. To legitimize them. To give the appearance to anyone who called that this wasn't some crank operation or dangerous prank.

"Poppy speakin', what can I dee for ye today?"

She…was British. Young. From somewhere near Newcastle, if her chipper Geordie accent was anything to go by. Adorable. Oblivious. Not bothered in the slightest by the fact that she was committing some sort of treason by working with the cult.

"Poppy? I'd really like to speak to Robine Danton please."

"Nah, can't dee that," she cooed. "She's busy, man. And she's not from roond here. French or summat. But you're American, yeah? Your accent's class! I proper love it, like."

"Thanks Poppy, uh, could you let someone know that Natalie Damarand is calling? See if they can put me in touch with Robine, please?"

"No wayyyy!" she suddenly squealed. "They telt us ye might ring, my lady. Never thought I'd be the lucky one to get ye. But before I can put ye through, I've gotta ask a quick question—and ye have to get it right, or I can't pass ye on."

"Okay."

"What was the name o' the fella leadin' the knights who attacked that village in Finland?" So casual. As if she was prying for a bit of gossip at the office watercooler instead of talking about a massacre.

"Antonio," I said.

"Aye, that's spot on! They said ye were sharp. I'll patch ye through now. Been dead canny chattin', like—proper honour, this. Hope I hear from ye again."

There was a click. Silence. Then one of Chopin's Nocturnes began to play.

The wait this time was quicker, though. The music cut off, replaced by a ring and then suddenly…

"It is *such a relief* to hear from you, my sovereign." It was the voice we'd heard on the television, melodic and low yet completely self-possessed. Comfortable. "I had hoped to speak with you first in person, but you were too quick for my men in Rome. Not easy to outrun a wolf *or* a vampire. Oded was quite heartbroken *and* impressed."

There was no point asking what she and the cult had been thinking, what she hoped to achieve. We already knew. Just like Idalia, Giselle, and I already knew what *we* were going to do. At least the first few steps as we prepared for the fallout from this.

So I asked, "What are you hoping happens now?"

She cooed. "You lead us into a brighter, safer, fairer future. One in which our people are able to lead free lives without being preyed upon all while building a strong, secure community that will stand the test of time no matter what the humans throw at us."

"*Our* people?" I asked to clarify.

"All alters, my sovereign. All witches. Every wild hair of magick still left in this world."

She knew about the wild magick. I wasn't surprised, but I was pleased she admitted it.

"Are you the one who's been making these tall wolves?" I asked.

She cooed again, pleased, before teasing, "The latest generations, yes, but I am no longer the only one."

She meant me. I could just tell she knew about what I had done for Cass somehow.

"Why did you announce me as your leader?" I asked.

"Because you *are* our leader," she said, unhelpfully.

I called that bluff. "So if I commanded you right now to have everyone in the Knights turn themselves into my custody, you'd do it? You'd tell each and every one to wrap a chain around their ankles and wait for my men to come throw them in prison."

"Hmm, in time, we would," she said, more seriously. "But the Order has made me its interim leader while you are…adjusting to your new place in this world. You have responsibilities, my sovereign, and you must rise to them, or you risk the entirety of your people being lost."

"*But. Why?*" I pressed. "Are you trying to blame me for all of this so I take the fall when things go wrong? I'm not even the leader of the Eighth Kingdom anymore. You know that, don't you? You understand I only have power right now because people believe in me. They chose to stay with me instead of accepting the new leader. That's fairy dust. That's not real authority. It could disappear any second."

"That's the most important kind of authority there is," she countered. "If you continue to be worthy of your people's loyalty, it won't disappear. The time for kings and queens is over. No more autocrats. No more oligarchs. No more corporatists. No more propaganda masquerading as truth. In time, you will understand your role in this. Until then, you must find acceptance for this new fate. Think of all of your gifts. Think of all you have already become, both as a leader and as an alter. Don't you see the pattern yet, my sovereign? You are the only one who can lead us."

"Robine, just tell me why."

She sighed. "To be completely honest, we thought you were ruined after Yule last year. We were so relieved to discover we were wrong and others were right."

Idalia and Giselle's gaze shot to me in question, but before I could think of what she might mean, Robine continued.

"The one to lead us could not have succumbed to the temptation of robbing another alter of their power. She might *accept* the power of others given freely. She might *give* power to others, but she could not feast on the corpse of their power as if it was hers to keep—"

I suddenly snorted in disbelief. I knew exactly what she meant by her comment about Yule. I'd never sacrificed anybody or consumed anyone. And the one bite I'd taken, my system purged anyway.

"You picked me…because I'm vegetarian and didn't eat anybody's heart?"

Robine didn't think it was funny.

"The one to lead us could not blaspheme against the Goddess by accepting a sacrifice falsely given in her name. *Because she is of all flesh, she couldn't cannibalize someone else's future.* And you have passed these tests without even trying because this is your destiny.

"It is your destiny to guide us into a great and wonderful future. You have made innocent mistakes you must correct before you take your rightful place as our leader, but I have faith you will very soon. You must, unless you wish to leave us leaderless…because there is no one who can replace you."

She finally took a breath.

"But we can discuss all of this when we finally meet, my sovereign. For now, you must come to terms with what you truly are. You cannot fear it, you cannot hide from it, *you must accept it.* Learn to use this great power that is only yours. You must push past the lies you have been fed to the truth at the heart of your greatest fear, and once you do, you will come to me."

The line clicked, and she was gone.

CHAPTER 28

The night after my call with Robine was one of forced rest. Boring by comparison to the days and weeks before, save for one more beat of existential horror I hadn't been prepared for. Even with that surprise, I needed it more than I could ever admit to myself in the moment.

After explaining the Yule comment to Giselle and Idalia, they'd told me they needed to decompress and prepare for tomorrow, which they warned would probably be atrocious as the dust after the explosion of the Great Secret started to settle. They commanded me to take a break as well, Giselle with the stern voice of a mother and Idalia with the playful voice of a naughty aunt.

"You cannot be a cult leader without your beauty rest, my sovereign," she teased.

As she spoke, Idalia kept moving backward toward Jasiri, who was waiting at the far corner of the hall for her.

I admit I watched them run up the stairs until they disappeared, admiring and envying what they had together.

Then, I found a kind bellhop who smelled of water and lilies—a frog alter—and who escorted me to my room up the stairs where I found my entire group of friends waiting for me. Well, *almost.* The suite was designed like an apartment, with a central living room and four bedrooms around the periphery. There, I found Fern, Yasmina, Millie, Jonesy, Scarlett, and Josh, on the sofas.

It was amazing how quickly my eye leapt to the one big vacant spot among them…where someone was missing. Someone who should've been there. I could almost see him there with his saffron mane of hair, smiling at me in relief and joy, reaching for me as if beckoning to just sit right on top of him; he would share the seat.

"Hey babe, come join us!" Scarlett said snapping me out of my fantasy.

"I will in a sec. Let me take a shower first."

I sealed myself away and took a *long, hot* shower, so I could wash away the grit of Rome and the spider silk strands still in my hair. Long enough I had a panicked realization that I hadn't spoken to my mother in *weeks* and that I'd need to go back up to the satellite phone room as soon as I could to call her, especially given what she'd probably seen on TV that day. But the water felt too good against my sore body to flee prematurely. I stayed so long that the water ran cold before I realized that I'd forgotten to grab a towel…but I stepped out to discover someone had brought one in for me.

Annnd then I discovered the towel was *also* made of spider silk. This kind had been woven into thread, so it was better—less *clingy*—but still. My exhausted mind spent too long wondering which alter had…produced it.

By the time I returned to the sitting room, I was so tired, I literally collapsed beside Scar half unconscious already. I wasn't built to outrun the Infestation of Rome *and* paralysis *and* an all-night G3 Summit meeting *plus* the utter annihilation of my public image without sleep. And it was slowly taking me over as I sat there, half listening to my friends talk about their reaction to what had happened this morning.

"It has to be a ploy. It can't be real," Millie said.

"If it *is* real, Natalie's going to be paraded out in front of the entire world to answer questions," Yasmina said. "There will be nowhere she can go where people don't recognize her face. We'll have to quadruple her guard at all times."

"King Elivagar will likely redouble his efforts to find her," Fern said, agreeing. "Whether it's to kill or claim her is anybody's guess."

Yasmina tutted with dismay and added, "We'll have to force Archer Mahon out of whatever throne he's stolen so you can return to Scotland. Maybe Kinloch Castle can be our initial headquarters."

"Ah, no, please," Jonesy said. "That place is haunted. And no chippy shops anywhere."

It was such an odd combination of words to say, I turned blearily to glance at him…and blinked several times in confusion as I realized what was sitting right beside him. Yasmina was there, cradling what I'd thought was a stuffed animal at first. It wasn't. There was a *bird* nestled in her arms, completely asleep. *Bright* blue, save for the head, which was ashy gray. About the size of a loaf of bread.

I couldn't help it. "Yasmina, are you holding a *live bird*?"

A look of amused annoyance passed between her and Fern before she answered me. "Yes. It is a *long* story."

But no sooner had we both spoken did the bird's eyes *snap open* and find me in the room as if I had shouted at it. It began to flap. It began to *squawk*. Until Yas released it in blank confusion. It darted straight for me, landed on my knee, and began frantically chirping at me.

"Oh-kay…somebody's Pokémon is mad at me."

"It has *never* done this before, my lady!" Yas said, blushing with embarrassment. She rushed to grab it, then recoiled as it pecked at her. "Excuse me, *вітрогон*. Unless you want me to cook you tomorrow, get off our lady!"

But…it wouldn't go.

And the moment it flapped its wings again, wafting its scent in my exhausted direction, I knew why. It smelled of floral honey.

"Wait, Yas."

"What is it?"

"This isn't a bird. It's an alter. Someone go into my room and grab my azurite, please. Long necklace on the dresser!"

Scar ran in and tossed the pendant at me, and the moment the bird saw the stone, it almost leaned in as I pressed the azurite to its body. My mind filled with an image…a *horrible* image of Corby screaming for help. I couldn't hear it, but I could see him there crying in some dark place. *Horrible.*

And then, there was an explosion of feathers and bits of flesh, utterly ruining the shower I'd taken, and I felt a body slide to the floor at my feet.

"Oh my god!" Scarlett yelped.

"Oh, Corby!" Yas said, rushing forward with a blanket to throw over his shaking shoulders.

He flinched away from her touch and began to weep.

"Corby?" I said. "What happened?!"

He gripped his head and clung as a stream of Spanish poured out of him at a speed that was almost incomprehensible, even to me.

"*…Trapped because-because-because…I don't know. I don't know! He told me nothing…fat…ground…Why are my feathers gone?…naked…no-no-NO!…too much remembering.*"

"Slower, Corby, please!" I tried, but he couldn't slow down, and his own language became a sort of choking chirp caught in his throat.

“Call the doctor!” I said.

“Can’t you heal him?” Fern suggested.

“No, I don’t have that power anymore. And I don’t think it’d work for…this.”

“Here, I’ll take him down,” Jonesy offered. “Josh, can you help?”

Josh…didn’t immediately move. He *hadn’t* moved the entire transformation; he seemed frozen where he sat. It was only when he saw me staring that he pushed himself out of his seat and reluctantly helped Corby to his feet.

“Sure, mate. Let’s get you some help, ay?”

“I’ll go too,” Scar added.

“Maybe I should go with them?” I offered.

“Nah, stay,” Josh said, guiding him away.

I turned to find Fern and Millie comforting Yasmina where she sat on the couch, wide-eyed with her hand over her mouth, sort of frozen. Not in fear, I realized, but in guilt. “Yas, are you okay?”

“Why didn’t I know?” she asked softly. “Why didn’t either of us guess…?”

Fern didn’t have an answer; her guilt was better hidden but I could see it there too, just under the surface.

“My lady, rest,” Fern said, after a moment, and I could tell they wanted to be alone with this. To think about it, talk about it, before telling the rest of us what had happened.

Even though I didn’t think I *could* sleep now, I nodded and turned toward my room. At the very least I could wash myself again of Corby’s blood and start some sort of decompression process sorely needed after…everything else.

Millie, though, caught me at the door. She waited until Fern and Yas retreated into their room and we were alone before her expression shifted, vulnerable and uncertain.

“My lady, I know with everything else, maybe this isn’t the right time, but…I know you know I was lying earlier when I told you what happened in Rome. I could *feel* your honesty gift leave my throat, if that makes sense. My muscles loosened and I could hide again. I wanted to thank you for that.”

“Mills, you don’t have to thank me,” I said. “I don’t think you even should. I’ve been leaving on my aura of honesty all the time now, after everything, to make myself feel safe. I need to remember to turn it off.”

“No, don’t. Leave it on, we understand.” Her eyes welled then with tears. "I also wanted to thank you for saving my life. I don't think I'd've made it if you hadn't helped me."

I shook my head at that in confusion. "Whoa, Millie, what are you talking about? I left you. I feel awful about it."

She leapt forward at that and gently took hold of my arm; through the touch I could feel her sincerity as she said, "I know—you had to. I swear I understand. But…*thank you* so much for leaving your power with me. That one you said looks like Cassian? Seriously, I almost died in that bar and if it wasn't for him—*for you*—I would have. He appeared out of nowhere and just…*eviscerated* the bat alters trying to reach me. Shredded their wings with his claws, tore out their throats with his teeth. I thought I was hallucinating, honestly. But then he helped me out of the hole in the wall, helped me get back to the apartment, and I understood what you were telling us—about the not blinking. The not talking. No smell. It's incredible. I just wanted to say that. I owe you my life, my lady. I swear I'll make it up to you."

Her muscled arms enveloped me then and nearly squeezed the life out of me with love, and I accepted it because I really needed it. I really needed to feel held, even if it was only for a few seconds.

But as I stepped into my room and shut the door behind me, I took a moment to let my exhausted brain process what she'd just said. I…hadn't thought about that power of mine at all as Jonesy and I ran for our lives through Rome. I had figured it probably returned to me after spiriting Oded away, and just hadn't shown itself in the interim because I'd been surrounded by people practically since leaving Rome.

To this point, the only power of mine that had continued to work that far away from me was my raven, when she'd gone off to follow Cass across the continent and keep him safe. Rav had also been able to borrow my wings for a time, but eventually he'd had to return to me to recharge.

Cass wasn't…*another form* of mine that could leave my body like my creatures and operate independently, was he?

I didn't know.

"Cass?" I whispered into the quiet bedroom. "Are you here?"

I stood there for a few minutes waiting. Then I crawled into the luscious, soft bed and called his name again and again until sleep stole me away.

CHAPTER 29

In the middle of the night, I woke to a rising sensation I'd felt before—my head lifting a few inches—and rolled to find Cass laying there beside me with his arm extended as my pillow. He was silhouetted in the silver light splashing through my window from the nearly full moon outside.

I couldn't help it. Relief swept in like a flood and even though I knew it wasn't really him, I threw my arm around him and tugged myself closer. My head slid into the curve of his neck under his head. My body pressed to his. My fingers swept around his back, lightly clawing for purchase on his shirt because I was afraid he was going to push me away. I was. I was.

But he didn't. He froze for a long moment until I settled and sighed; then his free arm wrapped itself around me, keeping me close.

"Thank you for saving, Millie," I whispered. "Thank you for protecting me and Jonesy."

He, of course, didn't reply, but I felt a weird little motion where his face was touching my hair and pulled back just enough to look him in the eye.

He was smiling. *Poking fun* at me.

"What?" I groaned.

His eyebrow waggled a little as if to say, *of course I protected you, what did you think I was going to do*? And I shoved my head back into the crook of his neck, savoring the way he nuzzled his head back into place against my hair.

It didn't matter if he wasn't real. Not really. The more I had him around, the more grateful I was to the Goddess, my psyche, or whoever had let me have this buffer to ease the loss of him. Just the thought that Giselle would never get to hold Aldric again welled bitter outrage in me; it was so unfair it made me want to puke. I at least got to see Cass.

And soon, I would get to talk to him.

Giselle could talk to Aldric too, once Idalia showed us how to talk to the dead.

"I wish I could smell you," I murmured. "I wish I could bring you back. I'd give anything to be able to do that. Even if I couldn't keep you. I'd give anything."

He tightened his hold on me.

"Maybe I should ask the Goddess for that," I said. "Maybe I could offer one of my powers? Or *all* of my powers, you know?"

But at that he pulled away from me, wearing that frustrated, almost angry, expression again. It was muddied with hurt and uncertainty, but there was more frustration.

He shook his head forcefully as if to say *stop saying that.*

I didn't. "You died saving me. I don't want people to die because of me."

His face softened and I hated the expression I saw there—that I had no control of that, and worse it would probably happen again.

"Do you…know what the cult did to me today?"

He gently nodded his head.

"Do you think it's real?"

He shrugged, and I almost smiled. Not even my subconscious knew what to make of the cult's choice.

"What do I do?" I asked him.

But at that, his expression sharpened again as if he knew *exactly* what I needed to do. He twisted, rising off the mattress and for a moment I thought he was going to roll on top of me. I didn't know what to think about the jolt of excitement and anticipation that shot through me at the thought, but…I definitely thought I needed to talk to a therapist *asap*.

Instead, Cass maneuvered off the bed, coaxing me to sit up with him to free his arm. Then he offered me his hand. As my fingers snapped into his, he guided me to the window, which faced north, and the towering mountains nearby which were still just foothills of the Italian Alps.

In the moon-drenched darkness, I could make out a trail leading up and away from the castle into the forest. Cass pointed to this, then slowly slid his finger up and to the northwest.

"I need to…go into the mountains?"

He rolled his hand over a "hump."

"Over the mountains. Past them."

He nodded.

"What's past the mountains?"

A soft expression of hope set across his cheeks…and he raised his flat hand to his heart.

Me, the gesture said. *I'm there.*

Let me tell you, the *storm* of competing emotions I felt in that moment could have knocked me clear off my feet. My lungs began to hitch. The back of my throat tightened around a ball of pain that wetted my eyes. My stomach sank into icy fear and boiling hope and dread and a longing so strong I felt drunk.

"*You're* over the mountains?"

He nodded. So confidently.

"What do you mean *you're* over the mountains?"

He pressed his hand tighter to his heart.

"You're saying you're alive," I pushed. "You're real."

He nodded again.

"*Is he telling the truth?*" I asked my creatures just in case.

"*Truth,*" they both said at once.

But I pushed again. "*Where is he?*"

"*Here.*"

"*There.*"

And tears rushed down my face as my mind tried to decide if this was more insanity, or a dream come true. But I wasn't strong enough to even entertain the hope of that dream. I called that bluff *immediately.*

"So, let's go then," I said, staring him down. "Right now. Show me the way and I'll go to you. I want to be where you are."

At that, he held his hand out, palm down and did that slow gesture again that meant *in time.*

I was so tired. And this wasn't enough. *It was cruel.* The concept of insanity was such an unfair, slippery, amorphous thing. And magick made it so much harder to navigate.

I needed proof that my brain wasn't lying to me!

Something.

Anything, for the love of all that was holy!

I shoved the tears from my cheek as I turned away and crawled back into bed, already sobbing even though I felt so silly for the tears.

Cass was there seconds later, lifting my head with his suddenly materializing arm. Then his fingers tenderly ran themselves through my hair and I didn't want to be mad at him, or myself.

I rolled back into him, in that safe place in the crook of his neck, with his head pressed against mine, and cried until I fell asleep again.

CHAPTER 30

I woke on a warpath in the morning. I had three goals for the day: call Mom, talk to Corby, and hold a magickal séance that was long, long overdue. Finally getting into the archives to begin the world's most important study session was fourth on the list, and the most intimidating; I would tackle that after the full moon came and went. Or maybe I'd ask Idalia to lock me in there all night so the moon couldn't find me and turn me into some other crazy thing.

"*Not insane*," my wolf growled as I knocked on Fern's door to grab the number I knew she would have for my mom.

And all I could say in response was, "*Prove it.*"

Seriously, I wished she would.

Number in hand, I practically jogged up the stairs to the cell reception room. Dialed with a shake in my fingers, antsy to hear—

"Hello?"

My mom's voice hit me like a wave of peace. Just that one word; I'd missed her so much. And it was one thing for my team to reassure me she was safe, another to know for sure.

"Mom?"

"Holy hell, Natalie, thank god!"

Those first few minutes were…emotional tennis, batting questions back and forth between us about how we were, where we were, how we were holding ourselves together. She told me she was warned not to say where she was, and I leapt to cut her off begging her not to tell me, but she let me know she was in a cottage in a wooded place surrounded by wildflowers. She'd spent most of her time since fleeing London building a garden of all things.

"There's a greenhouse here," she said. "So we'll have food in the winter."

I snorted. "Are you planning for the end of the world?"

But the second I said it, I could almost feel sadness in her silence. She was scared. I was too traumatized to be scared. Or maybe everything was so scary, even something like *survival* felt a little indulgent to think about. My survival, anyway, not hers.

"Oh Mom, I'm sorry," I said. "It's been a lot. A lot has happened."

"It has," she squeaked. "Why didn't you tell me you were…that you could…is shift the right word?"

"Shift is fine. Alter is the word we use most, though," I said, as an open-handed realization slapped me in the face. *She hadn't known.* I'd forgotten in the midst of all of this that she never knew I could alter in the first place. Then she'd been torn from her life again and woken up only yesterday to news that I was…some sort of cult's figurehead.

"What do you become?" she asked.

"A raven," I said. "A big black-purple raven."

"You can fly?"

A breathy laugh escaped me. "In more ways than one."

"Gah, that must be incredible," she almost sang. "I saw all those people transforming yesterday and as scary as it was, I was *so excited* seeing it! All my life, the world felt so small. Like it was shrinking. Just…uninspiring, you know? As you get older it's so much harder to find wonder in the world, and then I saw someone in front of parliament explode into a beautiful *deer* with antlers so tall they accidentally hit the streetlight over his head and I was so *relieved* to know something like that exists in the world. Does that sound crazy?"

"No! No, of course not!" I swore.

"Could…could someone like *me* do that?" Her voice lilted with…hope that I would say yes and fear that I would say no.

"Yes! Would you want that?"

Her breath blew out of her nervously. "I think so. D-Do I have to call that number the Knights are putting up on TV?"

My mind whited at that. "No! Mom, don't call them. They're dangerous. Just wait for me to come to you and I'll help you alter, okay?"

"But…why'd they call you their leader if they're dangerous?" she asked. "Are you falling into something you can't get out of?"

Yes, but not in the way she meant. "Mom, I'm not doing criminal stuff, if I can help it. It's…some political choice they made. It had nothing to do with me, but…"

"But?"

“I think I need to tell you what’s happened over the last year for you to understand, but you have to promise not to get mad,” I said, already knowing that was a tall order.

“I promise…” she said, teasing out the words slowly before finishing, “…that I won’t get mad right now. I’ll hold it in and let it marinate until we see each other again, okay?”

I chuffed. “Okay.”

“Tell me everything.”

***

It was tough condensing everything down to a two hour near uninterrupted monologue.

It was tougher listening to her cry when I told her the scary things that had happened.

“You should have told me,” she finally said. “I could have kept your secret. I could have joined you earlier. And if I had known, I could have protected you that day in London when Eike threatened you.”

“Eike’s dangerous,” I told her. “Even I wouldn’t fight her unless forced, Mom.”

“I know, but I’m your mother. Not only should you feel comfortable telling me anything; it’s my job to keep you safe, kid. Even when you’re forty, even when you’re sixty, even long after I’m dead and a ghost annoying the hell out of you.”

The best thing about the talk was how much it freed me from the secrecy I’d been forced to keep since this all started. I could share anything now. Dropping that weight from my shoulders, from my conscience, left me feeling like I could fly without wings.

And somewhere in that feeling, I wondered how many of the cultists and alters aching for the light had felt that enormous burden lift as well. How many people were going to celebrate their new-found freedom during the full moon? I didn’t feel afraid of that question or its consequences; I felt only joy at the possibility of so many people finally feeling free enough to share who they truly were with the world.

It almost had me wishing I didn’t have to see Corby. I knew that was selfish, but I felt so light as I walked the long halls and stairs to reach him in the infirmary. And nothing could have prepared me for what I saw when I got there.

He was…perched by the window, his head moving in tiny animalistic turns and tilts, as he stared out at everything. Even human, he moved like a bird. Like a creature. Like a starved creature, lonesome and hollow, even though Fern and Yasmina were already sitting with him. Whispering reassurances to him, it looked like.

The fact that he wasn't talking their ear off made me miss him while he was still in the room with me.

But the stillness in him was a mirage. The moment I stepped in and started walking toward them, his entire body spasmed with a panic I could feel and see from where I stood.

"No," he begged, sliding away across the bed. To get away from me, I realized. "No! Don't! He'll know! He'll put me back! No!"

I froze where I stood, hands raised in confusion. Yas and the doctor rounded the bed and reached for him, but that only made him frenzy more, until Fern snapped her attention away to me and nudged me out of the room before shutting the door behind her.

"What was that? What happened?" I asked.

"He's struggling," Fern said.

"Is it me?" She looked away from me, which was all the answer I needed. "What did I do?"

"I'm not sure I understood. He said he was punished for helping you."

I couldn't have stopped it even if I wanted to, but my mind flash-scrolled through memories, trying to find one that even remotely fit.

"How long was he trapped?" I asked, trying to narrow it down.

"Time's still confusing for him," she said. "Sounds like four months."

My heart seized with compassion for him—*four months* trapped inside his alter's body; it was a wonder he hadn't gone feral—but then memories started to fall into place along that timeline and vomit rose into my throat.

Punished for helping me four months ago.

Versailles.

He'd helped me by pretending to sleep with me during the wolf's holy day. And the words "*He'll know! He'll put me back!*" made a terrible sort of sense.

I thought I already knew the answer, but I asked anyway, "Fern, did he say who trapped him?"

"The king," she said. "It was the king."

Rav. Rav had trapped the man he'd once called his best friend in his creature for…lying about sleeping with me?

No. It was worse than that. I'd've bet my left hand, Rav trapped him because he believed Corby had actually slept with me.

***

An hour later, after I'd sat alone by myself for a while just…digesting what Rav had done, I found Idalia in a sitting room with Giselle, addressing a small group of her military leaders. A television that had been wheeled in for something was paused on a newscaster's serious face. The headline spot below him was in English and it read: *Who is Natalie Damarand?*

And under that was a tiny ticker tape headline that read: *World Leaders Demand Meeting with Damarand; Threaten Sanctions*

As I entered, Giselle motioned me into the seat beside her and we sat watching Idalia…"work." It was strange. She was moving around, pointing things out in a file each of her men and women had in front of them, but she wasn't speaking. People's heads were turning, they were flipping pages together as they moved through the file, but the room was *entirely silent*, or so it seemed at first…until Giselle nodded her head, as if responding to something someone had said.

"*What's going on?*" I asked my creatures.

"*Want to hear?*" my wolf asked.

"*Yes.*"

My wolf walked across my inner sanctum to a…hole I'd never noticed before. Small, but painted and difficult to ignore once I realized it was there. She took a deep breath…and she howled.

Howled.

The sound was lovely and resonant, but so loud I flinched away from it instinctively, anticipating pain. But there wasn't any. The ringing reverberated up into my ears and as it faded away, noises cut in. Sounds.

A fly buzzing in the corner.

A woman feeding geese in a yard somewhere.

"*What is this*?" I asked my creatures.

"*Wolf hearing.*"

It was disorienting, overwhelming. I could suddenly hear impossible things. Distant footsteps and vehicles and birds chirping and wind through tall grass and—

Voices.

Idalia's voice grew steadily louder and louder even though her mouth was barely moving.

"You say their headquarters were just…open to the public?"

"Yes, my lady," one of the military leaders said. "In Rome, on the Via del Corso. There was even a sign outside inviting visitors to take a tour."

"They have appeared in Paris and London as well, my lady," another said.

"Where in Paris?" Giselle asked, startling me for how loud she sounded despite the fact that her mouth was barely moving.

"On the Champs-Élysées," one of the women supplied. "I've heard it's quite an elegant building. Very…inviting."

"Mmm," Giselle hummed. "Legitimizing themselves to the masses. How long before they offer to alter people who walk in off the street?"

One of the men cleared his throat nervously. "They already are, your grace."

"Just like that?" she asked.

"They require you take a six-week course, but if you pass, I've been told it's arranged immediately. Whatever form you choose."

"They're letting people choose?" Idalia asked, genuinely surprised. "They're not just altering everyone into those wolfen things on two legs?"

"No, my lady." He cleared his throat. "You have to take additional coursework for that."

A giggle of disbelief escaped me, stealing attention across the room.

"Is this madness?" I offered, as explanation.

Idalia shrugged. "It's calculated. Methodical. Embassies. Paperwork. Representatives. They came prepared to dispel anyone's attempts to disenfranchise them."

"Impressive," Giselle murmured.

At that, Idalia shrugged again. "We will have to ask one of our spies to sit in on the course as soon as possible. Hear what propaganda they're feeding these *new recruits* before we decide either way."

A few minutes later, Idalia called the meeting and drew a chair up across from us, collapsing into it with a dramatic flop.

"I am *so glad* the cult chose you to be their leader instead of me," she sighed.

"You looked pretty great up there," I teased.

"Of course I did, *corvetta.* I do nothing without charisma. But! I have zero interest in being a '*wartime sovereign*.'" She mewled the words with all the disdain of an angsty teenager. "If you triumph, they will pick you apart after you die. And if you fail, they will pick you apart while you're still alive. It is not for me, although I will do it for my beloved but very young *Arch-Sovereign*."

I smirked at her. "I hope you know I don't want this either."

"Yes, well…something about having greatness forced upon you, and all that," she teased before growing a little quieter. A little more somber. "I would rather help rebuild. I would rather see the world through to better days than be the savior sacrificed to bring the old regime down."

"Idalia!" Giselle snapped.

"The girl should know," Idalia countered.

"What should I know?" I asked.

Giselle growled at Idalia once more before reluctantly saying, "We have another theory about why they chose you."

"…What?" I asked. "You think I'm a sacrifice?"

"I think there will be *many* sacrifices," Giselle said gently. "Robine spoke to you as if she genuinely wished to see you take your rightful, public place as the face of their cause, but… Throughout history there have been revolutions valiantly fought by those who were later executed to make sure the revolution…became permanent."

"Public figures are often consumed by the movements they lead," Idalia clarified.

"You are fragile in many respects," Giselle said. "You are a threat to the old rulers who do not know you are also a victim here. You are a threat to the new wave unless you decide to continue their game."

Idalia continued. "If you die you become a terrorist or a martyr depending on who wins in the end, and in the meantime everyone will expect perfection from you as the first of your kind—something which *is not possible*. They know that, and still they will enjoy ripping you apart for your mistakes."

I blinked, trying not to…just run screaming into the forest never to be heard from again.

"As I said, I would not trade places with you for the world," Idalia said.

"Don't be afraid yet," Giselle added, giving me a gentle hug from the side. "Save the fear for when you need it."

It was such a heady conversation I almost forgot why I'd entered the room in the first place. But the need for clarity came running back in as tired silence settled.

"Well, before I'm executed for crimes against humanity, I need to ask you a favor, Idalia."

"Ooh," she cooed, sitting up with interest. "A last request already?"

"I hope not. I really, *really* need to talk with the dead. Please."

Idalia smirked. "Well, since you said 'please,' let's do it."

"Really? Now? Tonight? Both Giselle and I need this, right?" I asked, turning to Giselle for confirmation. It was clear from the look on her face that she'd forgotten about last Ognianima too.

"No. Tonight is a full moon. We'll all be a little busy," Idalia said. "And if you are hoping to do this with more than one person, it must wait for the holy day when the magick is strong."

I sank at that. "*Next month?* We have to wait until Halloween for this? I guess we could start work in the library in the meantime."

"No, *corvetta*. I mean, yes of course we can go to the library after the full moon, but the equinox is nearly upon us. The twenty-second of September will work just as well for contacting the dead."

I almost leapt for joy. "That's only two weeks away!"

Idalia pulled a face before teasing, "Aw, our little Arch Sovereign can count, I am so proud."

"Hey!" I laughed.

"Given some of our politicians, that still puts you ahead of the pack," Giselle teased too.

***

I could feel the pre-moon energy thrumming through the building for the rest of the day. No one was worried about wars or cults. Or even the constantly shifting news cycle that ran headlines like:

Natalie Damarand Technically Eighth in Line for the British Throne

American Teenager New World Leader???

Asian Leaders Demand Public Registration of Shapeshifters

Kraken Spotted Off Hawaii Actually Man Trying to Attract Octopus Alter to Mate With

American Immigrant Threatens European Way of Life

New Industry Alert: Alter Tourism - Nearly Four Thousand People Have Signed Up to Alter in First 24 Hours Since Great Reveal

That last one didn't surprise me as much, given the chat I'd had with my mom.

But in the midst of those pre-moon jitters that had Scar and Josh running laps around the building, and spider alters plucking flies out of the air and eating them, I found a sort of peace I hadn't expected, given…everything.

I knew I wouldn't be altering, so I'd sneakily released my raven and wolf into the woods where they could exercise out their own zoomies to their hearts' content. I let them out at the far end of the castle promenade like alternate personalities I couldn't take with me to a slumber party.

I told Cass to go too, just in case, but he never appeared.

Then I followed my feet back to the infirmary and asked the doctor to have Corby moved down to a room Idalia helped prepare for me. It was a windowless chamber with two comfortable couches, a television, and a refrigerator her snackrifices had heave-hoed in there at her request. Along with more snacks and drinks than I'd ever seen in my life. Crunchy tarallini pugliesi, chocolate chip cookies, lemon shortbread cookies, Nutella, and tomato-flavored chips. Blood orange soda, orange juice, and the makings for something called a Hugo spritz.

"If you two feel like getting drunk, you are prepared, you're welcome," she explained.

Then at 7:35 on the dot, Fern and Yasmina delivered Corby into his lush prison cell for the evening. The one he'd have to share with me.

"No," he groaned the second he saw me, sitting there on the couch waiting for him.

He turned on the spot and tried to lunge between them back through the door.

"Corby, it's okay, we swear!" Yas said.

"She's trying to help you," Fern added.

They had to basically shove him inside before slamming the door shut and locking it. He stood there for a solid ten minutes yanking on the handle, his shoulders tight to his ears, moaning incoherently, until he finally gave up and sank to the floor.

"Corby? Corby please."

He shuddered at every word out of my mouth.

"Corby, I promise I won't hurt you," I said. "I *promise!* I will sit here on this couch all night and I won't talk to you at all, if that's what you want."

It took him ages to stop shivering before he finally whimpered, "I know you won't hurt me, *cuate*. It's not you I'm afraid of."

"I'm so sorry. I'm *so* sorry. If I had known what he was going to do, I would *never* have had you lie for me, I swear. *He* will never hurt you again. I won't allow it."

He dropped his head at that, and I doubted he believed me.

"If I have it my way, I'll never see Rav again," I added, in case it wasn't obvious. "After you disappeared, he trapped me too. Mine wasn't the same, but…I was terrified. He stranded me in the *actual magick of the Goddess*. There was no floor to stand on, Corby. No land, no sun or moon, no beginning and no end. I felt so alone I thought I would die and everyone who I cared about would think I just disappeared. And my mom would waste her life looking for me in all the places where I couldn't be found. And she'd wonder if she could have done something different to save me and hate herself making up scenarios until those bad fantasies ate her alive from the inside out."

It was a fear that had terrorized me in the magick. One I hadn't voiced to anybody, but which might help him, if he knew. I hoped, anyway? I hoped he didn't think I was trying to "out-sad" him, or diminish his own experience by describing mine.

"I just need you to know I know how it feels to beg for help and know nobody can hear you."

At that, a hand landed on my shoulder from behind, and I turned to find Cass there, brow bent as if he'd heard every word I said and desperately wanted to comfort me. It reassured me more than I could ever say. I squeezed his fingers on my shoulder gently before he disappeared again.

"If you *want* to alter tonight," I added to Corby, "I can let you—"

"No," he begged, still not looking at me.

"Okay, then at least take the other couch so you're comfortable, yeah? I'll be here when you're ready to talk."

Corby and I sat in silence for the rest of the night on those couches, scratching at the electric ant itchiness under our skin.

The next night, we did the same. Except this time, he turned on a Spanish telenovela called *La Riena del Sur* and we passed chips between us as we watched the first season straight through until dawn.

Then, on the final night of the full moon, Corby entered our evening sanctuary voluntarily.

He sat down on my couch and sank back into it, almost melting, so I did the same, offering him a lemon shortbread cookie. He brought it to his mouth like a teething ring, nibbling the tiniest bits at the edges as some idea percolated in his head.

"After Versailles, Rav changed," he eventually said. "In small ways. Ways that didn't…surprise me enough to mistrust."

"What ways?"

"He took me to drink in the Hamingja cantina one night after you were settled and…started asking all the questions I'd been dreading. If you had only been with me at Versailles. If I had properly satisfied you. If I had done anything in particular you liked."

I shivered, frowning. "I don't even like the *sound* of those questions."

"Nor did drunk me," he hummed. "But I also felt a *little* bad for the guy. He sounded so desperate to make sure you were happy. I just kept telling him what I thought he wanted to hear. 'Yes, she was just with me.'…'Of course, she was satisfied. I am a gentleman.'…'Use your tongue until it falls off, amigo. Find the parts of her that scream when you nibble them. Worship her. This is not that complex, you know?'"

I bit down on my lip trying not to laugh.

"I thought that was the end of it, but then he started asking even more questions about *where* we had been, which room, which…positions we had tried. He kept *hounding* me about whether I truly was the only one you had been with or if you'd had any time to yourself to be with someone else. I couldn't take any more of that. He had mentioned a special mission when we first arrived and I needed the conversation away from talk of you, so I pushed to know what it was. I told him I was ready to go."

"And what did he say?"

"He said he thought you were in danger." Corby shrugged. "He said he had good intel that someone in your inner court was betraying you and he wanted to know who. He asked me to spy for him. He altered me and sent me off to listen. Just to listen and report."

"Okay…"

Corby's eyes glossed with tears. His lips tipped down into a heartbreaking frown that made me want to hug him so badly, but I resisted.

"At first it was basic stuff and Eike changed me back at the end of every day when you went to sleep. But then…"

His eyes darted to meet mine before veering away again. He shoved the whole cookie into his mouth and reached for another.

"Then what?"

"I followed you to the witches, *cuate*," he said through stuffed cheeks.

I-I hadn't noticed a blue bird anywhere around us when we met the witches at the Hill of the Witch, but…I wouldn't have, would I? I was preoccupied and there were birds everywhere.

Betrayal-scented disappointment blew in like a low warm breeze. "Corby, you didn't."

He slammed his hands over his face. In pain. In shame. Probably both.

"I'm sorry," he said.

"Corby."

"I just told him what was said, that's it!" he swore.

"But you didn't understand why I was asking! He thought I was trying to break up with him! That's why he trapped me in the magick forty-five *bajillion* times."

"I'm sorry!" he said again. "Please don't hate me."

I scowled at him. "I don't hate you, you walnut. I'm just disappointed."

"That's worse!" he almost howled.

"Well, it's over now," I said, batting his hands away from his face. "Calm down. Just…tell me what happened after that."

His jaw clenched with pain then, and he looked away again. "Eike changed me back into a bird and…never came back for me. I didn't know what to do. I had never been Chaac for so long before."

"Chaac is your creature?"

He nodded. "He was afraid of the sun, and I was afraid of never having control of myself again and I had no blue stone to help myself. But then I started to lose bits of me in there. Little pieces began to fade and then the temple in my head began to disappear and I worried I might go feral. So…I found Yasmina and started pecking the heck out of her. I thought she'd figure it out eventually. Especially when I kept following her around. I mean, I was there at Lunasa for Goddess's sake!"

"But she didn't?"

"No! She started feeding Chaac crackers. Popcorn. Sunflower seeds. Gordito is *obsessed* with sunflower seeds. Suddenly he was her pet! Suddenly *it was okay* that she couldn't figure out we needed that stone in her friggen pocket. He was fine with it! Little traitor."

"At least she brought you along…" I said, trying to find the positive.

"*In a bag like a purse dog*, my lady!" he said, mortally offended. "She tried to make me wear a bowtie and a little hat. That's just not right."

"You think that's not right, just wait until I tell you about *my* summer."

I laughed at the thought, then he laughed a little, until we devolved into a lump of giggles on the couch, laughing at the state of our lives.

CHAPTER 31

When dawn broke after the last full moon, a call came in over the radio that none of us ever expected. One I heard from nearly a quarter mile away across the castle, thanks to my new wolfen hearing, a gift which my wolf told me I would have to ask permission to use as she hustled out of the forest and back into my body.

"*Why would I need permission? Giselle can use her hearing whenever,*" I pointed out.

"*Safer,*" my wolf explained. "*Avoid mania.*"

"*You're...trying to keep me sane?*" I asked, expecting some sweet reply that suggested she did really care about my continued sanity.

Instead, I got, "*More coming.*"

"*More animals?*" I asked just to clarify...and she nodded.

Great. The new redecorated cubbies in my inner sanctum hadn't changed since I'd first arrived at this Arachne's Revenge, but I'd be lying if I said I didn't feel...new energy there. Every time I walked past them I could feel them almost calling to me, to take a look, take a peek, touch them.

I wasn't ready to deal with any of that yet. Not with one of our remaining strays finally finding his way home.

"*My lady, we have Asterios Talon of the Fourth Kingdom here for you,*" the radio squawked around half past ten. "*He wishes to join you.*"

This single message required a whole meeting with everyone in our group gathered around one of the large dining tables on the ground floor, to debate. And it basically came down to an argument I hadn't had since grade school—would we let *Rav's best friend* come join us in our super cool hideaway castle or was it off limits to outsiders in a "no boys allowed" sort of way?

"It would be like letting a fox into a hen house," Idalia warned, shaking her head slowly like a wise, disappointed grandmother who already knew she was going to be overruled.

She wasn't. Not exactly. Fern, Millie, Corby, and Yasmina all agreed with her; it was too dangerous to let Asterios into our secret clubhouse.

Even Scarlett reached for my hand and whispered, "Nat, I don't think we're safe here *now*. Probably shouldn't give anyone any way of figuring out where we are."

Giselle and I were the only holdouts in the opposite direction, although for very different reasons.

"It is, how you Americans say, a 'win-win' for us, yes?" Giselle offered. "If he is turning on the king, he knows Rav better than anybody and we can interrogate him for information. And if not, we get a hostage."

I eyed her flatly at that. Not the most convincing argument.

"He saved me, in Greece," I told them. "He's the only reason I escaped Europe after the wedding at all."

I turned to Fern and Yas then. "And you know what happened at Lunasa. He helped us. He nearly died helping us get information."

"I'm not…ungrateful," Fern insisted. "But what if the king got to him? Used his power on him?"

It was a fair question. Would we even be able to tell?

But…maybe that was also an experiment worth the risk.

"Obviously, we can completely blind and deafen him while he's transported here," I said. "And we can put him in a room with no windows for a while until I interrogate him and we know for sure his motives are right, right? He'll do that. Offer him that option and I'd bet he'd take it."

As everyone hummed and hawed around me, it was a voice I never expected that offered its support.

"Nah yeah, I say we let the king's best mate in." Josh hauled himself off the couch and threw his arms around Scarlett and my shoulder. "Like Nat said, he did her a solid. And I reckon if he starts any drama, we've got heaps of ways to make his life a bloody nightmare, ain't that right, darl?"

I didn't like being called *darl*, but I let it slide and stayed quiet hoping the others would come around.

"Fine!" Idalia finally said, huffing and stomping like a teenager before heading for the door. "I will make him this offer of plucking out his eyes and ears to come here. If he accepts, he accepts, I guess."

"Wait, no, that's not what I meant!"

***

A couple hours later, Asterios arrived by helicopter bound, gagged, deafened, and blinded with spider silk so thick it took nearly ten minutes for Idalia's guards to unravel him in the windowless room Corby and I had used for the full moon.

When he was finally free, he looked *green*. "Ugh, did your pilot have to hit *every* bit of turbulence between here and Rome, Idalia?"

"I pay her extra for this," she purred.

Idalia stood against the far wall, her slender arms tucked across her chest, smiling at him. Her eyes flashed silver with each micromovement as she watched her guards re-tie him to the chair in which he was sitting. Giselle stood beside her, her shaggy curls already longer than they had been when I'd first reconnected with her, giving her a doll-like appearance. The contrast between the women was stark, almost comical—like a dominatrix standing beside her Lolita pet—but both wore an air of FAFO that I wouldn't have tested in my wildest dreams.

I stood across the room, behind Asterios. My aura of honesty was on. I was absolutely silent otherwise. Idalia had made it a condition of him being allowed to come there; that I would help in the interrogation but not reveal myself until the right time so we would know whether seeing me triggered anything in him.

"Hello Giselle," he said after a moment. "You are looking *very* well. Was that Natalie's doing?"

"Why? Did the king ask about it?" Idalia asked.

"He mentioned it, weeks ago, after I left Natalie in Alexandria," he said.

"I bet he was furious," Giselle said, smirking softly.

"He was that," Asterios admitted. "But he was also impressed. Natalie's choices have always been a mystery to him."

"We plan to keep them that way," Idalia said.

Asterios wasted no time. "I'm here to help her."

"Help her what?"

"Rise. I'm here to help her ascend to this new place in our history books."

"Why?" Giselle asked. "You have known Rav since he was born."

"I don't believe it is over between them," he said, coughing lightly and shaking his head as if he hadn't meant to say that. "What I mean is that, we all know he could be great with her by his side."

"And what if she chooses never to be by his side again?" Idalia asked. "Do you run back to him with your tail between your legs? Would you drag her back against her will?"

"No," he swore.

"Have you seen Rav since leaving Alexandria?" Idalia asked.

I smiled. She'd just set up a trip wire for him to trigger; a test for him to fail. Neither she nor Giselle had been at Lunasa, but I'd told them he had been. With my honesty gift on, even an attempt to lie would tell us a lot.

But he responded without hesitation. "Yes, at Natalie's holy day. He attacked me. I fled."

"How did you get away?" Giselle asked.

"While she was in Alexandria, Natalie told her team to carry azurite on them at all times just in case. I listened to that command. I had it in my hand when he reached for my throat. I transformed before anyone really knew what to do and I was gone, rampaging through the forest as fast as my hooves could carry me. I…"

He stuttered momentarily before adding, "I gored Ulric to get away. I'm sorry, Giselle. I don't know what happened to him."

My gaze snapped to Giselle, and the look I found on her face was heartbreaking. Caught between a mother's worry and a widow's wrath.

"And then?" Idalia asked. "Where have you been?"

He ducked his head at that. "I…got caught just outside a place called Kenmare. Farmer saw a massive bull with no mark of ownership and added me to his herd. Shot an ear tag into me."

"Saw more action than you have in your entire life, probably," Idalia teased.

And I gagged a little as I realized what she was implying. Giselle playfully smacked Idalia in the stomach with the back of her hand.

"We both know I won't be siring anything, Idalia," he said. "So there's no need to worry about that."

"You are no fun, Asterios," Idalia pouted.

"What I am is sincere," he said. "I had much to say to Natalie before she had to flee, and I want the chance to tell her those things now."

I decided that was my cue. "Like what?"

"Natalie?"

I rounded him at a distance, watching for any signs that Rav had…tainted him. Any twitch. Any lunge at his restraints to kill me. There wasn't one. But I supposed that in and of itself didn't prove anything. Asterios had told me in Alexandria that Rav's gift was one of inspiration and poison. Whispering tiny truths or lies that rippled into tsunamis over time. That became bigger than themselves.

At least, he didn't seem to want to harm me. That was a good starting point.

"It is good to see you," he said at the sight of me, and I believed him. "I'm sorry I never made it back to you."

But at that, I frowned. "Do you know how Eike found me in Alexandria?"

The light in his eyes died. "I have since learned how, yes."

I waited. The room waited. The whole friggen world waited for an answer.

"The Crocodile Lord told Eike where you were."

"Mesi's dad? So then, did she—"

"No! It was one of her guards. He has been dealt with, but…it was a terrible fallout for her. Her father wouldn't listen to any explanation she gave. She was simply removed from her position for the "irresponsible" choice to protect you rather than return you to your future husband."

For reasons it would probably take eons to unpack that saddened me more than a lot of little betrayals. The sexist undertones and implications. The complete disregard for her reasoning. The possessive language alone—"return you to your future husband." Uck.

"Where is Mesi now?"

"She's here, in Europe, hoping we'll call her to join us."

"That won't be happening for some time," Idalia said outright.

His eyes *lit up* at that. "She'll wait. Especially now that Natalie has been named the leader of that faction."

"Why are you so happy about that?"

"I'll tell you, but there's a story you must hear first."

"Ugh, is it a *long* one?" Idalia grumbled.

"Yes, but worth it," he said. "But in order to tell it, we must go down into your archives, Idalia."

"Out of the question!" she snapped, laughing.

"Carry me there wrapped in silk," he offered. "Kill me if you don't like what I have to say, but…*proof of what Natalie needs most in the world* is down there, and I can take you right to it."

CHAPTER 32

It was almost comical, what happened after Asterios made his bid to gain access to the archives. He was bound with silk again, more and tighter this time until he looked like a mummy sitting in that chair, so that even when Idalia went up and shouted in his face he barely flinched.

Idalia then commanded four of her spiderguards to pick his silken throne up between them, like they were hauling a heavy king, and a fifth guard she sent ahead to clear the path for us.

"So the archives are here," I said.

"Practically under the very ground on which we stand, my friend," she said, walking the long halls of the castle down to the cellar, where the fifth guard was already standing by a massive vault door. It was dark red and fifteen feet tall and embossed with the symbol of a spider. So large, it seemed like a cartoonish neon sign for any would-be thieves; X marks the spot.

Until Idalia typed in a passcode with her back turned and opened the door, revealing *a literal tunnel of spiders*.

Don't misunderstand. I don't mean a few made decorative webs in the dark. I mean every square inch of wall was crawling with them, wriggling and chittering in the lamp-lit dimness. Black widows, violin spiders, yellow sac spiders—all species Idalia reassured me were ruthlessly venomous.

All spiders who moved out of Idalia's way the second they saw her, leaving a narrow path for us to pass down. Even the men carrying Asterios had to tighten to two, one behind, one in front, to carry him.

"How do you *feed* them all?" I asked.

"Sometimes they get very large annoying treats, but otherwise they feed themselves. There are tiny spider-sized tunnels throughout the walls leading up into the forests and hills overhead. They're only here today because I requested they be. For the ambiance, you understand."

The tunnel went on for ages. Felt like miles, although maybe that was only because of the company we were keeping. Everywhere I looked there were eyes staring at me from the moving walls.

At a certain point, the tunnel shifted beneath our feet, inclining down-down-down into what I realized was some place under the mountains behind the castle. It had to be. The rock grew darker, slightly moist in places, and rougher. But it wasn't a cave. It never became a natural cave. Oh no, someone had taken *years* to carve this place into existence, and all the confirmation I needed of that fact I got the moment the tunnel leveled out and brought us into her library.

It was some sort of dark academic temple for the Goddess of Night and Knowledge. Purple walls, black marble floors, massive chandeliers depicting scenes from myth, I realized.

Arachne into the spider.

Daphne into a laurel tree.

Actaeon into a stag.

All caught in the moment before their humanity was transmuted into something else.

The whole place was stupidly enormous. I wouldn't have been surprised to learn this had once been a salt mine or something, repurposed to store books. *Fifteen million* books, Idalia had mentioned in passing like that was no big deal.

The books themselves lined the walls, of course, but many were stored in great, tall columns paired with equally tall revolving ladders. A fire roared in a whale-sized hearth. A breeze blew in like breath from thousands of not-exactly-little holes along the walls—artistic "cracks"—which spiders were pouring out of every second.

And the webbing? For a long moment, I thought I'd been transported into the Sistine Chapel version of *Charlotte's Web*.

Overhead along the ceiling, a *gorgeous* and *impossible* scene depicting a woman swimming across a river, leading other women away from what looked like a horde of angry men, was being woven out of spider silk by another of those beautiful half-spider women.

"Cloelia," Idalia said, stepping up beside me. "A Roman virgin who, along with many other young girls, was given to an invading Etruscan king as part of a peace treaty to save Rome. She tricked her guards, freed the others, and escaped with them to safety across a dangerous river."

"What happened to her?"

"She was lauded as a hero by the Romans…right before she was forced back to the Etruscan king from which she had escaped. By luck, the king was impressed with her bravery rather than humiliated by it, and as a reward he allowed her to free half of the rest of his hostages."

From the look in her eye, I could tell Idalia wanted me to take something from that story.

"She was called a hero by the very people who threw her away as a slave. She was granted her second freedom because she lucked into a tolerant king. One change, one twist of perspective, and she would have been branded a traitor or raped and killed by a king."

I dry swallowed as I absorbed her message loud and clear.

Still, she drove it home a little deeper. "Female agency is often only tolerated when it flatters male power…When you find yourself in danger, *corvetta*, remember it is always best never to rely on the generosity of an enemy, and throats are no match for your claws."

"Quite apropos, Idalia," Asterios said behind us.

I turned and found him standing nearby, loosed from his silken cocoon, save for his wrists which were bound in front of him.

"How so?" she asked.

He smiled and strolled forward, ignoring the four guards that clung to his every move as if they were tied to him by invisible strings.

"Stories are often tools of propaganda, and I have come to share several pieces of such with Natalie today."

"Ugh, are you going to be very long?" Idalia asked in a teasing way I knew meant she was actually excited to hear whatever he had to say.

He seemed to sense that. "So long, you'll grow bored of me."

"That happened many years ago," she snorted. "But fine. Bore us."

"Will you take us to the ancient section, please?"

Idalia smirked and turned, stomping ahead down a path through the stacks.

"King Rav and I were more than just friends by way of forced proximity," Asterios began as we followed her. "We were very often told the same stories together. Sometimes I'd heard them before him, sometimes we heard them for the first time together. And, as children do, we often didn't know the difference between what was myth and what was history, what was truth and what was…something like it. Not at first anyway. That sort of discernment comes with age and wisdom. Usually.

At a great stone carved archway, Idalia turned and led us toward a private side wing of books. A section sealed away behind a ceiling-tall wrought iron gate carved in the shape of a spider…that opened via fingerprint scanner at Idalia's approach.

The books were old there. *Ancient*. Precious. At our approach, a librarian who looked like she'd just stepped off the fashion runways of Milan rose from her desk carrying a massive tome and fell into step right behind Idalia until we came to the middle of the area.

"Rav's father had his favorite bedtime stories to tell us, and so did my father. One of Ivar's favorites was called *The First Gathering*." He turned to Idalia at that. "It would be found in a book called *The Fables of the Seven*."

Idalia nodded to the librarian who turned on the spot and strode away down the aisle, flipping through the tome in her hands.

"We also need the Erasmus Letters as well, please," Asterios called out before turning to me. "*The First Gathering* is an old fable."

He waggled his eyebrow at Idalia and Giselle until the first nodded and Giselle said, "Aldric told it to me when we were courting."

"It's the story of how our great families came to control the seven kingdoms of Europe. Very simple. Very…childlike, so I suppose I should start with *Once upon a time,* the continent was in turmoil, great roving bands of barbarians stole and pillaged at will, and so on. Until seven brave and noble souls were chosen by the Goddess herself and gifted great visions calling them to meet in a high alpine meadow in the Swiss Alps. A place not too far from here, in fact. There, the Goddess revealed their destiny to them. Their family lines were meant to unite these divided lands, she said. They were meant to protect alters across the continent from humans and witches trying to "dismantle the natural hierarchy of shapeshifter superiority." And all those who were trying to take away their freedom to roam in their animal form.

"So, the Goddess bestowed upon these seven leaders a gift. A direct line of communication with her, to be used as needed to strengthen themselves and their kingdoms. A sacrificial ritual that would allow them to take in magick and transform it into power the likes of which no creature on Earth had ever possessed.

"So, it came to be that each generation paid their ongoing tithe by selecting a sacrifice each sabbat and drinking of their blood, eating of their heart, appeasing the Goddess throughout history."

"And they all lived happily ever after," Idalia teased flatly, cutting to the quick.

"So the story goes," Asterios said. "But as I've told you before, Natalie, this story never made much sense to me."

"Of course not, Asterios," Idalia laughed. "It is a fairytale."

"It's actually worse than that," he said. "It's propaganda. *Incomplete* propaganda. History that has been shaved down throughout the centuries into a neat little story explaining why we hold our sabbat rituals. And I know that because long ago, when Rav was just a small boy, he accidentally revealed it wasn't the complete account of what happened. During one particular sleepover, when Ivar finished telling us his favorite tale, Rav asked him why he didn't tell me the rest of it, and Ivar shushed him in front of me. I'll never forget it. Ivar gripped Rav's shoulder tightly. I heard Rav hiss in pain, and…that moment *stuck* with me long after I went home.

"As I got older and I started to think for myself, I found myself wondering what the rest of the story was, so when Rav and I came together again, I asked him for the truth. The whole truth as he knew it."

Asterios turned his attention to the returning librarian. She carried three objects to the room's central table and carefully laid them out. One was a dusty old book clinging to its fragile, rapidly deteriorating spine like a security blanket long past its prime. The other two were a set of letters on delicate yellowed parchment, one marked by what looked like a royal seal, carefully preserved in plastic.

Asterios drew us over to them and watched as the librarian carefully opened the book to a story three quarters of the way through.

"This entire codex is worth reading, as it's the oldest copy I've found of *The Fables of the Seven* in any of our libraries. And unedited. Almost eighteen hundred years old. Handwritten on calfskin."

It wasn't just handwritten. It was *incomprehensible*. In Latin, for one thing. But the letters were also so tightly packed and uniform, it looked like some sort of robotic cursive.

"Can you read this?" I asked.

"Yes. It was one of the very first gifts I ever asked for from the Goddess. I was a nerd, what can I say."

It was a cute throwaway line…but Asterios followed it up with something I had not expected.

Very casually, he held out his bound hands as if asking to hold mine and said, "Come, I will share my gift with you today."

"Asterios…" Idalia purred in warning.

But there was a twinkle of need in Asterios's eye. I wanted to take his hand.

I grabbed it before she could protest. "It's okay. I can break his hand if he tries anything."

It took seconds—*seconds*—for the letters on the page to shift, rearranging themselves into English while I watched, a little queasy, from the motion.

Asterios seemed to know when the transition was done for me. He pulled my hand toward a section, drawing our eye and I read along as he spoke, "Now, *this* is what Rav told me when I asked for the whole story.

"It says that after the Seven "found each other," they cemented their alliance with a ritual to create a protective seal around the continent and bring all within under their rule. They forged seven objects of immense power that, when placed at specific intervals across the continent, spread peace and rule of law where there had once been war and lawlessness."

A spider of realization skittered up my spine. "The relics. They're talking about the animalmasses."

He nodded. "The Seven became rulers of Europe by conducting this ritual, forging these objects and then imbuing them with their blood." He motioned politely to the librarian. "The very beginning of this fable please."

She turned the pages for him.

"And there's something else. In this version of the story, the Seven weren't chosen by the Goddess at all. They were already rulers of their own land. They contacted each other and plotted to take control of the continent together. This happened because one of them had discovered a ritual from the witches to create those relics."

"I know. I've read how it all started in another book," I told them, carefully leaving out that it had been the witch Belina Saldo who'd told me about it. "It was a twist on a protection ritual the witches did to shelter their children."

Asterios motioned to the letters next and the librarian slid them into place in front of us. They were also written in Latin and he let his power rearrange it into English for me before continuing.

"They did not do this ritual only once. In fact, it was done multiple times, often when a Great Family was forced from their seat of power. It happened when the Equus Court of Rome fell to the Barbary Lions in 476 A.D.. It was done again in 1506 when Idalia's ancestor took over this region. We know this because the renowned human scholar

Erasmus of Rotterdam visited Italy and wrote about a strange and wonderous ritual he'd witnessed."

"The reforging of the relics," I supplied.

Asterios nodded. "This was particularly strange for him to write about as he was not only a *human* but a humanist. Someone who prioritizes the welfare of humankind to be of upmost importance, rather than the welfare of a supposed God or gods.

"The letter is one of gratitude. He thanks the Spider Lord for inviting him, although you can see by how he words this message that he's trying to thank him out of fear. The experience traumatized him. He was instructed to hide in the woods and watch from afar as *thousands of people were slaughtered* to make the ritual possible. But in the letter, he also warns the Spider Lord that the ritual did not sit well with him for a different reason. Here, he asks, "*If this Goddess of yours requires these sacrifices, why did she not appear to collect them herself?*"

"Of course, as you and I have already discussed, they're not for her. The sacrifices are greedy, done simply to steal power for the rulers who were already siphoning it away from the whole of Europe through these relics. But the Seven very early on understood this ritual was likely to be unjustifiable to anyone outside their small group, so instead they commissioned a fairytale version of it to be written and passed down to all Alter Supremes as they were raised, until the *real* reasons they did it faded into obscurity. So was written a version of this history in which they were selected as rulers by Divine Right and entitled to siphon power as they needed to "protect their devoted followers.""

It wasn't news to me, given everything Asterios and I had already discussed, but it hit Giselle and even Idalia rather hard. Giselle stepped away, almost bowled over with…nausea? Grief? Guilt? Idalia on the other hand was stock-still frozen like a statue, frowning and digesting this new reality of what she had probably done for many years.

"Why didn't you tell us the story had been altered, Asterios?" Idalia asked finally. "Why didn't you bring this original version up *years* ago?"

"Rav told me not to," he explained.

"Yes, but…" Giselle whimpered. "I would have *never…*"

She was going to pieces nearby, as her reality shifted, and I wanted to go to her. Comfort her.

But Asterios seemed to sense my movement and stopped me.

Without drawing any attention from the others, he tugged gently on my hand, until I looked down and saw his index finger was perched just above a section in the second letter. It read:

> *...Erasmus, ease your mind about these political games we must play. We must blanket our lands with our authority or risk it being stripped from us. Our Regent of Kalmar warns this is the only way to prevent a dangerous conflux of power. Of one earning many forms and uniting all under him so that he might burn our thrones to ash and return the magick to all. We must fear this beast more than any other threat to our kingdoms...*

It was…

It was an admission that beasts were something to fear, but not because they were physically or mentally dangerous. They were feared because…they were meant to be leaders. Was that right?

When I glanced over at Asterios, the smile on his face shined brighter than the sun. It was the happiest, clearest-eyed I'd ever seen him. Triumphant. Relieved.

And I called it a day right there on the spot.

"I think we all need a break, yeah?" I said, stepping out of his grasp. "Giselle? Idalia? Let's go back upstairs."

Asterios's smile disappeared. "But—"

"No, yes," Idalia said. "We can return at a later time."

I joined Idalia as she walked away, not daring to glance back at the disappointed face I expected to see on Asterios.

I couldn't tell him in front of the others the reason I wanted to leave. I also couldn't tell him that reason made me want to vomit right there on the black marble floors.

I'd had a more emotional revelation while he'd told us those intertwining tales. Rav knew about all of this long before he met me, and given the timeline of when new relics were created, The Gathering Table would have had to construct new ones anyway once I joined them, regardless of whether I'd given one to Marix to destroy. The blame for the mass spontaneous alterations still rested on my shoulders. But the blame he'd tried to lay on me for the sacrifices he had been so willing to make to reconstitute the relics? He'd pushed for murder first thing. He'd insisted on sacrificing thousands to "fix my mistake." And he would've let me carry that guilt forever without ever telling me what the relics were truly for or that those "sacrifices" would have been made regardless.

CHAPTER 33

In the days that followed, I fell into a routine that kept me safely away from the televisions in the building. I got up, went for a jog with the whole gang—even *Scarlett* joined us—before half my team and I descended into the archives to read more of the ancient texts and look for anything that might prove the beasts were what that "fairytale" of Asterios's claimed they were.

Something special instead of something damned.

Something that could unite people rather than terrifying them.

Leaders instead of insane monsters.

Asterios helped with this, once Idalia trusted him enough to let him accompany me down into the library with *only* a contingent of spider guards with us. Yes, I assumed they were also watching me.

But Asterios was smart enough to code his language so we could talk.

"Rest easy, I will find proof that you are blessed rather than cursed."

I told him flat out, "I need *proof* that I'm not going insane. That's it. Find that for me, and you'll be my third favorite person in the world."

"Third after…?"

"My mom and Scarlett."

But at that, his lips twisted playfully as he backed away to begin his search. "*Fourth* favorite."

I didn't get a chance to ask who he thought was ahead of him, or yell at him if he was talking about Rav.

Asterios ended up finding plenty, to my surprise, although not much in the way of proving my sanity still belonged to me.

He found and translated an ancient journal for me, which hinted that stories of "a beast child" had spread through Estonia and then concluded with the journal's owner burning a village to the ground and killing everyone "just in case."

He also brought me a short missive from one of Rav's long-distant ancestors to a knight warning him that any beast was to be delivered to the king *unharmed.*

That was a curious one.

But it was actually a conversation about my call with Rav in Rome that excited Asterios the most.

"He threatened my family if I chose to…bow out early," I told him one afternoon, when the books around me had begun to form a small fortress.

"Well, he still loves you," Asterios said dismissively, before adding, "But…as we've seen, these old documents suggest beasts weren't to be harmed if at all possible."

"Sure," I said. "Probably to make cures."

He shook his head. "These old rulers had a lot of *pride* in alteration. There was nothing to cure. And if they wanted anybody dead, they just killed them. What did Rav actually want?"

"Rav warned me he would finish the mating ritual and make me his queen as soon as he found me."

Asterios's brow rose. "How can beastliness be a dangerous horrible affliction if he's still willing to do that?"

I'd been wondering that very thing since Rome. In fact, of everything that had happened since the wedding, *that singular moment* had given me the most reason to believe there was more to this beast thing than anyone knew.

Mating was an eternal influential bond. There was just…*zero chance*…that a powerful shifter like Rav would forever "pollute" himself with something bad, right? More than anything else I knew about him, I knew that.

***

Fern and Yasmina also joined our research sessions, and two additional librarians had to be "remanded" to the castle to help search for how tall wolves were made and unmade.

I didn't find out *why* they were so obsessed with this until I found a moment alone with them one day and finally asked about their weird behavior all summer.

"Are you *really obsessed* with killing these alters, or something?" I asked jokingly. "They're apparently my people now, you know."

With a soft sad glimmer in her eye, Yasmina stepped toward me and said, "We were asking for Cass. My lady, his alteration went wrong from the start. First with the pain you helped him bear, then that night…"

"We were all waiting just outside the house for him when he first altered," Fern said. "What emerged from that house when he stepped into the moonlight? It was unlike anything I'd ever seen before. Nearly ten feet tall with silver hair and red eyes. It was *him* but it wasn't. And we could all tell he was struggling with it from the start. He howled in pain and ran away into the woods. Your raven followed, and we didn't know what happened to him until the next morning when he stumbled up to the house shaking and human again."

At that, I turned inward to yell at the creature that had kept something so important from me for so long.

"*Why didn't you tell me?!*" I practically screamed in my own head.

My raven didn't flinch. "*Mate.*"

"*What does that have to do with anything?*"

"*Nothing wrong with him,*" she said pointedly, before adding in a tone that sent a shiver down my spine, "*Glorious.*"

The fact that she was *still enamored* with him? I guessed that soul bond really was all-consuming, wasn't it?

"We had to tie Cass down when he came back to keep him from harming himself," Yas told me, breaking my heart. "He thought he was doomed. He thought he was turning into a beast."

"He made us swear not to tell you."

Tears tore at the back of my throat. "Why? I would have helped him."

Fern grimaced. "We know. He didn't want you to waste more time on him. He only wanted to help you. Protect you."

But that only angered me more. I didn't need to be protected into powerlessness. I needed people to stop seeing me as some priceless porcelain doll that must be set upon a shelf for fear any interaction at all would risk breaking me. Agency was the most important thing; it had always been the most important thing.

The anger in me faded abruptly, though, when I remembered Cass's words from right before he died.

"I only ever wanted the best for you. I thought I knew what that was, but it was never my place to decide that for you."

He had known he made that mistake and apologized for it. And I had zero doubt that if he'd survived that night, he would've changed his ways.

Remembering his apology brought Cass's last words to me to my mind too. *"This is a moment for grace, heart. Know that you carry me with you wherever you go."*

He'd kept that promise too.

***

Each night when I returned to my room in Arachne's Revenge, Cass was there waiting for me by the window, "on guard." And I'd be lying if I said my heart didn't *leap* with relief at the sight of him every time.

"I know what you became, Cass," I told him after my talk with Fern and Yasmina, as he crawled onto the bed beside me and held out his arm for me to rest my head. "I wish you would have told me what you were struggling with. I would've been there for you. I would've searched for answers with you."

He winced at that and studied me for a long beat, as if…he had another secret he wished he could tell me.

A secret that filled him with guilt.

And I wanted to know what it was more than I wanted almost anything else in my life.

"I can't wait to summon you on the holy day, Cass," I told him. "Then you won't be able to avoid talking to me."

He frowned at that too. But this time, he reached under me and took hold of my hip with his massive hand, turning me away before he curled around me and held on for dear life.

***

Not having Cass truly "with me" made me more perceptive in other areas of my life. It didn't take many days at all to notice I wasn't the only one having boy troubles.

A week into our time at Idalia's castle, I accidentally walked in on Scarlett and Josh arguing about something in the hall. With a quick request to my wolf, I could hear them from my distant location, but that didn't help me understand any better.

"I don't get why you won't just say it back," Josh said. "Do you know how that feels?"

"Josh, i-it's *not you*, I *swear*," Scarlett pled. It was a tone I rarely heard from her, vulnerable and afraid of losing something important. "It has *nothing* to do with you."

"Well, figure it out, yeah? I chose to betray the king to help you. The least you can do is act grateful for it."

That tone pissed me off something fierce.

Especially when I postponed my next trip down to the archives to pull Scar into an empty room with me to talk about it and she told me what had *really* been going on.

"I don't care that you eavesdropped, babe," she said, her voice sad and quiet. "Despite, ya know, the whole world imploding, he's just…really impatient for me to say I want to be his mate. He says he's already "declared it" or something so I have to too or it'll cost him. He won't tell me how."

My back bristled in anger, but I kept my darker thoughts to myself as I asked, "Do you *want* to mate with him?"

"I don't…know," she admitted, before lightly punching me in the arm. "No fair with the honesty thing, Nat!"

"Sorry!"

"Ugh, no, but I *shouldn't even want to keep this from you anyway*," she growled in frustration at herself. "The truth is…I don't…I don't *like* being a bird."

It was such an unexpected revelation, whispered as if it was a grave insult, that I almost laughed…until I saw the tears lining her eyes.

"Or something's missing?" she admitted. "It doesn't feel natural to me. You know it's like when one of your socks gets lodged in your shoe and you want to take it off and fix it? Except the shoe is, I don't know, welded to your foot, or something."

"Oh babe." I gave her a big ole hug. "I'm sorry."

"Me too. To everyone all the time. It's so unlike me. I hate it."

"I'm sorry you're stuck here because of me too," I told her.

"Yeah well, I don't think I could have escaped this…war, or whatever it is…no matter where I went. How can I focus on applying to schools and trying to mate with guys when the world might end tomorrow?"

I smirked at that. "Giselle once told me how we love is how we change the world. She said it matters just as much in the middle of chaos as at any other time." But then I added, "Don't agree with Josh just because he's pressuring you. You *might* be able to take mating back, but I haven't seen proof of that yet, you know? For all I know it's permanent."

"Yikes, well that's terrifying."

I winced at her gently. "I know you're exaggerating for fun, but if the thought of mating with him terrifies you, *definitely* don't do it. I don't know everything about mating, obviously, but I don't think you're supposed to feel…*reluctant* about it, you know?"

"I know. Thanks, babe."

She shouldn't have thanked me. A few hours later, I found Josh in one of the grand salons pacing back and forth by the window, staring out at the world like a caged animal and…something in me snapped.

"Josh, can we talk for a second?"

His eyes went wide and he took a step away from me, but he murmured, "Yeah, I guess?"

"Scarlett really likes you, but she's obviously under a lot of pressure right now. I know most of that is my fault, but she really needs you to be understanding right now."

A sneer of betrayal split his pretty face. "Did she tell you—"

"No, I overheard you making her feel bad about taking her time making that *life changing* decision to mate with you."

I'd had no expectations of his reaction before I spoke with him, but his response surprised me anyway.

"I knew you were a bad influence."

"Excuse me?"

That gift of honesty was hard at work.

"You abandon a fiancé who's obsessed with you *on your wedding day* to run off and play cult leader and you think *you're* in any position to give someone else advice on their love life? Get real. Just piss off and let her make her own decisions. Scarlett's a grown woman, and *my* mate, if you've forgotten."

Maybe a different version of me would have felt some guilt or embarrassment at what he was clearly saying to rile me, but I didn't.

"Oh right, and *why* is she your mate again?" I asked. "Is it because you surprised her in your altered form and scratched her without her permission during the *full moon* so she had no time to think about it let alone get used to it?"

Finally—*finally*—some realization dawned on him that he might not have to show me any respect as Scarlett's friend (although, he should have) but he *did* have to show me deference as an Alter Supreme.

"She wanted this," he said, backpedaling into a much nicer tone.

"Did she? Did she tell you that? Or did you presume she wanted it? Because we both know you didn't tell her."

"Well, she..."

I took a big step toward him, really feeling myself.

"Let's be very clear. You already took one of the most important choices in her life away from her, so you're going to pull your head right out of your own ass and stop pressuring her about the next one, mmkay? If there ever comes a day when I find out you forced her to do *anything* or pressured her to do something she didn't actually want to do, you're dead. I won't even hesitate. And after I've killed you, I will sleep like a baby."

A healthy dose of fear washed across his pretty face…for half a second before a mean little sneer replaced it.

"Let's go easy with the threats, *my lady*," he said mockingly. "You want to talk about taking an important choice away from her? I'm not the one who took her magick away back at Fylgja Castle, am I. Let's hope she never finds out, ay?"

My mouth opened and shut as he strutted away, sort of reeling in the wake of *one of the few decisions* that slopped guilt into my body like a bucket of mud. I'd stripped Scarlett of her wild magick, the melting goat that had taken residence in her body and saved her life after her fall in Luxembourg. Had…had he seen me take her magick?

I couldn't remember…and insecurity wrapped itself around my ribs at the thought of her finding out.

I'd have to tell her. I'd *have to* carve out time so she had a chance to yell at me properly for it.

But, just like so many personal things that had to take a backseat in the face of "the world imploding," it fell to the wayside before the day was even done.

That evening while reading in the archives, a spiderguard came skittering down the incline toward me and shouted, "*Lady Damarand, you've been summoned, you must come upstairs. You too, Lord Talon.*"

I was on my feet in a flash. Asterios was on my heel a second after that.

"*What is it?*" I asked. "*What's happening?*"

The guard's cheeks paled as he warned, "*The Sovereign Supremes have called an emergency meeting.*"

CHAPTER 34

The Sovereign Supremes. The global emperors of this world. Twelve secret leaders who I'd never met before. Well, *eleven* I'd never met before.

I walked into the conference room, surprised to see Idalia's setup. She'd…arranged it like a…dressing room, or a TV studio. There were three sound booths. In each, there was a camera and a computer, as well as a blank photography background, each one slightly different, meant to give nothing away about our location, or even that we were all in the same place together. Giselle was in one of these already.

Nearby, a bevy of important-looking people—some I knew were her military leaders, others I had never met before—sat at the conference table, silent as stones with their papers before them. One had a microphone; I guessed it was to feed Idalia information from the rest.

And across from that, an impromptu video village had been arranged where everyone else—all my people *and Rolfe* who had kept himself hidden away ever since arriving—were waiting in front of a large monitor to watch the meeting unfold.

Idalia was ready for us when we entered.

"Asterios, they have given us no time at all to prepare," she tutted, motioning away. "That is your booth. Go. Anna has your microphone."

"What about me?" I asked.

"You will watch," she said, snapping her fingers in the direction of my friends.

My shoulders seemed to move in opposite directions; one rose with relief, the other sagged with concern.

"And shut off your honesty gift as well," Idalia added. "As far as the Supremes go, they will talk about you, of course, but *they* will meet with *you* only when *you* are ready to meet with *them*."

"Okay, thank you, Idalia," I said. "You have no idea how grateful I am to all of you that you're helping me with this."

"*Corvetta*, please. Of course, we will help you." She was so casual about it, but her hand was on my shoulder, and those strange little threads of hers were wriggling around in my body, and I knew she could feel the kaleidoscopic emotions swirling around inside me. "Listen, the very first time I took your hand and read your emotions, do you know what I discovered? That even in the face of knowing *nothing* about our world, and *nothing* about me, and almost nothing in general, honestly, you were such a blank slate—"

"—*Idalia*—"

"—*Turn off your honesty gift if you do not want me to be honest, that is on you!*" she prattled in Italian before continuing. "What I *discovered* is that I had made the classic mistake of thinking I knew everything, but there you were with wide-eyed hope and sincerity and an outrageous amount of delusional self-confidence. I thought you were as likely to be served on our Gathering Table as sit at it. And yet here you are, not just surviving but *bringing us all together*. Rebelling simply by existing. I admire that. I also believe players are weaving their webs around us all the time as we speak. We must choose where we step carefully or risk getting caught in someone else's, and to that end, having you hidden in plain sight is a secret weapon we all desperately need. Now, let's make this as quick and painless as possible please. These people are boring on a good day."

Scarlett wrapped her arm around my waist as I joined everyone to watch, ignoring Josh's side eye.

"We descend into the lion's den," Rolfe murmured dramatically behind me, and the show began.

The screen before us slowly populated with faces, all somber and serious, but not entirely unknown. I'd met one of the other Sovereign Supremes without realizing it, which was my naïve mistake as much as a natural consequence of who she was. Months ago, when trying to send spontaneous alters off to their relevant courts, I'd met who I thought was the Alter Supreme of the Ameridelphia Court of South America. I mean, technically she *was*; she just had a second title too, which she'd never used with me. Her name was Benedita Costa and she was just as tiny as I remembered, just as "art teacher whimsical" looking. And she still had a papoose across her chest; the kid in it was just much older now and munching on a piece of…jerky, I think. And I enjoyed the sight of her for a moment, marveling at the fact that despite all the predator species South America had to offer, *a tiny marsupial lady* was their supreme leader.

Another I knew by association. The Octopus Queen Shio Umiko was in attendance—and I knew that because she had octopus suction cup tattoos across her exposed shoulders, as if one of her kin had wrapped its arms lovingly around her from the side and sucked at her skin until each individual cup left a little bruise. It was a beautiful pattern on an elegant woman with a surprisingly soft poker face contrasted against her quick gaze.

But the joy of them faded quickly as the rest of the solemn faces appeared.

It wasn't just a meeting among the Sovereign Supremes. The other Alter Supremes of Europe had been summoned too. Angry Oriol appeared with his serpents. Sorina arrived a second later, a pale pillar of elegance thinly masking deep insecurity. That new Deer Lord Oskar Lange was as smug as ever. Then gross Ulric with his sloppy oily hair appeared with Violette beside him. He seemed to notice his mother was in attendance *immediately*; his expressions shifted spastically for a few moments, as if trying to decide between arrogance and apology before he chose the former, sat back casually, and threw his arm around his mate.

I glanced at Giselle, surprised to see her warm, healthy face set with spine-tingling disappointment at the sight of him.

When I glanced back at the screen, Archer was there too…and Sarab Badawi—the Syrian Bear Court Alter Supreme who had taken advantage of Cass so many times—was seated right beside him. If I hadn't known any better, I might have thought they were *together*. But, given what she'd done to Cass, I realized they might actually be.

Turned out, I wasn't the only one who clocked her unexpected presence. "Is Lady Badawi joining us today?"

The voice was deep, rich, and oily. Hypermasculine but…whiny at the same time. The man it belonged to was the same. Enormous. Even on the video screen, he was clearly seven feet tall, bearded with mean little eyes, and built like a…well, like a bear. He was shirtless, hairy, sweaty, and wearing a giant gold revolver at his hip as he grabbed a shirt to throw on and sat down to face the camera.

And I hated him on sight, even though I'd never met him before. I hated him by association, because I knew who he was. Another predator like Sarab. The Russian monster bear who had given Cass his largest starburst scar.

"Yes, Dobrynya," Sarab said. "While I wait for my own kingdom to be recovered, I will be acting as Archer Mahon's Second."

"Suppose this *is* the only way for you to gain an invitation to this meeting without committing a war crime," Dobrynya teased.

"For now," Sarab hummed back. "I comfort myself knowing old men losing their teeth often die of starvation."

"Are you even an Alter Supreme, Master Mahon?" Dobrynya asked. "Isn't that the Damarand woman's court."

"Not anymore," Archer said too confidently. "And never should have been."

Uck. I didn't know who I hated more. Between the three of them, I wished it was possible to send a digital plague to wipe the mean faces off of every single one of them. Permanently.

And I genuinely didn't know what to make of all the threats I'd been making against people recently. I knew I'd have to think about the implication to my soul at some point, but in the moment, all I felt was rage and a self-righteous desire to see them all pay for what they had done to Cass.

Even my raven and wolf growled inside me at the sight of them.

And perhaps that was the answer. If I had truly been mated to Cass since last summer, maybe this was just residual loyalty and desire to protect him.

I thought it must be that, because a few moments later, Rav appeared on the screen with the rest of them and this twisted mating thing had my heart pulling toward him too. He didn't look like his strong, proud, steadfast self. Not like he did a few weeks ago anyway. He looked exhausted and cold and indifferent to everything that was happening around him.

I couldn't quite tell if he was genuinely struggling or wearing emotional armor for the occasion, though.

"There he is! The fallen man of the hour," Dobrynya said.

Rav's glacial eyes rose to the camera, boring into mine, and I shivered at the coldness in them. "Spare me your flirtations, Dobrynya, I am a taken man."

"Yes. Set to mate with the very alter who exposed our Great Secret to the world. The leader of this…new order. What a thing to be proud of."

"Natalie didn't do this," Rav said. "She's a distraction the cult is using to obscure their own ends."

"Ah, is that so? Is that why she's not here today to defend herself? We summoned her too."

To my surprise, Rav had to wait for his turn to reply.

"She was stolen, Dobrynya, you know that!" Sorina snapped, almost in offense for me.

"Hardly her fault those abominations are holding her somewhere," Oskar echoed, his slow smugness tempering her reaction a little bit.

It didn't do the same for Oriol's reaction. His face was a raw mask of anger and dark promise as his serpents held him back. "We *will* find them and rip our queen from their grasp before we burn them to ash for the insult!"

I shivered. *That* was brainwashing. Whatever Rav had said to them at the wedding, whatever amount of power he'd sacrificed to cover for me, it was on full display. And horrifying. Oriol's emotions were so high, it was as if *his own daughter* had been kidnapped.

"Oriol's right," Rav finally said, using it to his advantage…and mine. "Whoever has her will pay with more than their lives."

"It still doesn't fix the issue," Shio Umiko said calmly. "Our world has been forever altered. She *must* be recovered so that we can control how the Great Revelation is handled. Unaccounted for, anyone can claim to speak for her. With us, *we* can sway the political shifts in our favor."

"Giving into this new way of things so quickly?" Dobrynya asked.

Umiko's gaze cut to him. "This genie will never return to its bottle. It's done. The thing we have been warned to fear our entire lives has happened. There have already been reports of suspected alters being detained along the Pacific Rim. And after that *horrible* incident in Saudi Arabia? The only thing we can do is work to dictate our future, not return to the past."

"What horrible incident in Saudi Arabia?" I asked quietly.

"A man went out during the full moon and slaughtered every animal he came across in the hopes it would rid his town of shapeshifters," Rolfe whispered to me. Then he shrugged. "It worked. So far, sixteen people have been declared missing, and their homes were ransacked live on social media. The news has been covering it all week."

As selfish as it was, I was glad I'd avoided televisions. The Saudi Arabia tragedy wasn't my fault, of course, but…someone had done that *the first full moon* post-reveal. This was going to get so much worse before it got better. I held back that swell of fear that wanted so badly to escape me as a torrent of vomit.

My raven ran her feathers down my spine in reassurance.

"*Endure*," she said unhelpfully. As if I had any choice.

I snapped my attention back to the meeting to find they had been bickering about something and Scarlett was squeezing me tighter.

"There must be a reason they chose this young *child* as their leader," one of the Sovereigns said. "They could have picked anyone if they're just using her as a shield."

"I agree, she was a calculated choice," another said. "The question is why? She does not have the experience to truly lead, so it must be something else. Perhaps something physical. She might have a gift they desperately wish to possess."

"It's irrelevant why she was chosen or if she went willingly. She now represents a radical way of thinking that challenges our authority. Even just to send a message, we should eliminate her as soon as possible."

There was an uproar at that, especially from the European alters, both brainwashed and the ones here with me, but the dissent wasn't loud enough to reassure me.

"Hey. Hey! Killing is too final to be our first solution. Until we know for certain that Natalie Damarand is just being used and *not* a part of this conspiracy, *she is a fugitive* and will be treated as such," Dobrynya declared. "If she comes willingly, she will not be harmed, but if she resists being detained at all, well, it is what it is—"

Rav slammed his fist down on the table in front of him, rattling the camera. Then he rose from his seat, his eyes blazing as he stared us all down.

"Let me be understood," he snarled. "If *anyone* touches a hair on my mate's head, if any of you so much as step foot on European soil, looking for her or anyone else, I will erase you from the face of the Earth."

I shivered. He meant that physically *and* psychologically. Push come to shove, he'd kill them or use that terrifying erasure gift he'd mentioned back at Hamingja to make it as if they had never existed. It was a damning threat, one that seemed strange for him to use immediately like this, right? It was a nuclear reaction. One it felt like he shouldn't be able to get away with.

Unless…

Almost like a hackle rising inside my soul, I had this sudden horrible feeling at the back of my eyes as I stared at him. This wasn't just a threat. It was a…power. He was using some sort of power.

One which Scarlett—*Scarlett of all people*—seemed to pick up on as well.

With a whimper, she suddenly said, "Something bad is happening. Can you feel that?"

I could. The longer I stared into Rav's blazing blue eyes, the more I felt like I was being pulled into them. Or *they* were reaching into *me.*

And I was struck with a horrible realization. I'd mistakenly thought Rav's power of influence had to be used through touch. I had no idea why I'd thought that, considering he'd told me multiple times that he "didn't need to touch me" to make me feel things.

Whether this was a power he'd hidden from me, or just a heightened version of the same, that's what he was doing. He was using it against us.

"Shut off the monitor," I yelped suddenly.

"What?" Scar asked.

I didn't wait. I slammed my finger down on the off button before anyone could protest. It wasn't enough, though. The speakers in the room were still going, and I could still feel that prying sensation in Rav's voice as he said:

"Those of us in the European Kingdom will find her, we *will* destroy the leadership of this Noctaran Order and all traitors to our cause, and we will set the pace for this event horizon. That is what you've called us all here to hear me say, and now you've heard it. But make no mistake, your continued survival is entirely dependent on her safe return to me. And in that respect, every single one of you will heed my orders now…"

"Natalie, what are you doing?"

What was I doing? I was already moving. Darting around the long conference table toward the sound booths, shouting, "Turn off the speakers. Turn off the speakers!"

The only person that moved was Scarlett; everyone else seemed *captivated* by their nearest monitor or the nearest speaker, by Rav's scowl and his snarling voice.

"You will *exhaust* yourselves convincing your countrymen that Natalie Damarand is priceless, irreplaceable, untouchable…"

I ran to Asterios's booth and was relieved to see he already seemed to know what was happening. I gestured for him to shut off the feed. He did it instantly and emerged from the booth, already on alert.

"What do we do?" he asked.

"The speakers!" I shouted.

He and Scarlett bolted for them instantly.

Rav continued: "You will do the same with your human leaders. Warn them that they forfeit their lives if she's harmed in any way."

I banged on Giselle's booth next. I had to strike it until my hand ached, but she finally tore her gaze away from the computer. She slammed her laptop shut, shaking as she staggered to the door and threw it open. I ran on to Idalia.

Idalia didn't turn at all when I banged on her booth. Not even when I stood behind the computer, in her clear line of sight, and waved at her frantically.

"If any of you should find her, you will safeguard her life with your own…"

"Kill the audio!" I shouted to my friends.

"We're trying!"

I stopped wasting time, located the cords to Idalia's equipment, and yanked them clear out of the wall half a second before Rav said, "And you will bring all news of her to m—"

There was an amplified *POP* of noise from the speakers, then sudden silence as Rav's voice died. In the moments afterward, I turned to find nearly thirty people blinking strangely, as if waking from a daze, before their gaze landed on me and froze, sort of in awe. Fern. Yas. Corby. No one, save Scarlett and Asterios, and to lesser extents Giselle and Idalia, seemed immune from this sudden oppressive *interest* in me.

Idalia staggered toward me, shaking a little. Her hand went to my arm, almost for reassurance, as she commanded, "That's it. Thank you, everyone. Back to work protecting Nata—"

My gaze snapped to hers and the surprise I found there; she couldn't believe she'd said that either. But it was more than surprise; it was horror. She was *appalled* that she hadn't had control of herself for a few moments.

"Idalia…" I said gently.

"I-I need a moment," she said, reluctantly tearing her hand away from me, even though it seemed to make her shaking worse.

"I'm sorry," I offered again.

She simply shook her head and kept her eyes off me as she walked away. Giselle eyed me too but forced herself away with her.

CHAPTER 35

The oppressive interest in me didn't go away once I left the conference room after the call. No, it sneaked back in at random times whenever I entered rooms where one of the people who had been present during that call happened to be. They became *utterly distracted.* They would drop what they were doing to come ask me if I was okay or if I needed anything.

Sure, it "faded" after a few seconds, but any noise, any startling motion, sent them sprinting to protect me. At one point, I tripped over my own two feet in the hall and *Josh* of all people leapt forward to ask me if I was okay.

It made me uncomfortable!

And not just because I was a little introvert with fluctuating imposter syndrome depending on the day. If Rav could have *that sort of effect* on people through a web camera, who knew what he might do if given an international stage or the power of a holy day? What if the world was already filled with body-snatched people ready to "protect" and hand me over to Rav the moment they saw me? How could you ever hide from something like that?

I certainly couldn't. After that disastrous meeting, I learned the news had already released my picture to the global community, along with the rest of my history, going all the way back to Scotland and Pennsylvania before that. They dissected my life, picked it apart, and started making…conspiracy theories about me. That I was part of an abandoned government experiment. That I was AI. That I didn't actually exist.

I had no control over any of that.

Nor did I have control over the news that came in about the movement of troops across Europe, and how the human population had started to catch on to something going on in Italy.

Brodie, my most trusted link to the outside world, reported to Idalia, Giselle, Asterios, and I every day at dawn about new developments, and his fears that I would have to leave this queendom sooner than later.

"Tidebringer Rawan has been feedin' me fantastic intel, my lady," he said. "Thanks to her people, we now know they're doing something we call a "clear and hold" maneuver. Troops from every other court save yours, Lady da Carra, and Lord Talon's have been starting at the coasts, working their way inland systematically, sweeping sections of Italy for you and your fellow Supremes, and then claiming those sections for themselves, essentially eliminating places where you *aren't* until they know where you must be. There've been some run-ins between the cult and the king's forces because of it, but it's very clear to me he disnae care about them right now. He's just looking for you."

"What about our current location? How long before they reach us?" Idalia asked.

"Hard to say," Brodie said. "A month, maybe. I would prefer my lady *not* wait to the last second to leave this time. No repeats of Rome."

"Do *you* have any recommendation of where we should go?" I asked. "All four of us and our teams would have to relocate."

He sighed heavily. "With everyone aware of your face now? Honestly, lass, I think it's time to bully Archer off his stolen throne and return to your queendom. Our people are standing by across the Eighth Kingdom to secure it for ye the second ye touch down."

"Do you really think it's possible to secure our home when it's so close to Rav's kingdom?"

"I do, my lady. You need a solid foundation. On the run is no way to win a war. Let's regroup where you can establish yourself as ye truly are and defend against that manky king and all the rest of 'em."

That sounded wonderful, honestly. To finally be back on home soil where I could *settle* somewhere for the long haul until we knew what this new world would look like.

I glanced at my fellow Supremes for their reactions, but I already knew what I'd see there. We'd made peace with the fact that we'd be forced out at some point. Idalia had already issued a warning to the alters in her territory that they should make plans to leave; her soldiers would defend and fight while she moved on to our next location. The same for Asterios, who assured me the future of his own kingdom had already been secured, but wouldn't tell me *how* exactly. Giselle liked the idea, too; my queendom would give her and Rolfe a strategic base from which to launch an offensive into France to retake it from Ulric.

"Okay," I told Brodie. "Give the order."

"Will do. When do ye want to make your move?"

There were three days left until the Autumn Equinox. "Four days. Is that enough time?"

He purred with excitement. "Aye, we can work with that."

***

Everyone in Arachne's Revenge took advantage of those last three days.

My team got busy securing my way forward into my own kingdom. This included setting up an "interim" headquarters for us at Galdere by shutting the hotel down, arranging defenses and technological requirements so it could serve us until needed fortifications were carried out on the Isle of Rùm and Kinloch Castle. That would be our permanent base of operations once we implemented some of Brodie and Millie's recommendations for long-term defense. Things like vertical turret towers to take down flying attackers and mountaintop radar stations, as well as waiting for the U.K. Navy to send us a destroyer, a frigate, and smaller craft to defend the island from the sea.

They also reached out to the witches finally, promising a meeting with me as soon as we were on home turf again. And they triggered a kingdom-wide "Warning and Preparedness Campaign" that Cass had come up with months ago. A way of alerting and updating every alter in the kingdom to imminent dangers.

Idalia focused on readying Italy to expel Rav's invading forces in her absence.

Giselle and Rolfe began making their own in-roads with old Wolf Court allies, those who would support her bid to retake her queendom.

And Asterios helped me. He and I worked with the librarians to go through the stacks, locating any books that might have information about *beasts, the cult, tall wolves,* or *witches*. There was no time to read them now, but I'd fought so hard to reach this place, there was no way I was leaving without them. These were carefully packed into boxes and shipped out ahead of us, along with priceless works of art Idalia refused to let fall into the hands of whoever came snooping in her castle after we were gone.

By and by, the hours flew. Until, on the third day, a red sun set to the west heralding the start of the equinox holy day celebration.

I'd be lying if I said I got much done on the sabbat. I *couldn't concentrate* on anything other than the chance we were going to have to talk to the dead. I was finally going to get closure. I was finally going to talk with William Mahon, the man who'd changed my life forever. But that paled in comparison to the other person I was summoning. For one night, for however long I was allowed to keep him, I'd get to see Cass again. The *real* Cass.

I wanted to hear his voice.

I wanted to apologize.

…I *wanted* to pull him into a private place and discover whether ghosts could ravish the living…

More than any of that, though, I wanted a chance to say a proper goodbye, and ask him to be the one to come get me, when it was my time to go.

CHAPTER 36

Arachne's Revenge had a Celestial Temple of the Goddess on site. A simple white stucco "chapel" on the outside that hid a sanctuary of moonlit splendor within. The walls, the floors, even most of the ceiling—these were covered in a black marble with gold veining that had been shipped there hundreds of years ago from Porto Venere. Overhead, an enormous moon light fixture made of Murano glass hung from the rafters, splashing dazzling colors across the walls. It was a near perfect parallel to what was visible through my raven's eyes when she looked up at the full moon and saw the night sky's neon colors that were invisible to humans.

Idalia had explained that Celestial Temples were rare things nowadays, due to the destruction of so many during inquisitions, crusades, and invasions, but this one had survived simply because the castle had never fallen.

It was fit to burst with magick, which filled my lungs like humid air as we entered. Idalia said it accrued naturally over time in this place, which was why the temple had been built there to begin with.

Gorgeous.

Magnificent.

Humbling.

It was a simple space, otherwise empty save for the plinth and circles of stones located in the temple's apse.

Idalia didn't move us in that direction as we entered. No, she took us to the very center of the temple, right under the giant moon, and commanded us to back up half a dozen paces, so we were spread out in a wide circle of curious faces.

Then she gave us her version of a warning.

"Remember, you may contact anybody you wish tonight, but you don't *have* to if you'd rather leave the past where it belongs, okay? This can be very intense emotionally, so make sure it's worth it to you. They are their own people and there is no telling whether they will like being disturbed or not."

There'd been no time to learn the ritual with her beforehand, which saddened me a little bit, but as we'd made our way here from the main building, Idalia had assured me she'd tucked the book with the ritual instructions into one of the crates of books we'd sent to England. And with the little time we had, she was only going to tell us what part *we* had to play to summon the dead.

We simply had to wait for the "magick to rise" and then call for the person we wished to speak with.

"They *will* appear," she told us. "They have no choice, which is why I warn you to be careful who you call. Catherine the Great was an incredible woman and also an absolute bitch. Made me cry. Would *not* recommend."

With a loud, magick scattering clap of her hands, she added, "Let's do this," and began.

Last year at Ognianima, Rav had forced me away before I could see *how* contacting the dead actually worked. Watching it now, it shared a lot in common with how we had conjured the animalmasses together at Versailles. Idalia whispered words under her breath, engaged in soft tai-chi-like movements, and slowly *molded* the magick around us.

The orange-pink energy swelled and swirled around itself until a distinct "mass" of magick began to take shape in front of each of us. In my case, it was a mass shaped like a human with medium-length gray-brown hair and blue eyes I'd once thought were so sincere.

"Will?" I asked when it felt right.

"Hello, my dear girl."

He stepped *through* the magick and appeared before me exactly as I remembered, give or take a few wrinkles and gray hairs. To my surprise, I didn't feel resentment toward him, or even anger. Not really.

There was a…*gone*…quality to him. Faded. Like this ghost before me was an approximation of him. I felt sorrow for the man I'd once called my stepfather. I felt *relief* that I'd accomplished another seemingly impossible goal in summoning him. And I felt confusion. How could he face me after everything he'd done?

"Are you really Will?" I asked.

"Yes."

"The man who abandoned his kingdom for almost forty years?"

"Yes."

"The Knight—" I dropped my voice to a whisper "—and Bear Lord who married a wolf?"

"Yes." He offered me a theatrical little shrug. "I am he."

"What the *hell* were you thinking?"

"As a general answer, I was thinking the world was overdue for a change."

"Well you got what you wanted, eh? At my expense, but congratulations I guess."

"Natalie…" He let the name hang between us for a moment before he reset. "How long has it been since you inherited?"

"Almost a year and a half."

"And in that time, have you never questioned the things you've been called upon to do? The person you've been called upon to be?"

"Of course I have. I've questioned everything constantly."

"Good, then you're halfway there already."

"Halfway where? Insanity?" My voice broke as I added, "Do you…know…what I'm becoming?"

He didn't answer right away, but there was no confusion in his eye, only generosity and maybe pity.

"You knew, didn't you," I pushed. "Somehow. You knew what I was before you made me your heir."

"I did," he said, and this time there was remorse in his voice. "Natalie, if it's any consolation, I was part of the resistance long before you even existed. I'd been searching for someone…*like you*…since before you were born. I didn't choose you flippantly. I didn't "do this to you." *You* were a lucky coincidence. Or fate, maybe. Stumbling upon you was the greatest piece of luck I ever experienced in my life."

"But…*how* did you know? No one else did until the wedding. Not even me."

Will stepped forward, grimacing playfully. "Well, since we're in mixed company and you wouldn't believe me anyway if I just told you, I suppose I'll show you instead."

I didn't have time to ask what he meant by 'mixed company' before his hand rose and landed on the crown of my head.

It wasn't quite like one of the Goddess's visions; I didn't move through the stream of my life until one of my memories pulled me under. It wasn't *my* memory he wanted to show me.

My vision whited momentarily before I found myself in a dark space facing two viewing windows very similar to the ones in my inner sanctum. I was…in Will, I realized. A passenger in his mind. And through the viewing windows, I could see snow.

So much snow.

A forest.

It was nighttime. And Will was shouting.

"NATALIE!" It sounded slightly muffled inside his head. "NATALIE, CAN YOU HEAR ME?!"

He plodded deeper into the forest, calling my name again and again until a sound drew his attention. His gaze snapped to a pair of eyes shining in the dark a few dozen feet away. As we watched, a deer stepped out of the woods and eyed us before walking on.

But it wasn't just a deer, I realized. As we stood there observing, other animals began to *pour* out of the woods all moving in a single direction. Raccoons. Opossums. Beavers. Squirrels. Birds darted past in near constant streams overhead.

And then…a bear. The black bear was rotund in the winter snow, lumbering slower than the rest as if he'd been woken from his hibernation by something.

This one, Will followed.

He walked behind it until tracks began to appear in the snow at his feet, mostly animal…gathered around a single pair of tiny human footprints.

Will had been right about one thing; I wouldn't have believed it unless he had shown me. Because no sooner had the footprints appeared but he stepped around an outcropping of stone to find…me. Ten-year-old me asleep at the base of a tree *completely swaddled* by animals.

A raven nestled on my bare feet. Squirrels with their tails wrapped around my legs. A raccoon and opossum pressed against each other across my chest. Birds on my head and a deer licking my cheek…trying to wake me up, maybe?

I looked like a living zoo. Or maybe an anthill swarmed in tiny animals. And in all directions around me, animals stood watching. On guard. Vigilant and dedicated.

It was beautiful and bizarre and impossible.

This was the third incident in my life where animals had gathered around me as if compelled. It had happened in Scotland and Denmark too.

And if it was real, it explained how I survived that frigid winter night in New York all those years ago when I'd sleepwalked out of our home.

A few moments later, the vision retreated into the dark and I blinked my eyes to find myself back in front of Will in the Celestial Temple, surrounded by my friends and allies, most of whom were speaking to their own spirit.

Scarlett and Josh seemed to have left the temple, but…

Giselle and Rolfe were with Aldric.

Corby was speaking with a dark-haired lady with a flower in her hair.

Asterios faced…an *actual minotaur* with the head, tail, and feet of a bull.

Fern was speaking with a young woman.

Yasmina with a young man.

And me with Will.

"Because of that, you thought I was a…" I gestured vaguely to keep from having to say the word '*beast*' out loud.

"I'd never seen that before," Will said. "I took a chance. It was the best chance I had when faced with either giving the kingdom to Ulric, or a son who could have been a great leader but not an alter, or another son who had the bear form but no other redeeming qualities that I could see.

"I had an impossible responsibility and *you* came from a different world. You understood struggle in a way those of the Gathering Table never could. The world doesn't *need* more elitism and privilege; it needs more people like you. It needs more people willing to say, '*We can do better*,' and then actually doing it. You happen to possess the singular quality the Knights were looking for in a leader—someone who could represent us all in this transitional phase of the world—but that's a technicality. You are capable of leading anyway. Not just leading, *leading well surrounded by those who are vastly different from you*. And you *know* in your heart that you don't have to fear what you are. You must simply trust yourself, the way you have always done."

"I don't know that that's enough," I admitted, trying to keep the fear from leeching into my voice. "Platitudes and vague campaign slogans aren't exactly proof of sanity. Gimme *something more*, Will."

He sighed. "My girl, insanity is feeding off your own kind for wealth and power when you possess most of it already. Insanity is repressing truth because you fear the freedom it could bring. Insanity is forcing some to live a lie so others can cling to some fantasy version of life that has never *actually* existed. Insanity is trying to bend *a Goddess* to your will. No-No. It was too much. I couldn't stand it any longer.

"Living in the shadows forced too many of us to hide the best we had to offer, and it made it too easy for some of us to hide our worst. At least in the sun, we are undeniable. We become impossible to silence. At least in the sun, they have to look us in the eye before they destroy us."

The only thing I could do in the wake of Will's impassioned speech was absorb it. Let it sit with me for several moments until I could finally admit, "I'm scared, Will."

At those words, all his grandstanding melted back to a stepfather's warmth I remembered fondly. "I know. I *am* sorry about what you've been called upon to do. But…this is a lesson I wish I'd learned at a much younger age. We have no control over the circumstances of the world into which we are born. We have *limited* control over the unfairnesses we face. But we have *immense control* over who we become, if we're brave enough to embrace ourselves as we truly are—in all our varied forms—not how we think we should be.

"All things being fair and equal, people would see themselves sorted to their thriving places in this world on their own. But things *aren't* equal and they have never been fair. The game was rigged long before any of us stepped onto the board. In your case, I have no doubt you would have done marvelously well for yourself if I'd left you to your own devices in Pennsylvania. But I chose to give you the chance to rise *before* this world made some of your choices for you. Your youth is a weapon, not an impediment. Your wide eyes are not a sign of weakness but of strength. My dear, for love of a metaphor, you are not the ship tossed about by currents and wayward winds. You are the moon-guided tide that raises all vessels great and small."

He stepped forward then and reached for my shoulders, pressing warmly.

"If it matters, we are so proud of you on this side," he said.

I smiled with embarrassing hope. "Cass too? He's not mad at me anymore?"

But at that, his brow quirked in a way I hadn't expected. "I'm sure he is. I've never seen him so happy as when he's with you."

I blinked. "You…haven't seen him over there?"

"Why would I have seen Cassian here?"

My mouth opened and shut in confusion. "Will, Cass was killed a few weeks ago. The king had him shot right in front of me. I'm going to summon him after you're gone."

Will stepped back toward the human-shaped magick waiting behind him with a chiding grin.

"My dear girl, with the gifts you've given him, it would take more than a *bullet* to pry him from your side."

He stepped back once-twice, and he was gone, back through that slip of magick to somewhere I couldn't follow.

And I was left reeling again, not just from the closure he'd given me, but the *brand new opening* he'd sliced right into my heart.

"Cass?" I called out just in case, staring at that magick, *willing* a mane of saffron orange hair to walk out of it. "Cassian."

But he didn't come. And my heart began to skip beats in panic and *desperate aching uncertainty.*

Until my chest felt light and hollow and swollen with hope that was difficult to qualify, and I asked that all-important question again, "*Is Cass alive?*"

In an exasperated tone that tipped me headlong into joy, my raven and wolf answered, "*Yes!*"

CHAPTER 37

I was a whirling dervish of energy when we left that temple at dawn. I…didn't know what to do with myself. I couldn't sleep. I couldn't eat. The helicopters were set to arrive in a few short hours and my *one* bag was packed and ready to go.

The only thing I could think to do to pass the time was go to my room and "speak" with Cass again. I would conduct my own "clear and hold" yes/no interrogation until I knew *down to the square yard* where that cunning mate of mine was hiding.

So I could yell at him for leaving me to think he was dead! Obviously!

Once the joy had settled inside me after speaking with Will, annoyance and…and…*vexation* came pouring into me next. *That jerk!*

How *dare* he leave me to mourn the loss of him. How *dare* he leave some silent part of himself behind to follow and protect me. He was part of the reason I thought I was going insane!

The most *infuriating* part of it all was that Cass had told me what he was doing! Those last words he'd spoken before he "died."

"This is a moment for grace, heart. Know that you carry me with you wherever you go."

He'd even used our special code. *Grace*, the word for emotional danger that meant we had something to say or do that the other wouldn't like, but we were asking for trust anyway.

Jerk!

And I was a friggen dummy. No, that wasn't fair. Too many things had been going on at once to parse code words from *actual death*, but what the heck! I was embarrassed; I'd helped to come up with the code word in the first place.

But there was just as much to actually be angry at him for. I realized quickly that things forgiven in death can be *un*forgiven post resurrection. He'd kept things from me. He hadn't confided in me about his fears, his plans, or his gifts!

My ghost guardian was a power, just like he'd told me he was, but he wasn't *my power*. He was Cass's.

So impressive and so annoying; I felt like a lava lamp of globular emotions moving around each other but never combining. I *could not wait* to find the real him and yell at him and hug him and—

A voice cut across the open plaza, pausing everyone in our tired group where they stood.

"Natalie!" It was Scarlett. I heard her before I saw her, and when I did, what I saw confused me.

She appeared at the far doorway, but as she went to step out, she *caught* on something.

No, someone inside had hold of her. They were trying to stop her from leaving.

As I watched, she wrenched herself away from whoever it was and leapt down the few stairs to the gravel below, shouting, "Natalie! We have to go! Now! They're coming! Rav is coming!"

There was a split second of hesitation in me, as I shifted gears, but then I was moving toward her, reaching for her, to understand. Her cheeks were puffy and slick with tears.

"What do you mean? How do you know?"

"Josh! I-I saw him leave the temple and I followed him and…he called. He told them where we are."

A growl escaped Giselle and Idalia at the exact same time, and in a voice straight from the gut of a general, Idalia shouted, "*GUARDS! INCOMING!*"

Hands were suddenly on me in all directions. *Smothering* me with touch. And I was moving, but not of my own free will this time. My friends surrounded me like a wall, hustling me up and into the building, then down again into the cellar.

"Stop, guys! Hey! Let me go!"

They didn't. Idalia stepped away just long enough for her to open the library's giant red door. It creaked open and I was moving again, almost lifted off my feet by my friends. We were a conga-line of people moving down into the dark. Fern. Corby. Yasmina. Rolfe. Giselle. Scarlett was there as well, caught in the center of the net with me. Asterios was there, too, behind us all, closing the door, following quickly, glancing back as if he expected the door he'd *just closed* to suddenly spring open again.

Down-Down-Down we marched in near silence. There weren't as many spiders this time, but for reasons I wasn't in a place to pick apart, that made me *more* nervous, not less.

Until we finally bottomed out and arrived in the library. One of the librarians was already coming toward us, but at an unheard command from Idalia, she turned and ran in the opposite direction.

"What are we doing here, Idalia?" I asked when no one else did.

"Patience," was all she said.

And then, like something out of a Ghibli movie, *spiders* began to emerge from her clothes—the sleeves, the V neckline, the pant cuffs. Like lemon-plum-and-orange-sized soldiers, dozens of them scrambled down her body to the floor, then turned to line up in front of her. Idalia removed a piece of azurite from her pocket and with a bippity-boppity-*boop* on the head of each one, they transformed into very naked human-sized snackrifices.

Just like the librarian, with an unspoken word from the Lady of Silks and Secrets, they all took off running to…find clothing, I hoped.

But there was one spider she *didn't* change. No, this one, she let crawl into her hand. Again, some silent exchange took place as she walked to the wall and held the spider up to one of the cracks there. It stepped off her hand and took her piece of azurite, and then it was gone into the wall and Idalia ushered us into a smaller reading room with a large window through which we could see the main hall and shut the door.

"Idalia!" I finally snapped. "Why are we down here?"

"If the king's guard is already on its way, the helicopters wouldn't have reached us in time. We will wait here until reinforcements arrive, relax. Shouldn't be long."

"Should we move deeper into the library?" Fern asked.

"No," was all Idalia said.

"Why not?" Giselle asked when it wasn't answer enough for anybody.

"This room is fortified."

I blinked at the implications of that sentence. "What does that mean? The rest of the library *isn't*?"

"Of course it is, I am just saying if it collapses on top of us, this room will lock down, there will still be air in here, and my people know to dig this spot up first."

"Reassuring." I turned to Scarlett. "How long ago did he call? How long did he say we had?"

"I don't know. Josh told me we had to go. He was trying to make me leave *right then*. He said they were already on their way and we didn't want to be here when they arrived."

I nodded and turned to speak to my creatures, but Scar pulled me back.

"I'm sorry," she said.

"Sorry for what?"

"For him? For this? For not telling you how weird he's been ever since we got here. Please don't hate me."

I eyed her generously. "People need to stop begging me not to hate them. I don't hate anybody… Well, that's not true, but the list is very short and you couldn't be on that. Stupid sexy Josh is stupid, okay? We knew this from the beginning. This doesn't help his case, but he was already on my shitlist anyway for turning you into something you don't want to be. And I'm just going to say the obvious thing out loud—*you* earned my trust a long time ago. I *know* you'd never hurt me on purpose, okay?"

"Same," Scar said, and I threw my arms around her, squeezing some reassurance into her.

Then I turned to the others.

"What's the plan if you have to flee? Yasmina, Corby, you have your azurite, right?"

"Y-Yes!" they both yelped.

"Idalia, could a polecat and birds get through those cracks in the rocks?"

"Probably," she said. "Use the western holes. There will be some tight fits, but they open into small caves overhead."

I turned back to Scar. "Maybe you should go now. Up and through the rock. Yas? Corby? You too. While there's still time."

"What!" Scar squeaked. "No! We're staying with you."

"At least until we must flee," Yas said before I could protest.

I turned to the others who I knew were too big to use their animal forms to escape. "Fern? Giselle? Rolfe? Asterios? What about you?"

"We fight," Fern said. "If we have to, we transform and we fight, yes?"

"To the death, my sovereign," Asterios swore.

Giselle and Rolfe nodded too, but I hated the thought of any of it.

So I said, "If any of you are in danger, I'll surrender myself."

A sound I'd never heard before erupted out of Idalia; it was halfway between a sneeze and an old man grumble. There was suddenly a hand slapping the back of my head.

"Ow Idalia!"

"What is this nonsense?" she barked at me. "You think we do all this for you to *surrender* yourself, you idiot?"

"That's all he wants. He just wants me. I am not worth your lives."

She raised her hand as if to smack me again before grumbling, "*Goddess give me patience*."

And something in me snapped. "Look, let's just cut this out now. I'm not *trying* to make stupid selfless decisions, all right? I'm trying to make *incredibly selfish* decisions and keep you all alive so I don't have to carry that guilt for the rest of my life."

"We know that!" Idalia barked. "But whether you like it or not you are a keystone in all of this. Remove you and the whole structure of the world crumbles, understand?"

"If we're in danger, you leave us," Giselle said, more quietly.

"You leave," Asterios echoed.

"You don't even look back, *choupette*," Rolfe said.

"We're staying," Scarlett said, as if she was punctuating the moment.

She wasn't.

"*You*," I said to her, "are leaving. Now. I couldn't leave you even if I wanted to, all right?" I turned to her and Corby and Yas. "*Please* leave. *Please*."

Like a horrible omen inside me, my raven warned, "*Must be now.*"

"You're running out of time. Please."

"Go!" Idalia barked again, and all three jolted to their feet. "Come here, look where I am pointing. Do you see that hole there?"

"I see it!" Corby said.

"That one. It will take you to the northwest, into the forest. Go now."

I gave them each one more big hug, and then I watched on shaking knees as Idalia opened the door and let them all out into the main room. At the wall, they each took out the azurite they had hanging around their neck and used it to alter and skitter and fly up and away.

They looked back, though. They each glanced back once and…it had to be enough.

I turned away and called my creatures. "*Where's Cass?*"

"*Fighting*."

"*Go help him*."

They erupted from my body instantly and disappeared through the rock, but they were gone all of ten seconds before I heard…

"*Three…*"

I recoiled. "*Three*?"

"*Two…One…*"

BOOM. BOOM-BOOM-BOOM.

A tremor like a faint heartbeat went through the rock around us. Distantly above, it sounded like popcorn. Like fireworks.

I stepped toward the window as a faint movement caught my eye right along the ceiling in the main room.

"Idalia!"

"I see it!"

As if they'd heard us, there were suddenly spiderguards and the half-spider artist who'd captured the history of Cloelia in the webs overhead climbing up the walls to investigate.

They didn't reach the spot in time. They couldn't. The movement became a *wriggling*, became a *skittering*, as *thousands* of gray shapes began to pour into the room, coming from those cracks in the walls. It looked as if stones were crawling along the ceiling.

But they weren't stones.

They were… "Rats. Rats! *Ratsratsrats!*"

Everywhere. *Everywhere.*

Goddess, I could only hope Scar and the others had made it through the rock before those things stampeded inside!

One of the spiderguards was overrun. He screamed and fell like the "stones" he was covered with. The others were lobbing them away left and right. Until the half-spider lady began to weave. More and more and more silk emerged from her, and she cast it away like a net until everything *including* the guards were coated in it. It did the trick. Most of the rats were caught like flies, and the new ones clogged the web-coated cracks, unable to go any further.

"Do they know this is down here?" I asked.

"They shouldn't," Giselle murmured.

"They don't," Idalia said, lapsing quickly into Italian. "*These aren't alters. They're just rats. He is trying to scare us out of hiding. Damn it all, I should have killed the boy.*"

"What is she saying?" Fern asked.

"What boy, Idalia?" I asked in English.

Her eyes burned with disapproval. "We should have killed Scarlett's boytoy. He's the only one up there who would reveal we're still here without pressure. We have to assume he's told them by now. The door *should* hold them off until more of our people arrive—"

But a scream drew our attention back to the ceiling as a spiderguard fell from the wall and disappeared behind a stack of books.

As we watched, rats began to *pour* out of a larger crack nearby, as if they were all getting shoved past the spider silk holding them in by something bigger behind them.

One of the spiderguards began to flail frantically where he clung to the wall. Some large red thing with a brown zigzag pattern was around his neck, squeezing. *Slithering.*

It was a snake, and not an unaltered kind.

Chaos.

The rats. The snake. The spiderguards seemed to be winning, until suddenly, like a strange rainfall, the guards plummeted until there was only one left alongside the half-spider woman, who was having far more luck stabbing at the rats than her kin were using her many pointed legs.

But another serpent, same coloring as the first, lunged *instantly* for her throat, sank its teeth in and she fell, *crashing* into the table far below with a heartbreaking shatter.

No sooner was she still then the serpent slithered away from her…toward us. Whether he had brought azurite with him or he could transform at will, I couldn't tell, but there was suddenly a very naked bloody man standing on the other side of the glass, smiling at us.

A very naked Spaniard who I recoiled from instinctively.

Gaspar.

Or…was he Marcelo?

Whichever one this was, he was one of Oriol's twin shadows. And he was having fun playing the invading villain. Instead of covering himself, he dipped a finger into the blood on his hard abdomen and began to paint with it on the glass. Just one word—*Hola*—but that felt like enough to tell me he was enjoying this too much.

SLAM!

The sudden impact of a table into the glass beside the closest twin nearly startled the wits out of me.

Then they were both there, naked and bloody, wailing on the glass with whatever they could find.

"Will it hold?" I asked.

"No," Idalia said. "Let's just initiate the lockdown of this room now."

She turned and raced to a control panel on the wall. Her fingers flew across the keypad, entering some long password…only to be met with a red flashing light of failure.

Her fingers sped across the keypad again. Red again.

The twins had stopped to watch, one smiling, one simply observing, as Idalia reentered it again and again.

"It's not working. It's not working!"

Only once she stopped trying did the twins pick up the next object to throw. This time, it took one weird angular paperweight thrown like a baseball to crack the glass. And once it cracked, we watched with sinking dread as each blow to the glass spread the fissure wider and wider again. Until the shatter was inevitable.

"Rolfe, prepare to fight," Giselle said. "Natalie, prepare to flee."

The second the words left her mouth, I heard a strange, muffled noise—one I'd heard before at my wedding. The sound of an asteroid striking the earth.

And there, behind the twins…was Cass.

Idalia managed "Is that…?"

Asterios smiled beside me and said, "Yes, it is."

"I thought he was dead."

My voice erupted high and happier than it had any right to be. "No. He's not."

There was a sudden blur and one of the twins was gone, tossed away across the room. He struck one of the tall pillars of books like a ragdoll and fell straight down. But he was up again just as quickly, *bolting* deeper into the library as Cass chased him…

Just as his twin burst in the opposite direction, sprinting straight for that incline toward the surface.

"Idalia, he's going for the door!" Asterios shouted.

"*Merda!* Stop him!"

Idalia tore open our sanctuary's door and like a sinking ship, they fled from me after the viper. Idalia, Asterios, Giselle, and Rolfe—they were gone up the slope in an instant, but Fern remained in the library, right at the cusp of the tunnel. Waiting for something.

"Go, my lady!" she shouted at me. "Go now!"

I…wanted to go after them. Fight with them. For them.

I…*forced* myself the opposite way. Toward the wall where Scar and Corby and Yas had gone. It was the hardest thing I'd ever done.

Especially since I could *hear* the fight in the tunnel. I could *see* Fern's desperate desire to help them, even though her feet seemed rooted to the spot where she stood.

"NATALIE! GO!"

I yanked my azurite out of my shirt, nearly fumbling it. I pulled the cord and brought the buzzing piece of blue rock into my fingers, and when I felt it ask me whether I wanted to transform I yielded to it, expecting the unraveling pain, expecting the icy unzippering agony of my human suit unfurling and my smaller raven body giving me the gift of flight. Of escape.

But that wasn't what happened.

Oh no, I altered all right, but not into a beast of feather or fur.

As the azurite obliterated my human shell and I found myself a passenger in my own inner sanctum, I peered up to find a beast of oily darkness the color of garnets had emerged to take my place.

CHAPTER 38

Just like with my wolf, being inside this *new creature* was a wholly different experience than the others. Its vision alone—*technicolor*. The world through the viewing windows *exploded* with shades I never knew existed before, with a depth so rich it was like seeing a fourth dimension. Smooth surfaces now had texture to them. The basic wood of a nearby table was patterned boldly with stripes that hadn't been there moments before. I had trouble looking at lights now, and every human or creature I could see had an aura to them of bright yellow-orange-red, and I knew they would be hot to the touch just by looking at them.

I had razor sharp claws.

I had wings, but they were *far* too massive to be useful for escape through the tiny holes in the wall.

And I had…*teeth* like a shark. No, like a crocodile or some other reptile.

Then it hit me. I knew what I was.

"*Dragon*?" I whispered in my head.

"*Yes*," he said back, in a purr so low I felt it in my diaphragm.

I was a dragon. A vampire. Wonder and terror tore my mind in two.

On the one hand, it was new and strange and incredible. On the other, it was *obvious*, as I glanced at my expanded cubbies and knew the one that was slick and black and shined with colors belonged to this version of me. He'd been there all along, patiently waiting for a moment like this one.

A moment when both my raven and wolf were outside my body, leaving a chance for *some other form* to fill that absence.

Just like with my wolf, I felt trust in him, and a reliance that scared me. But unlike my first few moments with my wolf, I understood faster. And post-speaking with Will, I accepted faster too.

"*Keep me safe*," I said.

"*Yes*."

Our claws clicked against the marble as we turned toward the tunnel and my friends in need at the other end—

"So the rumors are true!"

I turned back to find the twin Cass had chased strutting confidently toward me without any fear whatsoever. Before I could blink, he raised his hand to my scales. I caught sight of a flash of blue azurite in his palm before I felt the icy unraveling again.

My mind scrambled.

My whole inner sanctum tilted sideways.

My dragon appeared in the inner sanctum with me, upside down in pain, scratching frantically to be righted.

And then I looked up to find *another form* erupting out of me through the viewing windows. This one was bigger. This one wore a coat of heavy fur. And its growl was unmistakable.

"*Bear?*"

"*Yes*," she said. "*Confused*."

I didn't get the chance to comfort her before the twin *laughed* that maniacal shrill insane laugh again and pressed his azurite to my body a second time.

I split *again*, and my creatures writhed, and the inner sanctum swayed as if I'd been at sea for twenty years.

This time, though, when I got ahold of myself, I found I'd been ejected from the inner sanctum, back into the library.

My form had changed again to something so beautiful I felt delight even through my disorientation.

I was shirtless, sitting on the floor, draped in my own curtain of obsidian hair. My legs were gone. Fused into a tail of orange pink, smooth with scales, and tapered to a scalloped fin of lightest blue so thin I could see through it.

I felt a need for water so desperate I thought I was suffocating until I manually forced air into my throat…through frilly gills that tickled as I struggled to breathe.

"*Incredible!*" the twin almost sang as he reached down for the azurite pendant around my neck and tore it off, tossing it aside. "Stay like that. I'd hate for my brother to miss you like this—"

Then there was a sudden grunt from above me and I realized through my swimming vision that Fern was there with her hand wrapped in his hair from behind, yanking on his head with her knees pressed to his back.

He hurled her away, but she rolled as she hit the floor and he had to face her, giving me a chance to get ahold of myself, my faculties. This form wasn't like the others. It was me, there was no creature here, but my identity was different. Colder. Sharper. But less focused. My eyes darted from one object in the room to the next to the next, seeking…

Seeking comfort, I realized. This version of me *desperately* wanted comfort. There was a pillow on a chair that called to me. A blanket that someone had left behind on a table. A feather on the floor either Corby or Scarlett had left behind.

And there! Right there, a few dozen feet away, I could see my azurite pendant.

I rolled onto my belly and began to crawl for it, dragging this tail, which I could tell was *never* meant to be dry. Still, I pulled myself forward inch by inch as Fern fought for me.

I made it halfway across the floor before a hand latched onto the narrow ankle-area of my tail and flipped me over rudely.

"*Que bonic* you are."

It was the other twin. And without feet or knees to use for defense, I was helpless as he dragged me back across the floor away from my pendant.

This was the *worst* form I could have gotten trapped in!

But…perhaps it was the best, given what I suddenly saw laying at the mouth of the tunnel leading upstairs. There were bodies. Two of them.

Idalia was still as death, eyes open and lifeless…across from Asterios who was broken and struggling, trying to crawl toward me across the floor. I couldn't see Giselle or Rolfe, but if they weren't there, if they weren't coming…

I knew I had a mermaid's heart the moment pain tried to coil around me like a straitjacket and something inside me tamped that sorrow down. Squashed it flat *instantly* as if it knew I couldn't afford to feel it right now. The coldness of this hybrid creature shielded my heart from the horror of seeing Idalia dead, seeing Asterios struggling, so blue and bloody, barely able to move but still trying to reach me despite everything.

And then…

Ugh, Goddess—*horrible.*

The twin that had me followed my line of sight to Asterios. Gaspar-

Marcelo released me easily, strolled over to my struggling friend, and pressed his gross hairy foot to the top of Asterios's head, pinning him to the floor.

"Natalie!" Asterios strained. "Remember what you must do…af-af-after I'm dead. *I-I-I* give you permission."

"Awwww," Gaspar-Marcelo chuckled. "He gives you permission to what, princess?"

"Please leave him alone! I'll go with you. Please!"

The twin ignored me. "I am supposed to save him for the king to kill, but…"

With a coldness that chilled even my mermaid heart, the viper bent down, gripped Asterios's curly hair, wrapped a forearm around his throat, and began to squeeze.

"No. *No-No-NO!*"

I crawled! I crawled as fast as I could, digging my breaking, bloody nails into the marble to pull myself along faster!

But Asterios was blue and fading and I couldn't reach him! I couldn't reach him in time!

And mere feet from Asterios's body, Gaspar-Marcelo tightened his grip brutally.

I heard Asterios's final, frantic gasp.

Heard his neck break.

And the twin dropped my friend's sweet, lifeless head to the marble floor.

CHAPTER 39

Just two.

It'd only taken *two* of them to kill my allies.

Not even an army. Just two.

Was that right? That couldn't be right, could it?

No. It wasn't. I still had allies. Fern, for one. My creatures…

My creatures!

As my friend's murderer turned his rancid gaze back to me, I met it with pure hatred in mine.

"You really should smile more, princess," he said, strutting toward me. "Especially now that we can return you to your king. A little worse for wear, but still in working condition. And much easier to keep locked away without feet to run on."

Just like that, my hate list expanded by one.

Then I heard a yelp of pain and turned to see Fern stuck in a brutal hold with a vile man dangling her own azurite just out of reach like some sort of fun little toy.

And my hate list expanded again.

The coldness in my heart rose to my brain. To my inner sanctum as I gave the order I wished I'd thought to give at the start.

"Kill them both."

"And who is going to do that, princess?"

It happened all at once in an eruption of color and magick and motion. Out of me climbed my bear. My dragon. From the tunnel came my wolf, my raven. And where there had once been a viper standing before me, there was suddenly a blur of flesh and pummeled bone as my creatures tore into him from four different directions.

"No!" I heard his twin shout, dropping Fern to the floor.

He ran for his brother, roaring, but he didn't get far. A blur stopped him in his tracks and lifted him off his feet and I looked up to find Cass there with his hand around the twin's throat.

It happened so fast I could barely follow the movement as Cass *slammed* the twin into the ground, then picked him up and slammed him down once more.

The earth *quaked* with each strike of his body as it broke the marble beneath it.

Until finally, Cass picked him up again and *hurled* him toward the tunnel.

I anticipated the strike of his head against the marble. Looked forward to it, honestly.

But I never heard the *hollow thunk* of his empty skull upon the stone. No, he transformed midair back into a serpent and disappeared into the tunnel as his human flesh sloughed to the floor.

I couldn't care. I stopped Cass from going after him with a quick, "No! Check Fern. Bring me my azurite. Then Asterios."

Cass nodded and did as I said in a blur that was difficult to follow. Fern was suddenly on her feet, recovering. The azurite was in my hand. And Asterios's body was right beside me.

With a quick touch of the blue stone, I returned my human lower half back to me, and reached for the nearby blanket to cover myself before I knelt beside the body of my friend.

"He's dead, my lady," Fern said, even though I already knew that. "They're all dead. We have to go."

"One second," I said, trying to decide how I was going to honor the final request Asterios had made of me without vomiting all over his body.

Weeks ago, he'd given me permission to eat his heart if he died. Commanded it of me. And I knew why. With it, I could ask to have his shielding power. The one that would protect me from Rav and his powers of inspiration.

But the longer I sat there trying to work up the courage to cut open this man's chest and rob him of that organ I'd only just begun to know, I couldn't do it. The whole ritual of it still felt wrong to me.

After all, I'd never *needed* to eat a heart to take power from the rituals or from other people. Giving and taking magick could be done with a touch and a request.

So instead, I pressed my head to Asterios's chest and asked "*Can I keep you?*" and accepted every drop of sudden magick that bolted like lightning into my brain.

My mind filled with blue and the taste of grass and the smell of the hot dry soil of Crete and the texture of that fried zucchini he'd once made for me. In the middle of these sensations, I saw a giant white bull—an aurochs twice as tall as I was—grazing peacefully in a pasture. I offered it my hand and it touched its snout to my palm and *power* coursed into me as a zap of static charge.

And then it was over, and I sat up blinking, wondering if it had worked. Let's be honest, wondering if I'd done it correctly.

Not that there was any time to worry about it. There was no delay at all before I heard the sound of stomping boots growing louder, echoing down the tunnel.

"Go, my lady," Fern said. "Leave me."

"Don't be ridiculous."

"You have to go, like Idalia said—"

"They'll *kill you*, Fern!"

"So what?!"

I was *so tired*, as I was every time I found myself in a fight, regardless of whether I used my creatures or not, but that seemed to be the way of war. Eike had told me once during training that it was possible to win a fight simply by wearing your opponent down. The relentlessness *was* the point, to numb you and pacify you. To convince you any resistance at all was futile. To pick off all your allies one by one until you felt truly alone.

But the sight of Idalia and Asterios's dead bodies was enough to bolster me. So was Cass who studied me with the same look of frustrated confusion as Fern. I kept my eyes pinned to his for a long moment until understanding dawned on him…and he nodded at me. His gaze snapped to the ceiling, then once more to me, before he disappeared from the room altogether.

The time for retreat had passed me by. And this was an unavoidable reunion—one that had been "on the calendars" since I'd fled that wedding in Greece. So as the boots drew closer, I stepped back and let my creatures form a *wall* between us and whoever was coming.

No, between us and who I *knew* was coming, as the approaching bodies pushed air out of the tunnel ahead of them and the scent of hot honey practically smacked me in the face.

CHAPTER 40

With my creatures in a tight defensive semicircle around the mouth of the tunnel, only four soldiers appeared, guns raised, before they realized the path was blocked and they had to back up to halt the flowing tide behind them. I couldn't tell how many of them there were in the passageway, but I could hear guttural protests as the ones at the back hit the wall of bodies ahead of them and were forced to stop.

One whispered into the radio at his shoulder at the sight of me. The men in the tunnel pressed to the narrow walls awkwardly to let someone pass through. And by and by, Rav's shock of white-blond hair stepped into view.

I wish I could say I stood tall at the sight of him. My fiancé. My…lost friend.

I wish I could say I didn't flinch or give any of my mixed emotions away.

I can't.

Seeing Rav again in person was so different from seeing him on the monitor during the Supremes meeting or hearing him over the phone. My heart still jangled in his presence. It still tightened with pain at the thought of the future it had wanted with him…and lost.

But my body couldn't forget how he had trapped me. My mind couldn't forget how he had lied. And being trapped again now at the bottom of a mountain with either the holes around me or him as my only means of escape didn't do the thought of 'us' any favors.

The look on his face, though? That…that hit me. The way his eyes widened with need and offered comfort. The way his brow rose out of its furrow with relief. The way his lips parted with longing.

The way he said my name, "Natalie," like it was the only word he knew.

"Hi Rav," I whispered.

Despite Fern and his men there listening, it was as if we were the only two people in the room, locked in a staring competition.

At least until a jumpy man just behind him suddenly whimpered, "One of 'em's a beast, your highness. Should we open fire?"

That word—that tainted word *beast*—spread to the men beside him, then deeper into the tunnel, spiking the energy sky high.

"No!" Rav snapped. "Hold your position or I'll take your head."

Turning away from the jumpy man, Rav pinned his gaze to me.

"It's time to come home, *min skat*," he said, his voice lilting with hope.

"You still want me, even like this?" I asked, gesturing to my creatures.

I had no expectation of what he would say, but he surprised me. "We can fix this!"

"Fix it? Fix it how?"

"We marry," he said. "We mate. I can take this burden from you, make you a raven alter again."

My brow quirked in scorn. Was he trying to say that he was *so powerful* our mating bond could suppress this *multitude* inside me? Did he actually believe that? Did he think *I* believed that? Or was this just something to say in front of his men, to hide me?

"Rav there's nothing to fix," I said. "If we mated, this would…"

The truth struck me like a pie launched from a tiny catapult.

"If we mated, you would get this gift too. That's what you mean by 'take this from me.' You *want* this power. You want it *badly*. Because it's not the great danger we've been led to believe it is, is it?"

Rav's mouth opened and shut instead of answering…because my aura of honesty was on and aimed straight at him. And he knew the only way to hide the truth was with silence.

That was it. All the fears I'd had that I was losing my mind, all the existential terrors that had left me feeling completely untethered and lost since that day in Greece. Asterios had been right. Will had been right. Robine had been right.

I wasn't going insane.

This was a gift. Perhaps *the* gift worth going to these extremes to possess.

It might even be a gift he didn't want to share. Not even with me.

"Let's discuss this back at Fylgja Castle," Rav pivoted. "Let's just go home—"

"I'm not going home with you."

I took a step back.

His eyes narrowed on me, in surprise, in longing. "You *will*, *min skat*, or I'll—"

"This isn't a negotiation, Rav."

I took another step back. He tried to move with me, but he couldn't with my creatures in the way, and the tiniest grin blossomed on his face.

"You're right," he countered. "Let's call it a trial of endurance. We'll stand here as long as it takes for exhaustion to bring you to your knees. And then I'll claim you as you have always wished to be claimed."

My brow rose in leery confusion.

And the smile on his face grew. "I told you on the phone. Hide and I would find you. Run and I would chase you. But either way, I would capture you, and when I did, I'd never let you go again."

With that, he leaned against the wall of the tunnel and crossed his arms, smirking.

"We both know how this ends. With you in my arms, and the world at our feet—or in ruins. Either way, *min skat*? You're mine."

THE END

Continue reading Natalie's story in

SAVAGE

Book Six of *The Garden of Beastly Delights* series

CHAPTER 1

A game.

This standoff in a great library at the bottom of a mountain surrounded by the bodies of our fallen friends is a game to him.

That was the first thought that went through my head as Rav settled into his position at the entrance to Idalia's library and began his torturous waiting game for me to…simply fall asleep. He genuinely seemed to think that was how I would lose this standoff.

No, I realized he wanted me to *surrender*. He wanted me to give in. Either physically—when I couldn't keep my eyes open any longer and my creatures currently holding him back blipped out of view like an electric fence slowly losing its charge. Or emotionally—by finally admitting that the lengths he'd gone to find me were proof of his love for me.

That wasn't how this was going to go, but it was cute that he thought it would.

If this was a game, I wanted to play too.

"Why are you smiling?" he asked after the silence between us grew long. "Undressing me with your eyes? You know we can do all of that and more in the comfort of our own home, *min skat*."

That was as good a way to pass the time as any. I let my eyes roam south, from his beautiful face, dancing across his Adam's apple, to the little notch between his neck and chest, and farther down, remembering the tattoos that were arranged like faded calligraphy across his skin, in blue ink with a bright spark of orange magick on top.

I'd always liked his hands; they were firm, yet soft to the touch, and well-manicured. And they were one of the few parts of his body not covered in tattoos.

His legs were lovely robust columns, guarding that pillar of marble between that seemed to be waking up to greet me the longer I left my gaze to roam across the stretched landscape of him.

"Goddess, I cannot wait to capture you," he purred, as if he couldn't help himself, and my gaze snapped back to his eyes, unsurprised to find heat and amusement in them.

"You haven't captured me yet," I teased. "And you won't."

"We'll see," he hummed.

"You're going to leave disappointed," I sang.

"Since I'll have you across my knees, I doubt it," he sang back, reveling in the chuffed low laughs of his men.

I wished I could chuckle too, since he clearly hadn't realized what I was doing yet. But I resisted the temptation.

"Natalie, you should *just go*."

My eyes jerked to Fern wishing I could speak directly into her mind and soothe away the fear that had her body tight and coiled. She hadn't yet realized what I was doing either, and there'd been no time to tell her before Rav's forces had stormed down the tunnel to the library and bottlenecked in this unfortunate way.

But she would understand soon enough.

So would he.

"Natalie's not going anywhere, Lady Saeli," Rav said with a smartass smirk on his face. "She can't. You're here. She'd never leave you to die. Isn't that right, *min skat*?"

He thought he knew me so well. He *did*. That *was* one of the reasons I was still standing there and not flying through the tiny tunnels in the rock overhead and out into the Italian Alps beyond. I couldn't leave Fern to die like our other friends. Not with Idalia and Asterios's bodies at my feet, gone too soon from the world because of me.

But it wasn't the only reason.

"My lady, plea—"

"Hush, Fern," I said calmly. "There's no point arguing about this."

"I disagree," Rav said. "I'd love to discuss the terms of your surrender while we have the time."

"Like I said, there's no point," I said, smiling.

"No?"

"I already know the terms of this surrender," I said. "You want to take me back to Denmark. To marry me."

"Among other things."

I pursed my lips playfully at that, buying time. I only needed time.

"Let me guess, you want to trap me in Hrafnagud," I teased again, relishing in the bolt of anger I saw flash across his eyes.

"No, I swore I would *never* do that again," escaped him in a hiss. "*Our home*. It's repaired and waiting for you. For us."

"And we'll what? Rule the world from there?"

That dazzling smile of his returned, delighting in the thought. "Yes."

"Together?"

"Yes."

I raised an eyebrow at that. "Even though I "lack the experience?""

"As I've told you before, that experience will come in time."

"How? You gave away my kingdom."

At that he sneered dismissively. "Archer's nothing. He's keeping the seat warm for you."

"And Ulric?"

"He's a good guard dog satisfied with the small yard he roams."

"And Idalia?" I asked, motioning to where one of his soldiers was practically standing on her body. "Asterios?"

"I already have their replacements picked, *min skat*." He said the words as if he was trying to reassure me everything would be okay. *He would handle it.*

"Everyone's just so easily replaceable?" I asked.

"Not you," he swore. "Never you."

But therein lied the rub. I was "irreplaceable" because I was literally one of a kind. Not because I had worth beyond my utility.

"On a scale of one to ten, Rav, how excited were you the moment the cult announced me as their ruler?"

A low chuckle escaped him. "Infinite."

"Even though they only chose me?"

"Once we mate, they'll have both of us. Together, we will be formidable. The world will have two pillars on which to build its new future. We'll give them more than they ever dreamed possible, *min skat*."

Oh Rav. He said so many things that almost sounded promising.

Some part of me wanted to give him the benefit of the doubt, believing that if we were in private, talking one-on-one, the conversation would be…deeper. Richer. And maybe it would have been.

But I'd only ever been trying to buy us time.

And as I stood there pretending to consider his offer, a tiny flicker of movement caught out of the corner of my eye, and I knew our latest "negotiation" was coming to an end.

There, just above the jumpy man to Rav's right, was a spider. As I watched, it let itself down its impossibly fine silk and crawled into the man's collar.

"Unfortunately, Rav, I don't think you've done enough to earn me yet," I said, stepping toward Fern and taking her hand, squeezing.

"I have time, *min skat*."

"Not as much as you think."

"S-S-SPIDER! SPIDER! SPIDER!"

There was a single moment, when the jumpy man began to flail and claw at his clothing, that I thought I might have jumped the gun a little bit on saying our time was coming to an end. For a moment, it was *only* him squirming, drawing Rav's annoyed attention like a child screaming for his mother.

But all at once, in a terrible tremble that sent tiny bits of rock falling to the floor around us, the wall above our would-be conquerors—and those of the passage itself—began to move, chitter, *skitter*.

And a tsunami of spiders poured into the tunnel, eager to meet their king.

RECEIVE A FREE PROLOGUE FOR *THE GARDEN OF BEASTLY DELIGHTS*

Building a relationship with my readers is one of my favorite things about writing. It feels like magic, connecting with someone through worlds created and stories shared.

I offer those on my mailing list a free bonus chapter or selection of free stories from other exciting new authors each month as well as details about new releases, special offers, giveaways, art reveals, and other bits of news about *The Garden of Beastly Delights* series.

You can join my enchanted circle of newsletter readers and receive *The Garden of Beastly Delight's* **free** prologue by signing up here: https://dl.bookfunnel.com/gegv95srvj

IF YOU ENJOYED *RABID*...

Reviews are insanely powerful for a self-publishing author like me because they help me draw attention to my stories. Someday, I might be lucky enough to have the financial might of a big wig publisher on my side, but for the moment it's just me.

Committed and loyal readers are an amazing gift. Honest reviews help me find other passionate readers, which in turn makes it possible for me to keep writing stories for you all.

If you've enjoyed this book, I would be eternally grateful if you could spend just five minutes leaving a review (it can be as short as you like) on the book's Amazon page.

Thank you so much!
Xoxo Sierra

ABOUT THE AUTHOR

Sierra Prynne is a cheeky little pen name inspired by a run-in with a lovely drunk lady who told me: "You can wake up ten years from now living the life you have or the life you want."

The women in my family have a tradition of using their middle names and Sierra is mine. Prynne is a gift to a certain complex and self-possessed literary character who deserved better. I'm learning about who I want to be as I write these stories and I think she'd respect that.

As for who I am, well, I'm a hopeful romantic who believes you can find true love if you're brave enough not to settle for less than extraordinary. Also, I probably like fantasy a little too much for my own good and when I'm not writing, I can be found wandering through theme parks, national parks, and book parks…those are a thing, right?

You can check out more of what I'm up to at www.sierraprynne.com or email me at sierra@sierraprynne.com.

And, if social media's your style, please support me with a follow:

Facebook: https://www.facebook.com/SierraPrynne
Instagram: https://www.instagram.com/sierraprynne/

COPYRIGHT

A LURING PRESS book.

First published in the United States in 2025
by LURING PRESS LLC

Cover art designed by the glorious Lisa Amowitz.

www.ingramcontent.com/pod-product-compliance
Lightning Source LLC
LaVergne TN
LVHW091118080826
845145LV00008B/1970
* 9 7 8 1 9 6 4 6 4 0 0 7 5 *